From Flag *to* Flag

The stories in this collection are works of fiction. All names, characters, historical events, places and scenes described herein are fictional (even the non-fictional ones). Any resemblance of characters (including actual persons) to actual persons, living or dead, or not yet born, is purely coincidental

These stories were published at a time when civilization was generally held as a positive value. Modern-day self-made savages will find these works politically incorrect and thus an abomination against nature. They are advised to go jump in the lake. The rational reader (for whom this book was lovingly compiled) will understand that these stories are the products of their times; will not react with a psychotic break to those aspects that are rationally in error; and will respond positively to those aspects that are rationally life-enhancing.

The text in this book is version 1.0. Loyal readers who find errors in the present version are encouraged to please send them to the e-mail below. You will be acknowledged (anonymously or by name, per your wish) in a subsequent version.

From Flag to Flag / Their Last Hope
ISBN: **978-1-945307-21-8**
Book compilation and design by Rodney Schroeter.

The Silver Creek Press
PO Box 334
Random Lake WI 53075-0334

rschroeter@silentreels.com

From Flag to Flag

SCP Tête-Bêche
Book 2

CHAPTER I.

CHECK AND COUNTERCHECK.

"HALT, there!"

I favored the fellow who had stopped me with a gaze of lofty contempt that I have known to impose upon far wiser men.

But this awkward militia sergeant was too stupid to be affected thereby. I saw that I must resort to some plainer measures.

"You have dared to stop me without warrant or excuse," I said, in what I intended for cold rebuke. "Your confounded crew of scarecrows are pointing their muskets at me so awkwardly that one or two of the guns are like to go off at any moment. Then it may be a hanging matter for somebody."

"It's like to be a hanging matter," he assented with a silly chuckle, "but not for *us*. Step out of that boat now, lively, or—"

"But," I protested with excellent indignation, "this is an outrage. I am rowing quietly up the Patuxent for morning exercise, when you suddenly appear at a curve of the stream and level a half dozen guns at me. I've rowed close to shore to humor your whim—and to save myself from a stray bullet. But I fail to see why I should consider myself under arrest, or—"

"You talk a lot, friend," grinned the sergeant, "but the weddin' ceremony's the only place I know about where talk ain't the cheapest thing on earth. If you've got a pass, hand it over, and I'll 'pologize and let you go ahead. If you haven't a pass, you've no call to be on the river, and we'll have to—"

"I saw no signs warning me off. Surely, the river is free to all. There can be no harm in—"

"That's where you're wrong. The Patuxent's a mighty unhealthy stream for strangers these days. They're liable to suffer a whole lot from rush of rope to the throat."

It was a grisly jest, and I did not echo the dutiful roar of laughter that convulsed the speaker's followers.

"I beg you will curb your pretty wit," I remonstrated with an irony that was quite thrown away. "Amid all those cackles some one's musket will be by way of exploding, and then I'll literally 'die of laughter!' "

The self-appreciative smirk faded from his lips.

"Friend," he drawled, his eyelids narrowing, "we Yankees don't use the phrase 'by way of.' That's redcoat talk. I'll trouble you to step out of that boat in a hurry. Potter! McQueen! Grab hold of that prow and run her ashore! You others keep your guns on him!"

I was fairly caught. For a wild instant I had thoughts of jumping into the water and seeking safety by diving. But I was close to the bank, where the muddy river was too shallow for my need.

Again, my eye fell on my fowling-piece strapped to the thwarts. But before I could have unfastened and lifted it, my body would have been riddled with bullets.

Militiamen are of little use in battle; but on patrol duty they have a stupid doggedness that often defies the cleverest man. In the case of disciplined soldiery, my own military training and custom of command might have stood me in good stead. But against these farm yokels, new to their ill-fitting regimentals, it was of no avail. I must yield to the inevitable.

I remember once hearing the great Marquis de Lafayette say he would rather face the rapiers of a dozen hired bravos than the cudgels of half as many angry peasants. I was now in like case.

To avoid a useless scuffle and undue rough handling, I leaped ashore. I had scarce touched bank, when four of the fellows were upon me, and had me trussed and bound like any spitted fowl.

I made no struggle. I think this surprised my captors.

"Please have my gun and my lunch-basket brought along," I requested the sergeant as calmly as I could. "I do not care to lose them. Where are you taking me to?"

"To headquarters," he answered, less truculently. "It's only a few miles back. You'll—"

"See that my belongings get there safely, then," said I. "You will have enough black marks against your record before I'm done with you without having to account for my fowling-piece and—"

"What were you doing when we caught you?"

"You saw what I was doing."

"You were rowing up the river. What for?"

"For snipe. I'd planned for a day's hunting."

"Are you sure it was snipe?"

"What other game is in season this time of year?" I asked with intentional misunderstanding.

"Gunboats, for one thing."

I gazed at him stupidly.

"Gunboats," he repeated. "Commodore Barney's. Whole flotilla of 'em. Your people are anxious enough to find out where they are. But *you* won't be the man to bring 'em the news. Not this trip. And if the provost marshal's the man I think he is, there won't be *any* return journey for you."

"Gunboats! Commodore Barney!" I gasped.

Then, fearing to seem to know too little of what was then the most talked-of theme in all the Chesapeake countryside, I added:

"Oh, you're speaking of the Barney flotilla that's been harrying Admiral Cockburn's war-ships all year and keeping the Chesapeake free from invasion? What have I to do with it?"

"Nothing now. Nor hereafter. Unless ghosts can spy."

" 'Spy' is an ugly word, even for a militia bumpkin to use," I retorted. "If you think I was rowing up the Patuxent trying to find and sink Barney's gunboats with a fowling-piece—"

"Or to tell your friends where his flotilla is?" he suggested. "Cockburn might pay good money for that bit of information. But he won't get a chance to pay it while three companies of Maryland militia are scattered along both banks to stop Britishers from getting too curious. You're the fifth that's been nabbed since 1814 began."

"Then," I broke in with an admirable pose of dawning comprehension, "I'm supposed to be a British spy and trying to find whereabouts on the Patuxent Barney has hidden his gunboats to keep them out of Cockburn's way till the mobilizing of the English fleet in the Chesapeake is over? Is that it?"

"That's it," he agreed with another prodigious grin. "And now, if you can walk as well as you can make guesses, let's see how quick we can get you to headquarters. Fall in!" he shouted to his men. "March!"

I walked along as carelessly as I might between two of the soldiers. But I was not yet minded to give up the game. So, as we plodded on under the broiling August sun, I spoke again.

"Have you been long in the service, sergeant?" I queried.

"Ten months," he rapped out. "Joined in November, 1813. Why?"

"And a sergeant already!" I exclaimed. "A sergeant in spite of your stupidity in thinking a spy would row up the Patuxent in broad daylight, where every addle-pated jack-in-office could catch him?"

"Tell that at headquarters."

"If I had less to tell at headquarters, you'd wear your sergeant stripes longer. It'll go hard with some one for this day's mistakes."

"Shut up!" he ordered gruffly, as he turned on me.

I was glad of his surliness, for it betokened a growing doubt. And doubt was what most I wished to instil into his mind. But for that cursed slip of mine about being "by way of," I think he would have been content merely to warn me back and let me go my homeward course in peace. Now was my chance to wipe out that unfortunate lapse.

"You accuse me of being a British spy," I resumed. "It may be well to have a clear understanding between us, so that my case, when I state it at headquarters, shall not be prejudicial to you. I am not a spy. I am not an Englishman. I am an American. Romney is my name. If you had orders to prevent any one from going up the river, you could have ordered me back, and no harm would have been done. Instead, you charge me with spying, and you tie me up and march me between your men like a convicted felon. Once more I deny my guilt and make formal demand on you for release."

He halted, hesitating. The loosely marching squad shambled to a full stop. All looked at me with varying degrees of heavy curiosity.

"You're American, hey?" grunted the sergeant at last. "Where are you from?"

"Baltimore."

"What are you doing down here on the Patuxent?"

"Visiting friends.   I went out this morning for a day's—"

"What friends?"

Racking my memory only for a moment, I spoke the first local name that sprang to my mind.

"I am guest at the manor-house of Colonel Jared Scholes," said I. "And he will see that you answer for your treatment of me."

The name produced an instant impression. But not quite the sort I had hoped for. The sergeant scratched his head and looked at me in frank perplexity; yet made no instant move to set me free.

"You're stopping at Colonel Scholes's?" he muttered.

"Yes. The manor-house crowning the hill above the Bladensburg Turnpike. If you know the neighborhood at all, you'll—"

"Oh, I know the neighborhood," he made haste to reply. "I've been on duty here all year. I know the Scholes house, too. How long have you been stopping there?"

"Not quite a week," I answered, glad to see that I was bringing him to reason.

"What time did you leave his house on this shooting picnic we just broke up?"

"At about seven this morning. I took a boat from Clarges Landing—you know where that is?—and had been rowing about an hour when you overhauled me."

I fairly beamed on him. For at each word of mine his bearing was growing more and more deferential.

"So?" he ruminated, as I paused. "Maybe we *have* made a mistake, sir. And I hope you'll overlook it. How many folks are there at the Scholes house now, sir? A large party or—"

"No. At present I am the only guest. There are no—"

"That's queer," he murmured. "Some one was telling me the colonel was expecting quite a party there, this week or next. Maybe—"

"He is," I answered glibly. "But they don't arrive till to-morrow night. At present there is no one but the colonel, his family, and myself. But it is hot standing here. If you will kindly release me and apologize for your overzealous error, I will not mention the affair to the colonel or to any one. I—"

"Now, that's real kind of you," he cried delightedly. "And just to show our appreciation, we'll escort you right to the colonel's door— and inside. It's no trouble to us to go there. We were on our way, anyhow. You see, Mr. Spy, that's our headquarters just now. For the past month the manor-house has been chock-full of off'cers. It's queer you didn't happen to notice any of 'em during the week you've spent there. Fall in there! March!"

CHAPTER II.
UNDER FALSE COLORS.

PERHAPS you whose eyes have followed my version of the fore-going scene may be as much at a loss concerning my status as I had hoped to make the thickheaded sergeant. So, briefly as may be, I will explain how I, Dick Romney, American, chanced, in this third year of the War of 1812, to fall captive to a squad of my own country's soldiers on charge of being a British spy.

I come of Colonial New Jersey stock and passed my childhood in my native State, varying this habitat by long visits to my mother's relatives in Bladensburg, six miles from Washington. (Hence my intimate knowledge of all the tract of country where now I found myself.)

My father—a former colonel in General Washington's own New Jersey brigade—dying when I was but fourteen, my mother went to live with a sister in England, and took me with her, my elder brother inheriting the broad New Jersey estates. Nor had I seen my native land again for full sixteen years.

I was educated in England, imbibing British customs and prejudices, as might any impressionable boy of my age; and had, through family influence, secured at nineteen a commission in King George's army.

Bonaparte kept his majesty's soldiers busy in those days, I can tell you. And the lieutenant with brains and pluck had rare chances of advancement.

I was a colonel at twenty-seven; and wore, as mementoes of the Peninsular wars, not only a sword-slash over the cheek, received at the assault of Ciudad Rodrigo, but a distinguished service order, pinned to my breast by no less a hand than that of Wellington, our "Iron Duke."

Well, by the spring of 1814 we had Bonaparte tied up safe and fast (as we thought) at Elba; and for the moment no other war save that with America menaced England. Some fourteen thousand of our Peninsular veterans were ordered to the United States to help reduce Uncle Sam's already hard-pressed armies to utter submission.

My own regiment was one of those shipped across seas on this mission. Then it was that, somewhat to my own amaze, I found I could not draw sword against the land my father had risked life and fortune to set free.

I had thought myself a thorough Englishman. If I had not joined in my fellow officers' sneers at America, I had at least felt that my loyalty was all to the British flag, under whose shadow I had so long and so successfully fought.

When, in 1812, war had broken out between the United States and Great Britain over the latter's high-handed insults to Yankee seamen and Yankee commerce, I had been too busy fighting Soult, Dupont, and Masséna in the Spanish Peninsula to trouble myself over any problem farther afield than the nearest French line. Beyond the fact that America's many losses by land had been partly atoned for by her brilliant success in sea fights, the "War of 1812" had meant comparatively little to me.

But when the question of taking up arms against the old homeland arose, something within me cried out against the deed. On impulse, I sold my commission and resigned from the British army.

As I was loafing drearily about London, a month later—for nothing is so wearisome to a soldier as the days of enforced idleness following active service—news reached me of my elder brother's death and of my own heirship to the New Jersey property.

I planned to set out at once for America to take possession. But at the same time I learned that my old commander, General Ross, was to take four regiments of our Peninsular veterans and reenforce Admiral Cockburn on the Chesapeake. Stirring times were promised; and at thought of missing so much of the martial excitement which for years had been as meat and drink to me, I hit on a very natural and simple plan.

I stated my case to Ross, explaining that, though I could not turn against the land of my birth, I longed to follow the future deeds of my old Peninsular comrades. The talk ended by his appointing me honorary major on his personal staff; in strictly non-combatant capacity, and with the thorough understanding that I should be employed merely in a clerical position and not expected to aid in any way in his plans against America. So it was that, late in July, I found myself with thirty-five hundred Peninsular veterans in Ross's camp at the mouth of the Chesapeake.

There, for the first time, I set eyes on that most picturesque dare-devil of the age—Admiral George Cockburn, commander of the blockade which England was enforcing along all the Atlantic coast.

I verily believe the man was a bit insane. How else explain his boundless generosity and ferocious cruelty; his kindnesses and bar-barities; his wild, gay boyishness and crafty strategic wiles? He was a mass of utter contradictions and, withal, the most lovable, grotesque figure of two continents.

It was at mess in the impromptu Army and Navy Club organized in our camp that the subject of Barney's flotilla had come up.

This fleet of gunboats had done more than everything else to mar Cockburn's blockading schemes. So he had mobilized his fleet in over-whelming numbers at the Chesapeake's mouth, not only to cooperate with Ross on an inland raid, but to crush Barney once and forever.

But, as though by magic the whole flotilla had vanished before his approach. Its whereabouts was a mystery and a decidedly needful thing to determine.

For neither Ross nor Cockburn relished the idea of stripping the British fleet of such mariners as would be necessary for the invasion if, in their absence, Barney's gunboats might be expected to bear down on the ill-defended shipping and destroy it, leaving the advancing army cut off from escape.

Accordingly, Cockburn had sent out a veritable swarm of spies in search of the flotilla. But such as had not been captured had returned as ignorant as they had set out.

Cockburn was in a fine rage, I can assure you, and his language was a liberal education to even the most voluble teamsters in camp.

I had a theory of my own. I knew the course of the near-by Patuxent, and realized how easy it would be to secrete a whole royal squadron in some of its sheltered upper reaches. This news I did not impart to my friends. For, was I not strictly non-combatant—a mere spectator?

But in reply to a wrathful declaration of Cockburn's that "Not a man who trod boot-leather had the wit to find the pestilent Yankee hulks," I had made shift to reply modestly that I would be willing to wager twenty guineas I could locate the flotilla within forty-eight hours.

Cockburn snapped up the bet before it was fairly made. So I hastened to add that, though I was certain I could find Barney's fleet, I had no intention whatsoever of divulging its whereabouts. I offered, however, to seek it and, on my return, to state on my honor as an officer and gentleman whether or not I had discovered the flotilla.

Cockburn was vastly chapfallen at this addendum to my boast; but, like the insatiate gambler he was, took the wager on my own terms. Others of the mess, too, backed one or the other of us, until a goodly sum hung on the result.

I set forth, in civilian garb, on my own private quest, half the spare cash of the camp hanging on my success.

Lest you who read may judge this freak trivial, pray understand that it was an era of unbridled gambling, and that he who made and won the wildest wager stood highest in regimental fame. When the Constitution (Old Ironsides) fought and sank the Guerrière at sea, it is a historic fact that the battle was the outcome of a bet, and that the rival commanders, Hull and Dacre, had wagered a cocked-hat on the result.

Be all that as it may, I was but twelve hours on my search of the Patuxent's backwaters when my friend the sergeant, with his squad, overhauled me. My own folly had done the rest.

And now, thanks to silly blunders and overconfidence, I found myself under arrest as a spy.

At first, as the irritation wore off, I was inclined to laugh at my plight. Then, studying the matter more closely, I grew grave.

I could foresee that it would be no simple matter to explain to some prejudiced United States provost marshal's satisfaction that I had embarked on this mission merely to win a bet, and that I had given my word not to divulge to Cockburn—in event of my success—the whereabouts of the fleet. Also, that I, though on the British major-general's staff, was a non-combatant and had no designs against my country.

Yes, the whole thing would sound unconvincing. Disgustingly so. Instinctively, I tried to loosen my neck-cloth. It had begun to feel uncomfortably like a rope.

CHAPTER III.

THE GIRL.

IT was high noon when we drew up in front of Colonel Scholes's great manor-house on the hill-crest overlooking the Bladensburg Turnpike. The sergeant left us standing there in the scorching sun of the driveway, the curious center of a hundred loafing soldiers, while he entered the house to report.

Five minutes later he returned and ushered me up the steps, across the deep porch and through the wide-open doorway into the central hall of the manor.

The cool and gloom of the place were grateful after our long, hot tramp. My eyes, growing used to the dim light as I was brought to a halt, showed me a stout man seated at a table in the center of the hall. About the place sat or lounged several officers and a civilian or two.

"This is the prisoner, general," reported the sergeant, saluting and falling back a pace at my side.

The man at the table looked up and surveyed my perspiring, dusty self with mechanical interest. Even in that brief instant of mutual scrutiny, I noted how harassed and bothered was his wrinkled face.

He had the air of a man who has been nagged almost to desperation. Nor, as I was later to learn, did this aspect belie him.

But there was something else in his face that set my heart to jumping in a fashion wholly unconnected with any fear. It was a resemblance—of expression rather than feature—that made me forget my present danger and sent my mind flying back to the other side of the ocean.

Another moment, and I knew of what the man's not especially handsome visage reminded me.

A winding garden path beyond the mission guest-house near Madrid—a meeting with one I had not seen since childhood—the pressure of a girlish hand, the clear, frank look of a girl's eyes—a few days' acquaintanceship, whose memory I had never been wholly able to lose.

Why did this plump, middle-aged man recall all these visions to me? To me who stood in the shadow of the rope?

"Who are you?" I blurted out, even as his lips had parted to make the initial query of his examination.

It was the oddest, least-expected happening in the world—this inquisition of a general by his prisoner. And a ruffle of quickly checked laughter ran through the group of spectators.

One man—a civilian who, from a sofa near by, had been scanning a close-written document—looked up with eager, amused interest and thrust his paper into his pocket.

I did not expect the general to reply to my impertinence, unless to chide it. But he, as well as myself, seemed momentarily off guard.

For he answered, apparently before the peculiarity of my question had the opportunity to strike him:

"I am General Winder, in command of the—"

Then, checking himself with a frown, he added hastily:

"The examination will begin."

I scarcely heard him.

"Winder!" Now it was explained, this haunting likeness.

The Winders—doubtless relatives of his — had owned the estate next my father's in New Jersey. On the day when I, a hobbledehoy youth of fourteen, left for England, I had received a solemn, ardent proposal of marriage—my first and last—from no less a person than seven-year-old Dorothy Winder, my neighbor's only daughter and my own best beloved playmate.

She had on that day of parting tearfully begged me to come back as soon as I should be grown up, and marry her. With the pitying condescension of a big boy for a little girl I had gravely promised.

Nor had I given her, I fear, a second thought, for the next fourteen years. Then, two years before my return to America, we had met by pure chance at the guest-house outside Madrid.

She was making the "grand tour" with her father. For two blissful days I had prolonged my stay at the tumbledown old guest-house, seeking Dorothy's company at every moment and postponing dangerously long my return to duty.

For there was something about that tall, willowy girl, with her level gray eyes, that one does not find in European damsels. We had talked over old times, she had told me of the old home and of all that had happened in the uneventful routine of life there since my departure, and had listened with flattering interest to the tale of my few petty war experiences.

Then I had ridden away. But fast as I might ride or hard as I might fight, I could never thenceforth wholly rid myself of that odd, "hidden-laughter" expression of hers, nor the level, clear look of her eyes.

Those same eyes had stayed in my mind to the prohibition of many a gay escapade in which my comrades reveled. And more than once I had half wished I might rid myself of their memory.

When the chance had come to go to my own country again and settle down among the hills of my childhood, I had all along recognized my chief, if unconfessed, motive in taking advantage of it. Was I in love with Dorothy Winder? How can I say?

It never so occurred to me in those days. To think ever of her seemed natural. That was all.

I was still tracing idly that faint family likeness in my inquisitor's face, and he was forced to repeat a question I had let pass unheard.

"Your name?"

"Richard Romney."

"From—?"

"New Jersey."

"Jerseymen pronounce the 'r' in their State's name somewhat more distinctly than you do," he commented. "What section?"

"Pompton."

"Pompton, eh?" he snapped, looking up at me with a new cunning. "I chance to have relatives there."

"Squire Gabriel Winder?" I suggested. "His place adjoins mine on the right. On the left are the lands of the old patroon—Petrus Ryerson. The Winder estate on the other side touches the Schuylers'."

General Winder leaned back, clearly puzzled. The others, too, seemed more interested. The young man on the sofa was frankly enjoying the scene.

"You seem to have some knowledge of Jersey topography," admitted the general, "but it proves nothing. You say you are one of the Pompton Romneys. Yet you are several hundred miles away from home and talking like an Englishman. How do you account for that?"

"You must be William Winder, attorney at law, of Philadelphia,"

I countered. "Yet you also are some distance from home, and in the uniform of a general. Is the one harder to understand than the other?"

"Insolence will not save you, sir!" cried the general, flushing. "I warn you you will not help your case by such talk. You are under grave suspicion and—"

"Then, sir," said I, "if I might suggest, suppose we get down to business. I can lift that same 'grave suspicion' more easily when I know its nature. Up to the present time, we seem to be engaging in a rather useless genealogical contest. Can't we go faster? I merely suggest it."

"Sir!" thundered the now thoroughly irate general, "are you aware of your position? Are you informed who and what I am, that you—"

"I have had much useless information thrust upon me from time to time," I yawned.

There was a stifled snicker from the officers. But I saw the man on the sofa frown slightly. His bright, interested face showed a trace of disappointment, and I was almost sorry for my gross flippancy.

"I shall ask you to answer my questions truthfully," proceeded Winder, swallowing his wrath with a certain stiff dignity. "Remember, sir, truth will be best for you in the end. If you try to deceive me as to—"

"If I answer your questions at all," I retorted, "I shall do so truthfully. But up to now, permit me to remind you, the only questions you've done me the honor to ask were concerning my name and the geography of northern New Jersey. On neither of those counts, I take it, am I under arrest."

"You are under arrest, sir, on the charge of being a British spy."

"I can answer that accusation in one sentence. I am not a spy, and I am not British."

"You were found inside the lines in civilian dress. You speak with a strong English accent."

"There are probably several thousand civilians like myself inside the lines in civilian dress," I answered. "That gentleman on the sofa over there, for instance. Yet no one arrests them. As for my English accent, I was educated in England, like many another native-born American."

"If you are a soldier at all," pursued Winder, "you are not in the ranks. Your bearing and education prove that. Do you hold a commission in the British army?"

"I do not."

"Commanding officer to inspect guard mount!" called the man on the sofa, mimicking the high-pitched, nasal tone and clipping words of an English aide-de-camp.

At the sound, before I could recollect my pose of civilian, I had clicked my heels together, dropped my left hand to where my saber had been wont to hang, and made a half-face-about toward the door.

Then, too late, I saw the trap wherein I had fallen. It did not need the bellow of amusement from the others to tell me how habit had betrayed me into a maneuver which no civilian could have thought of executing.

I turned wrathfully toward the sofa. Its occupant, alone of all the bystanders, was not laughing.

His handsome young face showed genuine regret. Before Winder could open his mouth, the man was on his feet beside me.

"I spoke without thinking, general!" he pleaded, his deep voice vibrant with contrition. "It was a scurvy trick to play, and"—with a graceful bow to me—"I ask this gentleman's pardon. May I beg that you will not take his impulsive act into consideration?"

"I am sorry, Mr. Key," replied the general, "but you must see how impossible it is for me to comply with your wish. You very cleverly stripped the mask from this fellow, and I thank you. The investigation now will be easier."

"But it is not fair," protested Key. "I took him unaware, and by recalling an order I used to hear when I was in England years ago. If I have prejudiced his case, will you let me make amends by acting as his counsel? Though I am not a military judge-advocate, yet, as you know, I am a member in good standing of the Washington bar. May I serve as his lawyer?"

"Tush!" fumed Winder. "The whole thing's cursedly irregular as it stands! We've caught a British officer in civilian dress inside our lines. What else is there to it? The case is clear. Prisoner!"—waving the protesting Mr. Key aside and wheeling about to face me—"have you any logical reason to offer why sentence should not be passed upon you?"

I had not. I knew how futile would be my plea were I to tell the whole truth. I was in a vise. Again that curious tightness of my neck-cloth and the sensation as of rope about my throat.

Well, it was the chance of war. Had it come in the regular performance of my military duties, I should not have murmured. But to have fought unscathed through the fearful Peninsular campaigns, and now, having laid down my sword, to die by hanging! To have braved Napoleon Bonaparte only to fall into the hands of William H. Winder, ex-attorney at law!

"The sentence of the court," began the general solemnly, "is that you be taken from this spot to the guard-house, and that at sunset—"

"I protest!" broke in Key. "The prisoner's guilt is not conclusively proven. That being the case, I warn you that I shall ride at once to Washington and lay the matter before President Madison. I believe he will grant a stay, if not a pardon."

I saw that shadow of worry and almost of fear creep back over Winder's puckered brow at mention of the President. He hesitated. Then broke into petty rage.

"Mr. Key," he stormed, "you are interfering where you have no business. I must request you to be silent and withdraw at once from this case. If you do not, I shall place you under arrest. I am master here! I am commander of the army of defense in the—"

"*Are* you?"

Key's brief query was respectful. Almost deferential. Quite free from slur or sneer. Yet it sent the blood to Winder's face, and his look of worry deepened.

What peevish retort he made, I know not. For just then I saw her.

She was coming slowly down the broad stair, her clinging white dress swishing gently at each step, her dainty little high-heeled shoes clicking a soft tattoo against the polished wood.

Down she came, the cool green light filtering through the closed blinds and seeming to caress the willowy lines of her figure. A single ray of sunshine through a nick in the shutters struck athwart her dusky hair, turning it golden and throwing a shimmering aura about her proud little head.

Oh, it was good to have seen her thus—cool, regal, girlish, infinitely lovely! It was good to have seen her, if for the last time on earth.

Forgotten was the death that loomed heavy above me; forgotten that mortal fear that had sanded my throat; the clash and quarrel of the two men over my tenuous life.

All I saw, all I knew, all I *cared,* was that she was coming toward me down the stairway. How she chanced to be there I no more paused to wonder than one wonders at the strange persons and places heaped together in some wonder-dream.

She reached the stair-foot, not ten feet away from me, evidently unaware that business was going forward. It was then that both Winder and Key stopped their squabble and looked at me.

I suppose one of them had asked me some question I had not heard, and that, wondering at my silence, they had turned to note the cause.

For their eyes now followed the direction of mine. I felt, rather than noted, Key's little involuntary start of joyous surprise. Winder blustered pettishly:

"Please don't interrupt me just now, Dorothy. We are very busy."

She bowed and passed on. She had not so much as seen me. All the world grew at once very dark.

Winder was beginning to address me again when I heard a young officer, who had risen and bowed at the girl's approach, whisper in loud self-importance to Dorothy:

"The general's trying a spy!"

She turned, curious, toward our group at the table. And our eyes met!

CHAPTER IV.

A HAPPY RESPITE.

How Dorothy Winder recognized the spruce dragoon colonel of the Madrid days in the disheveled, dusty prisoner who leaned across her uncle's table, staring dazedly at her, I do not know. Women's eyes are better than men's for piercing mere externals.

But certain it is that, after one instant's survey, she swept forward with both hands outstretched.

"Colonel Romney! Dick!" she cried, dropping back, in the excitement of the moment, to the familiar address of our childhood.

And I, shouldering my way past the two guards who stood beside me, had sprung forward and grasped those cool, white little hands in my own hot, eager grip.

"Dorothy!" I muttered, confused, unreasonably happy.

It was my loss of self-control, I think, that brought her to herself and to the fact that others were present to whom my ecstatic, gawky greeting must be making us both ridiculous.

It is always the woman who first recovers self-possession. So it was now. She drew back slightly and, turning to me, said:

"You have come home at last? We hoped, in Pompton, you'd return, now that the estate is yours. But how did you run the blockade?"

"In the simplest possible way," answered I loudly, an inspiration coming to me. "I crossed with Ross's transports. You know I used to be in his brigade in Spain. After I left the army I wanted to come back and settle at the old home. So I put my case to Ross, and he gave me transportation, landing me safe at the Chesapeake. As soon as this invasion-scare is over and I can get conveyance of some sort, I shall start north."

It was not to her, but *through* her to the others, that I was talking. All at once the hitherto tangled affair had become absurdly simple. With Dorothy to identify me, my case took on quite a new color.

And even as I spoke I realized my words carried weight. The two guards had moved toward me again, but General Winder motioned them back, and himself rose and stepped forward.

"You know this gentleman, it seems?" he said rather unnecessarily to Dorothy.

"Why, of course!" she replied. "We were children together at Pompton. Then we met in Madrid, two years ago. This is Lieutenant-Colonel Richard Romney—General Winder, my uncle."

There was a somewhat awkward pause. I broke it by saying in explanation:

"Your arrival was decidedly timely, Miss Winder. Your uncle, under a misapprehension, was about to—"

The general purpled and tugged surreptitiously at my sleeve. But Key caught up my story at exactly the proper point, and went on, with a half laugh.

"Colonel Romney was met by a squad of skirmishers and brought here on suspicion. His own story and your recognition, Miss Winder, turn an annoying situation into a capital joke."

"I—I remember now!" exclaimed Dorothy with a little gasp. "Captain Vokes said you were trying a spy. Surely you didn't think—"

"Vokes was mistaken," rapped out Winder hastily. "Colonel Romney, I suppose we owe you an apology. I hope you'll keep our unfortunate error to yourself. You see, in troublous times like these—"

He paused. The harassed, almost cowed look was again on his face. I was yet to learn how cruelly the man was hampered at every step, how severely and persistently the administration nagged and harried him.

From a naturally good soldier he was fast degenerating into a badgered, uncertain subaltern. To this trait, perhaps, I owed in part his willingness to drop the case against me rather than run the risk of a reprimand from the War Department for molesting an important New Jersey landowner.

"'Scuse me, gen'ral," muttered the sergeant who had captured me, tiptoeing forward and trying to gain Winder's private ear, "but that ain't the story he—"

"Pooh-pooh, man!" sputtered the general testily. "That will do. You've made a blunder that ought to cost you your rank, Sergeant McCrea. Be off! Next time, learn to discriminate between a spy and a gentleman."

As the discomfited McCrea shuffled back among his fellows, his lowering gaze met mine. I took no great pains to check a smile of malicious triumph. He caught the look, and I knew in a flash he still believed me a spy, and held me responsible for his reprimand.

His was one of those narrow, long heads that belong, as a rule, to a man who does not forget. Mentally, I made a note to be on guard against him should we meet again, and I felt it would be no fault of his if we did not.

I accepted Winder's invitation to remain to lunch, and until the heat of the day should be past. He went further by offering me a horse and a passport, to insure my speedier and safe journey north.

In the afternoon I had a long, delightful talk with Dorothy in the shaded gallery above-stairs. She was to have ridden across to an aunt's in Bladensburg directly after luncheon, she told me, as her visit to General Winder and his wife was at an end. And Key was to have been her escort.

She delayed the departure until sundown, at my urgent plea. Key was forced reluctantly to set off without her, for he had affairs of moment in Bladensburg.

He showed no outward chagrin at having to go alone; though I could see how unwillingly he gave up the prospect of the five-mile ride with her.

There was something very winning about the young lawyer who had so gallantly come to my defense. One could not help liking him. It was with genuine regret that I bade him farewell for what I then foolishly supposed was the last time.

It was a dreamy, utterly happy afternoon I spent on the long veranda at Dorothy's side. We talked of every conceivable subject save that which lay close to my heart. That could—*must*—wait until I had had chance to woo her in due form.

I foresaw a pastoral, beautiful courtship amid my quiet Jersey hills, when her visit to her Southern relatives should be finished and we should both find ourselves in the dear old Northern State again.

In the meantime I told her of the end of my soldiering and of my determination to live in America. It was on my tongue-tip to confess the ridiculous story of my twenty-guinea bet with Cockburn.

But the wager, which had seemed so amusing when made amid the riot and song of a mess-table, did not now appeal to me as the kind of thing of which this clear-eyed New Jersey girl would approve. So, like a fool, I let pass the opportunity.

Dorothy had much to tell me of the war. I was surprised at her ardent patriotism; for such was not then the tone of the country at large.

As history shows, the general feeling up to this time, in the War of 1812, had been of a decidedly lukewarm, passionless sort. It was hard to believe this faction-wrung, "moderate" nation was made up of the sons of men who had conquered at Yorktown, starved at Valley Forge, and died for their freedom at Concord and Lexington.

I commented on this to Dorothy.

"It will come!" she cried with cheeks aglow. "It will come! The spirit of '76 is not dead. When it awakens, England will be made to feel it as she felt it once before; and she will be the first to cry for peace."

A faint curl of smoke smeared the southern horizon. It caught our gaze and Dorothy pointed toward it.

"Look!" she exclaimed, "another village sacked and burnt! More of 'Demon' Cockburn's horrible work. He has ravaged our coasts as mercilessly as though we lived in the days of the Norse pirates."

"Aren't you hard upon Cockburn? War is war."

"Is it war to burn defenseless villages and murder unarmed people? If so—"

"But Cockburn is an awfully good chap in his way."

"You know him?" she asked in pained amaze.

"I have met him," said I, with a belated caution.

She shuddered.

"I wonder," she went on, "if it is really true that he and General Ross mean to march on Washington."

It was *my* turn for amazement. Ross fondly hoped no American knew of his daring project to strike inland and attack the nation's capital. He and Cockburn had resolved to make the dash before sufficient troops could be massed to block their progress. Should they be successfully opposed—as even in their most sanguine moments they feared they would—it could be explained to the government as a mere reconnaissance.

If, on the other hand, by rare good luck they could seize Washington, it meant unheard-of glory for both.

"Is there talk of such an attempt?" I asked.

"That is why my uncle has been sent here," she returned, "and why the militia for miles around are concentrating. They say it is only the fear of Commodore Barney that holds the British back. If once they could find where his flotilla is hidden—"

Oh, what a temptation to put the question! To ask: "*Where* is it hidden?" But I could not use this pure girl's confidence as means toward the winning of my wretched bet. So I changed the subject and the conversation drifted pleasantly from politics to self.

"I go North next month," she said at last, as the sun hung low and I rose to depart; "I shall expect to find you settled as squire, peace justice, and all other titles that go with your position, by the time I reach

Pompton. But won't you find it stupid to rust as a country gentleman after all your years of adventure?"

"No," I answered shortly.

"I should think you would," she persisted idly.

"*You* should think nothing of the sort," I retorted as I held out my hand in farewell. "It rests with you."

She seemed to understand all that lay behind my words. Or, perhaps it was the glow of sunset that flushed her wonderful face.

"In a month, then," said I, as, my good-byes to the others all spoken, I ran down the steps to where a trooper held my horse.

"In a month!" she replied gaily.

And there was no warning spirit to whisper to either of us a hint of the myriad stirring events wherein we two, side by side, were to play our part before that short month was at an end.

CHAPTER V.

ON RISKY WORK.

I HAD turned out of the grounds of the manor-house and was about to put my horse to a canter when, along the road toward me, advanced Sergeant McCrea. He had evidently been awaiting my exit, in order to speak to me on neutral ground.

The sight of the man touched me with compunction. He had made a clever arrest and had, in reward, received unjust rebuke and had seen his prey escape.

I drew up and awaited him.

"I'm sorry you got the reprimand," I said, tossing him a gold guinea. "You mus'n't let it discourage you, my man."

Now, in England, so condescending a speech combined with so lavish a gift from a colonel to a mere "non-com" would in those days have filled the latter with almost slavish gratitude. Hence—for I knew little of my own countrymen—his reply astounded me.

Catching the coin deftly in air he spat contemptuously upon it and then, letting the golden disk fall to the road, ground it into the dust with his hobnailed heel.

"I'm not your 'man,' Mr. Spy," he growled, "but you're the 'man' of King George whose face is stamped on that guinea. I've showed you how we Yankees treat his face. Maybe my time'll come to do the same to your own. When it does—"

"Do you realize," I broke in, controlling my hot temper at his insolence and speaking quietly, "do you realize I could repeat that speech to General Winder and have you not only degraded from rank, but flogged as well?"

"You can get me 'broke,'" he retorted, "and I s'pose you will. But we don't flog free men in the American army. We leave that to John Bull and his officers who spy because they're too cowardly to fight. I've been waiting for you, mister. I wanted to tell you that you wriggled out of trouble pretty slick to-day, but I'm laying for you, and some day or other *I'll get you.* Understand? Some day when there won't be a petticoat for you to hide behind."

I saw nothing would suit him better than a furious verbal wrangle. But I had neither time nor wish to bandy words further with a Yankee sergeant. So I put spurs to my horse and, without a second thought for the fellow's threat, galloped off.

But the brief colloquy had had the effect of banishing from my mind the glamour of the long, happy afternoon. And I found myself riding on in a decidedly black, reckless mood. Then it was that my insensate idea came to me.

For a mile or so my northward road lay alongside the river. What was to prevent my continuing for a few miles farther along its banks on the chance of coming upon traces of Barney's flotilla? Could I but find the little fleet's whereabouts, I might, under cover of night, ride back to Ross's camp, arrive there by dawn, claim my wager, and at once continue my northern journey.

Armed as I was with Winder's pass, none could turn me back. It irked me to think of having boastfully declared to Cockburn that I could locate Barney's gunboats—and then to go North with my boast unfulfilled. Moreover, dozens of men at the mess, relying on my pledge and on my reputation for resource, had backed my wager heavily.

Why should I be the cause of these old friends losing money many of them could ill spare?

It was not as though I were going to reveal to Cockburn the whereabouts of the flotilla. As I have said, he had agreed to take my unsupported word that I had succeeded where his best spies had failed.

No, I do not pretend to excuse the folly of my whim. I am not a hero or a wise man. I have never claimed to be either. Perhaps that is why the mad notion took strong and stronger hold of me the more I thought it over.

Dusk had long fallen and the full moon stood low and red in the east when I halted my horse at last, after a two-hour reconnaissance of the upper reaches of the Patuxent. I had spent the intervening time scouring the shore, peering through the dim light into every sheltered cove. But I had seen no sign of the hidden flotilla.

My wild mood had died and I was about to turn back, unsuccessful, toward the turnpike; then strike off to the northern road.

Even as I came to the resolve my eye was caught by a distant spot of yellow light. Not that of fire, but a gleam as of moonlight reflected on some polished surface.

The gleam shone through a mass of foliage in a scrub-oak grove, perhaps a hundred yards from the road. The river ran parallel to the highway. This grove was at right angles to it. Yet, memory of the countless backwaters and bays along the stream's course started a train of reasoning in my mind.

The gleam I had seen was yellowish. Not like that from glass, but from bright metal. What metal body could be concealed in the grove?

I dismounted, tied my horse and advanced on foot, crouching and moving with the silent caution learned by long scouting trips; taking advantage of every bit of shadow along my route.

Coming to the grove's edge I saw that it was no ordinary patch of woodland, but a well-nigh impenetrable thicket bordering a lagoon of considerable size. The spot of light I had long since lost and I was now walking by my recollection of its general locality.

So, creeping along in the shade, I skirted the wood, catching now and then a glimmer of water ahead of me, between the low-lying branches.

At a point a few rods from where I had reached the grove's edge, I noted a thinning of foliage and underbrush, barely three feet wide, from whence I could command a fair view of the expanse of lagoon. But the moon was still too low to permit me to gain more than a general idea of a shimmering, watery surface.

I must wait until the luminary should arise high enough to top that screen of leafage and shine unobscured upon the lagoon. Then I should be able to solve my doubts and to learn whether or not that spot of light had really come from some bit of brass-work on a gunboat.

I dared not advance into the wood, meanwhile, for fear of running foul of any shore-picket who might be stationed there.

Little by little the moon edged upward. I did not stand with bated breath, as do scouts in story-books. The whir of summer insects and the calls of whippoorwills drowned any ordinary low sound.

At last a clear bar of moonlight fell across the lagoon, spreading until the waters were silver bright. I caught my breath as I watched.

For, on that gleaming surface, at regular intervals, and with no lantern showing, lay black, moveless hulks, their fantom spars rising like ghosts above the silent decks.

"One—two—three—four—five," I counted, and so on until I came to the full quota.

My bet was won! The whole missing flotilla was tucked away, safe and hidden out of Cockburn's reach, and awaiting its time to rush back to the scene of war.

With a smothered laugh at my own cleverness, I drew back out of the frame of boughs and—turned to confront a leveled pistol not eight inches from my head.

CHAPTER VI.

IN STRANGE PREDICAMENT.

SO absorbed had I been in my contemplation of the hidden flotilla that it is scant wonder I had heard no one's approach.

The apparition of the silent figure in the long riding-cloak, standing so close to me and covering me with a pistol, was enough to jar any man's steady nerve.

I did not speak. What was there to say? I was fairly caught.

For a mad instant I had some thought of dropping suddenly to my knees in the hope that my opponent might be flurried into firing over my head; then of grappling the fellow and escaping to my distant horse before pickets from the flotilla could come up. My antagonist was smaller and slighter than I, and might be overpowered before he could draw a second pistol—if he had one.

But, even as the plan flashed through my mind, I noted the presence of a second and larger man standing close at the heels of the first. How many others there might be in the vicinity I could not tell. For we stood in the dense shade of the grove's border.

At any rate, the odds were too great for me, unarmed as I was. I must count on my wit to free me later. At present—

The figure with the pistol spoke no word, but stood with motionless, outstretched arm, the pistol-barrel steady as a rock. There is at times something terribly disconcerting about silence.

We stood there thus for perhaps five seconds. To me it seemed an hour.

Then the second figure moved forward through the gloom. Still keeping me covered, the first whispered something. The other nodded and whipped out a leather bridle concealed under his coat.

Stepping around behind me, he deftly passed the bridle about my arms, pinioning them to my sides at the elbow and securing the knot behind with what seemed to me quite unnecessary force.

There I was, for the second time in twelve hours, not only prisoner in my own countrymen's hands, but tied up in most humiliating fashion.

I fancied at first that McCrea might have followed me. But one of my captors was far too short, and the other too broad for the lanky sergeant. No, I had probably fallen into the hands of a couple of Barney's pickets.

And at the instant I remembered that in my pocket I carried Winder's pass. In the excitement of the sudden apparition I had wholly forgotten the precious document, and now at the memory of its possession I could have shouted aloud in sheer relief.

As the bonds drew my arms to my sides my cloaked captor lowered his pistol with what sounded like a sigh of relief. With soldierly instinct, I at once divined he was unused to this sort of business and terribly nervous over its performance. So I said lightly:

"If you are highwaymen, you will gain little, I'm afraid. My wallet is light. In fact, its chief contents is a pass signed by General Winder."

At my speech, the pistol-arm fell limply and its owner bent forward with sudden, sharp interest, as though to pierce the gloom and read my face. Then the pistol-bearer spoke, in a curious, muffled voice:

"Cato! A light!"

Flint struck steel in a tiny shower of sparks. And ere their brief gleam died out I had started back with an incredulous cry. For my captor was no man.

It was Dorothy Winder!

Her big negro groom, Cato, struck flint and steel again, and yet again, in his effort to secure a light. But I did not look a second time. Nor, I felt, did she. For from her little cry of horror I knew the recognition had been mutual.

At last she spoke again. This time with a weary, dead quality in her usually clear young voice.

"Never mind the light, Cato," she said. "Lead your prisoner back to the road. Some of Commodore Barney's sentinels might find us here."

"Will I untie de gem'm'n,' Miss Dor'thy?" queried the groom.

"No. Bring him as he is."

Turning her back on us, the girl walked swiftly, with bent head, in the direction of the road. At Cato's side I stumbled on in her wake, wondering, confused, wholly at a loss, yet oddly content to obey her capricious order.

We came finally to the highway, at a point near where my mount still stood tethered. I noted that two other horses—one of them carrying a side-saddle, the other bearing valise saddle-bags strapped to the crupper—were standing close by. Dorothy was there in the moonlight awaiting us.

"Ride up the road beyond the curve, Cato," she ordered, in the same lifeless tone. "I will call when I want you."

The groom obeyed. Nor did either of us speak until he was out of earshot. Then Dorothy turned slowly toward me, her lovely face strangely white and stern in the uncertain light.

"You *spy!*"

There was no wrath, no sharpness in the two short syllables. Nothing but sadness fraught with an infinite scorn.

The words cut me like a whiplash, which is odd, since the number of times they had been applied to me that day ought to have robbed their opprobrium of some of its novelty. They also awoke in me an unreasoning anger.

"You are mistaken," I said stiffly. "I am—"

"You are the man I saved to-day from the fate he deserved," she cut in coldly. "The man whom I believed honorable and all that a soldier and gentleman should be. I vouched for you to my uncle. I made him think—as I myself was foolish enough to think—that the charges against you were absurd. That your story was true, and that you were above the contemptible act of seeking to learn your country's secrets and then selling them to its enemies. I believed all that. I made others believe it. I set you free. And you reward me by—"

"Stop!" I cried. "You are unjust. You have no right to assume that I—"

"That you are not at this moment on the northern road instead of miles out of your alleged course? Is it that I have no right to assume? Or that you were, five minutes ago, skulking over there, spying upon Commodore Barney's little fleet, counting their number aloud and laughing at your success in outwitting us poor provincials? Is it in *that* assumption that I am wrong?"

She paused, her level voice choking. But for the instant I could not reply.

How explain away these two horribly obvious facts? How make her understand?

She went on, regaining her self-control:

"It will be an excellent camp-fire story, won't it? A fine tale of how a smart British officer wriggled out of danger by a girl's help, hoodwinked that girl into telling him the army's plans, borrowed one of his host's horses, and cajoled the patriot general into giving him a safe conduct through the lines! How he did all this and then went gleefully on with his noble task of spying!

"Oh, a charming romance, on my soul! Fit companion story to the adventures of 'Demon' Cockburn in giving over our helpless villages to flame and sword! But"—with sudden change from bitter badinage to determination—"this particular story will never be told in British camps."

"You mean I shall not return to tell it?" I asked coolly.

The scorching contempt of her words had turned me stonily indifferent to all save the pain they caused me. I was in a ready frame of mind to end the whole wretched game there and then.

"I am your prisoner, it seems," I continued. "It is perhaps more humiliating than you imagine to stand bound before a woman and listen to what I have just had to hear. May I beg you to make an end to it by sending your groom for the guard, or else letting me go direct to Barney's headquarters?"

"They would hang you!" she murmured.

"The chances of war," said I. "I am less anxious to live than I was a few hours ago. Why wait longer?" as she still stood motionless in the road before me.

"You have—you have *no* defense?" she asked faintly.

"None that you would believe," I sneered. "Since you have chosen to make up your mind as to my guilt, why unsettle your opinion by listening to any pleas for the defendant? Fire your pistol! That will bring some of Barney's men on the run. And let us end this interview that cannot be especially pleasant to either of us."

"You have *nothing* to say for yourself?"

And there was almost an appeal in the question.

"Why should I? You would not believe me."

"I'm afraid I should," she answered softly. "You see, from the time we were children I used to look up to you as a hero. After you went away I used to think about you and try to picture what sort of man you had grown into. Then two years ago, when I saw you in Madrid, in your colonel's uniform and with that saber slash across your bronzed face, and with those medals of honor—and when people told me what a dashing, gallant soldier you were—why, it all seemed the fulfilment of my childish dreams. You appeared everything that was brave and splendid in a man. And now—to find you—"

"*Don't!*" I begged. "If I were really the dirty spy you think me, your words could not hurt more. I—"

"You deny you are one?"

There was hope in the sweet voice. But almost at once she added, with a return of the old scorn:

"Then, how do I find you watching the flotilla when you are supposed to be far on your way north? Crouched in the bushes, counting the number of ships, and—"

"I did it on a wager."

Yes, I said it! Even while I recognized how crassly asinine and unconvincing the defense must sound.

She looked at me in astonishment.

"On a wager?" she echoed incredulously. "You deceived us all and spied upon our ships—on a *bet?*"

"On a bet," I repeated doggedly, "with Admiral Cockburn."

She shivered slightly at the abhorred name.

"Do you mean"—she asked after a pause—"do you mean to tell me that you were betraying your country on a wager? And with the man who—"

"Not betraying my country at all!" I cried, awkward as a schoolboy before his master. "I was not to tell the whereabouts—"

I paused. How was I to explain? At every step I only floundered deeper.

Would she, hating Cockburn as did every American, credit the odd terms of my fantastic bet? I saw she believed I was lying. Why make matters worse by saying more?

"I am not a spy!" I reiterated sullenly. "Believe it or not as you like. I can't explain my presence here. But on my honor—"

"On your—*what?*"

I winced under the scorn in her question, but made swift to reply:

"My *honor*. It is clean, as my father's son's should be. You do not believe that. There is no way I can make you believe it. But it is true. There is nothing more to say."

She was looking intently at me, straining her eyes in the elusive moonshine to read my face more clearly. When she broke the short silence her voice had momentarily lost its hardness and held a hint of something wistful.

"I left the manor-house half an hour after you," she said, "on my way to my aunt's in Bladensburg. I hoped to reach there before dark. Half-way my horse cast a shoe and we rode slowly across to this road, to the blacksmith-shop a mile below. The moon was rising by the time we started again.

"We passed your horse at the roadside. I stopped, wondering if he had thrown his rider. Then I saw he was tied. I was about to go on, when I saw a man's crouching figure outlined against the little patch of moonlit water at that opening in the trees. I knew it was a spy, and I feared he would get away before I could summon any of the guard. I couldn't have him carry back news of the flotilla to the British, so I took the pistol from Cato's holster and made him come along with a spare bridle to—"

"And, having caught the 'spy,' why distress yourself by further parley with him? Why not follow out your original intent and turn him over to the nearest sentry?"

"They would hang you."

"So you said before. And they undoubtedly would. That is the fate of a spy. If I am one, as you believe, I deserve nothing better."

"But," with delightful inconsistency, "you *said* you were innocent and—"

"Then why not cut these very unpleasant bonds and—"

"And let you go back to tell the British where our gunboats are? Never!"

I had a weird longing to laugh.

"You *believe* me guilty. You *think* I may be innocent," suggested I. "You won't let me go. Yet you won't have me hanged. What, then, may I ask do you intend to do with me? You can hardly expect to keep me here on the road indefinitely, tied and menaced by your pistol. Soon, some of Barney's men must pass by, and—"

She glanced about her in swift apprehension. Then faced me again, irresolute, frowning.

While I surveyed her discomfiture with a rising pity for the brave, perplexed little patriot, she straightened and drew a long breath. Her resolve, whatever it was, had been taken. I felt that in one way or another she had surmounted the obstacle.

"I have it!" she exclaimed triumphantly.

CHAPTER VII.

ON PAROLE.

"WELL?" I asked, as Dorothy paused in a silence of pride at her own sudden idea.

"I have it!" she reiterated. "The solution!"

"Yes?"

"You are my prisoner!"

"That is quite apparent," I acknowledged, with a rueful glance at my pinioned arms.

"You don't understand," she explained. "Listen—I can't turn you over to the provost guard to be hanged. I can't let you go to Admiral Cockburn with the story of what you have learned. So—I must hold you prisoner. Don't you see?"

"I am afraid I don't—quite—"

"Will you give me your parole not to try to escape? To surrender yourself to me, rescue or no rescue? To remain with me and at my orders until I see fit to release you at the close of this campaign?"

I stared at her, round-eyed, awkward as any booby at a fair.

"How stupid you are!" she exclaimed pettishly. "Can't you grasp what I am driving at? Because a thing is unusual, it's no sign it isn't just the only thing possible under the circumstances. Do you give me your parole?"

"My parole—my word of honor?" I retorted, memory of her earlier scorn stinging through my present surprise. "Of what good is the parole of a 'spy'? Of a man who abuses his host's confidence and betrays his country and induces a trusting girl to confide state secrets to him, only to—"

"Don't!" she broke in.

"They are almost your own words, Miss Winder."

"But—but you said you weren't—"

"Weren't what?"

"All those things."

"If you believe me, let me go. Barney's secret will be safe with me."

"No. I—I dare not."

"In other words, you aren't *sure* I'm a traitor and a cur; but you aren't sure I'm *not*. I think, if it's quite the same to you, I prefer the provost guard. *Hallo!*"

I raised my voice, with the last word, to a shout that split the quiet of the summer night like a gunshot.

Before the sound had fairly sped, her warm little hand was clapped across my mouth. Her soft voice—a note of terror vibrating through it—was imploring me to be silent.

"Are you *quite* mad?" she panted. "You will bring the nearest sentries down upon you!"

"So I planned," I answered as soon as that delicious touch left my lips free.

"But why? *Why?*" she whispered.

"Why not?" I countered, reckless now of results. "Let me tell you one more of the many 'lies' I have favored you with to-day, and perhaps you will understand. It was for a woman I came back to America. I have seen her. She thinks me a traitor—a common spy—all that is lowest in man. Somehow, life does not seem especially well worth while after that. If I am a spy, let me pay the cost of my filthy trade."

Again I drew in my breath as for another shout, and once more—as I had earnestly hoped—that dear little hand was pressed over my mouth.

But the patter of running feet down the road checked whatever word she would have spoken. Catching up the beaded "housewife" that swung at her side, she whipped out a small pair of shears and cut desperately at the slender leathern band that confined my arms. I could hear her breath come fast and irregularly as she bent to the task. And a feather-light strand of her hair brushed my face.

In an instant, under the keen shear-edge, the bridle parted and my arms were free.

"Run! *Run!*" she gasped, as the hastening feet neared the sharp turn of the road just beyond. "Oh, *why* don't you—"

"I shall stay where I am, thank you," I answered. "I called on the chance that some picket of Barney's—"

"But you are *safe!*" she exclaimed with a sudden thrill of exultation in her voice. "The pass my uncle gave you—"

"True!" I assented. "I had forgotten."

I drew the precious document from my pocket, tore it across and across, and let the fragments flutter to the ground. Then, as Dorothy cried out in sharp, belated protest at my mad act, I turned to confront a man who came charging at full run around the corner toward us.

Then—oh, the pitiable, ludicrous anticlimax of my cheap heroics!—the runner halted before us, asking:

"Anything wrong, Miss Dor'thy? I heard someb'dy holler an' I lef' de hosses an'—"

"No, Cato," returned Dorothy, in a breathless, indistinct effort at clear speech, "nothing is the matter. Go back!"

As the discomfited negro moved away, sheathing the crooked knife he had drawn, the girl and I looked at each other. And the pent-up emotion she had so hardly curbed in Cato's presence found vent.

There we stood, we two—one of us in the shadow of death—facing each other and fairly reeling with utterly helpless laughter. Yes, *laughter*—unrestrained, childish, immoderate!

It was not what either of us had meant to do. It is what no hero and heroine would have thought of doing. But oh, it was intensely human! And it relieved our overstrung nerves and brought us back to sanity as nothing else on earth could have done. After that, neither of us to save our lives could have continued on our lofty plane of melodramatics.

"We must go," I said when I got back breath. "If my shout and our laugh don't stir up Barney's outposts like a veritable hornet's nest, they're all dead. Come! Let me take you back to the horses."

"One minute," she cut in, stopping me. "Do you give me your parole not to—"

"Most solemnly and faithfully," I replied, at vast ado not to break out again into laughter. "Rescue or no rescue—I yield myself your prisoner at discretion."

"I accept your parole," she said with due gravity.

"And now—" I began.

"And now," said she as we hurried forward in search of the horses, "I must think what to do with you."

"To do with me? Why, I—"

"I can't let you go back to the British fleet. For—"

A faint return of my former bitter resentment caught me.

"If you accepted my parole—" I began stiffly.

"Oh, don't be cross!" she begged. "You know I believe in you. No spy could have laughed as you did. And, in my heart, I think I believed you at the very first. But if you go back and say you've found the flotilla—even if you don't tell where it is—'Demon' Cockburn knows the general direction you have taken. And he will naturally send some one else along the same route. A spy next time, who may find the flotilla as easily as you did."

"Very good," I sighed in resignation. "I'll lie to him and say I couldn't find it—that I've lost my bet."

"What good would that do? He could send out another man just the same. No, the only hope is for you not to go back at all. Then he will think one of two things: either that we keep so sharp a watch that you've been captured, or else that you found the flotilla was not in these waters at all and were ashamed to go back and confess you'd lost the wager. In either event, he won't be likely to send any one else in *this* direction."

"So I must go north?"

"Without a pass?"

"But surely General Winder will—"

"Write you out another? Is it the custom in the British army, in war times, to duplicate a 'general pass,' so that a man receiving one can pretend he has lost it and secure others until he has enough to pass any number of spies through the lines?"

"No. The rule is fixed over there. But I thought—"

"That we didn't know enough to make such a rule in provincial America? Well, we do. You threw away your one chance. I can see my uncle's face if you go to him and say you've torn up or thrown away or lost your pass. Why, he'd order you to the guard-house.

"No, no. The only course is to do as I said. You are my prisoner. And I have, I think, enough influence to keep you safe as long as you are with me. And I can see you aren't molested, even if you have no pass. When the campaign shifts to some other section you can easily go North. Until then—"

"Until then," I laughed, "I am wholly in your hands."

"It isn't a joke, please," she interrupted unsmilingly. "In spite of my influence, your neck is still in the noose unless we are both very careful. A man of martial appearance and British accent is not oversafe just now in the Yankee lines—with no pass. Does that throw any new light on the 'joke'?"

"I have faced death a few times before," I said lightly, "though never in such congenial company. If—"

"Please don't jest about such things. It's either bravado or else very bad form. In either case, I don't like it."

I saw her nerves were beginning to suffer reaction from the cruel strain thrown on them.

"I'm sorry," I hastened to say. "And now, what is my captor's next order?"

"I was on my way to my aunt's, in Bladensburg, as I told you," she answered. "Come there with me. She will be glad to welcome you for my sake. You can stay until—"

"Until you release me from parole? In the meantime do you realize that all the noise I made hasn't wakened one of Barney's men?"

I was lifting her to the saddle as I spoke. It was Cato who answered. With the familiarity of an old family servant, he chuckled:

"I clean f'got to tell yo', Miss Dor'thy! De gener'l done ordeh de flotilla crews to Bladensbu'g in a tearin' hurry dis noon. I seen de o'dehly wot cyar'd de ordeh. De gener'l's massin' all de men he kin lay han's on. Dey's shuah gwine be gre't doin's down Bladensbu'g way mighty soon."

We swung off down the moonlit road at a hand-gallop. With soldierly mind, I marveled at the odd move which had left a whole fleet defenseless. But it was only the first of many like marvels I was to see.

And so it was that I, ex-colonel of British dragoons, rode as sworn prisoner to the woman I loved. Side by side we galloped on toward Bladensburg—and to a stranger fate than had ever entered into my most fantastic dreams.

CHAPTER VIII.

A NOTE OF ALARM.

"His Excellency the President of the United States! Mrs. Madison!"
At the footman's announcement the dozen or more of us, already gathered in the wide drawing-room of the Gaines mansion, rose to

our feet and glanced toward the doorway near which Dorothy and her aunt, Mrs. Gaines, had just taken their places to receive these most distinguished of the dinner guests.

Across the threshold stepped a strikingly handsome man of dignified mien. The black official dress set off his fine, portly figure to perfection. The powdered queue wig—which had by most been discarded before now—framed features almost cameo-like in their regularity.

I fancied, however, that I could detect a faint trace of weakness about the full mouth; an expression that savored of pomposity rather than true dignity in the wide-open eyes.

But it was less at him than at the woman who glided lightly along at his side that most glances were directed. Like every other American, I had seen scores of pictures of dainty Dolly Madison. But none had given me a hint of the woman herself.

Small almost as a child, bewitchingly graceful, her flower-face, with its saucily tip-tilted nose and dancing eyes, vying in light and color with the billowy flowered satin of her court gown—she was a picture to live long in a man's memory.

Head over heels in love as I was, it needed a quick glance at Dorothy's tall, regal figure and serene beauty to restore me to my allegiance, after my first glimpse of this little fairy-like vision of loveliness. A thousand anecdotes of the daring, scintillating, wholly captivating Dolly Madison flashed into my mind, and, like half the other men in the room, I pressed forward.

The other guests were old acquaintances of the President's capricious little wife. To this fact I suppose I owe the fact that she singled me out, after her first greetings to the rest.

"You do not need an introduction to me, sir," she said, laughing daringly up at me, while his excellency was still exchanging ponderous compliments with Mrs. Gaines, "for I saw by your look when I came in that you had heard of me even as far away as England. And I need no one to tell me who *you* are. You are the ex-British hero who can't decide which way to fight, and so stays on as guest of Mrs. Gaines for a whole week, while every other man for twenty miles around is rushing to arms. Fie, sir!"

She tapped me rebukingly on the arm with her fan, but her mischievous eyes held no real reproof.

"Have you no shame, no regret, for such sluggard indecision?" she went on severely.

"I *had*," I made shift to reply, "until to-night. But if I were under arms I should be down in the valley yonder, in camp. No patriot there but would give his life to change places just now with the 'sluggard indecision' that permits me to be here."

Yes, it was a heavy, long-winded compliment. But it was the day of such talk. And, labored as they were, my words did not seem greatly to offend Dolly Madison. Yet she affected vast indignation.

"Tut, Colonel Romney!" she frowned. "You are evading my question by pretty speeches. And you don't look like the sort of man to be so moonstruck."

"No," I assented, looking down into her eyes, "I find I prefer to gaze at twin stars rather than at a moon. I—"

"*The Honorable Secretary of State! The Honorable Secretary of War!*" announced the footman.

We turned at the interruption and glanced at the two newcomers.

"Which is which?" I asked.

"The slender one with the periwig is Colonel Monroe, Secretary of State," she explained. "The tall man who is bowing over Miss Winder's hand is Mr. Armstrong, the War Secretary."

I was so interested in her news that I quite lapsed in my incipient attempts at amusing her. For these two men's names were on all lips.

James Monroe was already a power in politics, and the irreverent referred to President Madison and himself as "James I and James II." Of Armstrong, too, I had lately heard much. A politician rather than a soldier, he had up to then succeeded chiefly in hampering the movements of generals wiser than himself and in interfering arbitrarily with their most carefully laid plans.

Looking at his querulous, peaked face, I could readily understand why he was perhaps the best-hated man in the army.

From the statesmen my glance drifted—as it ever had a way of doing—to Dorothy. She looked like some young goddess, standing there at the doorway, in her simple white gown.

Dolly Madison watched me covertly, swinging a rose between her fingers. The stem broke and the blossom fell to the floor. I picked it up and kept it.

"There!" she exclaimed pettishly. "My poor rose is quite spoiled."

"Do you blame it for losing its head under the circumstances?" I asked, with what show of gallantry seemed expected.

"Colonel Romney!" she pouted, stamping her tiny foot. "You are making fun of me!"

"Madam!" I cried in civil disclaimer.

"You are making fun of me," she insisted. "You pay me compliments with your lips, while your eyes are always straying to Miss Winder. Well, behold your punishment!"

With mock majesty she pointed toward the doorway. Mr. Key had just entered. Instead of bowing deeply, as was our custom in those days, he had clasped Dorothy's slim white hand with what seemed to me a wholly unnecessary fervor and duration.

"My punishment!" I echoed, forcing my gaze back to Mrs. Madison's laughing face. "I don't understand."

"You mean to say," she mocked, "that you have been guest here a whole week without knowing?"

"Knowing what?" I queried, sick at heart.

"About Dorothy and Mr. Key. No announcement has been made, of course. In war-times marriage engagements must give precedence to campaigns. But I thought all her friends knew."

"I did not know," I said gravely, "or I should not have waited until now to congratulate him."

"Oh, you *mustn't!*" she protested, wide-eyed in childish appeal. "What a babbler I am! Always letting the cat out of the bag like any garrulous old fishwife! Now I come to think of it, the thing's a secret. And I vowed solemnly not to tell. And—lackaday!—they'll never confide in me again, either of them."

"Be quite easy," I assured her, forcing the pain back from my voice, "I shall say nothing, if you wish me not to. I am—very happy for them both. I have known Dorothy since we were children together. And Key tried to save my life when I stood in dire peril barely a week ago. May they be happy always!"

"You mean 'may they be miserable!'" she accused. "For, if ever a man's glance said one thing and his words another, it was when you wished them joy just now. Still," she added, with reflective malice, "it will be a good lesson to you in future not to breathe sweet nothings to a woman while you are looking your soul out to some one else. No, I'm not sorry I punished you. You deserved it. But I'll be merciful. Dine with us in Washington one week from to-night, and I'll give you other news that will make you forget this."

Other news, indeed! As if tidings that I had been chosen dictator of the universe could have compensated me for that downfall of my every hope in life!

So much for a fool's dream of heaven! I wondered if ever before had man's whole future outlook been changed in so brief a space.

Well, it was over! To-morrow I would ride away—turn my back forever on the closed gates of paradise and—

Then my morbidly galloping plans received another nasty check. How could I ride away? By my parole, I must remain with my fair captor, willy-nilly, until she should see fit to release me.

Was ever luckless lover in such a quandary? To be tied by parole to the presence of the woman he loved and who loved another!

Mrs. Madison was viewing my discomfiture with evident relish. The Lord deliver us from the mercies of these merciless little flower-faced women!

But almost at once dinner was announced, and my active ordeal was ended. Through the long, formal meal I found myself forced to chat on inane topics with a scrawny Carolina matron, who opened the conversation by asking me gushingly if it were true that Bonaparte always dined upon raw meat? I told her it was, and, after adding the information that he preferred a meal of live children, I lapsed into morose silence.

From time to time I caught Dolly Madison's laughing glance flashing momentarily upon me. Now and again, too, Dorothy's calm, level gaze seemed to search me in reproachful wonder at my sulks.

Dinner over, the party broke up into groups. Madison, Armstrong, Monroe, and General Winder, in one corner, were arguing heatedly in low tones, of which I caught but part of a single sentence, when Winder—harassed, apparently, into a louder pitch of voice exclaimed:

"But *how* can we be 'certain of victory' when my most important battle formation has just been utterly countermanded by Secretary Armstrong, and my—?"

I heard no more, but realized that the War Secretary was up to his old habits once more, and that, as usual, poor Winder was being badgered past endurance.

Another group had gathered about the piano—an instrument that had but very lately replaced the harpsichord and was still a rarity in our country. Key had seated himself at the keyboard, and several of the guests were begging Dorothy to sing.

Key broke into the prelude of the popular old martial air which was then usually sung to the somewhat maudlin and inappropriate words of "Anacreon in Heaven"—and which has since found an immortal verbal setting.

Dorothy's fresh young voice rose through the great room, with a compelling sweetness and power that hushed as by magic the hum of conversation. It swelled and soared like a call to battle, then sank to infinite tenderness.

I could not, in my wretched mood, listen to it. So I stole quietly out on the adjoining veranda, to be alone.

Down in the valley just below me ran the turnpike, white in the moonlight. Behind, twinkled the fires of the militia-camp. Just beyond were pitched the tents of Barney's marines and sailors.

Farther off—a bare six miles to the southwest—the lights of Washington were luridly reflected on the sky. Just beneath the mansion-hill nestled the little town of Bladensburg, along the river-bank, the broad, shining ribbon of water spanned by a single black bridge.

All was quiet, infinitely peaceful on that August night. Yet somewhere beyond to the east, across the river, I knew the British host, nearly five thousand strong, were massed, awaiting the word to make their dash upon Washington.

When the invasion would begin none in the patriot cause knew. Few seemed to care. So distant or so uncertain did it seem that the President, his wife, and members of his Cabinet had felt no fear in driving out from the capital to Mrs. Gaines's dinner that night.

The American forces at Bladensburg, they knew, as did I, probably outnumbered the threatening British. But *I* took into consideration one far less comforting thought that did not occur to the others, namely, that the bulk of the invaders were seasoned veterans, while three out of four of the defenders were raw militiamen who had never seen service and scarce understood the rudiments of drill.

Such things make all the difference in the world when two armies come to death-grips.

I stood there, leaning on the veranda-rail, I know not how long, gazing out over the valley-mists to where, unseen, my old Peninsular comrades were entrenched. Then a hand laid on my arm broke my reverie and a light little laugh shook off the night's spell of silence.

"Poor hopeless *Romeo* woos the moon alone," murmured Dolly Madison, laughing up at me, "and after what he said about preferring 'twin stars,' too! Poor lovelorn youth! Your penance is ended. I haven't the heart to make you wait a whole long week for the news I promised. That is why I ran away from the rest and sought you out. Prepare for happiness!" she ordered in quaint imitation of a military order. "Ready! Present! Listen! Let me inform you—"

"Mrs. Madison," called Key, appearing at the veranda door, "his excellency is looking everywhere for you. May I take you back to him?"

The man's usually gay voice was vibrant with excitement.

"What is it?" asked Mrs. Madison. "Is anything the matter?"

"I'm afraid there is," he replied. "The carriages are ordered and his excellency and yourself are to drive back to Washington as quickly as possible."

"But why? We had expected to stay until—"

"A courier has just brought word that the British are on the march. They will reach Bladensburg by dawn."

CHAPTER IX.

THE ATTACK.

WILL you be patient with me while I give rein to my military habit in very, *very* few words, to explain the situation that faced us on that dawn of August 24, 1814? For it is, after all, a matter of history. And you, as good Americans, should have a clear understanding of what is perhaps one of the darkest blots on our nation's fame.

So let me describe army affairs as quickly as may be, and then hurry on to my story:

The British raid on Washington was no sudden maneuver. The President and the Secretary of War had had warning of it full two months earlier—in time to have mustered twenty thousand men to the spot, had they so chosen, to check the invasion.

They did nothing of the sort. Time dragged on, and at last some five thousand militiamen, with untrained officers, were collected for defense. Not near Benedict on the lower Patuxent where Ross landed, but at Bladensburg, thirty-five miles inland and a bare six miles northeast of Washington.

Ross declared in a letter to England—and Cockburn told me afterward—that he could not understand such crass negligence, nor believe that our War Department would be so careless as to make no effort to check the landing or early marches of the invaders. So, ever fearing an ambush, Ross advanced slowly and with infinite care until reliable scouts told him there were not a score of Yankees between Benedict and Bladensburg.

Then, on he came with a rush, though still fearful of ambuscade or other trap.

To reach Bladensburg—and, incidentally, Washington beyond—the broad river must be crossed. A single bridge spanned it at this point. And on the Washington side of it were nearly six thousand militia, to say nothing of Barney's six hundred marines, detailed to defend that bridge and Bladensburg.

Winder, who commanded them, had laid out a plan of campaign that might well have checked the onset. Indeed—as Cockburn afterward confessed—a determined resistance at any point along the line must inevitably have turned the British attack to rout.

But, at the critical moment, every one in power seemed to have lost his head. Jones, Secretary of the Navy, had ordered Barney to desert his gallant, dangerous little flotilla of gunboats and join Winder. Then the Navy Secretary, in panic lest the British should discover the whereabouts of the deserted flotilla, ordered every vessel in it burned to the water's edge.

Inexcusable madness? Quite so. But historic. Jones thus robbed his country of the Chesapeake's most powerful means of defense.

Armstrong, too, arriving at Bladensburg, as I have told, on the eve of the British attack, promptly countermanded all Winder's plans of defense, forbade him to destroy the bridge whereby the British might cross, and otherwise so confused the original order of battle as to turn the already agitated little army into something perilously approaching a disorganized rabble. Nor was this all.

Lack of sufficient scout service left the Americans ignorant of their advancing foes' numbers. The British were variously quoted as from three thousand to seventeen thousand strong. As a matter of fact the assailants consisted of Ross's three thousand five hundred Peninsular veterans and one thousand marines from Cockburn's blockading squadron.

Truly, the whole affair was the worst blunder of the many which characterized what the peace party were wont to call "Mr. Madison's war." But for what followed a few weeks later we might well be ashamed of this phase of our country's history.

As it was, shame quickly gave place to glowing pride. But this was yet to come. At the moment the dark days were setting in.

I myself heard Madison say as he, with his wife and Cabinet, departed to hurry back to Washington, in the gray dawn of the battle morning: "Well, Colonel Monroe, let us leave it to the commanding general now."

And poor old Winder, his every plan smashed, must needs do his best, unsupported. But as the Presidential carriage rolled off, his excellency thrust his head out of the window and bawled back to the general's staff on the lawn:

"A banquet shall be prepared at the Presidential Mansion in honor of today's victory. I shall expect you all to dinner to-morrow."

There! The "history" is done. Now for my story again:

It was close to noon when, from the cupola of the Gaines house, Dorothy, Mrs. Gaines, Mr. Key, and myself saw the approaching dust-cloud from the east suddenly pierced by points of reflected light and then resolve itself into platoons of red-coated Englishmen.

To the right flank of the red lines was a column of blue—Cockburn's marines.

On they came, with swinging, clock-like stride, the whole host one splendid fighting machine. Their trundling field-pieces gleamed in the scorching sunlight. Apart from all partizanship, my heart beat high at sight of my old comrades in battle array once more.

True, I had refused to join them against the country of my birth, and at heart I was slowly—and unconsciously—beginning to feel the blood-call of my fatherland. But how could I forget that these invaders were the men at whose side I had fought on many a stricken field?

I think Dorothy read my thoughts. For now and then she eyed me furtively, and I thought I read a hint of pity in her soft glance. I had had no private speech with her since Mrs. Madison's revelation. Nor did I wish to have. There was but one thing I wished to say to her. And now that could never be said.

"Romney," said Key, handing me his spy-glass as the British column bore in view through the flying dust, "*you* know these men. Point them out to us, like a good chap, won't you?"

I took the glass and leveled it on the advancing battalions.

"His Majesty's Rifles—the Sixtieth—hold the center—" I began. "To the left are the Twelfth Fusileers and the Royal Fencibles. To the right, Cockburn's marines. So much for the vanguard. The reserves are too far back for me to distinguish. The batteries, too, I can't make out.

"That man riding in advance on the gray horse, with two aides behind him, is General Robert Ross. The man leading the marines—on foot, waving a cutlas—is Cockburn himself. Just behind him is Captain Wainwright, his second in command. One seldom sees a general and an admiral leading in person, and—"

But at the hated name of Cockburn all heads had leaned forward for a better glance at our country's most dreaded foe, and my further words went unheeded. Noting this, I handed Dorothy the glass. She peered through it eagerly. Then, with a shiver of disgust, passed it to her aunt.

Yet there was nothing outwardly to inspire repulsion in the erect, dandified figure of the daredevil admiral. Clad as for a court ball, he strode along in the ankle-deep dust, whirling his cutlas in fantastic flourishes.

His flaming red hair was uncovered. His florid face was alight with excitement. His great beak of a nose, laughing mouth, and blazing blue eyes were all working convulsively as he shouted out orders, jests, and encouragement to his men.

Ross, though showily mounted and decked in the gorgeous panoply of scarlet and gold lace, was a far less impressive figure.

"They will be within carronade range in another five minutes or so," said I. "Then it will be time for you ladies to go below. This cupola offers too tempting a mark for some cannoneer, who might imagine General Winder's staff had chosen it for a lookout."

"*I* shall stay here," announced Dorothy with a delightful finality.

There is no use in facing an argument before it is necessary. So, pretending not to hear her, I went on:

"I can't see baggage wagons anywhere. The British are marching without luggage. That is sign of a swift raid, not a campaign. By the way, Key, you're familiar with the American forces here. I'm not. What part of the force is that drawn up just this side of the bridge?"

"Winder's main militia body," he answered. "His artillery is to center and left center, to command the bridge. It—"

"It *should* be right and left, to sweep the bridge with a cross-fire," I commented. "Every recruit knows that. Go on."

"Captain Doughty's company holds the right wing. On the left are the cavalry. That band of bluecoats down the road, about a mile below, are our only reserves. They are Barney's sailors. And in the orchard to the left of the bridge—"

His words were lost in a roar of artillery. The American field batteries had opened fire before the foe was fairly within range.

The fusillade was practically harmless. But the British columns halted. Then a detachment of redcoats left the main body and struck off to the north, parallel with the river, while the rest continued their onward march.

"What's that for, I wonder?" queried Key.

"A flank movement," I cried, catching the import in an instant. "They'll follow the stream till they come to the ford at the old Baltimore road, cross there and take Winder's army on the flank while he's busy repulsing the vanguard. Doesn't the general see it? He ought to send a counter-force along this bank to block the move. But—"

A flash, a whirl of white-and-black smoke. The field batteries of both little armies had begun long-range operations in sober earnest.

Under the storm of cannon-shot the British column pressed unceasingly on. It came to the bridge-head. Muskets now as well as field-pieces were at work. The militia were holding their ground.

I was stirred with the old-time thrill of battle. Oh, to be in it! Not skulking here in safety with women and noncombatants!

But the safety was not so complete as, in my self-contempt, I had deemed. With a long, crooning note like that of a tired child humming itself to sleep, a shell sailed over our heads and burst.

Through the crash of the explosion sounded the rending of wood and downpour of an avalanche of broken glass. The cupola, all in a twinkling, was roofless. Down upon our heads and shoulders fluttered splinters and wood-dust.

Mrs. Gaines screamed. Dorothy said no word, made no sign. Yet with a sort of uncomprehending joy I noted it was toward myself, not Key, that her startled eyes instinctively turned.

"Come!" I ordered. "You must go below, both of you. That may have been a stray shot. But if it wasn't, the gunner will get the range more accurately next time. Come!"

I held open the door leading to the stairway. Mrs. Gaines bustled through before it was wide open, but Dorothy paused.

"Go down, Miss Winder," insisted Key. "Colonel Romney is right. There is danger. And—"

"I *won't*," declared Dorothy. "My countrymen are exposing their lives on the field of battle over yonder. And why should *I* crouch in safety while—"

"But, my dear girl," urged Key, "that's absurd. What good can it do your country to have you stay up here and be a target for shells? Go down!"

"No!" she insisted, the innate stubbornness of a really gentle nature aroused and with all a good woman's charming dearth of logic. "No, I shall—"

"You will go down *at once*," I interrupted.

It was no place of mine to interfere between a man and his betrothed. But while they were discussing the matter a second shell was likely to burst there. So I took matters into my own hands. It was no time for bickering.

"Go down at once," I repeated, and there was no argument in my imperative demand.

She looked at me wonderingly, then rebelliously—then—

"*Must* I?" she asked, like a doubting child.

"Instantly," I ordered. "If you don't, I shall carry you. Will you go?"

For a fraction of a second, rebellion flared up in her lovely face at my masterful tone. But as my eyes held hers—stern, compelling, unyielding—I saw I had conquered.

"You are a *brute!*" she cried, with a little flame of hot resentment that made my heart go out to her in a world of tender pity. Then she moved in angry obedience to the stair-head. I could scarcely repress a smile at my own petty victory, and, turning to the man at my side, I began apologetically:

"I didn't mean to usurp your authority, Key, but—"

"Colonel Romney," interrupted Dorothy, half-way down the stair, "you will come with me, please. If there is danger for me, there certainly is also danger for you."

I laughed aloud. I was not likely to consent to miss so splendid a bird's-eye view of a battle. Already the volleying and the reek of smoke had gone to my brain, and I returned to the outer edge of the roofless cupola without vouchsafing a reply.

But that sweet, insistent voice from below called again. And, faith, there was scarce less of command in it than I myself had shown a few moments earlier.

"Colonel Romney," summoned Dorothy, "I want to speak to you."

Reluctantly I left my view-point and stepped back to the stair-head, my mouth open to protest against the interruption of the spectacle.

"Dick," she said, before I could speak, her voice so modulated as barely to reach my ears and to be wholly inaudible to Key, "you are my prisoner and under pledge to remain at my side. I order you, in the name of your parole, to leave the cupola and come down here at once."

And—yes, I—Colonel Richard Romney, wearer of three war medals and hero of a dozen battles—meekly crept down-stairs out of danger—at a woman's word.

But I doubt if ever Cockburn's most picturesque profanity was a match for the lurid vocabulary that whirled through my thoughts as I obeyed that wretched parole.

"Well," I panted, white with fury, as I faced Dorothy in the room below, "I hope you are quite satisfied at making me turn coward and sneak down out of the range of fire."

"Yes," she smiled, "I am *quite* satisfied. Thank you."

"How about Key?" I asked, pettily seeking to rob the other man of the spectacle I was myself debarred from witnessing.

I don't excuse myself at all. But how many men would have behaved better?

"Mr. Key," she called, "won't you please come down, too? I'm sure it's safer here."

"No, thanks," he answered from above, a faint trace of impatient excitement in his pleasant voice. "It's quite safe enough for me up here, and I wouldn't miss this sight for worlds, you know. Aren't you coming back, Romney?"

"No," I snarled, in a hideously babyish access of impotent fury, "I'm afraid."

CHAPTER X.

IN THE THICK OF BATTLE.

I HAD the grace to be ashamed of my surly outbreak by the time it was spoken. I glanced, abashed, toward Dorothy. The look I met in those big dark eyes of hers banished what was left of my sulks.

"I don't blame you," she said, in reply to my unspoken apology, and added hastily: "But you mustn't blame me, either. I couldn't have you run into useless peril when it is my fault you are here at all. Won't Mr. Key come down, do you suppose?"

"If *you* weren't able to make him come," I retorted significantly, "he isn't likely to come for me. Key!" I shouted, as the firing swelled to a deafening volume that jarred the whole house, "won't you tell us something of what's going on? The windows here all face the other way. How are they holding the bridge?"

"They're standing firm," he reported, "but there's been nothing but cross-river musketry and a little long-range artillery to shake them yet. The British have halted again, almost at the very head of the bridge. I don't understand. There's a line of redcoats moving forward with some queer contrivances in their arms. By Jove! It's Congreve rockets they're preparing to set off. Right in the faces of our men. They'll scare the militia as gunshots startle a horse."

A whirring sound broke in on his words, followed by a distant clamor of screams, shouts, and commands.

"The rockets," cried Key, "discharged straight into our troops' faces! The militia are wavering. Doughty's company is on the full run. Winder's trying to rally them and—"

A second louder, more prolonged whizzing and crackling. Then Key's voice in what sounded like a sob:

"*Broken!* Everywhere broken! And they're running like stampeded sheep!"

"Who?" chorused Dorothy and I in one breath.

"Our whole line," he groaned. "It's crumpled and pouring back along the fields and road. No discipline at all. The few officers that aren't on the gallop can't rally a single company. The whole bridge is open to the enemy. Cockburn's massing his marines to cross. And not twenty men to oppose him. Say! I'm going to get a pistol or a scythe, if I can, and go out to take a hand. This is too much for—*Hurrah!*"

His despairing plaint had changed in a trice to wild jubilation.

"Barney!" he yelled; "Barney and his six hundred on the double-quick! They're at the bridge and they're forcing Cockburn's black-guards into the water and helter-skelter back to their own side. Good! *Good!* Barney forever!"

I do not know how it happened. I have no memory—certainly had no intent—of bounding up the stair. But all at once I found myself close by Key's side, on the cupola, with Dorothy just behind me. Both of us had forgotten my parole.

The valley below was choked with the panic-stricken, retreating remnants of Winder's army. By the thousand they fled, weapons thrown aside and discipline hurled to the four winds. Toward Washington—the capital they had been detailed to save from attack—the scared rabble scrambled, each man in mad haste to put as much distance as might be between him and the pursuing British.

Oh, the black shame of it! Non-partizan as I thought myself, my cheeks burned at the sight.

But the British were not pursuing. Indeed, at the bridge they barely held their own against the knot of blue-clad Yankee sailors.

The Americans were led by a broad, grizzle-haired man who was risking his life with all the abandon of Cockburn himself. I had seen the gray-headed fighter but once before. Yet even at that distance I recognized him as Commodore Barney.

His little band of sailors were fighting like demons. Yes, and holding their own on the bridge against nearly ten times their number.

History speaks of the battle of Bladensburg as a disgrace to American arms. It is not true. No battle where six hundred Yankee sailors fought as did Barney's men—and slew seven hundred English foes—can be termed disgraceful.

The lack of sane plans of defense, the rout of the militia, the nerveless abandonment of Washington to the advancing foe—these were disgraceful if you will. But Barney and his men showed the whole world what a brave American can achieve against fearful odds.

Again and again the British column rolled to the bridge's head. And again and again it was hurled back shattered.

With field-piece, musket, pistol, and cutlas the sailors beat against that mighty wall of redcoat veterans. Yes, the Peninsular heroes, who had smashed the proudest brigades of Napoleon, were balked, demoralized, beaten by a handful of Yankee tars, barely one-tenth their own numerical strength.

It is incredible, but it is history. Had the defenders received the slightest support from Winder—but they did not.

And so the fight went on.

"If Barney can hold them another half-hour," I said, "they must fall back. For they'll be afraid of a rally and reenforcements. They have no luggage or ammunition wagons. Thirty minutes more and the invasion will be over. If—"

"Look!" interrupted Dorothy, grasping my arm and pointing northward. On our own side of the stream, keeping close to the riverbank, a British column was advancing at the "double-quick." They were a scant half mile away.

I had clean forgotten the flanking party Ross had sent out an hour earlier. And here they came, to catch Barney's heroes in a vise between two fires—between two overwhelming forces.

Key was half-way down the ladder before I noticed he had left my side.

"Where are you going?" cried Dorothy.

"To warn Barney," he called back. "He may have time to retreat if—"

The rest was lost. I looked at Dorothy.

"Yes!" she panted. "Go! And God be with you! It's for the cause!"

How I got down-stairs, out of the house, and down the hill I hardly recall. I remember passing Key on the way and leaping high over the bodies that were strewed along the road. Then I was in the thick of it.

I made my way to Barney's side, in the press, and raised my voice to a yell. The old man did not hear. I caught him by the shoulder. His lieutenant, Miller, noting my action and, in the roar and confusion, mistaking it, struck at my bare head with his cutlas.

But the blow did not fall. In the instant of its delivery a musket-ball in the thigh sent him pitching forward into my arms.

I caught the cutlas as it slipped from between his numbed fingers, and let his body slide to the ground as I fought my way once more to Barney's side.

"Commodore," I roared, "flanking party falling on you from the rear! Call a retreat or—"

"Ammunition's out, sir!" bawled a quartermaster in his other ear at the same time.

The old war-dog turned to catch my words and—for the front rank by this time was fighting hand to hand—a slash from Cockburn's saber cut him down. And I—how it happened I can no more make clear than can any man explain the drunkenness of battle—was cross-ing swords with Cockburn myself, standing astride the fallen commo-dore's body and striving to fight back the onrush of that human tide of redcoats which had surged forward as Barney fell.

Our swords flashed sparks with the force of their impact. Cock-burn, blind with the fury of conflict and in no wise recognizing me, aimed a downward sweep at my head. I parried it, cut over the point, and reached his shoulder.

My cutlas-edge barely bit through the gold lace and broadcloth of his dress-uniform coat. But it sheared away one of his epaulets.

Again our blades crossed; and as they did so, I was swept back-ward off my feet. At Barney's fall, his bluejackets—out of ammunition, worn down by fatigue and terribly depleted in numbers—suddenly gave ground.

In that whirlpool of charging and retreating men I was spun about like a teetotum. Cockburn vanished, and I was fighting madly for life in an indiscriminate tangle of British and Americans.

Back over the bridge the struggling sailors were driven. At the far end we all came to a halt with a shock. Renewed musket-fire broke out, and a hundred voices were raised in cries of angry surprise.

The flanking column had come up. We were caught in a trap.

My saber was red—but from what cause I could not, to save my soul, imagine. For I had no clear memory of my own part in that mêlée.

Then I saw a red-faced dragoon lunge at me. I turned his point and he disappeared. In his place was a long, lean man, whirling a clubbed musket aloft. In a flash I recognized his distorted, furious features as those of my old enemy and former captor, the Yankee sergeant, McCrea. There was no time to shout—to explain. With murder in his little red eyes, he brought down his heavy gunstock with all the force he could at my head.

The press was too great for me to leap back out of reach. I whirled up my cutlas to ward off the blow.

Down came the gun-butt, striking my sword with a force that set my whole arm a tingle. The blade snapped in my hand, and—a queer, sickening blackness poured in upon me from every side.

CHAPTER XI.

THE ADMIRAL AND THE LADY.

WHEN I came to myself I was in no vast haste to renew the duties of this world. I was decidedly comfortable, in fact.

Looking straight upward from where I lay, as is the custom of those who newly regain their senses, my eyes instantly lost themselves in two other eyes that were gazing down into them with a world of tender concern.

Surely, it was quite natural that such eyes should be the first to greet me in paradise. If, indeed, I were in paradise. For certain slowly dawning pains in my head and body imparted to me a sort of dull doubt as to that—a doubt which only those eyes—Dorothy's eyes—dispelled.

And now I could see her whole face—pale and anxious with its aureole of soft, wavy hair. My aching head lay in her lap. She was bathing my forehead with a light touch that robbed the contact of its pain. Another voice was speaking, not hers.

"He's coming around all right," said Key. "It was a glancing blow. His sword partly checked its force, and my gripping McCrea's arm at the same time helped deflect the gun-stock's force. There's an abrasion. Nothing worse. Except for dizziness and headache, he'll be as good as ever in another ten minutes or so."

"I saw it all," murmured the girl. "How brave of you to throw yourself unarmed upon that horrible man with the gun! If—"

I started, reeling, to my feet, with a sudden recollection.

"Key!" I gasped. "What do you mean by letting Miss Winder come on the battle-field? It's madness!"

"There is no longer any battle, old friend," Key responded mournfully, catching me as I staggered. "And this is not the field where it was fought. Look around you."

The mist cleared gradually from my eyes. I saw we were on a little orchard knoll, about a hundred yards to the right of the bridge. Below, in front of us were strewn long swaths and scattered knots of slain soldiers in blue or red. Beyond, separate companies were standing about.

A group of officers of both little armies stood gathered in consultation under a cannon-blasted pine-tree near the Bladensburg side of the bridge.

"Surrender?" I asked.

Key nodded, in utter dejection.

"What else was left?" he protested. "Barney and Miller were down. The sailors' ammunition was gone. They were hemmed in. They surrendered not ten minutes ago; almost as soon as I had managed to drag you up this knoll, out of the rabble. Miss Winder had come down from the house. I found her waiting here."

"I can't try to thank either of you," I made answer. "But for you I should—"

Dorothy shuddered. I went on:

"Key, this is the second time you've intervened to save my life. The debt is growing rather heavy."

"Then cancel it by forgetting!" he laughed in embarrassment, adding:

"And now if you're perfectly sure you're all right, I must go. I'll leave Miss Winder in your care. Better get her back to the house at once, and—"

"But where are you going?" inquired Dorothy.

"To Washington as fast as I can ride. General Winder and his excellency must be informed at once of the surrender so they can take measures to defend the capital. In the confusion here there seems no one to send a courier. Good-by. There are surely enough troops in Washington to hold the city against such a small force."

He was gone. As I looked after his lithe, running figure, I am glad to remember that admiration drove out for the time all my hopeless, insane jealousy.

"A man in a million!" I exclaimed. "Dorothy, you should be very proud of him. He—"

I stopped. Three soldiers were hurrying toward us, leading a disheveled, blood-stained, struggling man with a rope around his neck.

With some difficulty I recognized the prisoner as Sergeant McCrea. I also knew the British corporal who was directing McCrea's two other captors up our knoll. He was a man who had served for years as my orderly in Spain, and to my influence he owed his promotion from the ranks.

"Here's a tree that'll bear his weight," the corporal was saying, pointing to the gnarled apple boughs under which Dorothy and I were standing. "String him up, boys! Excuse me, miss," he continued, speaking to the girl beside me, "but I'll have to trouble you and the gentleman to move. We have a good bit of use for this tree now."

"Simmons!" I cried sharply.

At sound of my voice, with its official ring, the trio of soldiers, as though galvanized, halted and stood at attention. McCrea, too, looked up through the tangled mat of hair on his wet forehead and gaped in dull rage.

The corporal, who had scarce glanced in my direction, now looked more closely and recognized me.

"Beg pardon, sir!" he said, saluting. "I didn't know you, sir. Not badly hurt, I hope?" as he noticed my cut forehead.

I was coatless, and there was little in my dress, as I now stood, to indicate the civilian. Simmons could scarcely know I was no longer his superior officer.

It is easy, as I have said, to deal with disciplined men. I hit on a bold idea.

"What were you going to do with this prisoner?" I asked, though I already knew quite well from experience with cases of the sort.

"Hang him, sir," was the prompt, indifferent reply.

"What has he done?"

"Refused to stop fighting after the signal for surrender, sir. Had to overpower him."

"By whose orders are you hanging him?"

He stared at me in genuine wonder.

"Nobody's, sir," he answered, puzzled. "It's the custom under the circumstances, as you know, sir. Shall I—"

"Let him go!" I commanded, and my voice allowed no leeway for argument.

The corporal and his men stared in astonishment. Such clemency was not customary to the British army in those days. But officers were often capricious. To this latter well-known fact I owed success in my present ruse.

The corporal dropped the halter.

"Fall in!" I ordered. "Right-about-face! March!"

The machine-like regulars obeyed. I could scarcely restrain a grin as they moved off, marching stiffly and in unison.

If nobody halted them they were like enough to march thus till doomsday. The British private soldier of the period did little individual thinking.

"Now, then," said I, turning on the dumfounded McCrea, "get rid of that rope and take to your heels!"

He gaped at me, stupid, unbelieving. I repeated the command.

"You—*you* got me out of being hanged?" he sputtered.

"So it seems. Now, be off, before you're caught and made prisoner. You were one of the few militiamen who stood by Barney's men to-day. That's why I give you your life. Hurry, now."

He wriggled out of the noose and took a hasty step or two toward the distant woods. Then he stopped.

"It's—it's only square to tell you," he began sullenly, "that it was me who—"

"That you tried to brain me?" I finished. "Yes, I know. Don't stop to talk about it. Here comes a company of regulars. Run!"

He glanced back over his shoulder at an advancing group of red-coats. Then he broke into a fast, shambling run, and was gone.

"How splendid of you!" cried Dorothy, with glowing eyes. "You were—"

"I played him a dirty trick once and got him an unjust reprimand," I answered, tingling with her praise. "I owed him something for that. And it has bothered me. I think we're even now, he and I."

The Englishmen to whom I had called McCrea's attention were passing the knoll. They carried a litter on which, conscious but deathly pale, lay Commodore Barney.

Walking alongside the wounded old man was Cockburn. With a coat he was shielding the commodore's face from the sun and was talking to him with all the sympathetic gentleness of a woman.

"My own surgeon shall take all care of you," Cockburn was saying as the bearers shuffled slowly past with the litter. "And if you don't get well in a hurry it won't be for lack of nursing and attention. I take it, sir, as a compliment to be of use to a man who can fight so gallantly. Command me for anything that—"

"I want nothing from you or yours!" groaned Barney. "Take yourself out of my sight and leave me to my own men. You've licked us. Be content with that."

Cockburn made no word of retort. Simply transferring the sheltering coat to a soldier, he stepped back. As he did so his eye caught mine. With a boyish halloo he ran lightly up the slope and gripped both my hands.

"Why, Dick!" he roared. "Old Dick Romney! What shower rained you down here? You're in civilian clothes and yet you've been barked over the head, eh? Noncombatant forgetting not to fight? Same old story. By the way, did you win that bet, or did I? And why didn't you—"

"I won it," I laughed, breaking in on his endless volley of rapid-fire questions. "You owe me twenty guineas."

"The deuce I do! Come along to Washington and I'll pay you as soon as I catch up with the valise my orderly is carrying ahead for me. Come along! We're on the march. Another three hours and we'll be there."

"I regret, admiral," said I, with ponderous decorum, "that I cannot accept your invitation. I am a prisoner."

"Prisoner?" he guffawed. "Well, Dick, I wouldn't let that bother me or turn my hair prematurely gray if I were you. Your captors are on the way to Washington or beyond, as fast as they can scuttle. You'll need a speedy horse to catch up with the army that holds you. Zounds, man! With all due respect for parole—"

"My captor is not in flight, admiral," I interrupted, stepping aside to disclose Dorothy, who at Cockburn's approach had shrunk back in disgust and was sheltered half behind the thick tree-trunk.

"My captor," I went on gravely, "is here. Have I your permission, Miss Winder, to present Admiral George Cockburn of his majesty's navy?"

Well, I was at last revenged on Dorothy for the stern use she had made of her office of jailer over me. For she now colored to the roots of her wavy hair as I so staidly announced our military relationship toward each other.

Cockburn made a profound bow, his blue eyes widening in palpable admiration at sight of the lovely girl who seemed to have sprung out of nowhere at his approach. Dorothy instinctively curtsied; then, remembering who and what this dust-strewn man was, she straightened herself indignantly and made as though to turn away.

"I am Miss Winder's prisoner, admiral," I resumed. "She caught me ferreting out the whereabouts of Barney's fleet, and at pistol-point forced me to surrender on parole. So I cannot accompany—"

"Forced you to surrender—at pistol-point!" echoed Cockburn in amaze.

Then his head went back in a wild roar of delight.

"Oh, the gallant, *gallant* lass!" he laughed. "To capture a peninsular colonel at pistol point! 'Fore Gad, though," he added, checking his mirth, "I cannot see why the pistol was needed. Miss Winder, you seem quite unarmed just now. Yet I am mightily tempted to follow

Romney's example and yield myself your prisoner, at discretion. Tell me," he added, his rich voice musical with pleading, half jesting, half earnest, "what should be my fate if I did?"

She looked him full in the eyes and answered slowly:

"It would not be for *me* to determine your fate, Admiral Cockburn. I should leave it to the women whose defenseless husbands you have murdered, whose little homes you have burned through wanton cruelty, whose children your brutal forages have forced to starve to death."

His bright face went cold and stern as Fate itself under her terrible words. Noting the change and knowing the man's wild, undiscliplined nature, I nerved myself for—I knew not what.

But Dorothy, never flinching, nor so much as lowering those great level, accusing eyes from his, coolly faced the invader whose name other American women of that day paled to hear.

And thus for full ten seconds we three stood, before the strange silence that had fallen among us was still more strangely shattered.

CHAPTER XII.

COCKBURN'S REVENGE.

I DO not know quite what I expected Cockburn to do. But I was ready to resent—at life's cost if must be—any outburst which Dorothy's calm, deadly arraignment of himself might call forth.

I was prepared, in fact, for any move whatever—save that which, in his own inimitably erratic fashion, he hit upon.

For, even as I watched their duel of eyes—hers bravely accusing, his wrathful and vindictive—the admiral's mercurial mood underwent a lightning change. Stepping back, he gracefully drew his cutlas, dropped on one knee and offered her the stained, battered weapon, hilt foremost.

"You have read me my faults," quoth he, in a sepulchral, sing-song voice; "pray follow up your duties as judge by those of executioner. Ne'er was sinful man wafted into the hereafter by fairer hands. My punishment is with you, Mistress Winder."

The girl was as nonplused as I over this sudden freak. It was plain that, for a moment, she did not know whether he were in jest or earnest. Nor, I veritable believe, did Cockburn himself. It was part and parcel of the man's mad nature.

But at sight of the red blotches on the sword she recoiled. The gesture brought Cockburn to himself—and to his feet.

Tossing the cutlas in air, catching it deftly by the hilt, and dropping it back with a clank into its sheath, he said in a lighter, more bantering tone:

"So, after my conviction, the lovely judge refuses to carry out her own sentence? Alas, for the inconsistency of your dear sex, *mademoiselle!* I stand accused, yet unpunished. What shall you do with me?"

Dorothy fought desperately with a sense of the ridiculous that twitched at the corners of her set mouth at sight of Cockburn's mock despair.

"Is there no atonement?" he pleaded.

And even the undercurrent of amusement could not rob his deep voice of its wondrous melody and appeal.

"Yes," she retorted, "there is atonement. Turn back! What is done cannot be undone. But you can save our nation the needless shame of attacking its capital. And," her sweet voice thrilling, "I warn you, Admiral Cockburn, if you pursue this campaign of fire and sword to the point of laying impious hands on Washington, you will strike a heavier blow on England than on America."

Her eyes glowed out of her pale face like those of an inspired prophetess of old. Cockburn caught his breath at sight of her flaming beauty.

"I don't understand you," he said, almost humbly.

"By carrying the torch and sword to Washington," she answered, "you cannot greatly injure our country—except in the pride of its sons. But you can and will be abhorred and condemned for the deed in every quarter of the earth to which the tidings may be carried. And you will do more: You will awaken the spirit that never sleeps too soundly in American hearts. The spirit that once made our ragged, ill-armed grandfathers sweep Great Britain's armies into the sea. Remember Yorktown and Saratoga, Admiral Cockburn! History will repeat itself if you drive us too far. Turn back while there is time, and—"

The hoarse notes of a dozen bugles broke in on her wild plea. At the sound, Cockburn's rugged face lost the look of superstitious wonder that had stolen over it as he listened to her. The bugle call seemed to wake him as from a compelling dream.

Something of the old, reckless humor flashed up in his eyes, together with an impatience, akin to shame, that a mere woman should have worked thus strongly upon his emotions.

"Too late, Mistress Winder!" he snapped, his hand dropping to his sword-hilt, his shoulders squaring.

He was once more the dashing, ruthless warrior.

"Too late!" he repeated. "Those bugles sounded the 'advance.' See! The men are falling into line. And their faces are turned, not seaward, but to Washington. What is to be is to be. Forward!"

She made no reply. The light of inspiration had died from her eyes, and she was pale and trembling from the gust of prophecy that had mastered her. She swayed slightly. I thought for a second she was about to faint, and I sprang to her side.

Something in my look or action seemed to strike Cockburn's notice, even as he was turning away to rejoin his army. For he halted, grinned in whimsical fashion, swung on his heel, and came back to us.

"I had quite forgot," said he, surveying us, head on one side, eyes half shut. "It seems I have a count against you, Mistress Winder. You have captured and paroled one of the honorary members of our general staff. True, he came to us under agreement not to draw sword against the Yankees; but, none the less, he was good company and something of an ornament to our mess. I must wreak vengeance on the pretty rebel who took him from us. Is that your house up yonder, on the hill, Mistress Winder?" pointing toward the Gaines mansion.

"It is my aunt's house," she answered, bewildered at the odd question; "I am staying there."

"And Bladensburg at large?" he went on. "You have friends living here?"

"Many," she replied, still bewildered; though *I,* knowing the man, began to see the drift of his questions.

"You would not care to see your aunt's house and the rest of Bladensburg in ashes?"

The brutal inquiry was put with a gentle indifference. She vouchsafed no reply. But even Cockburn's effrontery winced under her silent look.

"Mistress Winder," he went on, repeating his use of the quaint old form of address that was fast going out of fashion, "you are my prisoner. You, your doubtless very worthy aunt, every other Yankee here. I want something you have given Dick Romney—namely, your parole."

I looked across at him angrily and made as though to arrest his speech. For I was not minded to have Dorothy made the butt of his eccentric wit. But, unseen by her, he dropped me a wink and reassuring grin that halted me. I began once more to follow his crazy train of thought.

"My parole?" she echoed. "I don't know what you mean."

"I mean this: You have robbed us of Romney's society. We want to take him along with us. He can't come, because he is held prisoner by you, and must remain at your side. Don't you see yet? It's really very simple. If we want Romney, we must take you, too. Hence, I formally make you my prisoner and ask your promise to come to Washington. Bringing Romney along, of course. As 'prisoner's prisoner.' Now—"

"I think," she broke in, with a slow wonder, "I *think* you are insane."

"So I have been told," he replied carelessly. "But it is utterly beside the point. There was a Jamaica planter I once foregathered with. He had a slave he intended to kill for some crime. Says he to the slave: 'Will you die by hanging or shooting?' And the slave blubbers: 'Please, sir, I don't want to die at all.' And my friend the planter flies into a rage on hearing that and squeals: 'Tut, tut, man! *Ye're evading the question!*' And that's what you are doing, Mistress Winder. Have I your parole?"

She glanced at me as if for advice in dealing with this odd inquisitor. From my face and from my non-interference she must have seen she had nothing to dread. She was about to speak when Cockburn resumed:

"I'll bend my high and mighty dignity to barter with you. Come to Washington. Bring your excellent and no doubt bewitching aunt along for propriety. You and she and Romney shall travel thither in the first comfortable carriage we can levy from one of these village barns. Remain there till we return to the coast, and the day we leave Washington I'll release you from your parole. Do this and I'll revoke my order to burn Bladensburg to the ground. A rear guard was to attend to that little detail after we'd marched out. Is it a bargain?"

"But why should you want—" she began.

"The charm of your presence in Washington?" he finished. "Set it down to an insane man's whim, if it so please you. Do you agree? See, the vanguard is setting off, and I must follow. I'm plain George Cockburn to-day, at your service. But if I have the credit of marching a victorious army into Washington to-morrow, hang me but I'll be made Sir George Cockburn, baronet, when the tale of my triumph reaches His Very Gracious—if very ungraceful—Majesty King George. So, I've no time to waste. Come, give me your answer, I beg, and let me hurry to catch up with my baronetcy."

"I agree," replied Dorothy, after a sidelong glance at my face. "I give you my parole—under the conditions mentioned."

"I kiss your hand!" cried Cockburn with another sweeping bow. "And on the honor of an officer and a gentleman, I believe you'll have no cause to repent. One word with you, Dick."

He pulled me aside and whispered, chuckling:

"Am I not Dan Cupid's own true ally, lad? Ne'er say again I'm not thy best friend. Fie! Don't speak. I saw it all in your eyes as you looked at her. And I vowed to myself you twain should stay together a space longer, till the lass had chance to say 'aye' or 'nay' to your suit. If you find no opportunity to win favor and secure her promise during the days ye're in Washington together, then blast me if I don't have you hanged for sheer stupidity. Oh, a wondrous woman, Dick! God grant you the joy you don't deserve."

All this queer speech was rattled off too quickly for me to interpose one syllable of protest or explanation. At its conclusion he gave me a prodigious dig in the ribs and ran off, laughing aloud.

"He laughs like a child that has just planned some masterpiece of mischief," commented the amazed Dorothy.

"He has!" I rejoined grimly.

CHAPTER XIII.

WHEN WASHINGTON WAS SACKED.

"We be shipwrecked mar-i-ners
    New-ly come from the se-e-eas!
We spends our lives in mis-er-ee
    While landfolk dwells at ee-ee-ease!
Shall we go dance around-around-ar-?"

HERE the singer paused and glanced about him.

No, it was not a drunken marine who gleefully bellowed the whining old Elizabethan deep-sea chantey. The singer was no less a personage than Admiral George Cockburn of the royal navy. And the scene of his song was no waterside tavern, but the wide entrance-hall of the Capitol at Washington.

Into the newly erected building he strode, a mob of grenadiers and marines at his heels waving torches in unison to their roaring accompaniment of his song.

Cockburn was one of those rare characters who could revel and joke with his men—to the horror of stiff-necked British military leaders—and at the same time retain not only their absolute, adoring devotion, but, when necessary, an iron discipline such as no other arm of the service could boast. This was for him an hour of relaxation. And he led his vandals to their work of wanton destruction as though to a drinking bout.

When we—Dorothy, Mrs. Gaines, and I—had driven into Washington under the hated protection of a file of redcoats, the two ladies had gone to the house of a friend at some distance from the Capitol. By Cockburn's orders a squad of marines had been placed on guard before their door, to insure the fair prisoners against molestation. I, with a sort of morbid curiosity as to what might follow, accompanied the admiral on his tour of the city.

Washington in those days was quite another place from the Washington of later years. It consisted of a rambling, scattered collection of houses—from hovel to Presidential mansion—strewn over an inordinately large tract of ground. Sidewalks were of loose boards, and the unpaved streets were alternately a knee-deep mire of red mud and a wilderness of brick-hued dust, according to the weather.

On our approach no move had been made to check the British march. Winder's army the night before had poured pell-mell into Washington and pell-mell out again on the other side.

The President, his family, and his Cabinet had fled with them. The nation's capital was practically deserted.

From the Potomac, just below the city, rose a great reek of black smoke. Secretary Jones, in one last burst of official incompetence, had set fire to the navy-yard, destroying all its shipping, stores of provisions, stacks of arms and ammunition.

The whole thing was unbelievable. Never before in civilized history had a nation been thus grossly humiliated. The capital seized and looted by a foreign foe, the President and his Cabinet in fugitive flight, the army of defense shattered and demoralized!

It was the moment of our country's lowest ebb-tide. Were my story to end here, I should break my pen and refuse to record such degradation. But, in contrast to it, what was to follow shone with the purer luster.

Cockburn, as I have said, swaggered into the Capitol, his cocked hat askew, a drinking-song on his lips. Through the echoing corridor he passed, his motley crew shouting at his heels.

Into the hall of Congress he strode, and up to the Speaker's desk. Congress had so hurriedly departed that official papers and letters still strewed the tables.

Cockburn sprang lightly up on the Speaker's red-velvet chair of office. With one foot on the seat and the other on one of its upholstered arms, he surveyed his torch-waving, laughing followers. Then, removing his cocked hat with elaborate ceremony, he declaimed in true Senatorial oratory:

"My lords and gentlemen of the administration: We be now assembled in these sacred halls to discuss a monstrous, important matter. I will not weary you with rhetoric, but put the question forthwith: Shall this harbor of Yankee democracy be burned? All for it, say 'aye'!"

A bellow of jubilant "ayes" greeted his sally.

"Then, why create ill feeling by calling for 'noes'?" he yelled, in gloriously high spirits. "The 'ayes' have it. Get to work, my dainty little fireflies."

He set the example by seizing a blazing torch from a pot-hatted grenadier and thrusting it among the governmental papers heaped high on the Speaker's desk. In a minute the hall was ablaze in twenty places.

Out through the smoke and flame trooped the destroyers. At the main entrance Cockburn espied a negro in the street below leading a cart-mare whose little colt trotted at its mother's heels.

With a whoop of glee, Cockburn bore down upon the negro, thrust a fistful of guineas into his hand, and with a single bound was on the mare's strong back.

"A sailor on horseback!" he cried, seizing the bridle and wheeling his bareback steed about to face his convulsed marines. "In a light wind like this,who could ask for nobler craft? My transport and," with a glance at the bewildered colt, "her convoy! Forward!"

He clapped heels to his ludicrous mount's sides and off she set at a lumbering gallop, the baby colt cantering along trustingly in her wake; the mob of howling, merrymaking soldiery trailing on behind.

And all that day, as Cockburn rode up one street and down another, he refused the use of more showy nags, and stuck to his original, barebacked cart-mare. All day, too, the long-legged, gawky little colt frisked joyously at its dam's heels, capering with infantile playfulness through scenes of loot and pillage and flame such as never before our land had witnessed.

Those muddy boulevards, accustomed to stately Presidential progresses and the rumble of Senatorial carriages, never return to my memory without bringing back the spectacle of the gorgeously clad destroyer, his clumsy mount and the capering colt. These and the mob of whooping vandals, and stinging fumes and acrid smell of blazing houses.

Into the Presidential mansion streamed the horde. In the big banquet-hall a state repast was laid, the feast prepared for Winder and his staff in honor of the prospective "victory" at Bladensburg.

Well, the banquet was gobbled by redcoats and British marines, and several regimental humorists went so far as to mount the wine-stained table and dance a quadrille, fantastically clad in silk and satin ball gowns looted from Dolly Madison's dainty wardrobe.

Into the ugly state drawing-room wandered Cockburn. Catching sight of Mrs. Madison's grand piano, he made a flying spring, landed with a jangling and crash on the ivories, and ran, singing, up and down the discordantly protesting keyboard. His heavy heels smashed the keys and ruined the rare instrument forever. The ax-blows of one of his drunken satellites reduced the rosewood case to splinters.

After this the Presidential mansion was burned to the ground. So were all other public buildings—except two—and many a private dwelling. The two exceptions to the holocaust of national property were due to one of Cockburn's lightning whims.

"Children," he shouted, pausing in front of the post-office, "this is a hideous shanty, but it contains the patent-office. And the Yankee, with all his failings, has a way of inventing things that prove a blessing to England and the world at large. So, on the chance that some such designs are stored herein, let the shack stand. And, to even matters up—so that none of you may lack for a lodging-place should you ever revisit the place—we'll leave the city jail standing, too."

These two structures, therefore, were spared—one through a really decent impulse of Cockburn's, the other to point one of his crude jokes.

Lest any may think my love of a good story has led me to exaggerate these details, I say they may all be found—even to the incident of the colt—in any of the many great history books of America that have since been compiled.

And, so through the day, the abomination continued. And nightfall found the stricken capital city lurid from a hundred blazing houses.

Then it was that Ross sought out Cockburn, with worry and somewhat tardy remorse on his handsome face.

"Admiral," he said, "we've gone too far. This day's work will set the whole Yankee nation buzzing about our ears. Give order for retreat. Leave fires burning in the camps beyond the town, and then, for sanity's sake, let's be off to our ships. We'll be lucky to reach them."

"It seems a shame to spoil a pleasant party just as we were fairly beginning to enjoy ourselves," sighed Cockburn.

But he was only second in command, Ross being leader. So, reluctantly, he obeyed.

Out marched the troops, under cover of nightfall, on their forty-mile eastward journey to the shore camp.

Cockburn halted a moment at the door of the house where Dorothy and Mrs. Gaines were domiciled.

"I must bid you farewell, Mistress Winder," said he. "I had hoped for at least a week here, and for chance to make your better acquaintance. But Fate—and Ross—will not have it so.

"I return your swain to you in good order," he went on, laying his hand on my shoulder as I stood beside him, "and I am not sorry to lose him. At every turn to-day the fellow opposed me. Actually challenged me to a duel for daring to make a bonfire of your President's house, and fought like a wildcat to turn back my honest fellows from cremating your Capitol. He has no sportsmanship left—he who was once so good a fellow. I fear me you have cast an evil spell on him, Mistress Winder. 'Tis lucky I am flying from your wiles and releasing you from parole. Else I, too, might become a cooing turtle-dove. Good-by!"

He held out his hand. She made no move to take it.

"And no word of farewell, either?" he asked, in coaxing despondency.

"Yes," she answered coldly, "one word. This day's work has done England ten thousand times greater injury than Bladensburg and all our other defeats have wrought to America's cause."

"I think," he corrected, "it has won me a baronetcy."

"And I *know*," she retorted, "it has won you infamy."

Without a word he turned on his heel and left us. Indignant, horror-struck as I was by what I had witnessed during the sack of the city, I could not hate the man. Looking after his jaunty, graceful figure as the darkness engulfed it, I was once more conscious of the old-time attraction and magnetism that ever drew all hearts to him.

"He is a monster," murmured Dorothy, seeming to read my unwritten thought; "a *monster!* And I loath him. But, oh—he is a *man!*"

Her voice roused me from my maze of conflicting reveries.

"Dorothy!" I cried, turning suddenly on her, "I want you to release me from my parole."

She started, then eyed me in keen disappointment.

"You want to go back?" she cried, incredulous. "Back to—*them?*"

"No," I retorted; "I want to go back to my true self. To draw my sword for my fatherland. To-day my eyes have been opened. In the dregs of my country's shame I have learned at last that it *is* my country! If the United States army will have me, I shall enlist to-morrow. As private soldier, if need be. Don't you understand, Dorothy? *I am an American!*"

CHAPTER XIV.

PLAYING WITH FIRE.

DOROTHY impulsively caught both my hands.

"You are *with* us?" she cried.

"Heart and soul!" I answered. "What I saw to-day has taught me there is only one country, one allegiance for an American-born man. Release me from my parole and I'm off for Baltimore before dawn, to offer my services to General Stricker."

"Why to him? Why not stay here and accept a commission under my uncle, General Winder?"

"I think," I said evasively, "hotter service will be found under some leader who is not quite so closely harried by the War Secretary. If I can get a mount, I'll start at once."

I did not have heart to tell her that, after the Washington disaster, her uncle would probably be in no position to take the field, but would more likely serve as scapegoat for more exalted incompetents. I had met General Stricker at the Gaines house, and liked him.

After the first instinctive pressure, I had dropped Dorothy's eagerly proffered hands. Their touch had gone through me like strong wine. I could not—would not—play with temptation.

She was promised to another man. I could not grasp her adored hands in mere friendship. For my own sake, I *would* not grasp them in love.

The rush and confusion of the past two days had dulled the keen pain at my heart. Now that momentary reaction had set in, it all rushed back on me. I loved Dorothy Winder. And she—I had it on no less authority than Dolly Madison's own word—was betrothed to Key.

There was the situation, the difference between light and darkness to my whole life. I had lived perhaps little better than the other rough soldiers among whom my fighting days had been spent. Yet now, at the age of thirty, I could say with honesty that no woman but Dorothy Winder had ever made my pulse quicken. And having gone through the hothead years of youth without frittering away my heart in the countless little "affairs" which usually throng that period, I had brought the undiminished love of my whole existence to one perfect girl—only to find her hand preempted.

I am not given to self-pity nor to morbid reflections. But as I looked ahead into the lonely, loveless years that seemed to stretch before me, I felt a keen, bitter sorrow for the lot that was to be mine.

It is sad, at thirty, to believe that one has forever lost the only thing that makes the old world worth inhabiting.

The moon was rising, the night warm. Dorothy had sunk down on one of the broad porch-benches, and, pulling her skirt aside, had made place for me by her there. But I ignored the inviting gesture and seated myself on the top step at her feet.

The house was on the outskirts of the city, in a district far from the center of the day's desolation. It was odd to think that pillage had so lately swept past that quiet, moonlit scene.

Moonlight is bad for Spartan resolutions. That is why I sat on the step, instead of sharing Dorothy's bench. I was once more avoiding temptation, to the best of my feeble power.

Dorothy, I saw, noticed my choice of a seat. She had also, doubtless, deemed me churlish in the matter of the handclasp. She looked down at me, puzzled.

"You aren't angry with me, are you?" she asked, presently.

"*I?* What an idea!"

"Then why—" she began.

"Do you notice the lamp in the open window, over there?" I broke in. "See that great, blundering moth beating his heart out trying to pierce through the gauze shade to the flame within! He's what we children used to call a 'soldier-moth.' See the bright bars on his wings.

Pretty, aren't they?"

"But," she asked, "what has that to do with—"

"Nothing, especially," I replied. "Only soon or late the moth will find his way past the shade to the beautiful, lovable, warm light. And when he does—Piff! A pinch of ashes—and the flame will shine on just as gloriously as ever. Poor silly, suicidal moth!"

"Dick," she commented, as I paused, "this entomology lesson is very interesting, I've no doubt. But I don't quite catch its drift. First, you tell me you are going to be a soldier again. And then you begin—"

"I *am* going to be a soldier," I explained; "but not a soldier-moth."

"Oh!" she panted; and again silence fell between us.

Out of my black brooding I ventured at last to glance at her.

Her big eyes were fixed on me. In the dim light I caught a look in them that set my brain whirling. I braced myself to the belief that I had misread the expression which transfigured her lovely face. Even as I gazed, she quickly averted her head.

"Look!" said I, nodding toward the lamp. "The poor soldier-moth has quite disappeared. He dared face the light, and it destroyed him. *Human* moths have more sense, more caution—sometimes. That is why I am going to ride away to-night—why I dare not risk my wings here another twenty-four hours. Do you understand? It's good-by, Dorothy."

Her lips moved. From them, rather than from the barely audible spoken words, I read her reply:

"Don't go!"

I rose to my feet.

"Playing with fire may amuse you," I said roughly. "To the moth it can bring but pain. Good-by."

She, too, had risen, and was facing me—white, appealing—in the soft moonlight. Slowly she lifted her eyes to mine. And in them I read a blissful heaven of love.

There could be no mistake. A fool could have seen and understood. Nor, on seeing the knowledge that must have leaped eagerly into my own countenance, did she turn away or lower that wonderful gaze. The truth was there, for all to see.

"*Why* do you go, Dick?"

There was an undernote of passionate appeal in the whisper.

And then I went mad!

With one sweep of my arms she was crushed against my breast and my kisses were raining down upon her glowing, upraised face. I felt her body shake with hysterical sobs, and the light of utter happiness in her swimming eyes turned me faint.

Was ever worthless man so divinely blessed?

Then—like a blow from white-hot iron across my heart—came sanity!

This woman whose love I had stolen was the betrothed wife of another man. Were that all, I could have beaten down any fine scruples and let the luckless lover settle his score with me in whatsoever way his chagrin might prompt him to demand.

But with Key it was quite different. Twice he had intervened at fearful personal risk to save me from death. Only yesterday he had dragged my senseless body from under the feet of the fighting redcoats and sailors, in the mêlée at the bridge. I owed life to him.

He had left Dorothy in my care. How was I justifying his trust? How paying my life-debt?

Nature cried aloud to me that honor was but a shell; that he who can win, may keep.

"'All's fair in love and war,' they say!" I muttered excusingly to myself.

And in the same breath, my better consciousness flashed back the blunt and savage answer:

"And they lie when they say it! That is no plea for a decent man to hide behind!"

And all at once I knew that I had mastered my baser self.

I had lost her. But I had retained my honor. Truly, a sorry, empty exchange! But such as it was, I had made it.

And I have a stupid habit of standing by my decisions, be they wise or otherwise.

Now I have written at some length (having less skill with pen than with sword) concerning my emotions and the train of thoughts that guided my plan of renunciation. But it must not be fancied that act of reasoning itself consumed any such time.

In little more than a second or so from the blissful instant my arms first clasped Dorothy Winder, the whole wretched matter had worked itself out to a conclusion, in my mind. My course was taken.

Gently, yet as though parting with life itself, I put Dorothy away from me. I stepped back, not daring to look into her glorified, expectant face.

"Moonlight and madness go too well together," I said, my voice harsh and discordant from the heartbreak that gripped me. "When the sun rises to-morrow, must both forget the dream from which we have just awakened. Or else remember it only as a dream that can never come true. I shall be far away by daylight and—oh, I hope I shall never look on your dear face again!"

"*Dick!*"

There was pain, tense and dismayed, in her cry.

"Dick!" she repeated incredulously. Then added, falteringly, as though to clear up the whole misunderstanding: "But I love you!

Women's ideas of honor are not men's ideas. Yet, even in my own anguish, it astonished me that this high-souled girl should be so blind to the duty she owed Key.

For his sake, for hers, for my own, I must end this, here and now. I must put it past doubt that she should still care for me.

"I—I love you, Dick," she said again, speaking like a pleading child.

Her appeal cut me to the very quick. And with all my strength I steeled myself to the reply that must turn her love to contempt.

"But," I answered coldly, "I *don't* love *you,* Dorothy. We have both been very, very foolish. It was the moonlight—the reaction—what you will! It is over. Let us both forget it. In time you may perhaps forgive what I did a few moments ago. It—it was the cursed moonlight that went to my brain. Good night."

After which masterpiece of brutality I ran down the steps and hurried away into the night with never a backward look at the paradise my own mad sense of honor had closed to me.

CHAPTER XV.

I FALL IN WITH AN ADVENTURE.

UP the unpaved street I ran through the hot silence of the August night.

I had no general sense of direction. My only clear idea was that I had thrown away my life happiness, and that I must put all the distance possible between Dorothy and myself before my resolution should falter. For it was an endless fight to prevent myself from returning, casting honor to the winds, and seizing the wondrous happiness Fate offered me.

I was brought back to my surroundings in decidedly sudden fashion. As I ran, a figure stepped out of the shadow into the moonlight and, with leveled musket, cried to me to halt.

The voice was American. Moreover, it was vaguely familiar. The attitude and tone left no alternative for an unarmed man but to obey.

"Trying to catch up with your regiment, I s'pose?" drawled the man. "Well, they'll march without you."

The mistake was plausible. I wore the semimilitary cocked hat that was then quite out of use in America. My coat, though a civilian's, was of military cut. The deceptive moonlight finished the imposition.

And I, on my way to join the American army, was likely to be shot dead by some straggler from the Yankee ranks who was thus seeking to wipe out, in part, the day's disgrace.

The musket was unpleasantly close to my head. At any moment its owner might fire.

"I am not a British soldier," said I. "And while I've no great objection to losing my life, I'd prefer to end it in battle, instead of here, if it's quite same to you."

The musket was lowered. The Yankee took a step closer and stared at me.

"McCrea!" I exclaimed, recognizing the lean, surly face.

"It's—it's Mr. Romney!" he muttered. "And in another minute I'd 'a' killed you."

"It looked that way," I assented cheerfully. "You're really contracting quite a bad habit of trying to murder me, McCrea. You'll have to break yourself of it. First, you attempt to hang me for spying. Then, to break my skull with a musket-butt. And now—"

"And now," he amended, "I would 'a' shot myself if I'd found it was *you* I'd bowled over. I'm sorry, sir. I—"

"But what were you doing here?" I inquired. "I thought all Winder's army was—"

"Was still running?" he finished, with an oath. "Most likely they are. But *I'm* not. After you got my head out of the noose at Bladensburg, yesterday, I caught up with 'em. But it was no crowd for a decent man to stay with. Scared sheep are brave as cat'mounts alongside that pack of cowards. So when they went through Washington on the dead run, I stayed behind and hid. I've done some good work since dusk. You'd 'a' been the eighth that I've stopped from doing any more harm to Uncle Sam. I—"

"You've been potting stragglers, eh?" I broke in. "That's no work for a soldier."

"Maybe burning an undefended city was the kind of work a soldier'd be better employed at," he sneered.

"If you'll come with me," said I, "I think I can get you braver work than this."

"With the Britishers?"

"No! Look here, my friend. Get that idea out of your head once and for all. I am an American, and I'm on my way to Baltimore to join General Stricker's army. There'll be chance for hot service around the Chesapeake, if I'm not mistaken. Now that they've wrecked Washington, the British won't leave Maryland without a try at Baltimore and Annapolis. Are you coming with me?"

"You're not lying?" he asked, still in doubt. "You won't march me into Ross's camp?"

"Lying isn't one of my accomplishments," I answered. "And as for marching you into the British camp, you were very much in their toils yesterday. All I had to do was to leave you there. Now, do you believe me?"

He dropped the musket and gripped my hands.

"Right or wrong, I'm with you," said he with a gruffness that masked an unwonted emotion. "I'm your man, now and always. You lead the way, and wherever it goes I'm there at your elbow."

"Very good!" I said, embarrassed by the stolid fellow's complete unbending. "Now, see if you can buy or hire horses for us. I have twenty guineas. I won it from Admiral Cockburn on a wager, and it's a joke he'd appreciate if only he knew I was using it to join the American cause. Can you find us horses here?"

"I guess so," he replied. "But between us and Baltimore lies the whole British army. How are we going to get past them?"

"Get the horses," I ordered, "and I'll attend to that part the moment we come to it."

From the fact that he made no objection, I saw I had won him, and that he trusted me. It was no slight victory. Here was a man who might one day be of use to me. But to what vast extent I did not at the moment dream.

Dawn was breaking when we rode into the rear-guard of the slowly retreating British army.

I was known to Wainwright, the officer in charge, and without difficulty made my way, McCrea at my heels, to Cockburn's division. The admiral himself rode, as ever, at the head of his men, alert and jolly, as though he had not been in almost constant action for the past forty-eight hours.

"Why, Dick!" he hailed me. "Was ever so recreant a wooer! Twelve hours ago I deposited you at your sweetheart's door. And now I find you riding at breakneck pace away from her. Zounds! You should be court-martialed for flagrant treason to Cupid!"

I think my face must have told him something. For he changed his tone on the instant, and said more gently:

"The fair one would not? Oh, well, keep your counsel, if you will. 'Tis no affair of mine, though I did for you what I could. And so you're back to make the sword win you glory when the heart can't win you joy?"

"Yes," I made rejoinder; "I am off to the war."

"And we'll give you royal welcome, Dick! Why, lad, we—"

"You mistake," I said. "I'm off to join the army of defense at Baltimore. I'm an American at last."

He stared in frank astonishment.

"The deuce you say!" he blurted out. "Off to join the Yankees against us, and yet here in my presence to tell me about it! Why?"

"Because I want your help."

"*My* help in getting to the Yankees?" he roared.

"Just so," I retorted with perfect coolness. "A passport for my friend and myself through your lines."

He stared an instant longer in utter bewilderment, then threw back his head in a great bellow of laughter.

I breathed easier. I saw I had not mistaken my man. It was just the sort of mad effrontery to appeal to Cockburn's eccentric soul.

"On my hopes of a baronetcy!" he panted, weak from laughing, "you're well-nigh as insane as I. Had you gone to Ross, he'd have clapped the pair of you in irons. As it is, if he catches glimpse of you, you'll be sent to the provost marshal. He's furious at your interference of yesterday. If you'd appealed to him for—"

"But I didn't. It was to *you* I appealed. Time presses, and we must get out of this place and on our way. The pass, admiral!"

"I suppose I am dreaming," he sighed; "but it gave me a good laugh, and I owe you somewhat for that. How got you horses? I thought we had nabbed them all."

"Money will do much," I responded. "I had the twenty guineas you—"

"The gold I lost to you!" he cried. "And you used it—used my own guineas to—"

Laughter smothered him again. Dumbly he beckoned up an aide, and, as soon as he could speak, commanded:

"Write out a general pass for colonel—I mean, *Mr.* Romney—and his friend."

The correction in my title made me wince.

The rank I had fought for years to win was lost to me forever. No longer had I the right to so much as the honorary prefix. The last bond was forever sundered between me and my old life, my old comrades-at-arms. I felt strangely desolate and alone.

Cockburn's voice recalled me to my every-day self.

"You know this section," he was saying. "What is that great house on the hill, yonder? There, to the rear, and far to our left. It is the finest I have seen hereabouts. And—see—there is something like a monument or tomb to one side."

I glanced back. The sun was rising. Though the level ground by the river, along which we were marching, was still in shadow, yet the distant hill toward which Cockburn pointed was bathed in golden light.

The stately, porticoed mansion crowning it, amid the gnarled old trees, gave back the dawn-light from a score of flashing panes. The tomb, near by, stood out clearly in the first rays of the sun. The hilltop was visible for miles around.

"If it is a Yankee notable's home," went on Cockburn, "it might perhaps be as well to send a battalion up to make bonfire of it—just for example's sake. Whose estate is it?"

I felt a wild thrill of fury against the man, and it was in no submissive, nor even civil, tone that I replied:

"You'll give such an order over my dead body, Admiral Cockburn. The place you speak of burning is a holy shrine to every true man in this country. That is Mount Vernon, birthplace and beloved home of George Washington. His tomb is—"

"*Halt!*"

Cockburn broke in on my angry speech with the ringing order which a dozen bugles caught up. The whole long line of tired, blue-clad marines came to a stop.

"Left face!" shouted the admiral.

The column half-wheeled, fronting Mount Vernon. If it were his intention to march against the beautiful place, the marines should go leaderless. Of that I was resolved. And I moved my horse nearer to Cockburn. Then I saw his expression, and hesitated.

For a light of solemn reverence transfigured his florid features.

"Present arms!" he commanded. "Lower flags! *Officers, uncover!*"

I could scarce believe my eyes. There stood the men who had but yesterday looted our capital. They were now presenting arms as though to a passing emperor.

Their officers' hats were off. The hated regimental standards were lowered as before a monarch's tomb. Cockburn himself had dismounted. His bared head was bowed in silent respect. Marines, flags, officers, admiral—all were at humble, deferential salute before the hillock on whose crest slept the Father of his Country.

Thus did "Demon Cockburn" and his band of pillagers pay reverence to the man who had made America free. Let this be remembered by those who curse the "mad admiral's" memory.

McCrea, who had followed the entire scene with gaping jaw and wondering, incredulous eyes, broke the silence with a great sob.

The spell was broken. Cockburn leaped into the saddle and, with a half-shamed laugh, shouted an order that set the column once more in motion.

And I, McCrea beside me, rode ahead to a new act of my life-drama—an act that was to make its earlier scenes tame and colorless by contrast.

CHAPTER XVI.

A MAN AND A MAID.

DOWN the dust-white road leading from Baltimore, twelve miles away, bumped and clattered a big traveling-carriage. As it came abreast of the field where my regiment was encamped, it lurched to a standstill, and a plump white hand beckoned imperiously to a militia trooper who lounged at the roadside.

The fellow advanced, and I heard a woman's voice questioning him. An agony of bashfulness seemed to possess the country youth, and he stuttered forth incoherent answers that grew the more confused under her questions.

My own tent was pitched not far from the highway, and as I sat in its entrance, studying a map, the talk attracted my notice.

I put down my parchment and strolled across to the carriage. I was just in time to hear the militiaman protest:

"I—I don't know, ma'am. I just got here yesterday. I don't know where any of the other camps are."

"Is there *no* one of average intelligence to be found?" appealed the lady, addressing the universe at large.

"I have some few vain claims to it, madam," said I, coming up. "How can I serve you?"

The trooper, at sight of me, saluted and shuffled away, evidently glad to be quit of the inquisition. The lady turned to me, thrusting a somewhat shiny, dust-powdered countenance from the window.

"We are looking for General Stricker's headquarters, sir," she began. "Perhaps you can—Why, bless my soul, if it isn't Colonel Romney!"

She stared amazedly at my militia-colonel's uniform and at the added tan which long hours on the drill-ground had stamped on my face during the two weeks or so since we had last met, on the day Washington was sacked.

For, as I now saw, my fair interlocutor was Dorothy Winder's aunt, Mrs. Gaines. The sunlight in my eyes had at first blurred her features.

"Colonel Romney!" she repeated, surprised. And I thought I heard a soft rustle in the carriage behind her.

"Does it astonish you?" I asked. "I rode direct from Washington to General Stricker. In view of the help my previous experience could give me as a drillmaster, he was so good as to appoint me acting lieutenant-colonel of cavalry. For the past fortnight we have been maneuvering hereabouts, and trying to lick into shape the new Pennsylvania and Maryland recruits that come pouring in every day."

"'Come pouring in'?" she echoed. "Why, it used to be hard to raise a single company. What is the magic of—"

"It is the spirit of '76, I think. And the burning of Washington awakened that spirit, just as Miss Winder once prophesied it would. All the way back to their ships the British were fired upon from behind fences and rocks and trees by farmers and villagers. It was Concord and Lexington over again. As soon as our scouts brought word, the other day, that nine thousand men, under Ross, and sixteen frigates, under Cockburn, were massing for a land-and-water attack on Baltimore, the whole countryside rushed to arms. Old men, boys, invalids. Every one who can carry a gun. Already we have three thousand encamped and—"

"Is it really true?" she asked in consternation. "Are the British advancing again?"

"It is only too true. Nothing but these volunteers and the forts, McHenry and Covington, stand between them and Baltimore. If we fail to check them—"

But my last words were not heeded.

"They are advancing!" repeated Mrs. Gaines to her unseen companion. "Whatever shall we do now?"

"Can I help you?" I asked.

"Why, you see," she explained, "my brother, Dr. Beane, of Marlboro, was taken prisoner last week. Mr. Key went to Washington as soon as I told him of it, and got his excellency to add my brother's name to the list of prisoners to be exchanged. Mr. Key was to meet us at North Point this afternoon and go down the Patapsco in a schooner to the British fleet under flag of truce to arrange the transfer. He got permission to take us with him. My brother is ill, and I wanted to go to him in person. But if the fleet and army are on the march—"

"They will respect a flag of truce, no doubt," I replied, "even if they are preparing for battle. You'll be quite safe. Follow this road to the forks and then turn to the right. North Point lies only two miles beyond. How many are in your party?"

"Just we two. I and—Why, Dorothy, you haven't spoken to Colonel Romney! What a garrulous old woman I am, to be sure, to cackle so fast and not give you chance for a word!"

My heart stood still.

There was nothing in the least surprising in Dorothy's accompanying her aunt. Yet, somehow, I had not expected it. I still thought of her as I had left her—white and beautiful, among the honeysuckles on the moonlit porch of the Washington house.

So I stood—hat in hand, hesitating, confused—while a second face appeared at the open carriage window. Dorothy was paler than when last I had seen her. And her great eyes wore a tired, haggard look that went to my heart.

I bowed, scarce knowing what to say or do. But a woman, I think, always has better control of an embarrassing situation than has the wisest man.

"Let me congratulate you, Colonel Romney," said she in a level, unfaltering voice, "on your commission and on the service you are likely to see."

"Thank you," I mumbled, awkward as any schoolboy.

"Aunt Lucia," went on Dorothy, turning to Mrs. Gaines, "I'm afraid we are detaining Colonel Romney from his duties. Sha'n't we drive on?"

"Oh, *please* don't!" I begged, then checked myself.

Why should she not drive out of my life, this regal, gentle girl whom I had for a glorious second held close to my breast, then insulted and left? Why prolong her grief and my own? Yet, from my very soul that plea had come.

My unusual earnestness must have struck Mrs. Gaines, for she favored me with a glance of sharp scrutiny.

"Are you ill, Colonel Romney?" she inquired. "You are bronzed, but your face is much thinner and older than when I last saw you. You look as if you had suffered, or had a sickness. Perhaps—"

"I am quite well, thanks," I lied, quite myself again. "A touch of Chesapeake fever has pulled me down a bit. That is all. One has not time to be ill just now."

Dorothy's face, which had softened into a moment of anxiety, on her aunt's question, hardened at my careless reply.

"Wouldn't you like to see Colonel Romney's camp, dear?" queried Mrs. Gaines, the born matchmaker, laying her fat hand on her niece's arm. "I am tired, and I'll wait here for you. Do! It will be interesting. I'm sure he will be glad to show you everything. Won't you, colonel?"

I could not keep the gladness out of my eyes. Playing with fire, and worse than futile, as it would be, yet my whole nature craved to walk once more by this wonderful girl's side, to be alone with her, to hear her speak to me—to *me* alone.

"Won't you come?" I entreated, flinging open the door and holding out my hand to assist her to alight.

For an instant she shrank back. Then she seemed to read the agony of appeal in my look, and to be moved by it.

She must scorn me as the lowest blackguard unhung. Yet, at my plea, a flush tinged her pale cheek, and, almost instinctively, she rose and placed her hand in mine.

I felt the dear fingers tremble ever so slightly. As though thinking better of her futile impulse of mercy, she hesitated once more, and again our eyes met. Hers were doubting, troubled; mine, I fear, told all that must never be spoken. It was a war of glances and of wills.

Her lips parted. What she was about to say, I never knew. Nor whether she or I had won that mute conflict. For McCrea—promoted lately through my intercession to a lieutenancy—bustled up, clicked his heels together in salute, and said to me:

"Courier from headquarters, sir! Personal despatches from the general commanding. I couldn't find your orderly, so I came myself. He's at your tent."

For the time, I could have consigned the excellent McCrea and the "general commanding" to the depths of the sea. But I mechanically replied to his salute. Then I turned to say good-by to Dorothy.

She had quite recovered her self-control, and was once more the pleasantly oblivious, formal acquaintance.

"Good-by, colonel," she said. "May we both wish you every success in the coming campaign?"

She gave the coachman an order. Leaving me standing uncovered, and with dejectedly hanging head, she moved—as I believed—forever out of my life.

CHAPTER XVII.

McCREA PAYS HIS DEBT.

"Father and I, we went to camp
Along with Captain Gooden.
And there we saw the men and boys
As thick as hasty-puddin'.
Yankee Doodle, keep it up!
Yankee—"

THE song, swelling discordant, thunderous, triumphant, from thousands of throats, to the rhythmic tread of myriad feet, broke off in a mighty "huzza!"

For General Stricker, his bald pate shining in the glare of September sunlight, his saber waving encouragement, galloped, shouting, across the front of the marching army.

"In another ten minutes, boys!" he bawled, as he passed to the farther wing of our little host.

And ever, as he rode, that long, ringing cheer followed him.

Seasoned campaigner as I was, my pulse beat higher at the whirlwind of enthusiasm, and I sat my horse with greater pride than even when I had led my machine-like Peninsular veterans on to their invincible course through Bonaparte's French legions.

I looked about me. Even the sight that met my gaze could not dampen that glow of patriotism. Though, truth to tell, there was more in our outward aspect to excite a veteran's derision than his delight.

Three thousand strong—or weak!—we were. But chiefly militia and, to a large extent, men who never before had seen battle nor a month of drill.

Men were there whose shoulders were bent, whose gnarled, twisted fingers could scarce handle the heavy muskets, blunderbusses, or old-fashioned fowling-pieces they carried; dotards, whose palsied heads bore the snows of ninety winters. Lads I saw, not yet in their teens, their round, childish faces alight with the jolly adventure whereon they were entering. Consumptives, cripples, sick men—all were to be found in our lines.

Every sort of weapon, from regulation musket to scythe, was on view. Every costume, too, from my own spruce cavalry uniform down to some shambling mountaineer recruit's ragged homespun. Every manner of steed, from Arab charger to spavined plow horse.

Fewer in numbers by half, and infinitely poorer in equipment and training, than had been Winder's army at Bladensburg, there was yet about us a confident resolution, a certainty of success, a flamboyant patriotism, that lifted us head and shoulders above those ill-starred defenders of Washington.

The spirit of '76 was blazing broadcast. These motley fighters marched, singing and cheering, into a battle against fearful odds, even as had their fathers at Bunker Hill and Trenton. And I—veteran of the Napoleonic wars—was proud to be with them.

Thus we marched—singing "Yankee Doodle" in a dozen different keys and cheering ourselves hoarse—until we reached the line of rude earthworks hastily thrown up the night before by General Sam Smyth's handful of troops, on news of the British intention to land next day off North Point.

The "Point" ran out into the Patapsco River. Its upper reaches, or "neck," was furrowed by our rough defenses. Below, the British were already swarming ashore from their transports.

It was Ross's plan to march his land force of nine thousand over the twelve-mile road that led to Baltimore, and to wreck that city as he had Washington. Cockburn, sailing up the Patapsco, was to cooperate with him.

Reinforced as they now were, this was to be no mere fly-by-night raid, but a determined occupation of the Maryland metropolis. Thence, with Baltimore as base of operations, a foothold would be gained that might stretch to Philadelphia or to New York itself. Great Britain's grip would then be fairly on the helpless throat of our country.

And we—three thousand undisciplined, ill-armed rustics—alone stood in the way of that wholesale conquest.

Too weak numerically to prevent the landing of the British, we yet manned our shallow trenches, every man of us determined that the chief invasion of all the War of 1812 should not pass our ragged lines.

As our foe—outnumbering us three to one—formed line of battle, an old man in a gray suit and broad-leafed hat ran up to where my regiment was posted. Peering eagerly into the dismounted troopers' faces, he called tremulously:

"Nathanael! Nathanael!"

McCrea caught sight of the old fellow, and left his place to run forward and greet him with affectionate concern. "Father!" he cried, "you don't mean to say you've come to enlist? And you a devout Quaker!"

"Son," returned the old man with dignity, "thee knows I came not to take part in this unseemly brawl. Does not our creed command us: 'Smite not'? War is sinful, and is bred of Satan. I come to tell thee that thee hast my prayers for thy safety, and my earnest hope that thee will see the error of thy ways and turn from thoughts of bloodshed to peace."

"Gladly, father," gently replied McCrea, scowling over his shoulder at the grinning troopers behind him, "gladly. As soon as the war is over. And now let me get you to the rear, for there will be a charge as soon as those redcoats get their formation. Keep safe and—thank you for coming to see me again!"

He pressed the old man's hands, then guided him toward the rear. Only once did he pause. Then it was to give one last word of admonition.

"Nathanael," said he, "I know full well 'tis for country and flag thee fights. For that reason I cannot wholly condemn thee. To smite is sinful, and is prompted of Satan. Yet, O my son, Nathanael, the spirit moves me to give thee this one last counsel: Smite not, if thee can overcome the temptation to punish thy country's foes. But, if Satan *compels* thee to smite, then smite *hard,* son Nathanael! *Smite hard!*"

The blare of British bugles sounding the charge drowned the laugh that ran along our vanguard at this human-nature sophistry of the old apostle of peace. The redcoats moved forward at the double-quick. A shower of shot and shell from their transports and shore batteries rained in upon us. Our own little clump of cannon replied valiantly.

The battle was on. The battle that was to decide a nation's fate.

Perhaps to you, who know little and care less for war, the tale of a battle may grow wearisome in the telling. So I will touch but lightly on this one. The redcoats rolled like some mighty scarlet wave straight up against our earthworks. Then, like a wave, again they broke and surged back, followed by a leaden hail from our trenches.

"Yankee Doodle, keep it up!" sang the embattled militia, even as their fathers in Revolution days had sung the song which contemptuous British wits had originally devised for the ridicule of their American colonists.

Again and again charged the red line, and ever we smashed their formation and sent them tumbling helter-skelter back upon their reserves. Such defense, at Bladensburg, would easily have saved Washington.

A charge at last, with a stalwart, white-periwigged horseman at its head! Ross was leading his troops in person. And his presence before them lent new valor and strength to the oncoming hosts.

Our volleys crashed into their ranks again and again with murderous force and accuracy. Lesser opposition had beaten them back more than once. But now, with that stern figure at their head, it seemed that nothing could stay them.

Straight up to our breastworks they came, while we tore huge gaps in their line, but could not check them. Men and horses fell by the score. Still, the rest hurled themselves onward. Up to the first line of earthworks—and *over* them!

This was the moment when, had we been regulars, we should

probably have retreated, realizing that our defenses were carried. But, being for the most part raw recruits, our men knew nothing of the sort, and stood their ground, bayoneting or clubbing as many as possible of their onrushing enemies.

The space just inside the first line of trenches thus became the scene of a hand-to-hand struggle almost approaching in confusion the mêlée on Bladensburg bridge.

Then it was that I—for it was over my regiment's part of the wall their center had broken—found myself face to face with Ross himself as he slid down the low fortifications in the midst of his swarming adherents.

With Ross down or captured, the advance must become a retreat. With Ross still at their head, his men, by sheer force of numbers, bade fair to beat us back to the open plain behind, where we would speedily be hemmed in and at their mercy.

On the happenings of the next sixty seconds rested victory or complete surrender. With this in mind, I leaped upon Ross, sword in hand, and engaged him in single combat. My men rallied at sight of our duel, and momentarily checked the redcoats' advance.

I had but a second or two of time, and I knew it. Yet, every drop of blood in me cried out against slaying this man on whose staff I had once served—by whose side I had fought on a dozen Spanish battle-fields.

I was the better swordsman. In fact, few could cross sabers successfully with me in my prime. I knew I had skill to cut Ross down. And yet—I could not.

But what was to be done must be done at once. Every second was worth a thousand men. And suddenly I found the solution to the difficulty.

Ross had recognized me on the instant. But he was apparently controlled by none of the scruples that held back my own sword-arm. He attacked me with a wild rage that more than once almost broke down my guard.

Then I put my plan into execution.

I stepped back. He lunged. I sent my blade running along his, in the parry, with a sweep that ended in a sharp twist, an old trick learned in boyhood from an Italian fencing-master. Unprepared for the move as he was, it tore his sword out of his hand as though I had wrenched it away by bodily force.

"Back!" I shouted to the redcoats as I put my saber-point to their disarmed general's throat. "Back, all, or I'll strike!"

The red line halted in doubt.

"Surrender, General Ross!" I ordered. "Surrender! Give me your parole."

His arms sank to his sides in resignation. Accordingly, I lowered my sword-point to the earth.

As I did so, he snatched a pistol from his belt. Shouting, "This is how England surrenders to traitors!" he fired pointblank at my head.

The range seemed too close by far to admit of missing. Yet, even as he fired, Ross lurched backward, his arm flew up, and the ball whistled harmless over my head.

A man beside me had fired at the same instant—or, rather, a fraction of an instant sooner—and Ross collapsed, stone-dead, to the ground.

My regiment shouted and sprang forward at their disheartened foes. Ross being down, his men had no heart for further attack. Back over the rampart they were driven, and once more the trenches were ours. For the time, danger of assault was over.

Then it was that McCrea, still clutching his smoking pistol, spoke in my ear.

"I said I was your man, didn't I?" he drawled in that quiet, countrified voice of his. "And I said I'd always be at your elbow. Well, I was. And it's lucky I had my pistol in hand before Ross drew his. I guess my debt to you is about wiped out, ain't it?"

"It was you who shot him?" I cried, stretching out my hand in gratitude.

"'Tisn't every man that gets to shoot a real live major-general," he grinned. "And he's likely to he my last. The debt—the debt's wiped out—and—"

With no change in his leathery face or drawling voice, McCrea quietly fell dead across my feet.

When the British had first swarmed into the trenches a rifle-ball had pierced the man's chest, going quite through his body. He had lived long enough thereafter to save me; and had died on his feet, fighting, grim, surly, to the last.

Thus did Lieutenant Nathanael McCrea pay his life-debt.

The British rallied and came back to the assault. Once more, urged on by their officers, they made their way, inch by inch, to the barricade. Again we fought them hand to hand. It was an indiscriminate tumult of shots, bayonet lunges, and sword flashes.

The chief defense and attack centered where I and my regiment were posted. As leader of that section of the defenders, I quickly became a target for sharpshooters. A ball carried away my hat. A second grazed my shoulder.

Fifty multicolored lights leaped before me, and I sank pleasantly to sleep.

CHAPTER XVIII.

IN STRANGE COMPANY.

"You see," the man was arguing, "we beat 'em. We made 'em retire. We drove 'em clean back from their trenches. An' yet, 'ere *we* are, retreatin'. 'Ow's that to be explained? Jest tell me that, will yer? We lands, and we starts for Balt'more to treat it to a visit like we done to Wash'n'ton. We finds the Yankees entrenched. They kills Ross—rest 'is soul!—an' they 'olds us orf fer three 'ole hours. Then they gets out of am'nition an' falls back, gentle an' careless-like. An' so does we. An' now its orf to our ships, an' th' invasion's over. 'Ow's that?"

"It's this way," spoke up a second Cockney voice. "It's like this, sergeant. We was too weak an' too badly crumpled up to foller our advantage. So we comes pilin' back. An', as you say, th' invasion's over."

"Any fool could see that!" retorted the sergeant. "But 'twas a *vict'ry*. An' if 'twas a vict'ry, w'y don't we push on to Baltimore?"

"Because a few sech 'vic'tries' would leave ol' King George without a soljer left in Hamerica. That's w'y. We carried the trenches, but we was licked fer all that, an'—"

"An' if we'd carried them same trenches as ork'ard as you sweeps is carryin' Colonel Romney," insisted the sergeant in fine irony, "we'd 'a' been licked afore we started. Easy with 'im, there, you gawks! 'E ain't a sack of straw."

"No," sneered one of the others; "'e's a bloomin' sight worse. 'E's a turncoat. That's wot 'e is."

"If you'll do me the favor of repeatin' them words back of the barracks when we gets to camp," politely retorted the sergeant, "I'll 'ave the reel pleasure of 'ammerin' your 'ead off. Colonel Romney's no more a turncoat than you are. 'E's a Hamerican, ain't 'e? And ain't 'e got a right to fight for 'is own flag? Jest answer me that."

No one *did* answer, and he resumed.

"I've knowed the colonel over ten year, an' fought under 'im many's the time. An' I ain't goin' to see 'im lugged off to no prison-'ulks to rot or starve. That's w'y I made you lads pick 'im up, w'en I comes acrost him under the trenches after the fight, an' bring 'im along wi' us, afore the provost's men could go over the wounded. Once we get 'im to quarters, I'll put 'im in with them three p'litical pris'ners that's to be shipped out to-night to Cockburn. Him an' th' admiral's pals. Cockburn'll see he gets away safe. Easy over that log, now! Break step!"

Then it was that I ceased to listen to the talk in a dreamingly impersonal fashion, and opened my eyes.

I was lying at full length on a field-stretcher, borne by four soldiers. Alongside my improvised litter strutted my old Peninsular orderly, Simmons, now arrayed in the dignity of very new sergeant's stripes.

I took in everything with perfect clearness. My head did not so much as ache. Nor was I sensible of any wound.

"Hallo, Simmons!" I remarked, sitting up. "Where are we now?"

The litter stopped, and the sergeant bustled to my side.

"All right again, sir?" he queried. "I couldn't find no wound or bruise on you. Concussion of one of them newfangled shells of our'n, I guess. I saw you a fightin', not twenty foot away from me. Then a shell burst right above your 'ead, an' down you went. Not a scratch, even! Just concussion. I've seed it lay a man out for a good two hours, an' then seed 'im git up as good as new."

"You—some one—said the battle is over," I suggested.

"All over. Yankees fallin' back to their camp, an' us to ours. Our part of the shindy's over. It's for Cockburn—beg pardon, sir, I mean *Admiral* Cockburn—to pass the forts with them sixteen heavy gun frigates of his'n, an' batter Balt'more to pieces from the river. We can't give 'im no more 'elp. But th' admiral will do it easy enough. 'E starts to-night. An' you with 'im, sir, I now s'pose."

"I?"

"Yessir. I'm takin' th' liberty of shippin' you out to 'im with three p'litical pris'ners. You'll make it all right with him about it, sir, won't you, an' see I don't get into trouble?"

I promised to make his peace with Cockburn. In addition, I emptied my pockets of their little pile of gold and silver and forced it into his reluctant hand.

We had reached the shore, and I clambered out of the litter and stood on my feet. Beyond a slight shakiness, I was almost my old self again.

Fifteen minutes later I was in the stern of a long-boat which eight seamen were rowing to the British frigate Surprise, in the outer stream. Beside me sat three Americans in civilian dress who were held by the British on some technical political charge, and thus were not included in the harsh treatment accorded military prisoners.

Indeed, I learned there were several such captives on the Surprise.

Dusk was settling. Through the twilight I could see the dim bulk and twinkling lights of the powerful invading fleet. When I remembered that no barrier, save the decrepit Fort Covington and the nearer Fort McHenry, lay betwixt this mighty armament and Baltimore, my heart sickened.

It seemed, all at once, as if our gallant defense of North Point had been worse than futile.

What profited it that we had stemmed the land invasion if Baltimore were to be crushed beneath the big guns of these sixteen ships-of-war? Truly, the odds against our country were unduly heavy! We came alongside the Surprise. The rowers shipped their oars, a ladder was run down to us, and we clambered aboard.

A large cabin, aft, had been set aside for the captives' use. Thither we were conducted. I made for one of the bunks ranging along the wall, flung myself down upon it, and in a minute was sound asleep.

We had been on the march long before dawn. For hours I had fought, and it was now nightfall. I had earned my rest. It was the first unbroken sleep I had enjoyed for weeks.

Miserable, worried, discouraged as I was, Nature clamored for her due of repose. So, like a drugged man, I slept the clock around.

It was broad daylight when I awoke. I sprang to my feet, bewildered. Sprang up, only to be tossed back into my berth again as, with a swift lurch, the ship came about. So! We were under way, then. Bound for Baltimore!

I fancied the first motions of the frigate had wakened me, and that we must be just leaving our anchorage at North Point. So, waiting only to wash, and to munch a handful of the ship-biscuits and slices of dried meat that were piled on a plate on the table, I made my way to the deck.

Somewhat to my surprise, no one barred my passage. In fact, we political prisoners were made as free of every inch of the vessel as were the officers themselves.

I reached the rail and looked out on the distant shore. No sign of North Point, or of any of its surrounding country. While I slept, we had traveled many miles up-stream.

I saw some of my fellow prisoners chatting in groups about the afterdeck, but was in no mood to join them. Sitting down on a coil of rope, I fell to watching the waters and the far-off banks, and to speculating whether or not the fort would make the rash attempt to bar our progress. Remembering their scanty resources and weak defense, I half decided that we would not so much as halt as we swept by in our onward rush toward the doomed city.

I was fated, it seemed, to witness my fatherland's worst disasters. Baltimore once taken, the enemy's further conquest would be ridiculously easy. The freedom our fathers had won with their life-blood would become a mockery. Thus I sat an interminable time, moodily brooding.

A change in the sailing course drew my notice. Hitherto, we had moved in single file. Now the sixteen ships maneuvered into regular battle formation. We must be nearing the forts.

A bend in the narrowing river. A low fortress perched almost on the water's edge, the Stars and Stripes flying above its walls—Fort McHenry. Farther ahead rose the lesser walls of Fort Covington.

A crash from the foremost frigate's bow gun. The fleet had opened fire!

A second crash. Then two frigates swung about, and with a deafening roar hurled in full broadsides.

Some of the shot whistled high above the waves, following a true course to their mark. Others bounded and ricochetted over the water like the flat stones that country boys "skip" across millponds. Shells, too, now and then rattled noisily through the air and fell, plump! into the river, raising man-high pyramids of snow-white foam, or sending up a whirling cascade of spray.

From Fort McHenry now broke out an answering volley. The gun-ports flashed and sputtered like a series of toy crackers. Covington, farther away, and less exposed to the fleet's fire, followed suit in somewhat less emphatic fashion. So did a line of connecting batteries.

It was clear the little forts were going to dispute vehemently, even if uselessly, the passage of their stronger foe. And it did me good to see the valiant show of defense.

All afternoon the bombardment dragged on. Fort McHenry, being nearest, suffered the brunt of this. Also, her guns were mainly short-distance carronades, and could make little effective retort. The fleet hung in the offing, striving to batter the fort to submission at long range. It seemed impossible the defenders could hold out long under such fearful onslaught.

It was nearly sunset when, as I sat on my rope-coil, I heard one passing officer say to another:

"The admiral's found this a tougher nut to crack than he imagined. I hear he's given orders for a large shore party to be landed as soon as it's dark, to get around behind McHenry's defenses and smash them under cross-fire. That ought to settle them before midnight."

"And then Baltimore! And even better pickings than we found in Washington!" laughed his companion. "It's odd, though, how the fellows fight. They could hardly be pluckier if they were English."

The two moved on out of earshot. But they had given me an inspiration.

I had abstractedly noted, ever since morning, that messengers would occasionally rush to the chart-house, bearing orders from Cockburn, who had spent the day in the foretop rigging of the Surprise. These orders were bawled through the half-open door in the high-pitched "sing-song" so prevalent in both the army and navy of

England.

The officer on duty inside would rig signal flags accordingly and hand them out to a seaman, who took the flags to the signal ropes, ran them up, and thus flashed the commands to the other vessels of the squadron.

In fact, the seaman on duty at the door had but a few minutes earlier departed with a set of such signals. In a trice I was on my feet.

Slipping around to the side of the chart-room, just out of view of the busy officer within, I sang out, copying easily the droning intonation with which long years of custom had made me familiar:

"Set signal: Shore party, twelve hundred strong, land at nightfall to attack fort from rear!"

Then I was back again on my rope-coil, barely in time to dodge the returning signal sailor.

I sat waiting during a period that seemed interminable. Suppose the signal officer had detected a false note in my voice? Suppose he had realized how mad a thing it was to set such a signal as I had dictated?

Could he be so stupid as not to know that every spyglass in the fort would be trained on those signal flags as they were hauled aloft? That each would be read by the defenders, from their code-book, as quickly and as accurately as by the commanders of the other ships?

In fact, that the Surprise herself would be the only frigate in the fleet from which the signals would not be at once read?

But discipline aboard ship is cast-iron in its firmness. On this I relied. Had the signal officer received the orders: "Blow up every ship at once!" he probably would have set the flags accordingly.

Nor was I mistaken in my estimation. In a minute he handed out a new ball of flags to the seaman. And by the sunset light the defenders read—and took the needful precautions.

So it was that I, as prisoner, did my country greater service than ever I had in field of battle.

I was still chuckling over my success, when a surprised voice called my name. I looked up to see Key standing before me.

"What under Heaven brings *you* here, old friend?" he cried, glancing at my militia uniform.

Much as I owed to this man, much as my every instinct taught me to like him, it was all I could do to be civil. He had won all I had lost.

If I owed him my life, he owed to me the fact he was still betrothed to Dorothy Winder.

As poor McCrea would have said: "I guess the debt's wiped out."

I answered him as briefly as might be.

"I'm here as Mr. Madison's commissioner," said he, when I had finished my story. "I have charge of all arrangements for the exchange of certain political prisoners. But Cockburn holds us aboard here until the battle is over and Baltimore is reached. So we have the misery of watching our brave forts destroyed. But, oh, how pluckily McHenry is holding out! I've watched the flag floating so proudly above it all day. Will it be there at dawn? Or will the fort be a heap of ruins—and the path to Baltimore unguarded?"

"Who can say?" I shrugged, turning away.

But he was at my side again before I had taken a step.

"By the way!" he exclaimed, drawing a letter from his pocket, "I almost forgot. I dined with his excellency and Mrs. Madison four nights ago. Mrs. Madison asked a monstrous number of questions about you. When I told her I had heard you were on duty with Stricker's force, and that I was to stop at his headquarters on my way to the British fleet, she ran to her escritoire, scribbled a few lines, and bade me find you and give you the letter. She babbled some mysterious nonsense about having barred you long enough from the joys of Parad—"

"I can't stay in my cabin any longer," interrupted a voice as a woman's form emerged from the companionway and moved across to Key. "Aunt Lucia is better, and it is so stuffy down there. One of the officers says this ship is far out of range of the fort's fire, and that there's no danger. So I've come up to—"

The speaker paused abruptly on sight of me. And thus, for a second of confused silence, Dorothy and I faced each other.

Then, thrusting Mrs. Madison's unopened letter into my coat, I doffed my hat and bowed without speaking.

Had she been alone, I would have welcomed the meeting with unspeakable delight. But it was like a knife-thrust to see Key and herself standing there together.

CHAPTER XIX.

THE IMMORTAL VERSE.

DAWN—pallid and dim—crept over the waters.

All night had we three stood by the rail, almost wholly silent, watching the streaks of red light from signal-rockets whose blaze split the darkness as with a sword. All night had the boom of guns from ship to ship reverberated in our ears. And we had strained every faculty to catch the dull, answering roar from the fort.

Once a deathly silence had followed the fleet's volleys, and we had listened, breathless, for any reply from McHenry. The silence lengthened.

"Have they struck their colors?" whispered Dorothy with something very like a sob.

As if in answer to her words, a bomb trailed through the night sky from the direction of the beleaguered fort and burst in a thousand flashes of light far above the squadron.

"No!" cried Key in triumph. "The flag is still there!"

Shortly after midnight the distant crackle of musketry had sounded angrily through the stillness. A few rapid cannon-volleys followed. All these from somewhere behind the fort on the landward side.

"A shore attack!" muttered Key. "That was the meaning of the boats we saw the Surprise and some of the nearer frigates lowering, early in the evening. If it should succeed!"

Again McHenry's gun-ports belched a line of living flame, and the air shook with the report.

"The flag is still there!" answered Dorothy, using his own words in glad rejoinder.

"As far as the shore party is concerned," I put in, speaking for nearly the first time, "the flag is likely to stay there for some centuries. I fancy Commander Armistead was ready for them."

And I told them what I had done to warn the fort.

As I finished, Dorothy's soft hand was laid in quick, involuntary praise upon my own. The light touch went through me agonizingly, and, even as she withdrew her hand in sudden remembrance of our relative positions, I moved away slightly, glancing at Key as I did so.

He had evidently noted her impulsive gesture, yet his handsome face showed no displeasure. Whereat I wondered.

It may have been an hour or so later that the splash of oars betokened the return of the shore party. As such survivors of it as belonged to the Surprise clambered aboard near where we stood, we could hear, amid muttered curses, such detached phrases as:

"Yes, they were ready for us—" "We walked straight into the trap—" "The miserable Yankees heated round-shot till it was red-hot and fired it into our platoon."

And so the night dragged on. As gray dawn appeared, ship after ship slackened fire. And now we listened in vain for sounds from the fort.

All along shore was as still as death. A light mist overhung the water, blotting out every glimpse of land.

"It's all over," said Key, "one way or another. Either Cockburn has given up his attempt at passing the fort, or—what is much more likely—the garrison have surrendered."

"After such a gallant defense? All day and all night!" exclaimed Dorothy. "Oh, they *wouldn't!*"

"Their fort may be razed to the ground by this time," gloomily returned Key. "If so, America's liberties are in greater danger than ever they were in Revolutionary days. Baltimore must fall. And then—"

A swirl of wind blew the words from his lips and sent the soft strands of loose hair flying about Dorothy's face. The same zephyr cut the water mists as one might scatter the smoke of a cigar.

In the struggling dawnlight the low, dark fort stood out clear against the paler background of sky. And, like a splash of vivid autumn color in a dull pine-wood, the Stars and Stripes fluttered lazily from the flagstaff.

The relief was too great. Key and I seized each other's shoulders and capered about the deck together like drunken sailors.

Forgot, for the second, was my bitterness, my insensate black jealousy. I knew but one thing—the flag of my country still floated victorious. The bombardment had failed. The flag was still there!

Dorothy, in the mighty reaction, had sunk down and buried her face in her hands, her slender figure shaken with sobs.

"Oh, the splendid, *splendid* flag!" she wept in ecstasy. "The beautiful star-spangled banner! I love it so!"

Key, at sound of her weeping, came to himself, as did I.

"Hush!" he comforted the girl. "This is no time for tears. You have seen the most glorious sight this country's day ever dawned on—the 'star-spangled banner,' as you call it! It has triumphed once more. The fatherland is safe! Safe, thanks to the star-spangled banner!"

"Long may it wave!" I added. "It floats to-day over a land of brave people who will forever be free."

Key caught at my boastful words, repeating them softly to himself. Then he began to pace the deck, muttering disconnected sentences under his breath.

"Oh, for a sheet of paper and a crayon, while the mood is on me!" I heard him murmur.

Without clearly following his idea, but moved by the passionate earnestness in his voice, I mechanically began to search my pockets. In one I readily found a pencil-stub I had used in map-marking. Then my fingers closed on a letter.

"Will these do?" I asked as he passed me once more in that restless, muttering walk of his.

He snatched the paper and pencil almost rudely, with a bare word of thanks. It was not until I saw him rip open the letter and begin to scribble feverishly in tiny, neat characters on the blank side of it, that I realized it was the missive he had given me from Mrs. Madison, and which I, in the excitement of the moment, had put aside unopened.

Still, I cared little, even were he to blot out its message with his scribblings. I felt scant interest in Dolly Madison, for I could not forget it was she who had first shown me the closed gate of happiness, that night at the Gaines mansion, when she took so mocking a delight in telling me of Dorothy's betrothal to Key.

I turned now to glance at Dorothy. Her eyes were upon Key, but in what seemed to me curiosity rather than love. I stepped toward the busily writing man, but she checked me by a gesture.

"*Don't!*" she whispered. "He is writing. One word might break the inspiration. And his poems are usually too good to be spoiled by an untimely breaking-off of his thoughts. He—"

"I have it!" exclaimed Key, springing up and coming toward us, his gay face fairly glowing, his hand atremble. "I *have* it! The first stanza. The rest will follow easily. 'Twas only the first I doubted for. Will you listen?"

And in that wondrous, melodious, deep voice of his, he began to read what he had scrawled on the back of my letter:

Oh, say, can you see by the dawn's early light
What so proudly we hailed at the twilight's last gleaming?
Whose broad stripes and bright stars through the perilous fight
O'er the ramparts we watched were so gallantly streaming?
And the rockets' red glare, the bombs bursting in air,
Gave proof through the night that our flag was still there!
Oh, say, does the star-spangled banner still wave
O'er the land of the free and the home of the brave?

He paused. Dorothy and I, with a single breath, cried out in admiration.

"It is genius!" I said briefly as we grew more coherent.

"It is more!" Dorothy asserted. "It is patriotism! It strikes the key-note of love and pride in the fatherland. It will live when we are forgotten. Yes, and when this night's battle is scarce recalled to memory."

"You are right," I assented. "I believe that the battle will live in men's minds because of the poem. Not the poem because of the battle. What shall you call it?"

Key seemed scarcely to have heard our plaudits. Now, at my question, he had roused himself.

"I shall give Miss Winder the naming of it, if she will do me the honor," said he. "It was her chance phrase of the 'star-spangled banner' that gave birth to the idea. What shall it be, Miss Dorothy?"

"Why not call it just that—'The Star-Spangled Banner'?" she suggested timidly. "It has a good, poetic sound. *'The Star-Spangled Banner, by Francis Scott Key,'*" she added, giving him his full name, with mock deference, in declaiming the title.

"And," she continued excitedly, "do you know you've unconsciously chosen the meter of 'Anacreon in Heaven'? Your song will go better to that grand air than to any other. Listen."

She hummed a bar of the martial tune to the first line of Key's poem. Words and music seemed indissolubly made for each other.

"So be it," said Key. "You have christened my verse."

"No," she contradicted with pretty wilfulness, "it has been christened in the blood of heroes. And it will live in the hearts of their children's children! I prophesy it!"

"With all my heart, I thank you," responded the poet. "I am already repaid, even if the kind forecast fail to come true. But, Romney," he added in a more commonplace tone, "I'm afraid I've spoiled your letter. Had you any further use for it?"

"None, especially," said I. "It is the one you gave me last night from Mrs. Madison. Nothing important, I fancy."

"You 'fancy'?" echoed Key. "Do you mean you hadn't read it?"

"Scarcely," I retorted, "since you just now broke the seal."

"Oh, a thousand pardons!" he cried, full of remorse. "What a boor I am! I trust you'll forgive my rudeness. I—"

"It's of no consequence at all," I cut him short, accepting the missive from him.

"After you've read the letter," interposed Dorothy, "may I read the verse on the back of it once more?"

"Certainly," I answered. "Read it now, if you will. The letter can wait," I went on, in answer to her protest. "It has waited long, and a little further delay will scarce cool its tidings. Besides, I'd like to hear the verse again. Won't you please read it aloud?"

I handed her the letter. She began: "'I have kept you in suspense far too long, you silly boy!'"

Then she paused, colored, and looked so pathetically confused that Key broke out laughing.

"I think," he chuckled, "the tidings may not be so cold, after all—if one may judge from the start! Perhaps it might be well to read it?"

"I—I'm sorry," protested Dorothy, giving the sheet of paper back to me, "I got the wrong side of the page."

"So I perceive," I answered dryly.

I took the wretched letter—angry at my own share in the foolish mistake—and glanced idly at the dainty chirography of the president's wife. In morbid fear lest the others think from the opening line that the flighty little woman and I were carrying on some senseless, innocuous flirtation, I read aloud, scarce noting at first the sense of the words:

> I have kept you in suspense far too long, you silly boy. I promised I would tell you great news one week from the night I talked with you at the Gaines dinner-party. But one week from then—where were we all? So I have had to let your punishment last till I could get word to you. Though, on my faith, you deserved to suffer, for breathing sweet nothings to one woman, while you looked love with all your soul at another. Do you blame one for avenging myself? But I generously forgive you! In token of which, I do hereby affirm most solemnly that Frank Key and Dorothy Winder are not—have never been—and are never likely to be—betrothed. I only—

The paper fluttered to the deck. Dazed, reeling under the wonder of my sudden happiness, I rushed toward Dorothy, scarce noting Key's look of comic bewilderment.

"Dorothy!" I cried.

From ship to ship, through the hush of early morning, rang the bugle-calls, sounding the retreat. The invasion was over. Baltimore was saved. The liberties of the country were preserved. England's hopes of American conquest were forever crushed.

At my feet, scrawled on the back of a letter, lay a poem that was to become immortal.

But did *I* give heed to any of these petty trifles? Not I! I had greater, far more marvelous—glorious—immortal —things to think of—

Dorothy Winder was in my arms!

THE END.

Appendix

Publication information
for the stories
in this book

This novel was serialized in four issues of Argosy, from November 1908 through February 1909.

November 1908
Chapter I through V.

Front text (repeated in the three subsequent issues):
Author of "With Sealed Lips," "On Glory's Trail," "Their Last Hope," etc.

An American's strange adventures in his own country during the War of 1812, with an account of a historic achievement under fire closely woven into the fabric of the story.

December 1908
Chapter VI through X.

Front text:
SYNOPSIS OF CHAPTERS PREVIOUSLY PUBLISHED.

IN the year 1814, Richard Romney, a young man of American parentage who has been brought up in England and served in the English army, falls heir to his father's estates in New Jersey and comes to America, serving in strictly noncombatant capacity on General Ross's staff. Upon a wager with Admiral Cockburn he sets out to find Barney's flotilla of gunboats, which is interfering with Cockburn's blockading schemes. One of the terms is that he will not betray the whereabouts of the fleet. Captured as a spy, he is brought before General Winder, and is about to be condemned to death when he is identified as an American by the general's niece, Dorothy Winder. Sergeant McCrea, Romney's captor, is rebuked by the general for his action, and swears vengeance.

Leaving Winder's headquarters, Romney determines yet to win his wager if he can. Searching along the river-bank, he discovers the boats in a hidden lagoon, and turns away—to confront a leveled pistol.

Bottom of page:
Began November ARGOSY. *Single copies, 10 cents.*

January 1909
Chapter XI through XV.

Front text:
SYNOPSIS OF CHAPTERS PREVIOUSLY PUBLISHED.

IN the year 1814, Richard Romney, a young man of American parentage who has been brought up in England and served in the English army, falls heir to his father's estates in New Jersey and comes to America, serving in strictly noncombatant capacity on General Ross's staff. Upon a wager with Admiral Cockburn he sets out to find Barney's flotilla of gunboats, which is interfering with Cockburn's blockading schemes. One of the terms is that he will not betray the whereabouts of the fleet. Captured as a spy, he is brought before General Winder, and is about to be condemned to death when he is identified as an American by the general's niece, Dorothy Winder. Sergeant McCrea, Romney's captor, is rebuked by the general for his action, and swears vengeance.

Leaving Winder's headquarters, Romney discovers the boats in a hidden lagoon, and turns away—to confront a leveled pistol in the hands of Dorothy Winder. Half-believing him to be a spy, Dorothy binds him to her as a prisoner on parole until the end of the campaign, and takes him with her to the home of her aunt, Mrs. Gaines, at Bladensburg. Here he learns that Dorothy is practically engaged to a young American named Key. In the battle which takes place a week later, Romney rushes out to join Barney's sailors, who are holding the Bladensburg bridge against overwhelming odds. Just as the handful of Americans are surrounded, Romney is struck down by a blow on the head, from his old enemy, Sergeant McCrea.

Bottom of page
* *Began November,* 1908, ARGOSY. *Single copies, 10 cents*

Editorial change: The word "duece" was changed to "deuce."

February 1909
Chapter XVI through Conclusion.

Front text:
* Began November, 1908, ARGOSY. Single copies, 10 cents.

Editorial change: In the original pulp, the title for Chapter XVII was "M'CREA PAYS HIS DEBT." This character's name in all other places was "McCrea," so the title was changed to reflect that.

General Notes
The original story was not illustrated.

Other books available
from the
Silver Creek Press

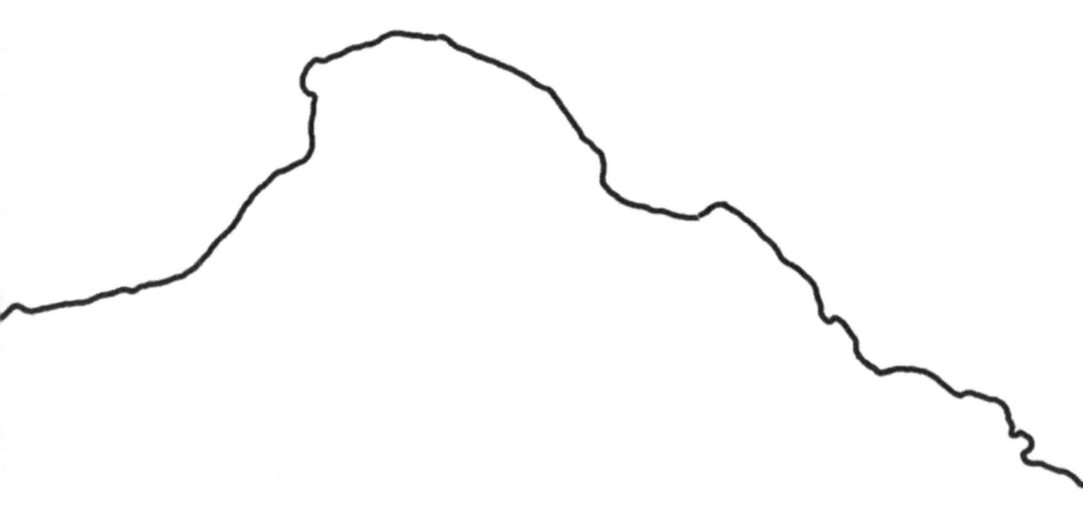

The *Albert Payson Terhune Reader* Series

Each reprints over 20 stories by Terhune
from pulp magazines of the 1900s through the 1920s,
with all original illustrations.

Other fiction by Terhune

The Flood Fighters
In Treason's Track
The White Way
First book publication for each

Their
Last Hope

Albert Payson TERHUNE

Their Last Hope

SCP Tête-Bêche
Book 2

Silver
Creek
Press

2019

CHAPTER I.

BLUNDERING INTO A TRAP.

A WHITE, dusty ribbon of road, lined with huge shade-trees. At one end, blurred by dust, three towering conical shapes, at whose base crouched a stone image—half lion, half woman.

At the opposite end of the thoroughfare a stone bridge, beyond which a hundred domes and minarets gave back the blaze of the afternoon sun. On either side, a dreary expanse of yellow sand, punctuated by discouraged-looking fields and terminating in a wide sinuous strip of verdure whose windings marked the course of the tawny river.

The highway was choked with carriages, camels, equestrians, and plodding peasants. For the Gizeh Road, leading from Cairo to the Pyramids, is the fashionable promenade and drive of Egypt.

A group of men and women, riding with more or less awkwardness on little mouse-colored donkeys, jogged westward toward the city; now moving abreast, now stretching out in single file or by twos to permit some unusually large cortège to pass.

Any one who had traveled in Europe or in the East would at a glance have recognized the party as Cook tourists. There were a round dozen of them, and at their head rode a swart-faced man in panoply of blue and gold—Halil Sadik-Ali, their dragoman.

A girl dressed in a dust-shedding costume of brown holland rode near the van. She was not very tall, and her brown eyes roved hither and thither among the unaccustomed sights with all the frank wonder and delight of a child's.

Observing this, more than one gaze which had turned on the tourists with amusement paused to linger with genuine pleasure on the trim brown-holland figure and joy-flushed face.

An elderly gentleman jogging beside the girl looked down at her with manifest approval.

"Miss Brant," said he half laughingly, wholly admiringly, "you're a model for us all. Here the rest of us are choking with dust and painfully conscious that we're making a show of ourselves on these wretched little donkeys, and yet *you* look as cool and as happy as a child on her

first holiday."

"It *is* my first holiday," she answered gaily; "my very first in four years, and I'm enjoying every minute of it. I—"

"Your first holiday in four years? Then you've been to college, I suppose? But I—"

"No," replied the girl, "I've been teaching school. And in summer vacation I've been tutoring girls who were preparing for college."

"Teaching school? You're the last sort of girl I should take for a school-ma'am."

"Oh, I can be *very* severe, I assure you. My scholars all hold me in awe. At least, I always like to think so. But I supposed you knew. The party has been together so long that we all know one another's histories and tastes and characters and most becoming clothes and—But I forgot! You only joined us at Port Saïd. So I suppose there are still a few incidents in our lives that you haven't learned."

"Yes, I took the Gibraltar-Tangier trip, you know. I hardly feel acquainted with my fellow voyagers. But your name is very familiar to me. Henry Brant, of Brant & Fitch, the brokerage house, you may have heard of. He was—"

"He was my father."

The gleam of fun had now quite died from Madge Brant's eyes, to be replaced by a momentary shade of sadness.

"Your father? Really, I—"

"You are surprised that his daughter should be a school-teacher? You know he failed; and soon after that he died. I was left alone, with my way to make, just as I was ready for college. I took up teaching, and I've been at it ever since."

"I am more glad than I can say to meet my old friend's daughter. I'd no idea of it. Seeing you so much with Mrs. Chittenden, I fancied—"

"No, she is no relation of mine. She is a wealthy New York woman whose daughter I prepared for college. Mrs. Chittenden seemed to take a liking to me. She was coming abroad for a year, and was kind enough to ask me to come along as her companion."

"I wish you joy of the employment!" the man exclaimed, real pity in his dusty face. "I know her well by reputation. One of the richest women in New York—and one of the stingiest. It was a joke at my club that she had invited that cub nephew of hers, Barry Clive, to make a

tour of the world with her, and that he was afraid of offending her by refusing; and then when he found she was economizing by making a Cook's tour of it he was furious. It—"

"Pardon me, Mr. Gault," intervened the girl, "but Mrs. Chittenden is my employer. If you don't object, sha'n't we talk of something else? I—"

She was interrupted. The little cavalcade had been brought to a stop to permit a troop of native cavalry to jingle past.

A fresh cloud of dust had been stirred up, and through it a man who had been riding at the rear urged his donkey at a canter, in order to be rid of the choking haze. He passed so close to Madge that the two donkeys collided, and the shock of the impact almost unseated the girl.

The youth, with no word of apology, nor so much as turning to see the result of his awkwardness, galloped on, the heels of his mount engulfing Madge and Gault in a second whirlwind of dust.

The elderly man coughed vehemently, his face purple with wrath. Digging his heels into his donkey's furry sides, he was about to speed after the youth, but a restraining voice checked him.

"Don't!" Madge begged. "He meant nothing by it. It's only his way."

"His way!" snorted the other, pulling back his donkey, nevertheless. "Well, it's a way I won't tolerate from any one, least of all from a whelp like Barry Clive! I'll make him come back and apologize to you!"

"Oh, I beg you won't!" cried Madge, in distress. "In the first place, he wouldn't do it, and there would only be a scene. Besides, I wasn't hurt. It's all right."

"I've heard quite a bit about that young man," observed Mr. Gault, eying contemptuously the broad shoulders and slender waist of the impulsive youth, who was beginning to slacken speed now that he was free from the dust-cloud—"quite a bit. And none of it was in his favor. According to all reports, he's about the worst specimen of unkicked puppy on record. They tell me he was a monument of selfishness and conceit at Harvard, and afterward at the law school; that he gave himself unbearable airs of superiority over the poorer men in his class, and that he's an all-around cad. And all just because he happens to have met no one with public spirit enough to give him a good thrash-

ing and teach him he doesn't rule the whole universe."

"Oh, come!" laughed the girl. "It isn't quite as bad as all that. He's been spoiled and petted until he doesn't quite understand the rights of other people. That's all. He's—"

"He's been toadied to, just because he is his uncle's heir and because he has more money than is good for any boy," amended Mr. Gault—"just because he happens to be the nephew of the great Jonas Fitch. By the way, Jonas Fitch was your father's former partner, wasn't he? Of course he was! I remember, now, hearing rumors that—"

"That he ruined my father and profited by the crash in which the Brant fortunes were swept away? It is quite true. Though there is nothing to be gained by brooding over that now."

"And that young beast is giving himself airs on money that ought to be yours!"

"As I said," resumed the girl, "there is nothing to be gained by bringing all that up now. I—"

"Madge!" called a querulous voice from behind; "the hotel is only about three blocks away. Ride ahead and tell Serene to prepare my bath."

Gault turned with amazement to face the old lady who had given so peremptory an order to Miss Brant; then, with still more amazement, he noted that Madge, without a word, had whipped up her donkey and ridden forward on her menial errand. As she passed Barry Clive the latter did not bow or in any way give sign of having recognized her.

"I don't know what salary that poor child receives," communed Mr. Gault within himself, "but whatever it is, she certainly earns it!"

* * * * *

To reach Shepheard's Hotel (the Waldorf-Astoria of Cairo) from the Gizeh Road one follows a transverse street. At a point a block or two east of the hotel this street forks.

The left-hand road continues on past the hotel; the right, after divers curves and windings, carries the traveler into the slums, or lower native quarter, of the city. The average stranger in Cairo is prone to mistake the latter and wider highway for the hotel street.

This is precisely what Madge Brant did. Spurring on ahead of

4

the cavalcade, her cheeks aflame at the humiliation of being publicly addressed as though she were a servant, she instinctively chose the wider road.

A passing string of camels had barred the way of the main party, causing a temporary halt and obstructing the view. Thus, Madge's blunder passed unseen.

Barry Clive alone, still riding in advance of the others, saw her pass him, and as she turned to the right he instinctively followed. His own knowledge of Cairo's topography was as limited as was Madge's, and seeing her go to the right, he supposed she was headed for the hotel. Thus they rode on, each thinking their fellow tourists were following at their heels.

Clive was in a thoroughly bad temper. From the very outset of the trip it had irked him to be associated with a mere Cook tour. It had seemed beneath him; he regarded his fellow travelers as hopelessly commonplace, and sternly repelled their friendly advances.

His aunt's parsimony was a daily trial to him; and but for fear of offending her, and of thereby marring his own financial prospects, he would long since have returned to America.

This afternoon the climax of annoyance had been reached when, in the passing throng on the Gizeh Road, he had encountered the wondering amusement in the eyes of a passer-by whom he had recognized as a Harvard classmate of his own—an ultrafastidious member of the university's ultraexclusive set.

That this man should have seen him in the guise of a "tripper" was as vitriol to Barry Clive's vanity. He pictured to himself the unction with which the story would be repeated in Cambridge, and the malicious joy it would afford the coterie of snobs among whom Clive had ever shone as the brightest star.

So absorbed was Barry in these wrathful musings that it was with a start he at length realized that the street through which he was jogging in Madge's wake bore absolutely no likeness to that on which the hotel fronted.

This same knowledge dawned on Madge at almost the same moment.

She reined in her donkey and glanced about her in bewilderment. She was at the entrance of a long, crooked rectangle into which a

number of filthy narrow alleys debouched.

The square was alive with activity, yet not one European face did she see. Natives everywhere; natives of both sexes; low-browed, evil of eye, and squalid of dress.

She had, although she did not realize it, penetrated to that vilest quarter of all Egypt, the Cairo "Fishmarket," an unspeakable section, wherein, even in this semi-enlightened age, no foreigner's life is safe, least of all if that foreigner be a woman, young, good to look upon, and defenseless.

CHAPTER II.

A SERVICE AND A REPULSE.

As Madge Brant glanced about her in perplexity she became aware that she had all at once become the cynosure of a thousand eyes. Comments of whose nature and phrasing she was luckily unaware were freely bandied back and forth among the frequenters of the square. A little knot of people, quickly increasing, began to gather about her donkey's head.

A native woman would have screamed; a European damsel would doubtless have fainted. Madge, being an American girl, with the fearless eyes and fearless soul of her type, felt only astonishment at the attention she attracted, and intense interest in the variegated costumes and odd faces that met her gaze.

Tall black Nubians in white robes and stolid faces; sullen Druses in white turbans and blue-tattooed eyelids; fat Cairenes of the lower type; *fellaheen* in ragged sheepskins; Turkish soldiers fat and dirty in their ill-fitting uniforms; shopmen, idlers, criminals, with here and there a man whose wild eyes and strange garb proclaimed him a dervish—all these congregated about the surprised girl.

She cast a hasty backward glance to see if any of her friends had followed. Her eyes encountered only Barry Clive, who had ridden up to within a few yards of her, and who was looking past her in evident perturbation at the motley assemblage in the square.

"I'm afraid we've lost our way," she began, when a hand on her arm caused her to turn suddenly.

A large man, bloated and yellow-brown of face, and who, by his dress, seemed a personage of some importance, had laid an unwashed paw upon her sleeve and was addressing her in halting French.

"*Mademoiselle* has come to view the charms of the Fishmarket?" he asked, with an unpleasant laugh.

"I—we have lost our way," replied Madge coldly, in the same language, as she withdrew her arm. "Will you kindly direct us to Shepheard's?"

Alone, the fellow's touch and words would have alarmed her. With a fellow countryman at her side—even so uncongenial a fellow countryman as Barry Clive—she felt no fear.

The man did not at once reply to her request. He said something in Arabic to the crowd, and a laugh arose—a laugh that was not reassuring. Nor were the distorted faces with their rows of grinning white teeth good to look upon.

The fat man, seeing evidently that the crowd expected something further from him by way of entertainment, again laid his hand on Madge's arm.

"Come!" he said persuasively; "*mademoiselle* must stop and have a glass of cognac as the Fishmarket's guest before she returns."

With a shudder, feeling as though some reptile had touched her, Madge attempted to withdraw her arm. But this time the grasp was not so easily shaken off.

An ugly look crept into the fat man's eyes as he tightened his grip and leered up into the face of the now thoroughly frightened girl. He opened his lips to speak, but a howl of pain cut short his words. Barry Clive had brought down his riding-stick smartly across the native's pudgy knuckles.

The fat man snatched away his hand and fell to nursing the bleeding fingers.

Before he or his fellows could recover from their astonishment Barry had caught the bridle of Madge's donkey, had swung the little quadruped about, and the two were galloping back up the alley by which they had arrived at the square. They had been only upon the threshold of the rectangle, and the crowd was wholly in front of them,

so the maneuver was executed with comparative ease.

Had the hour been later a hundred running feet would swiftly have outstripped the tired little donkeys and haled the pair of insolent foreigners back. But the sun had scarcely set, and the police were still abroad.

There was also the danger of running into a party of British or Egyptian soldiery. So the denizens of the Fishmarket prudently desisted from pursuit.

After galloping along at top speed for several hundred yards, Clive glanced back over his shoulder and perceived that they were not followed. He slackened his pace and dropped Madge's bridle.

For a brief space the two rode on through the tortuous alley in silence. Then Madge won the battle she had been waging against a longing to cry, and began to recover her scattered self-control.

With restored tranquillity came an impulse of gratitude toward the man who had extricated her from so awkward a predicament.

Moreover, she was aware of certain twinges of conscience at having misjudged him. The aloofness he had consistently shown toward herself and her friends doubtless arose from extreme diffidence. Otherwise, how account for this recent act of chivalry?

"Mr. Clive," she began timidly, yet with earnest gratitude, "I hardly know how to thank you for what you have just done. I—"

"Don't try," he answered shortly, urging his donkey forward through the labyrinth of alleys.

She brought her own mount alongside, secretly admiring him for the apparent modesty that made him seek to avoid her thanks, but none the less resolved to ease her mind and her conscience.

"I won't try to thank you," she continued, smiling across into his stolid face, "but I shall never forget how brave and how ready you were. And," as he made as though he would interrupt her, "there's another thing I want to say: I've misjudged you—your manner and your behavior toward the rest of us. I see now I was wrong and I ask your pardon for thinking—"

"It's quite immaterial to me what you or any one else thinks," he broke in crossly. "Look here, Miss Brant, we may as well understand each other at once and for all. What I did to help you a few minutes ago was no more than I—or any white man—would have done for

any washerwoman. As for my former behavior toward the others of the party my aunt forces me to travel with, that is no concern of yours. But concerning my manner to *you*, let me assure you I've never given you a further thought than I would have wasted on any other of Mrs. Chittenden's servants."

"Servants!"

She echoed the word almost inaudibly, the friendly smile dying on her childlike face as suddenly as if the man had struck her.

"Servants?" she repeated, not comprehending. "I—I don't understand."

"Then I must explain more clearly, and you'll excuse me if I speak with more plainness than perhaps you're used to. These people we travel with have made a pet of you, and have given you perhaps a rather magnified idea of your own importance. In other words, they've spoiled you. They have made you forget that you are a dependent of Mrs. Chittenden and have treated you as an equal. If they choose to it is their own affair. But I have noticed several times lately that you seem inclined to address *me* as if we were on the same social plane, and—"

"Mr. Clive!" broke forth Madge, but he waved her to silence and resumed:

"Please do not interrupt. I am sorry to have to speak so frankly, but you force me to it. Let it be settled henceforth that I shall accord to you the civility I would show to any woman, black or white, but that I do not choose to associate more than is absolutely necessary with my aunt's paid employee. The days of King Cophetua are past, and I—"

"You need not say anything further," interrupted the girl, and now all the surprise and indignation had gone from her voice, leaving it cold, metallic, deadly calm. "You speak of coming to an understanding. That is impossible at present, for you understand neither yourself nor me. But perhaps I can make both clearer to you."

She paused an instant, and he was about to speak, when she went on in the same cold, level tone:

"You look on me as a dependent of Mrs. Chittenden's and, as such, your inferior. I—like yourself—*am* a dependent. But with this difference: *I* work honorably to earn my living. *You* do not work at all. I give full value for every penny I receive. You accept a living for which

you give no return. Which of us is the inferior? No, please don't interrupt. I heard you patiently. I ask the same courtesy at your hands—the 'civility you would show any woman, black or white.' "

He winced, but listened in spite of himself.

"You look down on your fellow travelers and consider them beneath you. Yet they are kind-hearted, honest, and do what they can for one another's comfort. Can you say as much for yourself? You take advantage of the accident of fortune to make me feel keenly my position as an employee. By your own statement none of the others have treated me other than as an equal.

"You further insult me by hinting that I am seeking to play the roles of beggar maid to your King Cophetua. Just to prove to you how mistaken you are, I wish to tell you that I hold of you the same opinion that any sane and self-respecting woman would hold toward a man who can speak to a woman as you have just spoken. It can be condensed into one word: Mr. Barry Clive, you are a cad!"

The young man's bronzed face was purple. Thrice he opened his mouth to blurt out some angry torrent of retort, and thrice he checked himself. After waiting for an answer, she went on:

"I think that now we at last begin to understand each other. There are but two points more to clear up before we close this very unpleasant subject. First, I cannot, of course, continue in Mrs. Chittenden's service after this, even if your Bayard-like chivalry prevented you from repeating our conversation to her. But I shall not on that account let you spoil my long-planned trip. I have a little money laid by, and I shall continue the journey at my own expense. In other words, the fact of my being your aunt's 'dependent' need not force you to continue my acquaintance. So in future I beg that you will treat me as you treat the rest of us; in other words, ignore me. That is all, I think. We must be almost at the hotel; I won't trouble you to escort me farther."

Whipping up her weary donkey, she galloped on through the fast-gathering dusk. He made as if to follow, but his donkey stumbled on the slimy cobbles and fell to its knees.

By the time Clive had got the beast to its feet again Madge was out of sight around one of the sharp corners of the byway.

So engrossed had both been in their talk that they had failed to note the settling down of dark or the fact that the curving, tortuous

course of their path proved it to be one of those innumerable alleys which in the "native district" of Cairo merge into and depart from the main streets at so obtuse an angle as to mislead even the oldest foreign habitués of the city.

As a matter of fact, Clive and Miss Brant had been traveling almost in a circle. The alley forked almost directly in front of the spot where Clive's donkey stumbled. In doubt as to which road the girl had taken, Barry turned to the left, and in due course found himself within fifty yards of the hotel.

Madge, on the contrary, hot tears of rage and mortification dimming her sight and dulling her faculties, had wheeled into the right-hand fork.

As she rode on she fought back the unwonted resentment that filled her heart.

"They sha'n't spoil my good time! They *sha'n't!*" she told herself defiantly. "I've worked hard for four years, and I won't let a cross old woman and a cub of a boy ruin my trip. I'll forget all about it and enjoy the rest of the tour just as much as I can. Thank goodness, all the others are nice to me! I'd be foolish to let myself worry over what Mr. Clive chooses to think about me."

Having at last talked herself into her normal sunny temper, she fell to wondering at the length of the route she had chosen. It was now quite dark, and despite her Yankee fearlessness she began to grow a little nervous as the narrow black alley stretched out before her.

It was not wholly pleasant to feel that she might have missed her way and been lost in the slums of one of the vilest cities on earth. She quickened her pace, glancing apprehensively at the occasional dark forms that slunk past her.

Luckily, the night was as much her friend as her menace, in that it rendered her practically invisible to such frequenters of the quarter as she chanced to meet.

At length, coming around a curve in the road, she saw ahead of her, not one hundred yards distant, a welcome glare of light, an open space where hurrying figures passed and repassed.

"The hotel square at last!" she thought gaily, as, dazzled by the light, she urged the donkey forward—into the very center of the Fishmarket.

CHAPTER III.

THE MAN OF DESTINY.

MADGE BRANT, divining how fatally she had lost her way and to what a goal her last dash for refuge had led her, sat dazed, inert.

There, in the middle of that noisy, squalid square, she sat, a pathetic little huddled figure with white face and wide, frightened eyes. About her swirled the eddy and backwater of all that is lowest in Cairo's mixed population.

The air was vibrant with the monotonous *thud—thud—thud* of native drums in the various cafes and concert halls; shrill yells, laughter and song; thick with smoke and rank perfumes. The filthy pavements were swarming with the scum of the Mediterranean.

And in the center of it all, perched on a solitary small gray donkey, sat the trembling American girl.

Before she could frame a plan for escape one or two idlers had spied her. Drawing about her in open-mouthed curiosity, their actions attracted others. In less than thirty seconds the girl found herself once more surrounded.

Then came a shout from in front. She was recognized as the *Sitt* (foreign lady) who had been in the Fishmarket less than an hour before. The shout brought men running from all directions. It was seen that her escort was no longer with her, and this emboldened the throng to press closer.

Awakening to a sense of her peril, Madge sought to wheel her donkey to one side and to force a way through to the friendlier shadows of the alleys. But the crowd was thick and the little beast exhausted. A loud laugh greeted the failure of her attempt.

"Five medjidie to the man who will conduct me to Shepheard's Hotel," she cried in French, in a voice she pluckily strove to steady.

But even as she spoke there was a stir and confusion in the press, as of some one striving to force a way through. Men fell back respectfully to either side, and through the lane thus formed waddled the fat man who had addressed her on her previous involuntary visit.

His right hand was bound up in a dirty cloth where Clive's rid-

ing-stick had struck. His expression had not been improved by the experience.

"Let me be *mademoiselle's* escort," he said; "I shall be honored to conduct her to Shepheard's."

Such of the crowd as understood French laughed aloud as he waddled forward and with an air of mock gallantry held out his uninjured hand.

"And I shall not demand the five medjidie," he resumed, with a smirk, bringing his flabby face close to hers; "all the payment I shall ask is one little kiss—payable in advance, of course—"

She could feel his hot breath on her cheek. Tossing back her head just in time, she struck him full in the face with her little clenched fist.

He recoiled a step in amaze. Then, maddened by the amusement of his fellows more than by the sting of the blow, he sprang forward, gripping Madge by the shoulder.

"When payments are not made willingly," he snarled, with a sort of savage humor, "they must be collected by force!"

Regardless of her mad struggles, he once more bent his face toward her.

She cried out in horror, and—the fat man went spinning backward into the crowd like a tee-totum, caroming off from the impact with his comrades, and at last landing in a sitting posture on the dirt of the ground.

Almost before he fell he was up again, with an agility marvelous in one so obese. A curved knife was in his hand, and he was glaring about him like a wild beast. In a small cleared space directly in front of Madge stood a man in black. Of no great height or bulk, and dressed in plain civilian garb, his presence yet seemed to dominate that whole noisy rabble. His back was to the light; and the fat man, judging the stranger, from his attitude, to be the assailant who had balked him of his dainty sport of torturing a defenseless girl, gripped the knife tighter and took a step forward.

"Abou Saoud!" said the newcomer.

He did not speak loudly, nor threateningly, as he thus pronounced the other's name; but the effect was electrical. The fat man stopped in his tracks. By the torch-flare Madge could see the color ebb from his yellow-brown face, leaving it ashen. His very bulk seemed to collapse.

The knife dropped from his nerveless fingers and tinkled dully on the ground.

"*Saadat-el-Basha!*" (Excellency!) he gasped.

At the words a murmur, as of a rising wind, swept the mob. Madge could hear whispers of amazement, of fear, on every hand, mingled with cries of "*Effendi!*" "*Mamour!*" and "*Welee!*" (Lord! Master! Divine One!)

The crowd melted away as by magic, leaving in a moment none in the center of the erstwhile thronged square save the New York girl on her donkey, the stranger in black, and the trembling Abou Saoud.

And now the stranger was speaking again to the frightened native—speaking in deep-toned, guttural Arabic. Though Madge could not understand a syllable that was said, she noted the stinging effect of each stern word on the cringing Abou.

The fat man cowered wilting and crushed under the invective, attempting no reply, making no sign of remonstrance.

At length the stranger pointed to the knife on the ground, and then to the shadows beyond the radius of light. Like a whipped cur, Abou Saoud stooped, picked up the ugly weapon, and slunk away in silence.

As the darkness swallowed the departing native the stranger for the first time turned toward Madge Brant.

The torchlight fell full on his tanned face and slender, erect figure, the glare bringing out each detail of the high forehead, the stern yet kindly mouth half hidden by the crisp grizzled mustache, the level gray brows beneath which shone alert blue eyes of almost hypnotic keenness, yet in whose depths there lurked a profound gentleness mingled with a sort of fanaticism.

The whole face and bearing bespoke a strange blending of the warrior, the man of thought, and the mystic, while the key-note of the *ensemble* seemed an intense gentleness whose basis was granite strength.

At first glance, Madge leaped forward with an eager smile of welcome. Here was a friend, one whom she knew and loved. Then, on second thought, she blankly realized that she now looked on the man for the first time. Yet his face seemed as familiar to her as that of her own father.

Somewhere, she was sure, she had seen him; not once or twice, but often. For every line of the weather-stained handsome face was known to her.

"I—I know you," she faltered, lamely enough; "but who are you?"

Then, on the moment, recovering herself, she went on:

"Thank you a thousand times! If it had not been for you—"

She stopped with a little involuntary shudder at memory of the loathsome face that had been so close to her own. Then, again raising her eyes to the stranger's, she went on:

"I have met you somewhere—some time. Haven't I?"

"I think not," he replied, with a half-smile that began and ended in the depths of his strange blue eyes, "for I could hardly have failed to recall you."

There was a subtle compliment, an Old-World courtesy, in his tone that went to the girl's heart.

"Yet I knew your face the moment I saw you," she insisted. "Could I have met you in America or—"

"No. I have never had the good fortune to visit your country, though some of the pleasantest people I have met are Americans. But," he added, his tone changing to one of concern, "did those brutes hurt you in any way? I am thankful I arrived when I did."

"No," she answered, the shock and horror of the past scene now returning with double vividness, "but I owe my safety to you. I shall never forget what you did for me."

In a few words she explained her presence in so untoward a place, noting, as she did so, that he had refrained from questioning her on the subject, although the sight of an American girl in the Cairo Fishmarket after nightfall must have seemed to him a hopeless puzzle.

He heard her through in silence; then, laying his hand on her donkey's bridle, he said:

"We are less than half a mile from Shepheard's, though the streets are unsafe by night for a woman—or for a man, for that matter. Come, if you are strong enough to ride so far, I will be your guide."

"You say these streets are unsafe by night," she commented, as they threaded their way through the network of ill-smelling alleys, "yet you were here alone."

"No one in Egypt would molest me," he responded, a sort of fond

pride in his voice. "These people are my friends—my children."

"But I've heard there is only one European whom these crafty, suspicious Egyptians really trust," pursued Madge, "and that is 'Chinese' Gordon, the—"

She checked herself with an exclamation of wondering delight. Now she recalled the reason of the stranger's familiar aspect; why she had entertained that haunting idea of having met and known him.

The features that she had looked on in the torch-flare of the Fishmarket were those of the man whose pictures just then adorned the shop-windows and illustrated-magazine pages of a thousand cities.

"Yes," he said amusedly, reading her unspoken thought, "I am Gordon."

* * * * *

Meantime, in the upper room of a *khan,* just off the Fishmarket, sat three men. One was Abou Saoud; the second, a brown-faced man in the gorgeous blue-and-gold dress of a dragoman; the third, a gigantic negro whose solitary garment was a soiled white burnoose, and whose hair was piled in mattress-like tufts high above his head.

Abou Saoud's face bespoke utter and cowardly despair. He was rocking his fat body to and fro, and moaning.

"Ruined!" he wailed. "The whole Heaven-sent plan wrecked! It is hopeless now; and so you may tell your master; oh, Farragh."

The black man grunted, eying his shrinking ally with contempt.

"The gray jackals of the hills must have eaten your heart in babyhood, Abou Saoud," sneered he, "and left the heart of one of their whelps in its place. What is this Gordon Pasha that his coming should swerve the Mohammed-blessed plans of my master? What is he that all you Egyptians cringe at his very name?"

"What is he?" squealed Abou, in contempt at such ignorance. "He is the man whose life is charmed, that he may not be slain; the fool to whom boundless wealth has a thousand times been offered, and who has refused it because, forsooth, he deemed it against his honor to accept bribe or tribute! The saint who is poor because he gives his all to the poor! The wonder-man who, single-handed, wrenched the Sudan from its ancient masters and crushed our rich slave trade, and by his might swept the country clear of armies of fifty-fold his

numbers. The one Feringhee whose word is as the word of Allah for truth, whose heart is a lion's and a dove's. He is the wizard who will again swoop down on the Sudan and scatter like chaff the hordes of your master, El Mahdi, and bring El Mahdi himself whining for mercy at his feet. Do I not know him of old? *'What is he,'* do you ask?"

"Words!" grunted the Sudanese. "When this Gordon before conquered the Sudan his foes were mortal men. El Mahdi is the Son of Heaven, and his followers cannot be vanquished. So spake the Prophet to El Mahdi in a vision, and the promise has been proven true in twenty battles. You say this Gordon Pasha is a wizard—that he has learned of your plan, in far-off Feringhiston [England] and has flown hither on the lightning to thwart it? Bah! You call yourself one of the Faithful, and yet you place this wizardry above the power of the Prophet? Can he face the Chosen of Allah?"

Abou Saoud was visibly moved by this theological aspect of the case. A little color returned to his sallow face.

"Be it so!" he said at last. "Though my heart is turned to water at thought of Gordon Pasha. I deemed him ten thousand miles away!"

"One of the *cavasses* from the embassy tells me the pasha arrived but this afternoon and starts for Khartum on the second day," volunteered the dragoman, speaking for the first time.

"Then I must be gone before dawn," replied Farragh. "My mission here is accomplished. If you send us the tidings and give us the aid you have pledged, Abou Saoud, you shall be back at the rich slave trade within the year. And all Feringhi [foreigners] who pass beyond the First Cataract from now on shall be yours. For we rule, already, all the land beyond. Thus says our master, El Mahdi."

"Then, if Gordon Pasha goes directly to Khartum," spoke up the dragoman, "you will reap your first harvest before long, oh, Abou. For some members of the Feringhi party I conduct start next week up the Nile. They plan to pass Assouan and go on to the Second Cataract. I will lead them into your net—if it be made worth my while."

"Of what condition are they?" carelessly asked Abou.

"Of rank, I should judge, and able to pay ransom. Among them are the *howadji*, Clive, who is known to be rich; and the aged woman, his aunt, who also is rich, though meager in giving. Also the little

maid whom Gordon Pasha but now snatched from you, and—"

"It shall be made worth your while, oh, Halil!" interrupted Abou. "It shall be made worth your while!"

CHAPTER IV.

A MESSAGE FROM THE DARKNESS.

GREAT was the amazement and open the good-natured envy of the Cook party on the following day to learn that three of their number had actually been honored by invitations to the Khedive's levee at the palace that evening.

The levee was of a semi-informal nature, arranged on the spur of the moment (or as nearly so as anything in the lazy East may be said to deserve such a term), in honor of General Charles George Gordon's opportune arrival.

That beloved adopted son of the land was spending but two days in Cairo prior to his Sudan departure, and had expressed a wish to meet his former Egyptian comrades before leaving. Consequently, the levee was planned, "last-moment" invitations deluging the *élite* of all nationalities who dwelt in the Nile city.

Now, thus it was that three of these coveted invitations chanced to fall among the group of Americans at Shepheard's:

Mrs. Chittenden was the American consul-general's cousin. She had sent him her card on arriving at Cairo. Instead of calling—for he had vivid transatlantic memories of the old lady's crotchety ways—he salved his conscience by procuring for her and Clive two invitations to the forthcoming levee.

That the third invitation should be addressed to Miss Madge Brant was the true sensation of the whole affair, so far as the others of the party were concerned.

Madge had wisely refrained from mentioning to any one her adventure of the previous evening, understanding the difficulty of so doing without involving the fact and cause of her having broken away from Clive. Yet it was to that same adventure she owed her summons

to the Khedive's levee.

On the homeward journey from the Fishmarket to Shepheard's she and Gordon had fallen into pleasant talk. The general, noted always for his oft-expressed liking for Americans, was particularly charmed with this plucky American girl whom he had so opportunely rescued, and who to him seemed to combine the independence of a woman of the world with the unsophisticated freshness of a child.

Learning how short a time she had been in Egypt and how deeply interested she was in every phase of native life and customs, he had hit on the plan of giving her an insight into Cairene aristocracy such as she could not otherwise have gained. Hence the invitation.

"My dear Miss Brant," beamed old Mr. Gault across the table where the party were finishing their late breakfast in the great alcove dining-room of the hotel, "I shall begin to think you are a princess in disguise. How on earth do you happen to be going to the palace? I thought you said you were a stranger in Cairo?"

"I am," she laughed; "or was till last night."

"You haven't told us yet how you chanced to be invited," snapped Mrs. Chittenden, from farther down the table. "Of course you aren't going. You must realize there is a mistake somewhere, and—"

"There is," retorted Madge sweetly. "The mistake is in your thinking I'm not going. I *am*."

"Well," grumbled the old lady, "I suppose, if you insist, Barry and I *can* take you in our carriage. That is, if you will pay your share. But of course—"

"Oh, I shouldn't dream of troubling you, dear Mrs. Chittenden. General Gordon has very thoughtfully promised that his aide, Colonel Stewart, will take me. The colonel is to call this afternoon with a note of introduction from General—"

The whole tableful had been regarding her with wide-open eyes and mouths since her very casual mention of Gordon's name, but before she had finished speaking their amazement had found vent in a storm of questions.

All of these Madge parried with ease, and in such way as to give no offense, while at the same time leaving her hearers no wiser than before.

Mrs. Chittenden and Barry Clive alone of all the party did not join

in this chorus of query. The former was glaring in speechless incredulity at the girl, and finding it impossible to recognize in her the deferential, ever-obedient companion of the earlier part of the trip.

True, Madge was no longer in her service, having on the previous night (when Mrs. Chittenden had taken her to task for losing her way and reaching the hotel an hour late) resigned her position, and having gently refused, in the face of tears, threats, and recriminations, to reconsider that resignation. Yet Mrs. Chittenden could not thus soon adapt herself to the knowledge that she was no longer the absolute tyrant of her former employee. The idea came as a shock.

Clive, for far different reasons, held his peace. He had been doing a good deal of hard thinking during the past twelve hours, and Madge's recent arraignment of himself was the unwilling theme of his thoughts.

While he in no way agreed with nor admitted the truth of anything she had said to him on that belated ride, he involuntarily felt a new respect for her, somewhat as a snapping dog might feel for the man who has just kicked him.

Barry Clive, for the first time during their six weeks' acquaintance, found himself looking at her as if she were a human being and not merely a cog in his aunt's domestic machinery. To his surprise, he found that she was worth looking at—in fact, that she was decidedly pretty—and that everything about her, from the daintily aristocratic poise of her little head to the intonations of her soft voice, spoke of birth and breeding.

He wondered, dully, that he had not noticed this before. And even as he wondered the memory of her searing opinion of himself returned with renewed vividness, making him turn his face away from her with a scowl.

The queries of the others were interrupted by the entrance of the party's dragoman.

"Well, Halil," queried Mr. Gault, "how about the *dahabiyeh*? [a sort of house-boat propelled by steam or sail]. Has one been chartered? And when are we to start up the Nile?"

"It has been chartered, *howadji*," replied the native, in moderately good English, "and we can start as soon as you desire to. You must forgive my delay. These foolish rumors of uprisings among the back-

country tribes have made many of the boat-owners timid, and they would not rent out their *dahabiyehs*. The company's own boat, the only one now in commission, is too small to hold so many with comfort. So I have, on my own responsibility, hired another. If you will deign to inspect it, and if it meets the approval of all, we can provision and be ready to start within three days."

"You speak about uprisings among the tribes," quavered an angular spinster from Missouri, Miss Halpin by name. "Maybe we would be wiser to wait till we're sure everything is safe?"

"Pardon, *Sitt!* I spoke of 'foolish rumors of uprisings.' I have inquired closely. I have also consulted a very holy man—Farragh, a priest—who is but just returned from the upper Nile. All my investigations prove the country to be as safe as Chicago, the capital of America."

"In that case," dryly observed Mr. Gault, "I shall certainly carry two revolvers. Shall we go down and now take a look at this *dahabiyeh?*"

*　*　*　*　*

The vast, barn-like Presence Hall of the Khedival Palace was ablaze with lamps and full to suffocation with a throng that had gathered to bid farewell to Egypt's idol, "Chinese" Gordon, on the eve of his departure for the Sudan.

The only especial outward difference in appearance between this assemblage and any one of a hundred similar gatherings at any of the European capitals consisted in the fact that among the men present scarcely one in five was bareheaded, and an equally large percentage wore clothes so grotesquely ill-fitting as to cause an unaccustomed outsider like Madge Brant to stare in wonder.

In other words, four-fifths of the men present were Egyptian or Turkish officials, crowned with the never-absent fez or tarboosh, and dressed in a manner almost to justify the French diplomat's famous remark, "The Turk wears the cast-off clothes of Europe."

The remaining fifth of the male guests wore, for the most part, the uniforms of the various nations to whose diplomatic corps they belonged, while here and there the somber evening clothes of a civilian stood out like black smudges on the carnival of color.

The women—all of whom were European or American—were in

ball costume. Not a native woman was visible, but an occasional flutter of drapery from behind a high screen in the gallery betokened the unseen presence of the Khedive's wives and their attendants.

In a niche at one side of the vast hall sat Madge Brant. The excitement had brought warm color to her cheeks and a light to her brown eyes. All evening a little group of attachés had been clustered about her.

Mrs. Chittenden had glared at the girl in malignant envy from her own isolated position near by, while Barry Clive, behind his aunt's chair, had gazed on her in growing amaze and admiration.

He could not realize that the jolly, obedient little girl in brown holland was one and the same with this radiant creature to whom half the young diplomats of Cairo were struggling to speak. Twenty-four hours earlier he had attempted to teach her her place. Tonight she had found a place of her own, wherein he had no part.

So he stood, looking on morosely at the swirl of gaiety and beauty whence he was ostracized. He recalled his views of his own importance, his ideas of Madge's insignificance, and wondered how their respective positions had for the time become so completely reversed.

And as he wondered a sense of shame awoke within him at his own past behavior toward the girl.

Madge at last found herself momentarily alone with Colonel Stewart, a big, soldierly man of the dragoon type, who had stayed close by her side from the first.

"Tell me," she commanded, with pretty imperiousness, "who are some of these people? I mean the famous ones, you know. I've been so busy talking all evening I've had no time to look around. That stout old gentleman in the pirate make-up, over there, for instance. Is he—"

"Hush!" laughingly whispered Stewart; "he is a very important being, and his uniform is quite correct. Not in the least like a pirate's. That is Selamlik Pasha, the most powerful man in Egypt, next to the Khedive. See, he is speaking to His Highness the Khedive now. The heavily built fair man in the Guards' uniform, next to him, is Sir Herbert Stewart. And there, just beyond—"

"Oh, who is the giant over there?"

She was nodding toward a youngish man who strolled across their line of vision. He was in the dress uniform of a captain in the British

Royal Engineers, and stood head and shoulders above most of the natives about him, being at least six feet four inches in his stockings.

He was lean, with the leanness of vast endurance; his harsh face was burned brick-red by many months of desert campaigning, and between the sweeping sandy mustache and the shaggy sandy brows eyes as cold and as stern as a hawk's blazed keenly forth on the world at large.

"That?" queried Stewart, following the direction of Madge's gaze. "Oh, that's Captain Horace Kitchener, one of her majesty's officers out here on special duty. Odd chap, is Kitchener. Ideal soldier, but more like a machine than a man. The sort of fellow who is likely to make his mark some day. But there, just behind him, is one of the 'lions' of the levee."

"That pompous-looking officer with the wooden features? The one who just ignored the salute of those young subalterns? Who is he?"

"That is Sir Garnet Wolseley—or, rather, Viscount Wolseley, as he is now. You've heard of him, of course. He, like General Gordon, is merely making a flying visit to Cairo. He is the hero of Tel-el-Kebir, you know. There! those are all the real celebrities in sight just at this moment."

"Colonel Stewart," asked the girl suddenly, "did you ever hear of a man named Abou Saoud? "

The soldier's face darkened.

"Where did *you* ever hear of old Abou?" he inquired, surprised.

"I—I've heard the name, I think," evaded Madge. "Who or what is he?"

"He's a number of things. But they can all be summed up in the one word 'Blackguard.' He was one of the most notorious slave-traders in the old days in the Sudan. Then General Gordon stamped out the slave-trade there, and on Abou's solemn pledge of reform gave the man honorable employment on his staff. Soon he found Abou was betraying him, smuggling slaves through the lines, taking bribes, and extorting tribute in his employer's name, and even conspiring against the general's life. A less noble man would have had the cur shot. But Gordon Pasha contented himself with dismissing him on condition that he leave Egypt forever. Wherever he is now, he is doubtless hatching some new deviltry. Pardon me an instant. The general is signaling

me."

As he moved away, and before any of a half-dozen waiting swains could take his place, Barry Clive strode across.

"Miss Brant," he said curtly, as the girl looked up in surprised displeasure, "I wish to ask your forgiveness for my rudeness of last night. I was a cad. I should like you to give me an opportunity to prove how sorry I am."

His tone was ungracious, and robbed his words of much of their contrition. Yet Madge could see that in a measure he was in earnest.

"Please say no more about it," she said quietly.

"I never apologized to any one before," he went on, with the same sulky expression of face and voice, "and I hoped you'd meet me half-way."

"You forget," she said, "King Cophetua came *all* the way down from his throne, so the story goes, to meet the beggar maid."

"Oh, come!" he growled, "what's the use of rubbing it in? I said I was sorry, didn't I?"

"You said all that was necessary," she answered, "and so far as I am concerned the whole affair is forgotten. But may I offer you one little suggestion? If a thing is worth apologizing for, it is worth apologizing for gracefully. Not that it matters in this case, of course."

He was about to reply, but Colonel Stewart returned. With him was Gordon Pasha. Barry stood irresolute a moment, then backed away to give place to them.

He had sought in vain all evening for an introduction to the hero of the hour. And now Gordon had come of his own accord to seek out this girl whom Clive had looked on as a nonentity.

"Have you enjoyed it, Miss Brant?" asked Gordon, leaning against the open casement of the window and looking down at her.

"More than I can tell you," she answered eagerly. "It is all so new— so beautiful. A scene from fairy-land. I shall never forget it."

"Stewart tells me you are going up the Nile in a few days, as far as the Second Cataract. Why not come still farther south and bring your party to visit me at Khartum? You will be made very welcome there, I can assure you."

He spoke in idle kindliness. At a later, supreme, hour both were destined to recall his careless words as vividly as though they had been

written in letters of blood.

Madge was about to make some light reply, when, with a faint whirring sound, some object, apparently hurled from the moonlit garden below, whizzed through the window, struck Gordon on the shoulder, and bounded off into the girl's lap.

Gordon did not move a muscle of face or body; but at Madge's involuntary exclamation Colonel Stewart sprang forward and snatched up the missile.

It was a small stone around which was wrapped a sheet of paper. And on the crumpled page ran this sentence in Arabic:

To His Excellency, Gordon Pasha (on whom be peace!)
Death waits for you in the south.

Stewart ran to the window. The garden beneath was empty.

CHAPTER V.

THE RETORT DISCOURTEOUS.

GORDON PASHA had begun his southward journey to Khartum, starting up the Nile toward Berber, whence he was to strike inland.

Cairo, recovering from the little ripple of excitement occasioned by the idolized pasha's sudden arrival and early departure, had settled back once more into its habitual plethoric calm—a calm that overlies more intrigue, crime, and evil than any mere outsider dreams of.

Such members of the Cook party as were to make the Nile trip to the Second Cataract were busy with preparations. To every rumor of discontent among the up-country tribes there came from all sides a dozen emphatic denials of the possibility of anything of the sort.

For it is hard for the Englishman in the Orient to credit the idea of his subdued vassals venturing to rise up against him. And this despite the red memory of such exceptions as the Sepoy Mutiny, the insurrection of Araby Bey, the Zulu and Boer wars, and the Mahdist rebellion.

Soon or late all these uprisings have been crushed and terribly

avenged, but at the price of thousands of innocent lives.

At last all was ready for the Nile journey. The *dahabiyeh* was equipped from the tips of its lateen sails to the clumsy wooden hull.

Halil had engaged a particularly villainous-looking and incompetent crew, for the regular sailors attached to the Cook service were not permitted to make the journey. The tourists—a round dozen, all told—were assigned to their respective stuffy cabins opening out on the deck.

So it was that in the gray of the morning, when a malodorous and unwholesome mist hung low on the river, the order was given to get under way. At the last moment a rotund, puffing figure loomed up through the mist, making violent signals to those on board.

A man panting and perspiring ran up the gangplank and on to the deck. He was short, perilously fat, and of a sallow, pasty face, whose little round eyes had a furtive look.

He carried a big valise, and a negro *commissionaire* toiled up the plank behind him bearing a second.

Barry Clive hurried forward with both hands outstretched to welcome the newcomer and to relieve him of his luggage. Mrs. Chittenden, with a manner that dimly approached affability, bustled forward with equally ardent greeting.

"Why, Jonas!" she exclaimed. "When you didn't come last night we supposed you had changed your mind. We were going on without you. You wrote us to, you know, in case you didn't reach here by the twenty-first. You must have traveled all night."

"I did," answered the late arrival, his breath coming in great gulps as his laboring lungs sought to right themselves after their unwonted exertion. "Got here from Alexandria half an hour ago. Found you'd just left Shepheard's, and raced on after you. Where's that nigger of a dragoman? Here, you!" to the resplendent blue-and-gold Halil. "Take my things to my cabin."

Madge Brant and old Mr. Gault were standing by the rail about ten yards distant, whence they had been watching the gradual awakening of the river-front traffic.

As the newcomer bustled aboard Mr. Gault turned to the girl. She was pale, and her eyes shone.

"You recognized him?" queried he. "That's Jonas Fitch."

"I saw him," she replied, without emotion.

"When he didn't arrive by last night's train I hoped he had given up the trip," went on Mr. Gault. "I am very sorry, for your sake, that the man to whom you say your father owed his misfortunes should have come to break up the harmony of our party. But it needn't really matter, you know. He and Clive and Mrs. Chittenden can herd by themselves. He will hardly have the effrontery, of course, to address you."

Jonas Fitch was rolling along the deck in the wake of Halil, Clive following attentively at his heels. He came face to face with Madge, blinked unbelievingly, then held out a pudgy hand.

"Why, it's little Margery Brant!" he gurgled. "You've forgotten me, I see; but your father knew me—"

"My father," said Madge, in a low voice, looking him in the eyes and ignoring the fat hand, "knew you to his cost, Mr. Fitch. *I* do not purpose to know you at all. Please let that be very clearly understood from the start."

She turned away. As soon as Fitch could recover from the stupendous discovery that he had actually met some one who did not cringe before him and the wealth he commanded he took an involuntary step to bar her way. His yellow face was mottled with purple.

"D'ye know who you're speaking to?" he roared. "How dare you say—"

He got no further. Old Mr. Gault had stepped forward; but Barry Clive was before him.

The young man had heard the whole brief colloquy. With flushed face and eyes that could not meet Madge's, he laid a none too gentle hand on his uncle's shoulder, and wheeling that amazed personage to the right, propelled him toward his own cabin.

Jonas at first showed signs of balking, but the pressure on his plump shoulder was too strong.

"Here!" he squealed. "Don't you go hurrying me along like that, Barry! I've got something to say to this young person, and I mean to say it. I—"

"You've said quite enough," interrupted Clive, for the first time in his life venturing to cross his uncle's will. "Come to your cabin. You must be tired after your run."

Too aghast at this unwonted behavior on the part of his erstwhile dutiful nephew and heir, Fitch suffered himself to be assisted along without further comment.

As the uncle and nephew vanished around a corner Mr. Gault looked at Madge in genuine surprise.

"Well!" he ejaculated. "That young Clive actually has a latent spark of manhood in him, after all. And you, of all people, Miss Brant, have brought it to light."

Then, perceiving that the girl was still agitated, the old fellow tactfully began pointing out various sights along the shore, avoiding looking at her or making any remark that required an answer.

The *dahabiyeh,* under power of her little auxiliary engine, was heaving clumsily up the river; the turgid yellow waters parting sluggishly before her blunt bow. The mists were rising. From riverside fields came the creak of water-wheels, revolved by sleek, slope-horned Cape buffalo.

In the blue mud of the river's edge gray crows with black wings walked daintily, looking for garbage and insects. Lean scavenger-dogs prowled along the bank. A string of mangy camels wound in and out among the scrubby trees.

Farther away, to the left, where river herbage gave way to encroaching sand, the three pyramids—the Great Pyramid of Cheops in the center—rose ghostlike out of the lifting mist-shrouds. And in the yellow sand at their base, the Eternal Enigma forever lurking in her blank stone eyes, crouched the Sphinx. Still more distant, mere blurs in the haze, showed the lesser pyramids of Memphis.

"It's the Nile! The Nile of Cleopatra—of Ptolemy—of Rameses!" the old gentleman rambled on, "and every throb of the engine takes us farther away from Civilization and the Nineteenth Century, and farther into the Past! If only—"

Barry Clive swung around the corner of the deck-house. His face was still flushed. He had the air of a man coming from an unpleasant interview and anticipating one no pleasanter.

"Miss Brant," he began abruptly, not perceiving Mr. Gault, who was hidden from view by a flap of the bulging awning—"Miss Brant, it seems to be my fate to apologize to you every time we meet. I know how you feel toward me and toward Mr. Fitch, but I beg that you will

forgive and overlook his rudeness to you this morning. He was excited and overtired, and was scarcely himself. I sincerely hope you were not offended at his bruskness. I'll do all in my power to avert a recurrence of such a scene and to prevent your trip being spoiled in any way by him. Please believe that. Won't you? "

The abruptness had faded from his tone. It bore, moreover, no trace of its usual intolerant superiority.

Madge vaguely noted that his voice, thus stripped of its ordinary defects, was decidedly musical. Also that the look of honest concern in his eyes altered for the better their expression, and that of his entire face.

"It is all right," she answered, more gently than she was wont to speak to him, "and I thank you for the way you interfered in my behalf a few minutes ago. It was very—"

"It was fine of you, young man!" seconded Mr. Gault, quite ignorant of the fact that Clive had not seen he was present, "you really behaved most—"

Madge saw the old-time look of contempt rush back to Barry's face, and saw his eyes harden from their momentary gentleness.

"Mr. Gault," said he stiffly, "when I wish your opinion I will ask for it."

Turning on his heel, he retraced his way to Fitch's cabin, leaving the poor old gentleman staring blankly after him.

*　*　*　*　*

It was late the following evening. The sails had been run down, the engine stopped. The *dahabiyeh* lay moored to the bank. Above was a full moon.

The tourists, with the exception of Clive, Mrs. Chittenden, and Fitch, had been sitting on deck, beguiling the hours with banjo and song. They were a lighthearted group, and snatches of music and laughter were wafted to the stern, where Clive sat alone, smoking an unsolacing cigar.

His aunt and uncle had long since retired to their cabins. The merrymakers ignored him, having had unpleasant experiences in former kindly efforts to make him one of themselves.

Looking out on the vast solitude of the Egyptian night, the young

man suddenly felt pitiably alone. The ideals, the patrician standards, he had set for himself somehow seemed less exalted out here in the wilderness than they had appeared at Cambridge or in New York.

He fell to wondering. The music, the laughter, the wholesome good-fellowship of these people whom he had despised as middle-class Philistines—might there not be something in all this that he, in his higher, more exclusive, notions, had somehow missed? With conjecture came discontent.

He was aroused by some one walking toward him. Madge Brant, seeing the solitary figure seated in the stern, had, like himself, been struck by the contrast between it and the jolly group forward. Moved by a half-comprehended impulse, she had moved astern to speak with him.

"You look lonely," she began, commonplacely enough.

"I *am* lonely," he answered, rising; "deucedly lonely, and a bit blue, besides. Miss Brant," he continued, the odd query coming to his lips unbidden, "what is the matter with me?"

She looked at him in bewilderment.

"What is the matter with me?" he resumed. "I was always well satisfied with myself until lately. Yet since we've been in Egypt I've been ashamed of myself more than once. I never was before. I sit here tonight as lonely and shunned as if I were a pariah, and actually longing to join in the jollifications of that crowd up there that I wouldn't speak to at home. I'm as good as they. I used to think I was far better. Why am I ostracized? "

He had spoken incoherently, in puerile fashion, utterly unlike his ordinary self. Yet it never for the moment occurred to him that there was anything unnatural or unconventional in his appeal.

This childlike, big-eyed girl just now seemed different from all other people he had known. He could speak to her as he could not to others. He vaguely felt she would understand. And she did.

"You are not ostracized," she said, unconsciously speaking in the tone she might have employed toward one of her refractory but penitent pupils. "It is you who have ostracized *us*."

"I—I don't quite see—" he began, but she went on:

"You were brought up to believe yourself a man above the common herd. You took no pains to hide that belief from any of us. People don't

like to be looked down on and snubbed. They seldom give a stranger a second chance to do it. That is why no one risked another rebuff by courting your friendship."

"You said once that I was a cad. I was angry at the time. But—to-night—I've been wondering if I am. Do you really think so? "

"No," she replied reflectively, "I don't think I do. But, if you'll pardon my saying so, you will always be mistaken for one until you revise your mental list of the world's great men and give yourself a lower place in it. You speak of being lonely; of not being sure you were right in your treatment of me and my friends. Prove that we were wrong in our estimate of you."

"But how?"

"There are some of the singers still left up yonder. Come over and join us. Be one of us!"

Clive frowned; drew back; hesitated, and, by a mighty effort that none save Madge could have understood, obeyed. It was the hardest struggle he had ever undergone. But he won it.

Five minutes later, to every one's surprise—most of all, to his own—Barry Clive was on the deck-house, shamefacedly growling a horribly inharmonious bass to that classic ditty, "My Bonnie Lies Over the Ocean."

As the party broke up, an hour later, Clive and Madge walked down the deck together toward their respective cabins. At the gang-way they met old Mr. Gault, who had been taking a solitary ramble along the bank.

Madge walked forward to the head of the gangplank to greet him. She was still several feet away, when, with a gesture incredibly rapid for so old a man, he leaned forward and, with all his strength, thrust her to one side.

The next second he had brought down his stout walking-stick with a resounding thwack on the boards of the gangway.

Something black and sinuous writhed and doubled over. Another blow laid it motionless. Mr. Gault's quick eye had descried in the moonlight one of the deadly water-asps so common to the Nile, which had wriggled up the gangplank from the bank on a tour of investigation, and had lain coiled directly in the girl's path.

A glance made the situation clear to Clive and Madge. The latter

shuddered at the danger she had so narrowly avoided, and for the instant could not speak, but Clive, in open admiration of Mr. Gault's presence of mind, pressed forward.

"Splendidly done!" he cried. "You were—"

"Mr. Clive!" snapped the old gentleman, drawing himself up in ironic haughtiness, "when I wish your opinion I will ask for it!"

CHAPTER VI.

HEMMED IN.

ONE day passes much like another on a Nile *dahabiyeh*. From Cairo as far south as Assouan, at the First Cataract, the scenery of to-day is the scenery of yesterday and the scenery of to-morrow.

There are the same shelving or sloping banks; the same vistas of irregular yellow sand; the same oases with their feather-duster palms; the same mud villages; the gray crows, the gray donkeys, the yellow scavenger-dogs and mouse-colored, mangy camels; the same tawny, muddy water.

Incidentally there are the same long or short donkey-back journeys into the surrounding country at various points; to the age-hallowed ruins of Beni-Hassan, Abydos, Thebes, Karnak, etc., for a detailed and exhaustive description of each and all of which the reader is respectfully referred to any of a hundred weighty tomes of travel.

Despite the uneventfulness of the journey, Madge Brant saw nothing monotonous in the daily panorama. To her the gorgeous sunrises and sunsets, the ever-varying hues and forms of the desert, even the squalid villages, and their bovine inhabitants, afforded, daily, new revelations.

Steeped in the magic of the mystic past, she saw everything through wide eyes of wonder.

Such of her fellow travelers as did not fully share her enthusiasm were at least the happier for it, and dutifully admired everything, as good personally conducted tourists should. They made the rounds of the tombs and other ruins on their donkey-back excursions, loafed

about the awninged deck, and devised new pastimes to while away the tedium of the slow river miles.

After that moonlit night when Madge had succeeded in drawing Clive into the pleasant circle of merrymakers, she saw comparatively little of the young man, for Jonas Fitch and Mrs. Chittenden, feeling the time hang more and more heavily on their hands, levied with daily increasing extortion on his every waking moment. Thus it was that though his demeanor toward the party at large had undergone a slight but quite visible change for the better, he had scant opportunity to avail himself of their society.

Jonas Fitch, profiting, perhaps, by Madge's own warning, and perhaps by his nephew's influence, had not intruded himself upon Miss Brant since that first morning. Mrs. Chittenden, too, who had never been able to forgive Madge for not begging to reenter her service, turned a glassy eye of disapproval on the girl.

So the two cliques remained aloof one from the other, to the probable profit of both.

The First Cataract was passed. At Assouan, Halil, the dragoman, had received stringent orders from the local authorities to venture no farther south.

By dint of a goodly bribe (in the land where money will achieve any object save loyalty) he had been permitted to pass on, but was warned that he did so at his own risk, as the upper country was now alive with marauding tribesmen and with bands of Egyptian outlaws.

Needless to say, the trusty dragoman neglected to communicate these tidings to his passengers. Nor had he remembered to mention to them, at starting, that he was no longer a Cook man, but had fitted out the present expedition at his own cost—and that of Abou Saoud.

So the thirteen Americans, all unaware of the fate planned for them, pushed on up the river, daily encroaching on what, back in Cairo, was already referred to as "the danger zone."

*　*　*　*　*

The *dahabiyeh* lay moored off the village of Amelook, on the Nile's west bank. There had been no apparent reason for putting in at so unprepossessing a spot, and it was still early afternoon.

But Halil reported the engine in need of repairs, and had

announced that the *dahabiyeh* would not go on until the following morning.

The tourists, for the most part, had gone ashore, and were wandering with frank curiosity about the little Nile-side town, paying the natives exorbitant prices for bogus antiquities and tawdry bits of Egyptian needlework.

Halil had been the first to land, and he had bent his steps directly to the plastered abode of the Sheik-el-beled (head man of the village).

"Well," he said impatiently, in response to that civic dignitary's salaam, "what orders from my lord, Abou Saoud? I thought to find him here. Is he not ready?"

"No, effendi," returned the head man, "he is not. He passed through here four days ago, and bade me tell you that there are still squadrons of *Gippies* [native colloquialism for Egyptian troops] returning through the country toward Assouan and he dare not yet make the capture, lest he fall in with some of these. Within a week, he says, the last of them will be gone and all will be safe. He bids you go on to the Great [Second] Cataract, and to stop here on the return. All will then be ready."

Halil, with a grunt of disappointment at the thought that he must be servile for another ten days or more to the Unbelievers he despised, eased his ruffled feelings by imparting a resounding kick upon the cringing head man, and then strode out into the blazing glare of the filthy little street.

But what he saw there changed his majestic walk into a run. Jonas Fitch, Mrs. Chittenden, and Barry Clive had gone ashore with the rest, but had strayed off by themselves to a quarter of the local bazaar. There a bit of exceptionally gaudy lace had awakened Mrs. Chittenden's admiration.

She had priced it, and had been horrified to hear the shopman appraise it, in broken French, at something approximating its real value. With every sense of bargaining at once on the alert, the old lady had striven to beat down the price. Failing in reducing the figure fast enough to suit her, she had lost her temper.

Had she possessed enough knowledge of the East to walk quietly away, the shopman would doubtless have rushed after her and begged her to take the lace at her own price. Instead, she slammed down on

his table a medjidie (about eighty-four cents), snatched up the lace, and started off with it.

This was a method of shopping hitherto unheard of in that land where every innovation is regarded in the light of a personal insult. The shopman, slipping the medjidie into the fold of his scarf, screamed aloud that he had been robbed by the Unbelievers.

In an instant the space in front of his booth was alive with screaming, gesticulating villagers.

Here again the party's ignorance of the East led them into an error.

They did not know that the unarmed Oriental is harmless as long as he screams and makes gestures. As it was, they judged him by Occidental mobs, and foresaw themselves torn to pieces. So they did the one foolish thing that was left to do—they tried to escape.

Barry, as a vanguard, sought to force a passage where the crowd was thinnest, and the scared Mr. Fitch attempted to guide Mrs. Chittenden through the opening thus formed. The crowd hooted with joy at this new afternoon recreation, and a lump of mud flew past Barry's ear, plastering itself mushily across Fitch's sallow face.

Jonas howled in an access of fright. Mrs. Chittenden promptly fainted. It was at this juncture that Halil Sadik Ali fell upon the natives with the flat of his drawn saber, scattering them to the four winds.

The rescued trio were escorted in safety to the *dahabiyeh,* whither the others had some time preceded them. The story of their adventure lost nothing in oft-repeated telling, the one important result of the recital being that each and every man of the party solemnly resolved never again to set foot ashore on Egyptian soil without carrying along at least one revolver.

Halil was profuse in apologies for the mishap, and on his venturing to present Mrs. Chittenden with the luckless bit of lace (which he had picked up during the *mêlée)* he was graciously forgiven by Fitch and herself, but only on condition that he would start on at once, leaving that perilous village far behind before nightfall. This he readily assented to.

On the second morning, anchor was cast off Ibrim, on the border of the Bishareen Desert. Scattering groups of temples lie to the east, about two hours' journey by donkey-ride.

None of the party save Miss Halpin had ever heard of these

ruins or cared particularly to visit them. But that sentimental spinster averred that a "gentleman friend" of hers had been at the Ibrim ruins three years before and had scratched his name with a penknife directly beneath the great bas-relief of the cat-god Bubastis, and when he heard that she was coming to Egypt had made her promise to visit the sacred spot and see if the name was still there.

"It'll be so like home to see it," she pleaded; "and besides, it'll be better fun than sitting on deck and watching the sand go past."

For this reason it is to be feared more than for the former, the party fell in with her wishes, and the expedition was arranged.

Mrs. Chittenden did not care to go; neither did Barry; but Mr. Fitch loudly declared that no American was going to see more of Egypt than he or get more value for his money. So, his reluctant satellites accompanied him.

Mounted on their decrepit little donkeys, and headed by Halil in his full panoply of purple and gold, the Americans set forth, two donkey-boys following with big hampers of lunch.

Over the desert they wound their dusty way, Madge Brant and old Mr. Gault in the van, close at Halil's heels.

"It's queer," said Madge, as she glanced about at the knolls, ridges, and gullies of rock and sand amid which they rode—"it's queer what false ideas one gets of the nature of a desert. At home I always fancied it a flat area of sand, but it is as rough as an Adirondack forest. I wonder if we will meet with any such adventures to-day as befell poor Mrs. Chittenden at Amelook? "

"I hardly think so," replied the old gentleman. "There are too many of us. Besides, we men are all armed now. See?"

He pulled a neat little revolver from his hip-pocket.

"I never fired one of these things," he went on, "and I don't exactly understand their mechanism, but a friend gave it to me when I left home, and it really affords me quite a feeling of security."

They came at last to the temples—a rambling group, half buried in shifting sand, and stretching brokenly for nearly a mile in area. After a perfunctory examination of the first few the party gathered in the shade of a huge cornice for lunch.

The meal over, they wandered idly about among the ruins until the hour should arrive for the return ride. Madge and Mr. Gault, in

the course of their ramblings, came out upon a long avenue lined with broken pillars, fallen capitals, and partly buried monoliths.

A hundred yards ahead, and moving in the same direction, they descried Barry Clive, walking between his aunt and uncle.

"Mr. Fitch is evidently still resolved to see his money's worth," laughed Mr. Gault. "See how he drags along those two perspiring, bored protégés of his! Money must be very precious to them both to make them put up with such a man."

He and Madge loitered along on the shady side of the prehistoric highway, now and then pausing to admire some half-effaced carving or to avoid stumbling over a fallen pillar.

"I, for one, am saturated with ruins," Mr. Gault was saying. "After you've seen the first few you've seen all. I shall not be sorry to start back next week to civilization, a decent bed, and a bathtub. I am getting too old for—Here comes Halil! He must be rounding up the party. Hello, Halil!" as the dragoman came alongside. "Time to return to the *dahabiyeh,* eh? I'd no idea Miss Brant and I had walked so far. Why, we must have come almost a mile since we left the others."

The dragoman had passed on and was hailing Clive and his two companions. The three, at sound of his voice, turned and retraced their steps.

"Let's walk ahead of them," suggested Mr. Gault. "You won't care to trudge a whole mile in Mr. Fitch's company. Shall we start on?"

The others were but a few yards behind them as they turned— turned to confront some fifteen mounted men who had, unheard, ranged themselves across the ancient highway, between the six wanderers and the road that led to the rest of their party.

The equestrians made no hostile sign. They simply sat their horses in stolid silence and gazed without expression on the five Americans and the dragoman. Wild-looking fellows they were, in their flaring red burnooses, sheepskin under-vests, and close turbans.

From the belt of each peeped knife and horse-pistol. Long flint-lock guns with queer curved and inlaid stocks rested across their saddle-bows. They rode hairy, lean ponies whose rough coats were strangers to the currycomb.

The travelers turned involuntarily to Halil for an explanation of this sudden advent. It was their wont to look to him in all cases where

the Western mind could not at once grasp some Eastern situation.

There was no fear in the Americans' gaze; only curiosity as to the nature of this picturesque cavalcade. But one glance at the dragoman's face set their nerves to thrilling with vague uneasiness.

Halil Sadik Ali was the picture of dumb horror. His brown face was ash-color. The whites of his rolling eyes shone yellow. He shook from head to foot as with an ague.

"Well?" asked Fitch, breaking the momentary silence. "You're a pretty picture, ain't you, you pusillanimous nigger! Can't you speak? What are these folks on horseback?"

Mr. Jonas Fitch's hardly acquired education had an unfortunate way of deserting him in moments of stress. But now even the fastidious Barry Clive did not notice his breaks in English.

For both Clive and Madge had seen, over the trembling dragoman's shoulder, a second line of dusky horsemen emerge into the farther end of the highway. The little party were completely hemmed in.

CHAPTER VII.

THE MERCY OF THE MERCILESS.

THE dragoman, following the direction of Madge's eye, turned his head and beheld the second rank of horsemen. And now, moving quietly through the ruins at either side of the avenue, their horses picking their way among the debris, came more riders.

"There must be fully fifty of them, and they are all around us," whispered Madge to Mr. Gault. "Do you suppose they mean us any harm? They are so quiet, and they use none of the threatening gestures Mrs. Chittenden described the Amelook villagers as employing. Do you?"

"If I had not been told over and over that this country is as safe for travelers as America itself," answered the old gentleman in the same guarded tone, "I should take these picturesque-looking ruffians for brigands, and I should fancy they were about to make us their prisoners. And, on my soul, poor Halil's face seems to bear out this idea."

"Halil!"

It was Barry Clive who spoke, and his voice had a sharp, imperious ring as he wheeled on the cowering dragoman. The silence and the melodramatic advent and disquieting want of aggressiveness on the part of the intruders had begun to get on Clive's nerves.

"Halil!" he repeated, "what does all this mean? Why do these men block our way? Are they beggars or lepers looking for alms?"

The dragoman shook his head dumbly, looking with fresh apprehension at the strangers, as though fearing they might understand the uncomplimentary appellations in the foreign tongue.

"Then, what are they? You don't mean—you don't mean to say they are robbers?"

The whole party hung on the dragoman's answer as Clive voiced the unspoken dread of all. To them, Halil formed the only possible link of comprehension between themselves and this odd situation.

"Are they robbers?" repeated Clive more imperatively, as Halil's chalky lips twitched in spasmodic wordlessness.

The dragoman jerked his head forward acquiescently.

"Well!" observed Mr. Gault, with a rueful grin, breaking the little hush of horror that had followed on Halil's assent. "Here's a pretty kettle of fish! A mile away from our party, two hours' ride from our boat, and surrounded with half a hundred comic-opera banditti! What's to be done? Eh?" looking from face to face. "What's to be done?"

"What d'ye mean by draggin' us into such a hole?" shrieked Jonas Fitch, venting his panic in a burst of wrath at Halil, as the one man worse scared than himself. "What d'ye mean by it? And"—the immobility of the horsemen again impressing him—"if they're robbers, what are they waitin' for?"

"They are waiting for their leader," responded Halil from between chattering teeth. "For their sheik. They are Bishareen Arabs. Perhaps they were to await their sheik here at the tombs and came upon us by chance. They will not act without his orders."

"But you said the up-country tribes were harmless."

It was Mr. Gault who made the somewhat needless remark.

"They are Bishareens," repeated Halil; "wicked men of the desert! Outlaws!"

The dragoman had been edging to one side of the open space as he

spoke, toward a rift between two pillars of the nearest ruined temple. At the last word he bounded for the narrow opening with incredible alacrity.

A Bishareen six feet away swung his long gun about by the muzzle and struck the flying dragoman across the side of the head with the curved inlaid stock. Halil collapsed, a huddled heap of blue and gold, into the sandy avenue.

After this single deed of violence the ring of horsemen sat as inert as before.

"What's to be done?" quavered Fitch. "Shall we empty out our pockets and beg them to let us go? Maybe they'll do it, and—"

"No!" cried Clive, his tanned face reddening with wrath. "No! We're white men—Americans! Are we going to let ourselves be held up by a crowd of cowardly natives? We'll fight our way through them. They'll scatter at the first shot. Mr. Gault, stand beside me. You two ladies keep directly behind us; and you, uncle, guard the rear. Now, then!"

He drew his revolver, and old Mr. Gault, fired for the moment by the foolish young man's fury, followed his example.

"Don't!" cried Madge commandingly, stepping in front of them. "You will only be shot down like rabbits. What chance would you have against such odds? The only thing to do is not to rouse them, and to await an opportunity to escape or to make terms with them. To try to fight your way past fifty armed men isn't courage—it is suicide."

"She's right, Clive," urged Mr. Gault, pocketing his pistol. "We'd only throw our lives away uselessly, and then who'd be left to protect these ladies? No, no! We must find some safer way."

The riders had viewed this little scene with amused indifference, but their expression changed as Barry Clive, maddened by opposition and by the humiliating predicament, shook off Madge's detaining hand and fired pointblank at the nearest of the Bishareens.

Like the average American, he had not fired a revolver twenty times in all his life. Easy as was the mark, he scored a clean miss—the luckiest miss of his career, for it saved him from instant death.

But his shot had caused a marked change in the mental attitude of the horsemen among whom he had fired. By one impulse a dozen spurred forward.

"We're done for now!" gasped old Mr. Gault, pulling Madge behind him and once more fishing out his useless little revolver.

Clive was struggling madly with his own weapon. The rusty cylinder had become jammed, and refused to turn. Jonas Fitch crouched behind the shrieking Mrs. Chittenden.

It all occupied a bare second. The riders had been scarcely sixty feet distant, but before they could reach their prey the aisles of the templed ruins echoed with galloping hoofs. One of the Bishareens to the rear cried out, and the others checked their onrush.

A man who had been approaching in leisurely fashion had at sound of the shot urged his horse to a run, and now dashed into the very midst of the turmoil.

At his advent the riders drew back, saluting, and remained at attention. The newcomer brought his mount to a standstill and looked keenly about him, from his followers to the knot of frightened Americans.

He was, at first glance, the typical picture-book Arab. Of lighter skin than his comrades, he was tall, spare, and wiry, his face lean, hook-nosed and fierce of eye. The mouth alone softened the harshness of his stern visage.

In age he could have been little more than thirty. From the splendor of his dress and the stately beauty of his roan horse, as well as from the deference paid him by his compatriots, he was evidently a man of importance.

His quick gaze at once took in every detail of the situation, from the prone figure of the gaudy dragoman to the foolhardy Barry Clive, who was still working with angry ineffect to get his pistol in order. Last of all, the stranger's eye rested on Madge Brant.

She returned his look coldly, fearlessly, yet with a certain childlike curiosity awakened by his striking face and gaudy attire. As he gazed, the keen eyes seemed almost imperceptibly to soften, and a reflection of the girl's own frank curiosity dawned in them.

Apparently, this man of the desert was not wont to have women meet his eye in a manner so candid, so devoid of either fear or admiration.

From Madge he passed on to Fitch and Mrs. Chittenden. He appeared about to speak, when Clive, at length succeeding in restor-

ing his revolver to order, raised and cocked the weapon, leveling it straight at the leader.

What next occurred was accomplished before the onlookers fairly understood what was going on. A revolver in the stranger's sash was drawn and fired in what looked like a single lightning gesture. Clive's pistol went ricocheting over the rocks, and Clive himself, white with pain, was grasping his own numbed and quivering right arm.

The Arab, without touching the young man himself, had calmly shot the revolver out of his hand, at the very instant Barry had been about to fire on him.

Replacing the weapon in his sash, the native, without bestowing a second look on the American, gave a brief order in Arabic to one of his men. The latter, dismounting, walked to the prostrate Halil, kicked him none too gently in the ribs, and hauled him to a sitting posture.

The dragoman, who had come to his senses almost at once after falling (though none but the newcomer detected the sham of his unconsciousness), rose to his feet and prostrated himself before the leader.

The latter spoke a few curt sentences to him, and then asked him one or two questions, to which Halil replied with tearful servility.

The rider addressed the dragoman in the tone he might have used toward a pariah dog.

"He says," reported Halil to the Americans, "that he is Sheik Darah, of the Mekheir Bishareens. He and his tribe are in the service of El Mahdi, and he and these men with him are only a part of a larger body on the way to the Sudan. He says you are his prisoners. If you make resistance he will kill you all. You must come away with him at once, for the shots may have been heard by the others of your party, and he fears they may summon troops—"

"That is a lie," interrupted the sheik, in fairly intelligible English; "I fear no one."

"You don't, eh?" shouted Barry Clive. "Then get off your horse and fight me like a man! It's easy enough to talk about courage with fifty cutthroats at your back! But come down and fight if you dare!"

"Young man," said the sheik, with infinite composure, "you have much to learn. But I fear you will never live to learn it."

"Do you mean," asked Madge, "that we are to die?"

"That is not for me to judge," he replied more gently. "I must carry you all to camp. There your fate will be decided."

"I'm not any too rich," whined Jonas Fitch, gathering courage from the astounding fact that he was still alive, "but I'm willing to pay a fair price for my ransom."

"So am I," wailed Mrs. Chittenden. "Not too much, but—"

"And," went on Fitch, "I'll pay something for the release of my nephew, here. What's your terms?"

"And these others?" asked the sheik, paying no heed to the question, and glancing toward Madge and Mr. Gault. "They are doubtless as able to pay handsomely if it is a question of ransom?"

"We neither of us have much money," spoke up Madge, as Mr. Gault hesitated; "I am afraid it is hardly worth your while to make us prisoners."

A look of reluctant admiration again crept into the sheik's piercing eyes as the girl made her intentionally careless response.

"Then," he went on, a moment later, "as I understand, these three are rich and you two are poor? Am I correct?"

"That's it, sir," assented Jonas, with eagerness; "we three can pay whatever's right to be let go. I'll give you a check—"

Madge, through all her terror, could scarcely force back an hysterical laugh at the idea of the panic-stricken millionaire proffering this savage a check in payment for his deliverance. But the sheik resumed:

"And these others?" again indicating Madge and Mr. Gault. "You will surely not desert them to their death?"

"Who? Gault and that girl?" screamed Jonas. "What are they to me? I've nothing to do with their ransom. I—"

"And you would escape by the payment of money and leave them to die sooner than to pay out a little dirty gold to save their lives?" queried the sheik. "Truly you Americans are a noble race!"

"I beg that you will not judge my country by this man!" broke in Madge, her cheeks aflame at the slur on her nation. "Not one American in one thousand would behave like that at such a time. I, for one, would rather die than be beholden to him for my liberty and—"

"If you will do me the honor, Miss Brant," observed Clive, his rage against the sheik checked by these unlooked-for developments, "I shall throw in my fate with yours, just to show these Arab curs what a

real American is. Uncle, you can ransom yourself and my aunt, if you choose, but unless your offer includes the others I shall refuse to leave them."

"You talk like a fool!" stormed Fitch, who, now that the affair was apparently resolving itself into a mere matter of dollars and cents, was brave as a lion. "And maybe you think I won't pay you for it when we get back home. Your share of my estate may not be quite so large as you fancy, and—"

"Your estate has meant less and less to me for the past month," retorted Barry, "and if it can only be won by proving myself a coward you may keep it, for all of me."

"One moment!" intervened the sheik. "It appears to me you are all speaking much on matters of no concern. There is no talk of ransom. You are my prisoners, and we march at once for camp."

With a howl of terror, Jonas Fitch saw the cup of liberty snatched from his very lips. Mrs. Chittenden burst into tears. Clive, Madge, and Mr. Gault, in a little group by themselves, made no sign of disappointment.

A guttural order, and a dozen Arabs dismounted. Before the victims were fully aware of their captors' intentions, the three American men and Halil were seized and bound. A hand of each was strapped to the saddle-bow of one of the riders.

A rough litter, formed by swinging poles and saddle-cloths between a couple of the horses, was hastily arranged for the women. Then the horsemen closed in about the prisoners, and the march began.

CHAPTER VIII.

THE SON OF HEAVEN.

IN 1881, a Dongola carpenter's son, one Mohammed Achmed, hitherto a lazy dreamer and mystic, suddenly declared that he was the long-promised Redeemer for whose advent all Islam has waited for more than a thousand years—the Messiah, heaven-born, sent by Allah and the Prophet to sweep the world clear of unbelievers and

to give the faithful the earth as their heritage, with a sort of spiritual commutation ticket entitling bearer to all the vivid joys of the Moslem paradise.

Achmed accompanied this declaration with a few neat, hand-made miracles, took unto himself the title El Mahdi (the Redeemer), and set out to make converts.

He was successful beyond all measure. Within three years his doctrines had spread like wildfire throughout the whole of that vast fertile region bounded by the Sahara, Senegambia, Upper Guinea, and Abyssinia, and known as Belad-es-Sudan (literally, Country of the Black Man), or, more commonly, the Sudan. The entire region was transformed into a hotbed of Mahdists, and the false Prophet became at length so great a menace that active steps were taken for his destruction by the Egyptian government.

Expedition after expedition was launched against El Mahdi, and each failed. Every victory served to increase Achmed's fame and power.

The wandering desert tribes from the north—Nubians, Abyssinians, negroes, and Arabs, outlaws and political vermin from every quarter of Africa—flocked to his standard.

One after another, he subdued Egyptian garrisons throughout the Sudan until at last it became patent that the government could make no successful stand against him.

Then, at England's instigation, the Khedive resolved to withdraw all troops from the Sudan. To do this without great loss of life, and to wind up local governmental affairs there with any show of credit or profit, was a task beyond Egypt's power. There was but one man on earth who could possibly accomplish the feat. And that man was hastily summoned to the rescue.

Thus it was that "Chinese" Gordon, who had been in Brussels and on the point of departing on a diplomatic errand to the Congo Free State, had hastened to Egypt in response to the appeal, had paid a flying visit to Cairo, and had then gone at once to Khartum, capital and chief city of the Sudan.

The Khedive breathed a sigh of relief. He and the rest of the civilized world knew Gordon's total ignorance of the word "fail."

In bygone years, Gordon Pasha, fresh from his triumphs in China,

had come to Egypt to serve under the Khedive. He quickly made his mark, in that vilest and most corrupt of governments, by opposing fierce honesty and indomitable will-power to every subterfuge or plot of his enemies.

He was at last made governor-general of the Sudan, and in five years' time had crushed out that district's prosperous slave trade, put down the horrible abuses of the pashas, and made the whole land to blossom forth in newer and cleaner life.

His name became a word to conjure with, from the Mediterranean to Abyssinia. He was the one foreigner who had ever succeeded in winning the Oriental's full trust and love.

So it was that now he had entered on his new duties in the Sudan with full confidence of success, forgetting, as did the world at large, that a fanatical leader with fifty thousand fanatics at his back and a record of three years of unbroken victory is not as readily dealt with as are a mass of disorganized and unguided tribes.

It was Islam against progress; all barbarism against one man; the Prophet and his hordes against "Chinese" Gordon.

The sun was still high, and beat down with cruel intensity as the five Americans and their dragoman, surrounded by their captors, filed down the broad avenue and out into the Bishareen Desert, leaving the Temples of Ibrim behind them.

Darkness had long since descended before the cavalcade came to a halt. The way led over sand-dune and rock-hills; down cañons scooped out of the sand-drifts by the fingers of the wind; along ridge and over gully.

The desert horses kept their footing where a European or an American mount must have fallen or become utterly exhausted by the heavy going. The pace set was as brisk as possible under the circumstances, the perspiring captives slipping and sliding along with increasing fatigue, until each step became an agony and each breath a burden.

The litter which bore the two women was of the most primitive sort, and its uneven swaying and jolting called forth ever-increasing lamentations from Mrs. Chittenden. Madge, on the contrary, bore the keen discomfort in patience, breaking silence only now and then

to comfort or cheer the poor old lady, whose nerves were in a state of pitiable collapse, and on whom this primitive mode of travel told more severely than on the girl. But Mrs. Chittenden refused to be comforted or to see any bright side to the unknown future toward which they were moving.

At length Sheik Darah, who was riding in advance of the rest, turned back and checked his horse.

"Madam," said he, in a wholly impersonal manner, as though imparting a bit of interesting local knowledge, "in this country, when old women are too noisy we drown them."

He trotted ahead without awaiting a reply; but his threat sufficed to silence Mrs. Chittenden's complaints for the remainder of the day.

The men, toiling on painfully, had scant opportunity or breath for speech. Moreover, they walked for the first part of the journey as if in a nightmare.

None of them could clearly realize that the mishaps they were undergoing were not part of a horrible dream, from which they must soon awake.

The illimitable yellow-brown reaches of desert, the ferocious faces and bizarre dress of the men around them, the circumstances of their captivity—all went to enhance the unreality.

Barry Clive, youngest and strongest of the male prisoners, looked neither to right nor to left as he strode on. His eyes were downcast, and in his face was written a bitter mortification that drove out all thought of fear.

"Don't take it that way," begged Mr. Gault, as a stretch of smooth down-hill sand made conversation less impossible. "You did your best, old chap! It was no fault of yours—or anybody else's—that we were caught like rats in a trap."

"If I could be sure of that!" groaned Clive. "I can't help thinking I acted like an idiot. But for my foolhardiness we might have found some way out."

"It wouldn't have been possible. We were a mile away from our friends. These natives came on us in a breath. We had been told the country was safe. And once the Arabs got around us a troop of cavalry couldn't have rescued us alive. You showed pluck, my boy. And I hope," he continued, with an effort at gaiety, "you won't snub me *this*

time for praising you."

But Clive did not even hear him. His thoughts were elsewhere.

"Two pistol-shots were fired," he said. "I wonder why the rest of our party didn't hear. Perhaps they did," he added, more hopefully. "Perhaps they gave the alarm. Even now a squadron of 'Gippies' may be on the way to rescue us."

"Don't count on it," counseled the older man. "We were a mile away from them, and the wind was in our direction. In such a case no pistol-report would carry half the distance over such broken country. No; if we want to escape it's to ourselves, and not to our friends, we must look. My only wonder is that the sheik didn't go back for the rest. I suppose he didn't know how small and how defenseless a party they were, though."

"By the way," commented Barry, "I don't see how that sheik happens to speak such tolerable English. I didn't know the natives as far from Cairo as this knew a word of the language."

Halil, who was limping along just behind them, overheard, and answered:

"Sheik Darah was a pupil at El Azhar (the university at Cairo), where many great men from up the country send their sons. I saw him there twelve years ago, and he was pointed out to me as son of the great sheik of the Mekheir. It was there he learned English, and much else, until he slew a Syrian bey in a duel and had to fly. It is twelve years since then, but I knew him at sight."

"Do the rest of the troops know English?" asked Mr. Gault.

"Not they!" replied Halil, with fine scorn. "They are ignorant fools, born and bred in the desert."

The fact that Halil dared speak thus was sufficient proof of the truth of his words.

"What will they do with us?" queried Mr. Gault.

The terror returned to the dragoman's voice.

"Allah knows!" he quavered. "We may die by morning, or the wealthier may be held for ransom. It is as the council shall decide."

"The council?"

"The camp we are marching to is made up of the warriors of four or five tribes. They are on the way to join El Mahdi outside Khartum. The sheiks of these tribes sit in council on all matters. If perchance

they sell you your freedom, you will not forget the poor dragoman who has served you so faithfully, oh, *howadjis,* and who loves you all as his own brethren? You will intercede for me? You will pay my ransom?"

His voice had dropped into the whining note of the professional Oriental beggar. But his plea was unheard. For Barry and Mr. Gault had begun to talk again between themselves.

"If it were not for the women," said the former, "I should mind it less. What a brick that little Brant girl is, and how pluckily she answered the sheik's threats! She—"

"If you had shot her instead of trying to kill Darah you would have been wiser," broke in the old man sorrowfully. "Better die at the hand of her own countryman than be sold as a slave, as she must be if her life is spared and the ransom is beyond our means."

"That shall never happen! Never! Never!" panted Clive, carried out of himself for the moment. "If ever such an emergency arises I will kill her with my bare hands. I swear it!"

The old man glanced at him with interest. Then he said with irrelevance:

"Harvard and New York are a long way off—and pretty long ago, too—aren't they?"

Late in the evening the cavalcade topped a high ridge. In a cup-like valley at their feet blazed a dozen campfires. Between themselves and the camp the captives could discern the skulking figures of wolf, hyena, and jackal prowling suspiciously about just beyond the ring of firelight, drawn by the smell of food, yet fearing to approach the abode of so many men.

Dark silhouettes showed around the various camp-fires, and the party's approach was greeted by the neighing of horses and the howling of pariah dogs.

Into the radius of light rode Sheik Darah and his followers, the captives in their center. At sight of the new arrivals a thousand men of varying dress and racial aspect crowded forward to inspect the prisoners and to listen to the story of their capture.

Foremost among the throng was a man whose features stood out distinct in the fire-flare, and who was quickly recognized by two of the

unfortunates.

At sight of him Madge Brant could not repress a little cry of terror, while Halil, the dragoman, forgot his fears in a shout of joyous relief.

For the man was Abou Saoud, from whom Gordon had rescued Madge in the Cairo Fishmarket, and to whose roll of slaves Halil had bargained to add the entire passenger list of his *dahabiyeh*.

CHAPTER IX.

IN THE SCALES OF DEATH.

FOR an instant, so uncertain was the light, and so thick the jostling press of men, that Abou Saoud could gain no clear view of the prisoners.

When he was able to recognize Halil and saw the pale, troubled face of Madge close behind the dragoman he went black with fury.

"Dog of the gutter!" he yelled, hustling aside those between him and the Americans and advancing upon the shrinking Halil with upraised hands, "is it this way you earn your wage? Is this how you hold to your solemn agreement? I was to take these unbelievers and my own men—a week hence at Amelook! I was to take them and to profit by their ransom and sale. I, and I alone! And so it was that we bargained, I and you, scum of the Fishmarket that you art!"

"Oh, beloved of Allah!" wailed the terrified Halil, seeking to burrow a way of escape backward through the crowd. "Oh, Light of the Earth, it is no fault of mine. We were set upon this day by the illustrious Sheik Darah, to whom be honor, and by his noble followers. I would have followed the orders but for that mishap! "

The incensed Abou Saoud, unheeding the shrieked remonstrance and explanation, would have launched himself bodily upon Halil had not Darah barred the way.

"This man and the rest," said the sheik, in stern rebuke, "are my prisoners. They belong to me until the council shall decree their fate. So keep your money-changing talons off them, oh, Abou Saoud, or I

shall demand damages that all your filthy medjidies cannot satisfy."

The Americans had understood no word of this conference, which had, of course, been carried on in Arabic. But the pantomime was vivid, from Abou's first fierce onset to his sulky retreat under the cold wrath of the sheik's eyes.

Exhausted, bruised, footsore, and sick of body, and dazed and numb of mind, from the experiences of the day, the captives huddled, speechless, in the center of that jostling mass of armed natives, and at the close of the colloquy suffered themselves to be hustled unceremoniously into a tumbledown mud hut near the largest of the several campfires.

Here an ill-smelling, smoky oil-lamp was brought to them, and with it a scarce more savory concoction of lentils and lumps of goatflesh in a sort of pigskin trough. The captives were unbound and left to themselves, but a half-score rough-looking tribesmen had already mounted guard outside the hut.

Old Mr. Gault's legs gave way under him as the ropes that bound him were cut, and he sank to the ground from sheer weakness. Fitch was already rocking to and fro on the earthen floor, while Barry Clive leaned in moody silence against the adobe wall.

The hut had two rooms, separated by a hanging flap of goat's hair. In the second and smaller apartment Madge had laid the old lady tenderly down on a couch of piled stones covered with a sheep's skin. This was the only article of furniture the room possessed.

Though dizzy from fatigue, the girl busied herself with loosening the old woman's high, tightly laced boots and bathing her dusty, tear-streaked face with cool water.

"There!" she said, at length, cheerily, as Mrs. Chittenden recovered sufficiently to begin weeping, "you'll be all right in a few minutes, now. Lie still and try to rest, and I will get you something to eat. You must keep up your strength, you know."

"Oh, don't leave me!" gasped Mrs. Chittenden, clutching at her in dread. "I can't bear to be alone! All those horrible dark faces, and those savage eyes, and—oh, *what* will they do with us?"

"They won't harm any of us, but just hold us here until our ransom arrives," soothed Madge, stroking back the straggling gray hair from the old woman's brow and quieting her with the soft magnetic touch

of her white fingers.

"You're sure? You're *sure?* They won't kill us—won't burn us alive as an offering to their idols?" quavered Mrs. Chittenden, whose ideas on Mohammedan theology were not of the clearest. "You think they'll really spare us and let us ransom ourselves?"

"I'm sure of it," reiterated Madge, with a firm conviction of tone that was far from convincing herself.

"Well," grunted Mrs. Chittenden, somewhat calmed, "I only hope the ransoms won't be too large. I'm sorry for you and Mr. Gault, though. It must be dreadful to be poor at such a time as this. I hope," she added, with sudden suspicion, "that you haven't been fussing around me like this and currying favor in hopes of inducing *me* to pay your ransom, for I tell you flatly I *can't.* I'll be lucky if I've money enough to pay my own."

Utterly disgusted—too much so to make disclaimer or to meet the sharp old eyes that were peering at her so cunningly from beneath the tangle of thin gray hair—Madge moved toward the doorway leading into the other room of the hut.

"I will get you something to eat," she said quietly.

Barry Clive was already at the threshold. With a gesture he signed her to step back into the room she had been about to quit. He followed her, and advanced toward the couch. "Aunt Rachel," he began, "I could not help overhearing what you said just now to Miss Brant. I want to tell you in her presence how abominably you misjudge her, and that if you have one spark of womanliness in your heart you will ask her forgiveness. I wish also to repeat what I said to-day: unless Miss Brant and Mr. Gault are ransomed, I shall stay here with them.

"As for Miss Brant's seeking to 'curry favor' with you, there is but one person in all our party who has ever done such a thing. And that was not Miss Brant, but *I.* And, like every other sycophant, I have paid in self-respect for whatever favors I have won. I am just beginning to realize that. And the realization is not pleasant."

The unappetizing meal was at an end. At its conclusion Fitch fell asleep from sheer exhaustion, and snored resonantly. Madge had withdrawn to the room she shared with Mrs. Chittenden. Halil, of less steady nerve than the Americans, was crouched, monkey-fashion, in

the darkest corner of the hut, his face hidden in his bent arms.

Mr. Gault was about to stretch his aching bones on the clay floor, when Barry Clive touched him on the shoulder.

"Look out there," whispered Clive, his voice too low to penetrate to the adjoining room.

He was pointing to the camp-fire, barely twelve yards distant from their guarded door.

The sheik was seated at one side of it. Opposite him squatted Abou Saoud. Between them were several men who, by their dress and bearing, were apparently personages of consequence. As the Americans looked, one or two others joined the conclave.

"That must be the council Halil spoke of," conjectured Barry; "the council that is to decide on our fate. The chiefs are gathering for it now."

"If only we could hear what they say," muttered Mr. Gault, in the same tone. "It's hard to have one's life thrown in the balance and not even able to guess which way the scales are swinging. I've an idea! They're within easy earshot. Let's make Halil translate."

"I had thought of it. But I want to tell you something first: I suspect that dragoman's a scoundrel!"

"What? Poor old Halil a—"

"Just so. Do you remember when that fat man out there saw us? He was enraged for some reason, and rushed at Halil and said something in their infernal guttural jargon. I caught the word 'Amelook.' Now, Amelook was where Halil insisted on our stopping, three days ago. He said the engine was out of order and could not be fixed before next morning. He hurried ashore, on some errand of his own. After it was accomplished he got us out of that row with the natives, and then started off up-stream at once, in spite of the engine being, as he alleged, out of commission. How do you account for that?"

"You mean he had some understanding with this fat man?"

"He knew him. That was evident. And they said something about Amelook. There was a plot of some kind that our worthy dragoman was mixed up in. I mention my suspicions so that you will back me in what I'm about to do."

He crossed to where the dragoman crouched, leaned over him, and inserting a hand in the collar of the soiled blue-and-gold tonic,

jerked Halil to his feet.

"I want you," he said bruskly. "We have found out all about your plot—that Amelook scheme you and the fat man, out there, had hatched up for our benefit—and—"

The miserable Cairene fell on his knees. His face was ghastly.

"Mercy!" he groaned. "Forgiveness, *howadji!*"

Mr. Gault and Barry exchanged a quick glance. The latter went on in the same compelling tone of command:

"My friend was for killing you at once. But we have decided to give you one chance for life. Come to the doorway, here, and translate for us what those sheiks say. And remember, Mr. Gault has some knowledge of Arabic, although he has kept it to himself, and if you lie to us or translate wrongly he will know. So sit here, just within the shadow. I will be behind you, and at a word from Mr. Gault I shall strangle you. The truth is your one chance for life."

The dragoman sank down limply in the spot designated, Barry kneeling behind him and watching the firelit group over Halil's shoulder. Mr. Gault (whose knowledge of Arabic was limited to three single sentences he had laboriously conned from Baedeker) stood near, fixing the dragoman with an eye that seemed to defy that wretched creature to make one error in translation if he dared.

And thus they waited while the last members of the council arrived.

Around the more distant fires they could see rings of bearded, bronzed faces. The stamping of tethered horses and mules was clearly audible on the still air, while from the farther gloom of the foot-hills came unceasingly the sharp, yapping bark of jackals, interspersed by the occasional howl of a wolf or the hysterical "laugh" of a prowling hyena.

Sheik Darah opened the council. He spoke briefly, directly, authoritatively, Halil translating his words in a mumbling whisper between teeth that chattered like castanets.

The sheik merely recounted the accidental discovery of the detached party of Americans among the ruins of Ibrim and their capture. He said that they were seemingly persons of great wealth, as were all Americans, and that he intended to hold them as prisoners until a ransom could be agreed on and sent for.

Abou Saoud spoke next. With many gestures, and in a shrill voice, he pointed out the dangers of sending for a ransom and the risk of bringing down upon them a regiment of government cavalry. The far wiser course, he declared, was to attach the prisoners to his own company, which was to go shortly into the Sudan on a slave-hunt; to transport them to Abyssinia or Kordofan, and there sell them at a high price to some pasha or petty king.

He further offered to pay Sheik Darah, there and then, a fair price for the unbelievers.

As he sat down, flustered and out of breath, a third man spoke.

He was incredibly old and wrinkled. His head was hairless as a billiard-ball, and his yellow-white beard fell in unwashed waves below his waist. His skin was like parchment, and his hollow eyes glowed with the maniacal fire of fanaticism.

"He is Zebehr, the fakir—the greatest of the Bishareen dervishes!" whispered Halil. "He is inspired of Heaven!"

The old man began to speak in a crackling, harsh voice that as he proceeded began to throb with fanatic fervor until it rose almost to a roar.

In unmeasured tones he denounced the impulse for wealth which had led the two previous orators to forget the Prophet's maxim, "Slay the unbelievers, and spare not!"

He reminded the council that they were even now on the march to join El Mahdi, the Redeemer of Islam, and asked if they wished to incur the displeasure of Allah and bar the gates of Paradise against themselves by pausing to hold barter or traffic with heathen Feringhee.

On the other hand, would not the instant and agonizing death of each and all of these unbelievers be as a breath of roses in the nostrils of the Prophet, and would it not insure them a prosperous and triumphant campaign?

More he spoke to the same effect, his shriveled body thrilling to his own wild eloquence. And the fanatic light in his eyes began to find answer in those of more than one of his hearers.

With a shout of "Bismallah!" (in the name of the Most High!), a shock-haired Nubian next to Darah leaped up with drawn simitar. The sheik forced him back to his place. A babel of talk burst from about the circle.

Words and tones ran high. Many and mad were the gesticulations. The earlier dignity of the council was lost in the frenzy of excited debate. Through it all Sheik Darah alone sat speechless and unmoved.

Translation was out of the question. Halil gave up the effort and sat open-mouthed, forgetting his terror in the fascination of the scene before him.

At length the tumult died down almost as suddenly as it had broken out. For this is a peculiarity common to all Oriental disputes.

One man after another, apparently in order of rank, spoke a single word. Then the council broke up.

"That word?" asked Barry, shaking the paralyzed dragoman into sensibility. "That word each of them spoke in turn? It sounded as if it were some verdict. What was the word?"

And his parched lips writhing in the mere physical effort of articulation, Halil groaned brokenly:

"The word, *howadji,* was—*Death!*"

CHAPTER X.

ON THE WINGS OF THE GALE.

BARRY CLIVE and Mr. Gault looked into each other's eyes in the faint light from the dying camp-fire. The cowering dragoman was forgotten. They two were Americans, and in this moment race called to race.

"We are condemned to die," repeated the older man in an awestruck whisper. Barry nodded.

"I am old," went on Mr. Gault, looking curiously at Clive, "and I had not long to live at best. Most of the road lies behind me. With you, it is different. Your whole life should be ahead of you."

"If I were destined to make as much of a mess of the rest of it as I have of the part I've already lived," said Clive, with a quick throb of self-contempt, "I'd rather end it all at once. But—well, lately, life has taken on a different look, and the world seemed to hold so much more for me than I once dreamed of, and my ideas were beginning to

enlarge from their old narrow lines. It's hard to be cut off just at the threshold, isn't it?"

He spoke impersonally, as though commenting on some abstract proposition. He went on, a moment later:

"Shall we tell Miss Brant and—"

"There is no need to tell me," said Madge, close behind him in the gloom. "I was standing here and heard. I thought you both knew I was here. When—when is it to be, I wonder?"

"It may never be at all," spoke up Mr. Gault reassuringly, as he recovered from the surprise of her presence. "We may be rescued, or they may change their minds and accept a ransom, or—"

"You saw the look on that chief dervish's face and the excitement his words caused, and yet you speak of their changing their minds!" interrupted Madge. "And as for rescue, who is to find us here? It is kind of you to try to comfort me, and I appreciate it," laying her hand affectionately on the old man's, "but I am not a child, and I can stand the truth. If I must leave this dear old world, it is at least a joy to know that I go in company with two brave men—men of my own race, who would save me if they could."

At her simple words a wholly inexplicable thrill of pride in being thus included in her praise surged through Barry Clive. His head was erect and his shoulders squared. He felt that such a fate as awaited him might not, perhaps, in such companionship, be so very ignominious an ending to the troubled game of life.

"It is you who show us how to be brave," he replied. "You make it all much easier for us both. And now," he added, "let us try to get such rest as we can. Whatever ordeal is in store, we'll meet it better if our nerves are steadied by a few hours' sleep. I—"

He checked himself and peered out of the door. Noises of running feet and loud voices had caught his ear. Past the dim glow of the fading camp-fires he could see men hurrying in divers directions. The tethered animals farther away were snorting and neighing in terror.

Guttural shouts of command sounded here and there throughout the encampment. Above and through it all, from far to eastward, could be heard a faint, indefinable hum, as of thousands of far-off bees.

"What is it?" asked Madge, joining him in the doorway. "Is the camp attacked?"

The stars were blotted out, and a blackness that seemed almost tangible had settled down over the camp. The air was dead, and the heat of the atmosphere had perceptibly increased within the past few minutes.

The guards on duty outside the hut were talking to each other in an excited way, and, from voice and gesture, were evidently in a high state of nervousness.

"Is the camp attacked, do you suppose?" repeated Madge.

Instead of answering her, Clive turned on the dragoman, who, forgotten, had returned to his corner, where he was again crouching by himself in mortal terror.

"Come here!" ordered Barry.

Cringingly Halil obeyed. As he reached the doorway the new sights and sounds of the night struck him for the first time. Through his fear appeared traces of the same restless excitement that had affected the guards.

"What is the matter out there?" demanded Clive. "Ask the guards."

"No need to ask them, *howadji,*" returned the dragoman. "Any one who has ever crossed the desert knows what is afoot. Praise be to Allah, we are under shelter! May his breath wipe out these tribesmen like—"

"What is it?" repeated Barry more imperatively.

"Why, the simoom, *howadji,*" replied Halil, in wonder at such ignorance.

"The simoom?" echoed Mr. Gault. "What is that?"

"The sand-storm, *howadji!* The sandstorm of the desert, when Scarramouche and his wind-devils ride the gale and strangle all in their path. And may they destroy—"

The distant noise from the east that had resembled a bee-swarm had steadily increased in volume. Now it had grown so loud as to drown the remainder of the Cairene's imprecation.

The blackness of the night took on a livid, sulfurous tinge, and the still air was stirred by an occasional fitful gust of wind.

Here and there men could be seen, near the camp-fire embers, throwing themselves face downward on the ground, their heads sheltered by saddles or baskets, and their bodies swathed in voluminous burnouses. All these prostrate forms lay facing westward.

The lurid light that had no place in the midnight desert glowed brighter. Then, in an instant, it was extinguished.

Halil darted back from the doorway. The guards without threw themselves to the earth, their faces pressed close against the hut-walls. By instinct, or profiting by Halil's example, Clive flung his arm about Madge and dragged her into the interior of the hut.

At the same instant a roar and swirl of tempest burst deafeningly on the ear. The hut was full of stinging, whizzing particles of sand.

The scream of Mrs. Chittenden, and the hoarser note of Fitch's lamentations, as the two were thus suddenly aroused from their sleep of exhaustion, were unheard amid the wilder din of the elements. The sand-storm in all its fury was upon the camp.

For a few seconds there was merely that deafening, earth-shaking roar; the stifling darkness; the myriad burning pin-points of sand that whipped face and body and choked back both utterance and breath.

Barry had instinctively kept his arm about Madge's waist. He could feel the girl's slender body tremble as he pressed her close to him amid that bedlam of uproar. The sensation drove his own fears away and gave him a strange sense of protection, even in the face of the mighty tempest before whose force his poor human strength had not a featherweight of power.

Then, while the voice of the wind and the hiss of driven sand still banished every sense save that of touch, he felt the girl wrenched away from him.

He leaped forward, groping blindly for her. At his first step his arms were seized, dragged backward, and bound behind him.

He was snatched up as by the gale itself, and he felt himself moving rapidly through the air, the wind and sand-blast roaring past him like a cataract.

From the suddenly increased intensity of the gale, he knew that he was either outside the hut or the structure had blown to pieces about him.

Tossed and buffeted, his ear-drums in excruciating torture, the labor of breathing an intense agony, he felt himself slung upward. Then he struck against some unyielding substance.

The quick pressure of finger-tips could be felt here and there about his body. His arms, bound behind his back, swung again free at his

sides, and blindly he clutched a bar or rail, with which they came in contact.

Against his face he could feel a cloth. Then the hard substance on which he had been flung began to plunge forward in a heaving, jerky fashion, and once again the wind and sand whipped about him with redoubled force.

Too dazed by the roar to collect thoroughly his scattered wits, the young man continued to cling to the object his hands had by chance settled on. Then returned the memory of the girl torn from his side, and at the thought he struggled madly to rise. But he could not move the lower half of his body.

Powerless, deaf, dumb, blind, unaware of his direction or whereabouts, his mind like the mind of a man in a nightmare, Barry Clive felt himself whirled rapidly forward through illimitable space.

CHAPTER XI.

A CARAVAN OF GHOSTS.

FOR a period that might have been a half-hour or a half-century, so completely was time wiped out in that war of the elements, the storm raged on. And through it Barry Clive could still feel himself mysteriously propelled in that same plunging, swaying fashion.

Then—in the twinkling of an eye, as it seemed—the din of the gale died down. Died down so suddenly that the ensuing silence was well-nigh as painful to racked nerves and lacerated ear-drums as had been the Inferno of noise.

As the uproar subsided Clive ventured to remove one hand from the rail-like support to which he had been clinging. His object was to tear from his face the cloth or mask which shrouded it, and to learn where he might be—whether in this world or another.

But as he removed his hand another lurch of the great object on which he was perched nearly hurled him forward on his face. He renewed his grip on the rail, and clung there dully, while he felt himself whirled ever, ever onward.

So for a few minutes he remained inert, collecting his dazed faculties and wondering vainly what had befallen him.

At length, with awakening perceptions the suspense grew unbearable. Again he strove to rise, but could not. But now he knew the reason of his helplessness. His legs were strapped fast.

Just then he heard a most lamentable groan near by, that rose to a howl. The voice was the voice of Jonas Fitch.

This was too much for the maintenance of the unaccustomed awe that had taken hold on Clive's usually practical mind. Bracing himself with his left hand, he took advantage of a momentary slackening in the swaying and lurching movements of the object beneath him and lifted his right hand to his face.

His fingers came in contact with a coarse hood, its creases filled with sand. This hood hung loosely over his head and down to his shoulders. It appeared to be fastened only by a single drawstring passed about the neck.

One jerk of his fingers sufficed to break the string and to tear loose the hood. Then another heavy lurch brought his hand back in haste to the rail. The hood fell away, and he looked about him.

After the stifling darkness, his first sensation was one of a strong light. But a second look told him that day had not yet broken.

Above, the great white stars of the desert poured down a radiance never lavished north of the tropics. The waning moon, too, had risen, and its pallid light flooded a scene whose strangeness once more gave the young man the sensation of being in some weird nightmare.

About him, on every side, stretched the endless miles of starlit desert. To right and left of him rode a troop of fantastic gray ghosts mounted on camels. He glanced down. The ground was far beneath him. In front of him was a long, swaying neck, terminating in a hideous head.

The sight gave him a momentary start, but on the instant he realized that he was strapped to the saddle of a camel. To his left was a fat, squirming, hooded gray creature similarly mounted. This rider twisted about in impossible postures and emitted a series of melancholy wails.

"The—the voice is my uncle's!" mused Clive, in amaze, "but the shape—the color—"

Then he looked more closely. It was indeed Jonas Fitch, strapped to the great shapeless saddle of a racing-camel.

The man's hood was gray with sand. His clothing was of the same uniform hue, and mounded over in many places by the drifting sand in such a way as to give him the appearance of some grotesque prehistoric monster.

Every rider bore the same unusual aspect. They were more like a company of gray goblins than human beings. Only on the outskirts of the little central group had they cast back their hoods.

Clive could there recognize the thin dark faces of Arabs. His eyes searched the nearer riders for one especial figure. He soon descried her.

Almost directly beside him, to his immediate right, she rode; slender, childlike, graceful, despite the shapeless hood and burnoose that had been cast about her; silent, yet very evidently conscious.

Clive reached far across and cast back the hood from Madge Brant's face. Very white she was, but unflinching of countenance; and her great dark eyes glowed like stars as they met his.

Long the two glances met and mingled, though surely never before since the birth of time did man and maid under such bizarre circumstances read each other's souls.

Then, as Clive had done, Madge surveyed her surroundings, clinging the while to the saddle-rail of her camel.

In front of her rode old Mr. Gault, crouching low and grasping the rail for dear life, his hooded face bent almost to the pommel. Beside him, swinging limply back and forth with each motion of her camel, was Mrs. Chittenden.

She, like the rest of the prisoners, had been lashed securely to the saddle; and it was well, for she had fainted.

A score of Arabs surrounded the five captives, the bearing-reins of each of whose camels were attached to the pommel of one of these tribesmen's saddles. Behind and in front the cavalcade stretched out.

Fully a hundred riders were of the party. All were mounted on camels save, far in front, one man who rode a horse.

"Where are we?" questioned Madge dazedly. "We were in the hut. Then came that terrific noise and—and I was snatched up and—"

"Miss Brant!" called old Mr. Gault, hearing her voice. "You are still

alive, then? What has happened?"

He, too, began to claw at his hood, and after divers efforts wrenched it off.

"Oh, Mrs. Chittenden has fainted!" cried Madge, in distress, as her eyes fell on the inert figure before her. "Can't we—"

"Leave her as she is, for the present," counseled Clive. "She is happier so. Where can they be taking us?"

"Wherever it is, we are going like the wind," panted Mr. Gault, as he plunged to and fro in his saddle. "It is as if we were in flight from death itself. See how these men flog the camels on! Where is the camp?" he added, looking back into the trackless miles of waste behind them. "It is quite out of sight. Perhaps Halil can tell us something. Halil!"

But there was no reply. Closer scrutiny proved that the dragoman was not of the party.

"There's a man on horseback riding in front," suggested Mr. Gault. "Perhaps that's he?"

"No," corrected Madge. "It is too tall and too slender for Halil. Who—oh, he's turning and riding back toward us! It's—it's Sheik Darah!"

The equestrian had wheeled his galloping horse, and now brought the roan alongside the group of captives without slackening his speed.

"Ah!" he commented coolly. "You have come to your senses?"

He addressed the party in general, but his eyes were on Madge Brant.

"Where are you taking us?" she asked, as the rest hesitated for words.

"Away from death," was the terse reply.

"And to what? "

"To Khartum."

"Khartum?" she echoed in delight. "Then you are taking us to General Gordon?"

"I am taking you to El Mahdi, the Heaven-born. Gordon Pasha, by now, is a prisoner or dead. Khartum should be in the hands of Islam. El Mahdi rules there, as in time he shall rule the earth."

"Wait till he tackles that fragment of earth bossed by Uncle Sam!" growled Mr. Gault. "Then your divine friend El Mahdi will think he's

hit a sandstorm. He—"

"Do you mean," Madge broke in, as she saw the sheik's brow knit with anger, "that we are to be taken to El Mahdi as prisoners?"

"I am El Mahdi's man," returned the sheik. "You are my prisoners. I demanded the right to ransom you. That right was refused me by the council, and it was decreed that you should die at the morning call to prayer. The simoom came up. Being desert-born, I smelled it many miles away, and I made my plans.

"My men took, by stealth, the hundred riding-camels of Abou Saoud—for which I shall one day pay him, but not in coin—and as the storm burst we entered the prison-hut, bound you all to the camels, and bore you away under cover of the tempest. No horse save Massoud, here, who was bred in the sand-storm country"—he paused to stroke the roan's arched neck—"could live in so great a simoom. Only camels could survive. So, we feared no immediate pursuit. But we must travel at full speed, none the less, and in a circuitous course, if we would wholly escape."

"And when we reach the Mahdi?"

"Then I shall plead my past services to gain his permission to hold you until a messenger can be sent for ransom."

"But if he refuses?"

"If he refuse, you will be no more unfortunate than you would have been even now but for the simoom. But I think he will not refuse me."

"Where is Halil, our dragoman?"

The sheik's stern face relaxed into a grim smile.

"When I was at the English school in Cairo," said he, "before I went to El Azhar (the university), the head master bade us, at meals, not to empty our dishes wholly, but to 'leave something for manners.' I have taken Abou Saoud's camels and the rich folk that he would have sold into slavery, but I have left him Halil—'for manners!' Besides, the Cairene's ransom would not be worth his keep during the months we must travel."

"The *months?*"

"The months. Khartum lies a full five hundred miles to the southwest as the bird flies. And by the route we must take the distance is fully a thousand."

"But," broke in Mr. Gault, "if, on reaching Khartum, Miss Brant and I cannot pay a ransom that you demand, what then? "

"Then," returned the sheik, with unaffected brutal indifference, "you will be put to death. Perhaps by torture. El Mahdi is just. You will die."

There was the faintest imaginable emphasis on the personal pronoun, which arrested Clive's attention. Still more did he note the complete change in the sheik's manner when he turned from Madge to address Mr. Gault.

Madge, too, had noticed the emphasis on the "you."

"Mr. Gault did not speak only of himself, sheik, but of me as well," she said.

"I understood him," replied the Arab lightly, "but you are far too beautiful to die. A spirit of prophecy tells me that you will live to wed a sheik and be sublimely happy, far from your native land."

"Sheik Darah!" exclaimed Barry, his face black with rage as he observed Madge's flush of distress at the strange words and the look that accompanied them. "Sheik Darah, a spirit of prophecy tells *me* that *you* will die suddenly and with great violence in the very heart of your native land, and that *I* shall be most actively present at the time to see that the operation goes on without a hitch! "

CHAPTER XII.

FACE TO FACE WITH THE CRISIS.

THE events of the few succeeding months, while affording almost daily episodes of more or less vital interest to the five Americans, stretched out to too great multitude and volume to permit of detailed chronicling.

Each day comprised twenty-four hours of greater or lesser hardships and peril.

Southward, in a general way, the cavalcade journeyed; not in a straight line, but in a half-moon, whose northern horn was the camp to which the Americans had been taken on the day of the capture, and

whose southern terminal was to be the Nile city of Khartum.

The flight, especially for the first few days, was almost unintermittent. Brief snatches of time were allowed for food and sleep; then onward at the same ceaseless, mile-devouring, swinging trot of the long-legged racing-camels.

The motion experienced in riding a camel is not at all unlike that aboard ship in a heavy sea. At first it is sickening, then acutely painful, and at length well-nigh as easy as the sway of a rocking-chair.

There is also as great a difference between the various sorts of camels as between horses. The ordinary draft-camel is as rough to ride as a dray-horse. The riding, or racing, camel, on the other hand, is as easy of gait, in his way, as a Kentucky thoroughbred.

To the five Americans, for the most part unused to violent or prolonged exertion, the first few days of that wild flight were torture. Forced to ride at breakneck speed under a torrid sun; to sleep on scarce-covered sand and for unduly brief intervals; to eat sparingly of coarse and unfamiliar food; to feel themselves hopelessly in the power of their savage masters—all this was seemingly sufficient to break down their health or drive them mad.

As a matter of fact, it had no such effect. Strangely enough, after the first shock and the brief rebellion of nature against so sharp a departure from former habits they one and all throve on their hardships.

Twenty-four hours a day in the open air of a dry, windy country; exercise that stirred every muscle to activity; food which, if plain, contained nothing but nourishment, and which was, administered so seldom as to impart zest to each mouthful—these benefits at length overcame the handicaps of heat and overfatigue. Even Mrs. Chittenden grew stronger, and a faint flush—that owed nothing to cosmetics—settled in her withered cheeks.

All grew, at first, scarlet, and then brown as Arabs, beneath the blistering sun. Jonas Fitch alone derived no benefit from the enforced "cure."

Beneath the tan his cheeks daily became sallower, the pouches under his eyes larger, and his fat figure thinner and more bent.

After that first clash between Barry Clive and the sheik the captives agreed among themselves to do or say nothing further to awaken the wrath of their capricious captors, but to yield, for the present, to

the inevitable, trusting to chance, later on, to devise a mode of escape.

Thus, a sort of armed truce that in many respects approached good-fellowship sprang up at last between, captives and captors. The sheik, while seeking Madge's society as often as possible, gave no further hint of trying to win her hand. The question of the ransom, too, was tacitly tabooed.

At the end of the first week the headlong haste was abated. Darah evidently saw that he had outdistanced or outmaneuvered any pursuit.

The caravan traveled more slowly, stopping longer at the divers oases and wells that strew the Bishareen Desert.

The hundred men of Darah's troop, like the fifty who had rendezvoused at the ruins of Ibrim, were but a portion of his full command. The remainder of the Mekheir tribe were scattered, in parties of varying sizes, through the Bishareen Desert and to the south of it, raising recruits, collecting provisions and armament, and in other ways preparing for the march to the Mahdi's army.

From time to time the travelers would pick up some such waiting squadron, or turn aside to visit desert encampments where the local men of war were eagerly waiting to enroll themselves under the standard of so renowned a leader as Darah. Thus, the troop that originally numbered a bare hundred finally swelled to a thousand or more warriors, and the wild speed of the first week slowed down to an average of ten miles a day.

The journey also, lengthened by the many détours and halts, stretched far beyond the thousand miles Darah had originally mentioned as its limit.

Egypt was long since left behind; they were in Nubia, land of gigantic, jet-black men and of acacia-strewn wastes, sloping southerly to the rich, fertile Sudan.

Here it was that messages from the front began to reach Darah by Mahdist couriers. He gravely translated all these reports to his captives.

They were not of a nature to impart cheer to the Americans. Everywhere, it appeared, the Mahdi was triumphant. Gordon had reached Khartum in safety, but had almost at once been hemmed in there by the Mahdists. How he had since fared, whether or not he still lived, none of the besiegers knew.

On his arrival in the doomed city Gordon had found all his work of former years undone and the old-time abuses in full sway.

The prisons were jammed with innocent men; the magistrates and petty rulers were extorting money by means of bastinado and torture. The poor were homeless and starving; the rich living in unspeakable official corruption.

Gordon's first act was to set free the innocent prisoners; to hurl into a pile and set fire to the torture-implements and whips; to feed and house the needy, and to punish the corrupt officials. The city was in an uproar at his arrival. He was wildly hailed by ten thousand tongues as "Savior!" "Father!" "Blest Deliverer!"

Then the Mahdists had beleaguered the town, and from its interior no further news had come. The Egyptian government, urged thereto in a half-hearted way by Gladstone, had sent a relief expedition under Hicks Pasha.

Of this army's fate the outside world never learned, but Darah's messengers told rare tales of an outnumbered and fast dwindling force cut off from aid or supplies in the midst of a hostile country and at last annihilated.

Hot tears stood in Madge Brant's eyes as she heard how Colonel Stewart, heading a "forlorn hope" in a mad dash up the Nile valley to gain his beloved chief's side, had been routed and slain. She well recalled the aide's loyalty to Gordon. The memory brought back to her that evening of the Khedivial levee.

All Egypt had gathered to do honor to the man it loved. And then it had sent him to his death. Then all had been gaiety, light, and music. Now life was grim to desolation, and on all sides stalked the shadow of slaughter.

As Madge summoned up the thought of Gordon's grave, kindly face as it had bent above her that evening of the levee another face rose before her mental vision—the discontented, handsome, boyish face of a man who had stared incredulously at the attention lavished on the girl he was wont to regard as a mere upper servant.

At the recollection she now lifted her eyes. Lounging near her on the sand (it was during one of the noonday halts) was the same man.

The boyishness was wiped from his features by all he had under-gone; his eyes and mouth, behind the mask of tan and tangled beard,

were strong and alert. Decidedly, he was another person from the Barry Clive who had once sought so superciliously to "teach her her place."

The two had been thrown together in the closeness of enforced intimacy for many months. Yet no word anent their former differences had been spoken.

"King Cophetua," she observed, her laughing eyes denying the mock severity of her voice, "do you know your clothes would shame a rag-bag? Your hair is as long as a cowboy's, and your beard looks like a mane. Also, that you are the color of a mahogany bureau? Even the Beggar Maid of the poem would run and hide at sight of you!"

He looked puzzled as she addressed him by the fantastic title. Then, as she went on, memory returned, bringing with it a sting that was so faint as to be wholly swept away by a laugh.

"Beggar Maid!" he retorted, in the same exaggerated tone of disapproval, "do you know it is lese-majesty for you to criticize my august self like that? What is to hinder me from summoning my guards and casting you into the deepest dungeon of the keep?"

"Nothing, sire," she replied meekly, "except the unavoidable absence of the dungeon. I confess my guilt."

"Also," resumed Clive, in majestic sternness, "I may mention that when you were making up for the role of Beggar Maid you overdressed the part. No self-respecting Beggar Maid in poetry or real life ever wore a sheepskin tunic torn in seven places and a burlap skirt made by herself out of four meal-sacks and strewn with such an array of weird darns and patches! And as for your hair, I don't believe you've an idea how untidy it looks."

"Oh, my poor, *poor* hair!" sighed the girl, instinctively raising both hands to the shining mass of gold-brown tresses that crowned her little head; "I work over it so hard, too! But what is one to do, with scarcely a single real hairpin left? I fix it passably neat in the morning, and then by the time we've ridden a mile it's in my eyes."

"So!" he laughed triumphantly; "I've touched the one vulnerable spot in the Beggar Maid's armor! Now, perhaps you will treat my own appearance with more respect."

"Yes, sire," she admitted, with due submission. "And now that you have been pleased to criticize so freely my desert-made costume and

my unlucky locks, is there any other comment you care to make on my appearance?"

"Yes," he answered slowly, the lightness of his tone suddenly underlaid by a deeper note, "there's one thing I omitted to mention: Between the patchwork dress and the tangled-sunshine hair there's a face—the loveliest God ever made."

A bright wave of crimson swept through the olive of her cheek, bathing her from throat to brow. But she curtsied to the very ground, in mock reverence, to hide the telltale blush. Then she answered, in forced gaiety:

"The mighty Cophetua must not turn the Beggar Maid's poor rustic head with compliments. Come," she added in her primest school-teacher manner, "it's time for our daily Arabic lesson! Translate *'Nahar-ak koom sàid! Ha-yâal Sâlâh, Saädat!'*"

"'Peace be unto thee! It is the hour for prayer, Beloved,'" translated Barry, with due docility.

"No, no!" corrected the girl, "*'Saädat'* means 'Sir,' or 'Excellency.' *'Aleel'* is 'Beloved.'"

"So it is! So it is!" assented Clive quickly. "I must have been thinking of—in fact, I *was* thinking of—"

"Madge!" exclaimed Mr. Gault, hurrying up.

"Exactly that!" muttered Clive, under his breath, yet quite loudly enough for Madge to catch the words.

"Madge!" repeated the old gentleman excitedly, "Darah tells me we are not going to Hesuna for the cattle, as he had planned, for they have just been driven into camp. So he is going to march at once for Khartum. We'll reach the Nile by noon to-morrow, and by night we will be within El Mahdi's lines."

Madge and Clive were both on their feet at the news. The journey—the delays—the long waiting—all were at an end. Within the next two days their destinies would be settled.

El Mahdi might spare their lives, but if the tales they had heard during the past few months concerning his treatment of foreign captives were to be credited he was far more likely to order the five Americans torn to pieces at once by his horde of fanatics.

The earlier fears, worn blunt by months of imprisonment and by the varied happenings of the long journey, now rushed in on them

afresh. The trio looked back on the stress and toil of the pilgrimage as at some prolonged holiday.

For now they were, in one brief moment, to be brought to hand-grips with Fate.

One must needs have glanced twice at the tense, drawn faces of Madge and Clive before recognizing them as the man and girl who five minutes before had been playing at the world-old comedy of Cophetua and the Beggar Maid.

CHAPTER XIII.

A LOVE-QUEST.

"Do you know what day it is?" asked Barry Clive.

They were riding, he and Madge, along the winding native road that skirts the eastern bank of the Nile. Before them moved a hundred Arabs, Darah at their head. Behind trailed nearly a thousand more, followed by camp baggage, lines of cattle, sheep, and goats, and all the disordered equipment of an Oriental march.

Fitch, on the news that their long period of waiting was at an end, and that by the following day they would be judged by El Mahdi, had collapsed. In so bad a state was he that he could not remain in the saddle, and lay stretched on a pile of fodder in an oxcart.

Beside him sat Mrs. Chittenden; while Mr. Gault, who had some slight skill at surgery, was doing what he could for the comfort of the fear-sick man. Thus, Madge and Clive, so far as their own party was concerned, were left alone together.

"Do you know what day it is?" Clive repeated as she looked at him in doubt as to his meaning. During the march the exact periods of Occidental time had been largely ignored.

"It is the last day of our journey," she hazarded, "and—"

"And the first of the year," amended Clive. "New Year's Day! Happy New Year, Beggar Maid!"

"Happy New Year, King Cophetua!"

They both laughed; and on a sudden their laughter died as the

same thought crept into the heart of each—they saw the dawn of the new year. But how much of that year's progress were they destined to view with mortal eyes?

Since the first moment of mortal misgiving, on the previous day, when Mr. Gault had told them of their forthcoming appearance before El Mahdi, they had schooled themselves against giving way outwardly to the dread that possessed them.

"New Year's Day!" mused Clive. "Last New Year's we sailed from Brindisi for Port Saïd. I remember Miss Halpin called my attention to the gorgeous sunset over the Mediterranean, and I—"

"And you snubbed her unmercifully. I remember the poor thing cried when she got to her cabin."

"What a cad I was!" he growled disgustedly. "I remember feeling it a personal affront that any of those people should dare to address me. I wish—"

"What?" as he paused.

"I wish," he went on, a little wistfully, "that I could see some of them now for five minutes and tell them how sorry I am. It has been a hard school in which I've learned the divine gospel of friendliness and good-fellowship. And now that at last it is partially learned, I—well, it seems a pity I've so little time to practise it."

"Don't talk that way," she begged. "You may live to bless this 'hard school,' as you call it. And—"

"Whether I live or not, I *shall* bless it. For in it I have learned all that is really worth while in life. And the sum and substance of it all is—*you!*"

"The king is really coming down from his throne at last!" She tried to speak mockingly, but the laugh that accompanied the words had little true mirth in it.

"Madge!"—the man's voice was instinct with pain—"can't you see how much it means to me? Surely I have paid, and doubly paid, for my miserable snobbishness—for all my rudeness toward you in the old days! I was punished by the mere knowledge of having offended you. Then, during the long months in the desert when I watched you day by day—when I saw you bent to the saddle-bow with weariness and yet always ready to help or cheer the rest of us—when I saw how brightly you bore the fearful discomforts and fatigues and dangers

that would have broken down any other woman—when I saw those childlike big eyes of yours look so fearlessly on the horde of ruffians that surrounded us, and when I noted how you gave no thought to yourself, but all to the comfort of the others—when I saw all that and a thousand other things, then came my true punishment for the way I had treated you. For I realized at last the sort of woman I had insulted and looked down on. Ah, Madge, can you ever forgive me?"

"There is nothing to forgive, Barry," she answered, "or if there were, it is forgotten long ago. No one who had seen the splendid way you've borne yourself throughout all this trying journey could have kept on blaming you for what was, after all, only the fault of your ignorance. No woman could have helped admiring your courage and—"

"Then you really care? You—"

"Wait!" she commanded. "You must not speak of that. This is no time to talk of love or to plan for the future. Our lives are in God's hands, and we have no right, at the very threshold of the life-and-death crisis, to look forward beyond it."

"But, dearest," he pleaded, "I could meet whatever fate may have in store with such a blithe heart if only I were sure—"

"But *I* am not sure!" she interposed.

He winced at the words as though struck across the face. She went on gently:

"We have been together much, you and I, for nearly a year, and either of us might readily mistake mere good-friendship for love. But that is not all. I am the only girl you have seen in that length of time. You are only twenty-four. At such an age, they say, a man would fall in love with his own shadow if nothing lovelier presented itself. Suppose—just suppose—that we win our freedom and return to America. You will be surrounded once more by people of your own class—of your own social standing. The memory of this past year and the lessons it has taught you will quickly drop away.

"How would you like to introduce your Harvard friends to a prim little schoolmistress and say to them: She hasn't a penny; she has no social standing; she was my aunt's paid companion; for four years she worked for a living (which none of the women in my own set would deign to do). Seen beside girls of my own kind, she lacks distinction. She isn't even particularly pretty, now that I have a chance to com-

pare her with other women. I am going to marry a little, insignificant Cook's tourist schoolmarm.' How would—"

"Stop!" broke in Clive, hot with indignation. "You know that what you're saying is utter nonsense! There are two kinds of fools—the sort that see they have been fools and have sense enough to do better in future, and the sort that keep on being fools every time a new chance for idiocy offers itself. I like to believe *I* belong to the first sort. At any rate, even if you never look at me again, I shall forever be the better man for having known you, and for all you have taught me. And I could not, even if I chose to, look on life with the blind, fatuous, self-complacent eyes I once had. That is gone forever; believe it or not, as you like."

"I *do* believe it, Barry," Madge replied, a new tenderness in voice and eyes which wholly escaped the man's angry notice—"I do believe it. But you have had no means of testing it—of seeing me alongside other women. Think of what it would be to me if I—if I—cared for you as you want me to care and then lived to see you ashamed of me! To know you were bound to me only by honor, and not by love! You think that impossible now, but all things look clearer from a distance. Wait until we are free and our faces are set toward America, and then— then speak of this to me, again, if you must. But not till then. In the meantime—"

"In the meantime," interrupted Clive fiercely, "I've made an ass of myself. I might have known you could never stoop to loving a worthless chap like me. But I thank you for letting me down so easy. Somehow, it won't be so hard now to stand anything that devil of a Mahdi may decree. The game's played and over with forever so far as I'm concerned."

"Don't speak that way," begged Madge. "It's more like your old-time self than like the Barry Clive I know to get angry because you cannot have your way. Barry, we are riding to the Mahdist camp. Every step means one step nearer the end of the long, pleasant comradeship of the journey. Don't let's spoil the last few hours of it by quarreling. Sha'n't we try to forget everything except that we are chums?"

She stretched forth her little bronzed hand in appeal. He grasped it warmly.

"You're right," he said. "I'm a selfish brute. And I'm sorry."

In token whereof, before releasing her hand, he bent and kissed it. Again he missed the look in the brown eyes above him, for when he raised his head her face was averted.

The caress had passed unheeded by the Arabs about them, hand-kissing being a commonplace, every-day act of deference in the East. Only two men in all that cortege paid any special note to it. One was old Mr. Gault, who, riding forward from the hospital wagon, saw it, and smiled in a fatherly way behind his unkempt white beard.

The other was Sheik Darah, far in advance, who, unnoticed, had turned more than once to note the couple's prolonged colloquy, and who (at sight of the salutation which instinct told him held more of love than courtliness) began instinctively to toy with the hilt of his curved saber.

At sound of Mr. Gault's approach Madge turned in her saddle to greet him.

"We have made a discovery," she said, speaking rapidly to hide her embarrassment.

"So I gathered," he answered, beaming on them both, "and I—"

"We've discovered that it's New Year's Day."

"Oh!" grunted the old gentleman, his face falling.

"Imagine New Year's," went on Madge, "with the thermometer at one hundred, the palm-trees above us, and—*what's* that? There! Out there in the river! "

The Nile beside which they rode bore no likeness to the muddy, desert-lined river of the *dahabiyeh* days. Here it was narrower, bluer, its banks lush with rank tropical vegetation and dotted by groups of date-palms whose trunks were thick with vine and undergrowth.

Wild tropical country, beneath a scorching tropical sun, stretched away on every hand to where hot ether-waves pulsed and shimmered along the skyline.

Athwart the smoother waters of the river, where Madge pointed, ran a double ripple, at whose apex moved a black misshapen thing.

"It's—God bless my soul! It's a crocodile!" cried Mr. Gault. "From the size of his head he must be fifteen feet long. And see, there's another, half-way up the bank, just below, asleep in the sun. Looks like a log!"

"Crocodiles and New Year's Day!" murmured Madge. "Back in

New York the snow is a foot deep and the mercury near zero."

"And," added Mr. Gault, "the Christmas decorations are still in the windows there and the crowd has a holiday look, and there are broken tin horns lying in the gutter as remnants of last night's celebration of the birth of eighteen hundred and eighty-five! Can't you see it all?"

His old face was alight with sweet recollection.

"No," muttered Clive, "I can only see crocodiles—and Arabs."

"Well," laughed Mr. Gault, "we've got New York's August weather here, anyhow, to remind us of home. Lord! how hot it is there in August! But I'd give ten years' income to be coming home from work on an August day, just now, in little old Manhattan. I'd take the L up-town from Warren Street. People would have their hats in their laps, and their coats open and no vests on. And the car-windows would all be up.

"And when we got to my station I'd walk down the street toward my flat and I'd see the North River—worth fifty of this measly Nile— shining at the foot of the street. And there'd be a hand-organ man play-ing 'Mulligan Guards' half-way down the block and children trying to dance to it, and wives in cool white dresses would be leaning out of the upper windows or strolling up the sidewalk watching for their hus-bands to come home, and now and then one of them would wave her hand as some tired, perspiring chap with a wilted collar would come around the corner, and he'd wave back and walk a bit faster and forget all about the heat and the office bothers, and—oh, I'm an old imbecile to ramble on like this! Why don't you stop me when I get maudlin?"

He cleared his throat with an impatient sound and glared very savagely at the nearest crocodile. Madge leaned across, without speak-ing, and laid her fingers in quick caress on his cheek.

"Some day you must show us that street," she said.

"I—I don't live there any longer," he replied. "I—you see—there's no one to come to meet me or wave to me in the hot summer eve-nings. I'm a very old man, little girl, and sometimes I talk foolishly and forget how fast time flies. Here comes Sheik Darah."

Unconsciously they had for the past few minutes been ascending one of the few hills in that flat country. The sheik joined them as they neared the summit.

"At the crest," said he, "you will be able to see the hosts of the

Heaven-Born. And beyond, the city of Khartum itself."

"What are all those moving dots in the sky just over the hill?" asked Madge, pointing to innumerable circling specks far in front of them and just visible beyond the near-by hilltop.

"Those," replied the sheik, in matter-of-fact fashion, quite careless of the significance of his words, "are the kites and vultures above the army and city."

Madge shuddered in involuntary horror, and her two compatriots glanced furtively at her and at each other.

They breasted the last slope, and at the summit Darah drew rein. Below them lay a vast plain that melted away in haze to the far southward. At the hill's farther base, and stretching for miles in every direction, a mighty host lay encamped.

Not such an orderly, geometrical array of white tents, wagons, and other accouterment as one sees in pictures of American or European army camps, nor bright with the blazonry and pomp of medieval array, but a sullen, disordered, scattered mass of dull brown, ragged in outline, somber of hue. The sun here and there struck a glint from rusty field pieces or brought into clearer view some lurid-tinted standard.

In the center flapped a huge green banner, symbol of the "Holy" War. And above, in swarms like summer flies, flocked the myriad carrion birds of prey. Beyond—a mile or two distant along the river's bank—a little peninsula ran out into the water. It was thickly covered with mud huts, flat of roof, squalid of exterior. In several plates, above the dead level of the lesser houses, tall modern edifices reared their bulky height.

In the midst of the city stood a big stone-faced structure over whose parapet fluttered the Khedivial flag.

"Khartum!" announced the sheik. "The garrison still holds out," he added, pointing toward the distant flag. "But it is only a matter of days before the Heaven-Born shall sweep the infidel from his last foothold in the Sudan!"

Turning to his men, he gave the command to march.

Down the long hill rode the cavalcade, the Americans in a silent group in the van; down the hill toward the flapping green banner of the Prophet, toward the camp of the conquest-drunk fanatic who held

the lives of the five prisoners in the hollow of his hand.

"Be brave, dear," whispered Barry Clive to Madge as the foot of the hill was reached. "For better or for worse, it will all be decided in a few hours now."

CHAPTER XIV.

A TRANCE AND AN AWAKENING.

BUT Barry Clive's prophecy that within a few hours the captives would know their fate for better or for worse was in no way justified.

As they drew near to the great encampment a throng of soldiers, fakirs, unattached dervishes, and camp-followers straggled forth to meet them. Darah haughtily ignored the salutations of this rabble, closing his men in compact order about the prisoners and riding straight through the crowd.

At sight of the Americans a yell went up, followed by a myriad questions, shouts of menace, and bellowed insults. The disorganized mass pressed close on the flanks of the band, but wisely forbore any effort to push past the grim-visaged tribesmen and gain a nearer view of the five Feringhi.

"Sweet discipline they keep here," commented Mr. Gault. "But it's lucky we have these thousand Mekheirs to guard us. If we had less powerful protection the fanatics would tear us to bits."

Onward rode the desert band, Darah's red standard streaming in the van. And now from out the camp rode a group of men, gorgeously appareled, showily mounted—emirs (princes) serving under El Mahdi's banner.

Darah spurred forward, ahead of his command, to greet them, kissing each in turn on both cheeks, and receiving from each a similar mark of affection.

"Until I saw how ugly Eastern women are," observed Mr. Gault as he viewed this lengthy ceremony, "I never realized how Oriental men got into the silly habit of kissing each other."

No one answered him; for, the greetings being over, Darah was in

speech with a gigantic Abyssinian with the features and coloring of a negro. The Abyssinian's costume was aglitter with tarnished gold and fiery scarlet, and from his words and bearing he was evidently high in power in that motley host.

The emirs and Darah were within easy speaking distance of the Americans. Barry, Madge, and Gault, who had whiled away the long months of their captivity by a daily study of colloquial Arabic, had but little difficulty in catching the gist of the conversation.

The Heaven-Born Mahdi, according to the Abyssinian, could not receive his beloved disciple Darah on that day.

For the Heaven-Born was in one of his periodical divine trances, wherein he was wont to commune on terms of familiarity with the Prophet, with Ali, With Omar, and with other celestials who always returned his soul to his body, soon or late, in good order, and filled with new wisdom for the glory of Islam and the dire confusion of the Feringhee.

The present trance had already endured for forty-eight hours, and might continue anywhere from a week to a month longer, according (presumably) to the length of time Mohammed, Omar, etc., could spare from other heavenly matters to commune with him.

The Heaven-Born, however, according to the Abyssinian, had for weeks expected the Mekheirs, and had wearied of waiting for the joy of gazing on Darah's face. Also, certain of the Faithful who had arrived in camp some time before had pained the Holy One's ears with tales of an escapade of the sheik's wherein divers camels and infidel captives had been spirited away, under cover of a sand-storm, from a camp in the northern Bishareen Desert.

On all of which El Mahdi had in his infinite wisdom deferred judgment until Darah's version of the case should have been set forth. Yes, his chief accusers were Abou Saoud, the slave-merchant, and the holy Zebehr.

In the meantime, until it should please the Prophet to restore the Heaven-Born's soul to his earthly body, a section of the camp, near the river, had been set aside for the temporary quarters of the Mekheirs. Would the beloved Darah consent to be directed thither?

Through miles of encampment the party rode, their guards still close about them, while from all sides arose plaudits of welcome to the

great desert chieftain, mingled with curses and howls of execration leveled at his unbeliever prisoners.

The air was thick with the horrible odors of an Oriental camp. Here and there were clumps of black goat-hair tents and a few mud hovels, but for the most part the Faithful lived and slept on the open ground. As practically no rain falls in the Sudan between October and April, the latter arrangement entailed less hardship than might have been expected.

Men from every corner of the Dark Continent were jumbled in one wild, heterogeneous mass in that strange army—Arabs, Egyptians, Bedouins, Abyssinians, Turks, Nubians—but the predominating race were the Sudanese themselves. Wiry, coal-black men were these last named, clad in soiled white, fuzzy ridges of black wool piled high above their narrow foreheads, their eyes small and evil, their other features of a strong negro cast.

While thousands of them carried flintlocks and many had modern Winchester rifles slung across their shoulders, their favorite weapons appeared to be the long, shovel-bladed spears of their ancestors' time and crooked forked-blade daggers.

There was no semblance of order, as Occidentals understand the term, about that horde of fifty thousand barbarians. But what they lacked in discipline they atoned for in zeal.

They held together through no loyalty or patriotism, but because of insane fanaticism and a childlike reliance on Allah's glittering promises as interpreted to them by his mouthpiece, El Mahdi.

To keep up the zealous piety of the Faithful the camp was alive with fakirs and mad dervishes who (incited by hasheesh and self-hypnotism) performed miracles of a cheap sleight-of-hand type, cut themselves with knives, went through weird conjuring feats, and preached Paradise to all believers and destruction to the worldful of infidels.

It was an army chiefly, made up of homicidal maniacs lashed to greater fury by fellow madmen. Here and there were a few men, like Darah, actuated by simple religion and patriotism as they understood the words, and here and there men of the Abou Saoud type who viewed the Holy War, as a mere avenue to wealth and personal glory. But these were in the extreme minority.

In the midst of this concourse of violent incurables Madge Brant and her companions were domiciled. Their abode was a long low tent of woven hair, divided by partitions of the same material into three compartments. About the tent a hundred men of the Mekheirs, armed to the teeth, stood guard night and day, while on all sides the remainder of Darah's tribesmen were encamped, ready at a word to rush to the rescue of their lord's captives.

Nor was the post of these guards a sinecure. For no sooner did the news spread abroad that Feringhi were harbored in the camp than that section of the field was besieged by screaming fakirs calling down divine vengeance on the unbelievers whose presence defiled the sacred hosts and urging their fellow worshipers to rend them asunder.

Only Darah's fame and the prowess of Darah's men held back the "avengers" at the spearpoint.

And so the interminable days passed. The Mahdi still slept. His faithful disciples still raged impotently about Darah's tent. Once or twice from the beleaguered city to the south came the muffled reports of old-fashioned cannon—a forlorn defiance, but, to the Americans, evidence that Gordon still lived and successfully defied his religion's and adopted country's foes.

The period of waiting was hard upon all the captives, harder by far than any of the preceding months. For now they must sit in enforced inaction, uncertain of the moment when their summons might arrive.

New lines crept into Barry Clive's face; Madge was cheerful and buoyant as ever, yet there was pallor now instead of a flush beneath the deep olive tan of her cheek. Old Mrs. Chittenden had long since passed the stage where her shallow nature was capable of new emotion. She moved about silent, apathetic, in a sort of continual stupor.

It was upon Jonas Fitch that the suspense told most heavily. From the first, his health had steadily declined. The bracing life of the journey had only served to age and weaken him.

Ever since their arrival at El Mahdi's camp he had grown rapidly worse. At last Mr. Gault, with his smattering of medical lore, could see that the old millionaire's days, if not hours, were numbered. Without medicines or restoratives, in dire privation, weakened by successive shocks and by months of unabating terror, Fitch had fallen into a collapse, from which the primitive skill within the party's com-

mand could not arouse him.

One night Barry Clive was awakened to find Mr. Gault leaning over him.

"Get up and come with me," commanded the old man, pointing toward the central apartment, which had been set aside as Fitch's sick-room. "Your uncle is sinking fast. I have given him some *mastik* (an Oriental cordial), and he has rallied for the moment, but the end is very near."

Without a word Barry followed through the goat-hair hangings to the next room. There, stretched on a pallet of straw, covered with skins, lay Jonas Fitch. Beside him, on the ground, sat Madge, smoothing back the matted white hair from his forehead, and now and then raising the *mastik* cup to the twitching yellow lips.

In a corner, stupid, uncomprehending, stood Mrs. Chittenden.

"Gault tells me I'm going, Barry," croaked Fitch, rolling his hollow eyes toward his nephew. "I sent for you—for you—to tell you—about the property. It'll go to you. All of it. You—you ain't been the nephew to me you ought to have been this—this past year, but—but it's yours. Every penny of it. There's no one else to leave it to, and—"

"Uncle," interposed Clive, breaking in on the weak, gasping utterance, "forgive me for speaking as I must at such a time, but before you—before the end there is a wrong you must ease your soul by righting. Mr. Gault once told me that you—forgive me for saying it!—that you robbed Madge Brant's father of his fortune by a dishonest deal when he and you were partners, and that your great fortune is built up on the wreck of his. It—"

"Pshaw!" panted the dying man, with the peevish irritability of the very sick, "why bring up that old forgotten matter now? It's—it's long ago, and—and forgotten. Besides, it wasn't—wasn't robbery. Just a bit of business finesse. I—"

"Uncle!" cried Barry, his voice throbbing with an emotion he could not control, "can't you see the wrong you have done? The sin you have on your soul? Will you face God without atoning for it? Ah, can't—"

"Atoning?" echoed Fitch faintly, the word seeming to awaken a vague impression in his fading faculties. *"Atoning?* There's no use talking that way. Brant's dead. He—"

"He died crushed by the disgrace of the failure that made you rich," urged Barry, loathing himself for speaking thus brutally in the antechamber of death, yet nerving himself to the task. "He is dead, it is true, but his daughter is here."

For a long time Jonas Fitch lay with closed eyes, giving no sign by word or look that he had heard. Barry opened his lips to speak; but Madge, by a protesting gesture, urged him to silence.

The mere matter of wealth seemed to her, at this supreme crisis, of too slight moment to be worth the troubling of a dying man's ears.

At last Fitch's heavy lids lifted. And from the eyes beneath them the low cunning, the irritability, had fled, leaving a sort of awe, as though they gazed on the Unseen.

"You're right, lad," he whispered—"you're right. Do as you will, if—it isn't already too late."

"Whatever is done must be done quickly," said Mr. Gault in Clive's ear. "He will not rally again."

Barry darted out into the next apartment, and returned an instant later, bearing an inkhorn half full of the thick, malodorous fluid that Arabs miscall ink. In his other hand he held a long-empty fountain-pen.

Tearing a fly-leaf from the pocket Testament Mr. Gault had recently been reading to the reluctant invalid, Clive scrawled thereon three lines of writing. Signing his uncle's name to the document, he raised his uncle's head on his knee and read to him what he had written.

"All right! All right!" gasped Fitch. "It's lucky—lucky I gave you a law-school course, lad! Give me the pen."

By a mighty effort he closed his numbed fingers about the holder and affixed a straggling cross next to his signature. Then, as Mr. Gault and Barry witnessed the document, he sank back fainting. Again the *mastik* was poured between his withered lips and Madge chafed his death-cold hands.

It is perhaps the strongest proof of Mrs. Chittenden's stupefied condition that she neither moved nor spoke as she saw the cherished Fitch fortune willed away from the family.

Jonas suddenly opened his eyes with a feeble start.

"Barry," he whispered hoarsely, "you—you poor fool—*you've dis-*

inherited yourself!"

Again Jonas Fitch strove to speak, but could not. His head settled deeper in the pillow, and he lay very still. Mr. Gault leaned over him an instant, then rose, crossed the room and drew aside the outer flap of the tent.

The first gray tint of dawn was lighting up the blackness of the eastern sky. Madge, her face in her hands, fell to sobbing softly. Barry stood looking dully down at her bowed head, the precious scrap of paper still between his fingers.

Then from every quarter of the huge encampment arose a shout that echoed and reechoed far beyond the mist-choked river and the rolling plains beyond. Cannon and flint-locks were fired. Yells of joy mingled with tuneless hymns of thanksgiving from a thousand dervishes' throats.

The erstwhile silent dawn roared and throbbed with discordant tumult.

"What is it?" called Mr. Gault to one of the sentries. "Has the camp gone mad?"

"The Heaven-Born has awaked!" shouted the exultant Arab. "The divine trance is at an end!"

CHAPTER XV.

THE LAST HOPE.

FOUR days passed before El Mahdi found opportunity, in the dissemination of his latest batch of heavenly information, to devote any attention to the dispute between Darah and Abou Saoud.

In the meantime the remains of Jonas Fitch were interred by night and with such show of Christian burial as circumstances rendered possible.

His death, beyond the first shock, caused no great grief to any of the four survivors. Jonas had in no way endeared himself to anybody. To Clive he had always been a petty tyrant; to Mrs. Chittenden, the mere embodiment of great wealth. Thus, life in the goat-hair tent went

on much as before, the shadow of the approaching judgment at El Mahdi's hands crushing out all lesser thoughts and memories.

The camp, always noisy, had been in an unceasing uproar ever since the hour of El Mahdi's awaking. The Heaven-Born's first act was to call the entire host to arms, announcing that the Prophet had commanded him to abandon the policy of inactivity and storm the city.

The walls, Mohammed had assured him, would miraculously melt away before the first assault of the Faithful and the garrison be delivered paralyzed and helpless into their hands.

Despite the fact that in more than one previous vision El Mahdi had received precisely similar instruction and promises and had each time found an unexpected impediment to their fulfilment, the army went mad with joy at this latest repetition of the Prophet's orders. Forgotten were the previous disastrous assaults on the city, the incomprehensible failure of the divine pledges to materialize.

Arms were furbished up; the air was vibrant with the discordant prayers and shrieks of the dervishes; the Faithful were assured in a myriad tongues that Paradise awaited those who should fall, and that the whole earth should be the portion of the survivors.

Of all this preparation vague reports sifted to the captives. Ignorant of the failure of the many former futile attacks on the town, they trembled at the insane joy that swept through the encampment, and dreaded the loosing of such an avalanche of fanatic fury against the pitiful handful of English and Egyptian troops who defended the doomed city.

On the third morning the army streamed forth to battle. From the tent the Americans could see the clouds of fantastically dressed horsemen of the desert tribes file past, tossing their long guns high in air, screaming their uncouth war-cries, making their horses curvet and caracole madly. The scarlet burnooses, the white turbans, the gorgeous trappings, formed a blindingly brilliant carnival of color beneath the glare of the cloudless sky.

Behind the horsemen followed the mass of foot-soldiers, not marching in any semblance of order, but rushing onward in wild confusion, waving their weapons and calling on the name of Allah. Last came a disorganized throng of horsemen, infantry, camel-artillery, and dervishes.

Throughout the whole mob half-naked fakirs wormed their way, praying, exhorting, prophesying; slashing their own flesh with knives, hurling themselves on the ground in front of horses' feet, and in other mad ways arousing the fervor of the legions.

"It is a mob! A crazy rabble!" sneered Clive as he watched the human wave roll on in all its turgid force along the river-girt plain toward Khartum. "How can such men face organized troops? "

"How?" echoed Mr. Gault. "Because not one of those men fears death so long as he may slay before being slain. Because each of them is insane and knows no indecision or caution. Wherever they have met the Egyptian troops in open field they have borne them down and annihilated them by sheer force of numbers and by that same reckless courting of danger. They fare less well against walled towns. El Obeid held out against them for weeks, so Darah told me. But where their impetus cannot crush their patience starves out their enemies."

Thus it was that the hosts of the Mahdi rushed to the storming of Khartum at sunrise of January 20, 1885. Throughout the long, suspenseful day the waiting captives could hear the reverberation of distant cannon, the purring of Gatling, and the petulant snap-snap-snap of flint-lock and rifle. At times faint echoes of cheer or yell reached their straining ears.

And in the first gray of dusk backward reeled the broken fragments of that Heaven-directed assault, followed by the baffled, decimated main body. Not a kite nor a vulture was left soaring in the skies above.

The attack had failed. There was rich harvest for the birds of prey.

Against the furious onslaught of the hordes the walls of Khartum had stood firm; the plucky handful of defenders, guided by the veteran skill of their leader, had held their own against a force that outnumbered them by more than twenty to one.

All that long night the camp was shaken by desolate wailings and lamentations. In the morning, these died away, and the army gradually began to recover, through the fakirs' exhortations, a portion of its old-time confidence.

But the ever-present crowd of angry fanatics that besieged the captives' tent was visibly increased, and their threats and maledictions redoubled.

Darah, whom none of the Americans had seen for two days, visited them soon after sunrise. He was haggard of face, and across his cheek was a bullet-graze.

"The Heaven-Born," he began without preliminaries, "will judge you this morning. Prepare to go to him."

Stepping into the farther compartment, he beckoned Madge to follow him out of ear-shot of the rest.

"Miss Brant," he said as the surprised girl joined him, "Zebehr, Faragh, and others high in office have declared to the Heaven-Born that yesterday's attack failed because he harbored in his host four unbelievers. The Prophet, they swear, is wroth at such sacrilege and has turned his favor from us until you all be put to death."

"But," objected Madge, with sad irony, "surely this all-seeing Prophet of yours must have known, during El Mahdi's trance, that we were here! Isn't it strange he didn't mention his displeasure at the time?"

"It is not for me to question the wisdom of the Most High," returned the sheik, "nor have I come to speak of that. El Mahdi is incensed against me for sparing the lives of infidels and for bringing such folk here. He will order your death, yours and the others'. There can be no doubt of it. This, then, is what I have come to say to you before leading you to the Holy Tent. Will you hear me in patience?"

She bowed bewildered assent.

"Do you know why I snatched you and your friends from death in the Bishareen Desert?"

"For our ransom. It—"

"Ransom!" he repeated in infinite scorn. "The cattle and the wealth of a million *feddan* (acres) are mine. What need have I for dirty Feringhee gold?"

"Then, what reason had you for—"

"My reason was—yourself!"

"Sheik Darah!"

"Hear me to an end. When I captured your party at the temples of Ibrim I was minded to slay you all where you stood. But *you* looked me in the eye and answered my questions as no other woman ever dared to. And my heart was as water at thought of your death.

"That I might have time for decision I brought the Feringhi to

camp. There, because my will was opposed, and because a low slave-trader set at naught my wishes, I snatched you all from the grasp of those who had dared to gainsay me. Still was I minded to kill the others, for they but hindered me, and still was undecided what should be your fate.

"I planned, at first, to send you to my own village, in the mountains of Mekheir, there to await my return. But as days passed on I found I could not live far from you. And as the rest were your friends and you would sorrow for their absence, I spared them. Thus, a woman no larger than a child made weak the heart of a man who before had never known weakness."

He was speaking in Arabic, rapidly, fervently, as she had never before heard him speak.

"From month to month," he went on, "I planned to end the waiting; to slay the rest and to wed you—for I, alone of the great leaders of our land, have no wives—to wed you in the barbarous Feringhee Christian fashion, if need be, though Gehenna should claim my spirit in punishment for the blasphemy against our religion. Yet I forbore, because I feared you.

"Yes, *feared* you—slip of a girl as you are. I, who would have borne away any other woman were her whole tribe in pursuit, feared to wed you against your will. So it was until we came here. And now the hour has struck when I can delay no more, for fate rides hard behind us."

He paused, but the girl was speechless.

"There is but one hope for your life," he proceeded. "Outside this tent my own men are gathered. In the center of their ranks are the two fleetest horses in all the Sudan. We will mount them, you and I, and sweep through the camp and out to the north. My spirit will be forever accursed for turning from the field in the day of Holy War, but—my heart is even now in the center of the eternal fires, so, what matter! Come!"

"Sheik Darah!" gasped Madge, aghast, shrinking back to avoid his arms.

Then, gathering her senses, she asked dazedly:

"You would have me desert my friends—leave to death those who would protect me with their lives? Would such a woman be worthy any man's love?"

"It is as I feared," he muttered, "and I have made preparation. I knew you would not leave them. Let them come. I have power to save you all. It is a small price to pay for your love."

"For my—love!" echoed the girl.

She stood for an instant wordless, motionless, her mind alive with hurrying thoughts.

By this sacrifice of herself she could give freedom to three helpless fellow countrymen. Mrs. Chittenden, old, feeble, stupefied by fear; Mr. Gault, kindly, ever tender and thoughtful of her comfort; Barry Clive, the man whose mental and moral reincarnation she had effected—all these would be snatched from the jaws of death by her consent to become Darah's wife.

She had read of women who made equally great sacrifices for others, and—in books—she had admired (and had longed, woman-like, to emulate) their heroism. But in real life—

Clive's eyes as they had looked deathless love into her own rose before her mind with startling vividness. Ere she herself was aware of it, her resolve was taken.

"Sheik Darah," she said, all hesitation and fear gone, "I do not love you. If I married you without love I should commit mortal sin. Moreover, two of those whom I should thus save would far sooner face death than accept life at such a cost. If we must die, let us die as Americans and good Christians should. I cannot accept your offer."

He was looking at her, his deep eyes aglow, but even as he looked the glow died from them, and in place the dull, hopeless look of the Oriental fatalist settled over his features.

"*Tamam!*" (enough), he said shortly. "A lesser soul would have consented and either have learned to return my love—for women are pliable—or else have died, in time, of grief. A less honest woman would have seemed to accept, and when safe would have laughed in my face. *You* could have done neither. But," he went on, with a new flicker of the dead fire in his eyes, "what is to hinder me from carrying you by force to my waiting men and riding away with you?"

He stepped forward again, his arms outstretched as though to seize her. White as death, but unshrinking, she stood still and looked him fearlessly in the eyes. For a full half-minute they confronted each other thus, in a battle of eyes, a war of wills.

Darah lowered his gaze. His arms fell limp at his sides.

"Inshalla!" he murmured. "You were right. You knew I could not do it."

He turned away. Moved by an uncontrollable impulse of pity that so proud a spirit should stand thus humbled, she made as though to speak; but he checked her with a gesture.

"The bitterness of death is past," he said. "All that has been said is dead and forgotten. It is ill to wake the dead."

Moving into the central apartment, he gave curt directions to the others to prepare for the visit to El Mahdi.

Five minutes later, the quartet of Americans, surrounded by picked Mekheir guards, stepped out into the open air, for the first time in three weeks. Their advent was received with a fresh outburst of howls and curses from the Faithful.

The air was thick with missiles, and fanatics surged forward toward them. But at a shouted word from Darah a thousand fierce-eyed men of the Mekheir hurled themselves upon the rabble, driving them back at lance-point. Then they formed a close-packed cordon about the prisoners, and the march began.

The distance to El Mahdi's headquarters was a bare half-mile from the sheik's camping-ground. Yet the progress was slow, and every foot of the way was stubbornly disputed by fresh detachments of Suda-nese, dervishes, and fakirs, who hurled themselves furiously against that compact wedge of fighting men in a frenzied effort to get at the captives.

At length the prisoners and their escorts came out into a cleared space in whose center stood a great tent of green, ornate with tarnished cloth of gold. Above it waved the huge green banner of the Prophet; and at its door stood twenty white-robed Sudanese with drawn simitars.

As this sacred space was reached the mob fell back, leaving the Americans and their Mekheir guards to advance unmolested.

The Mekheirs halted, drawing aside on either hand. And down the lane thus formed Darah and his four prisoners made their way to the door of the great green tent and entered the presence of El Mahdi.

CHAPTER XVI.

THE SERPENT OF THE NILE.

FROM the glare of the outer day to the cool gloom of the tent was so sudden a transition that for an instant Madge Brant, who had entered slightly in advance of her three compatriots, could distinguish nothing clearly save a dim group of gaudily dressed forms grouped about a dais at the farther end of the pavilion.

Her vision clearing as she and her friends came to a halt at a signal from Darah, she began to glance with interest about the enclosure.

The tent was almost wholly devoid of furnishings, except for the raised platform and the solitary divan that crowned it. On every side of this platform men were standing, perhaps a dozen in all.

Some were black, some yellow, of face. Nearly all wore gorgeous apparel. Among these counselors of El Mahdi Madge's quick eye singled out Abou Saoud and the black Abyssinian who had welcomed Darah. Somewhat to the rear she distinguished the bald head, parchment visage, and waist-long white beard of Zebehr, the chief fakir, who a year before had pleaded for the death of the Americans.

Before the dais stood six armed Sudanese guards—the "Fuzzy-Wuzzy" type which Kipling has since immortalized. They leaned on their long spears and eyed the prisoners with malevolent curiosity.

On the divan reclined a man the elaborate negligence of whose dress sharply contrasted with the brilliant costumes of those about him. At first glance there was little to remark in this ill-clad native's appearance.

Thin almost to emaciation, his brown face revealed an odd mingling of mysticism and cunning. A straggling black beard covered the lower half of it, scarcely concealing the cruel lines of the well-nigh lipless mouth. The head was crowned by an enormous green turban, and the man's only other garment was a soiled white robe hanging loosely about his figure.

But it was when he slowly raised his lowered lids to gaze on the newcomers that Madge realized the tremendous power and intellect that lay behind his indifferent stare. The forehead was flat and retreat-

ing, but the expression of the eyes belied any hint of stupidity.

These eyes were small, unwinking, intensely bright. But their oddest characteristic lay in the fact that while one was as black as a negro's the other was a pale blue.

Madge dimly remembered reading in school that the Prophet Mohammed had been possessed of this ocular peculiarity, as had his successor, Ali. She recalled, too, having heard Darah say that the mere fact of those ill-matched eyes had of themselves convinced many a waverer that the Dongola carpenter's son was the true successor to Mohammed.

So, this insignificant man with the odd eyes and dirty robe was the Heaven-Born Mahdi, at whose word a whole continent had been convulsed! Curiosity, for the moment, drove fear from the girl's brain, and she stood gazing with frank intentness at the epileptic genius on the dais before her.

"Beloved of Allah!" spoke Abou Saoud, breaking the silence that had fallen since the entrance of the Americans, "these are the Feringhi. And there," pointing to Darah, "is the man who stole them from me."

El Mahdi made no immediate reply; but lay gazing with moody interest on the four foreigners, his bicolored eyes drifting from one face to another, taking in every detail of dress and feature, and seeming to read the very souls of the quartet. At length, the scrutiny over, he looked at Darah, who, erect and expressionless, stood in front of his captives.

Then the Heaven-Born spoke, in a high, light voice that held, none the less, a carrying quality of great penetration.

"You have heard the charge," he said, his eyes still bent on Darah; "is it the truth?"

"Most holy," replied Darah, his voice betraying none of the submission of his words, "I have already told you all. It is for you to judge. I demand these prisoners. They are mine, not Abou Saoud's. Yet I bow to your judgment."

"Do you know their barbarous speech?" pursued the Mahdi. "I would question them."

"Three of them have learned the Prophet's tongue, holiness."

"It is well." He turned suddenly on Mr. Gault. *"Lá ilâhâ-llah"* (There

is but one God), he droned, after the manner of a muezzin calling the Faithful to prayer.

"God is God, by whatever name He be called," acquiesced Mr. Gault, somewhat puzzled. "And there is but one God."

"Siädnah Mahmoud râsoul Allah" (Our lord, Mohammed, is God's Prophet), continued El Mahdi, apparently surprised by the "infidel's" prompt assent to the former statement.

"I have no belief in the so-called Prophet," replied the old gentleman, a trifle hotly.

After his words a gasp of horror shook the gaudy group about the dais. Hands flew to sword-hilt, and Zebehr shrieked aloud for the instant destruction of the blasphemers.

"Were your life to be spared by my infinite clemency," queried the Mahdi when the clamor had subsided, "would you abandon your pagan fetish of Christianity and embrace the true faith? Think well on the joys of Paradise and reply."

"I am already of the true faith," was the quick response. "The faith for which my ancestors suffered martyrdom."

"He means the faith of the Christians, oh, Son of Heaven," interpolated Zebehr. "The dog blasphemes! "

"And *you*," urged El Mahdi, turning from Mr. Gault to Barry Clive, "will you renounce your false creed and be of the Prophet's children? "

"No," retorted Clive, with tactless candor, "I will not. I have given all too little thought to religion in my day. Once I was fool enough to think I was an agnostic. But here for the first time I understand all that Christianity means. And when I see the 'Prophet's children,' as you call them, I prefer the beliefs of my countrymen. If I am to die I will die a Christian, not an unwashed heathen."

He spoke boldly, expecting at each word to feel a score of swords meet in his body. But he was in the mood to die bravely. His love, as he felt, rejected, his fortune gone, the faith of his fathers slandered—all tended to arouse in him a devil of desperation that cast out fear, and even common prudence, from his heart.

At his rash speech a murmur again arose from about the dais, but a faint smile contorted El Mahdi's features. The young man's courage, apparently, seemed to him something mildly amusing.

"And your women?" he asked, with the slight accent of contempt a

true Oriental always imparts to any reference to the weaker sex.

Madge opened her lips, but Clive forestalled her.

"They think as we think," he answered. "Our creed is their creed."

"As you will," answered the Heaven-Born carelessly. "I have already wasted much breath on mere unbelievers. The sentence—I speak with the tongue of the Prophet—is death! "

Darah, through all his armor of stoicism, flinched at the word. The gesture was so slight as to escape all eyes but El Mahdi's.

"The sentence will be carried out under my orders, oh, Darah," he said. "This morning I gave orders for videttes to be thrown southward beyond the city, toward Shederrah. Follow them—you and your whole command—at once. I place the expedition under your command in proof that my face is not hidden from you because of your late sin. Go, oh, son."

Darah hesitated for the remotest fraction of a second, his eyes on Madge Brant. His face was cold as a stone mask of despair, but his eyes smoldered like dull embers. Then he salaamed to the Heaven-Born and departed.

For in that day no true Mussulman would so much as dream of disobeying or questioning the inspired one's lightest decree.

With Darah's departure all the Americans felt vaguely that they had been cut off from the last link that bound them to earth. Their own world lay far behind them. Between themselves and it stretched the fanatic forces of all Islam.

Death looked them in the eyes. And with the calm born of great crises they returned look for look.

Scarce had Darah passed out between the double row of guards when Abou Saoud, relieved of the fear occasioned by the formidable Mekheir sheik's presence, cast himself face downward on the earthen floor at the foot of the dais.

"Holy One," he wailed, "I cry for justice! These unbelievers were delivered into my hands as slaves. I have given much to the sacred cause, and will give more. But is it just that I be robbed—first by that desert thief, then by your decree?"

Clive could scarcely believe his ears. Where Darah, who knew no fear, had not dared to plead against the Mahdi's decision, this fat slave-merchant was actually questioning the divine justice.

Yet even Zebehr raised no outcry at the sacrilege, nor did El Mahdi at once rebuke his rash follower. The Heaven-Born sat for a full minute in silence, glancing from the prostrate Abou to the Americans, his uncanny, varicolored eyes inscrutable.

"The Faithful," said he, at length, "from Cairo to Kordofan, have named me The Serpent of the Nile. And the Prophet has mercifully endowed me with a wisdom great as that of the serpent god of Memnon that our ancestors in bygone ages were wont to worship. The trail of my armies is from the rising to the setting of the sun, and the earth rests within their coils. Yet a slave-merchant arises at the last to doubt my wisdom."

He paused. Though Abou Saoud still lay prostrate on his face, Madge could see that he had not paled as he formerly did under Gordon's few stern words of rebuke; nor did the fat body tremble.

Moreover, the excitable group about the dais looked on with indifference. And at all this the girl wondered.

"I do not doubt your Wisdom, Holiness, in decreeing these infidels' death," replied Abou, with sullen persistence, "but they are my slaves, and I ask justice—the justice that Gordon Pasha ever accorded to the meanest."

"You name *me*—the mouthpiece of Allah—with that infidel hound!" cried El Mahdi, while this time the knot of emirs murmured angrily.

Yet, to Madge's womanly intuition, there appeared something forced in El Mahdi's indignation; something perfunctory in the emirs' answering wrath.

"Nay, Holiness," protested Abou, "I name you with Gordon Pasha because of all living men Gordon Pasha has ever seemed to me the highest, the noblest. I say it—*I,* who once and again repaid his generosity with treachery, ingrate that I was. Now that I shall never see him again, I—"

"Peace!" commanded the Mahdi, his high, thin voice ringing out piercing and compelling as the note of a fife. "Abou Saoud, I would have raised you from the dust to the very gates of Paradise and made your name a power in the land. But you turn as did the wife of Lot and look back with longing on the foul corruption you have quitted. Such men are not for me and for the empire that Allah shall give me

to rule over. From my presence and from my holy host shall you go, an outcast. And more—the abode of the Faithful shall not be defiled with your presence. You have sighed for Gordon Pasha—on whom be confusion!—and to Gordon Pasha you shall go.

"Yes," the shrill voice rising in a pitch of grim, ironic humor, "to Gordon Pasha shall you go this very day, and with you you shall take the four Feringhi you claim as your slaves. Twice of old did Gordon Pasha crush out the slave-trade, and the thought of slavery is an abomination to him. Go to him with these your slaves and learn how he will receive you!"

Abou Saoud had scrambled to his feet, and now he faced his judge not without a certain defiant dignity.

"Be it so!" he said. "I go gladly. Even should my lord, Gordon Pasha, slay me in his wrath, I shall at least die at the hand of the earth's greatest."

Though the emirs still stood calmly looking on, the Mahdi's brow contracted at these words and a blaze of wrath sprang into his strange eyes. But he controlled himself, and repeated:

"Go! I will give orders, and the way shall lie clear before you, as though you were a leper. Go, and"—with a gesture of contempt toward the prisoners—"take these with you. But your wealth in gold and camels and servants is the Prophet's, and with the Prophet's host it shall remain. All save the Cairene, your body-servant. He is idle and worthless. Bear him as a gift from El Mahdi to the dog whom presently I shall slay. Go!"

Somehow—in just what manner or order they never clearly remembered—the four Americans found themselves outside the presence-tent, once more in the glare of daylight. With them was Abou Saoud, and behind him skulked a pitiable figure in ragged remnants of what had once been the resplendent blue-and-gold livery of a Cook dragoman.

The excitement they had undergone had robbed the four, temporarily, of any great power of surprise or other sensation. So it was merely with a vague thrill of passing amazement that they recognized in Abou's wretched body-servant the once ornate Halil.

Above, the afternoon sun beat down pitilessly from a copper sky, and over their heads wheeled and screamed the myriad kites, ravens,

and vultures that were so inseparable and so significant a part of the Mahdi's horde.

But where an hour before they had been assailed by vituperations and threats, the outcasts saw now on all sides naught but averted faces.

No crowd awaited their appearance. No man so much as looked at them as, following dumbly in the wake of Abou Saoud, they made their way through the interminable camp and out into the wide water-side field that separated it from Khartum.

Madge, gradually recovering her wits, whispered in Barry Clive's ear as they trudged along:

"I do not understand this wonderful good fortune, but I do not trust it. There is something behind it all. What can it mean? "

"Nonsense!" replied Clive. "It means that by the rarest stroke of luck we are free. It's like waking from some horrible nightmare to find oneself safe."

"Perhaps so," assented Madge, looking about her with a little involuntary shudder. "But—but I'm not yet quite sure we're really awake."

CHAPTER XVII.

THE CITY OF SILENCE.

ON the little peninsula formed by the juncture of the White and the Blue Nile stands the town of Khartum, capital, chief city, and key of the whole Sudan.

Within its walls for nearly a year General Charles George Gordon had been closely besieged. Although all attempts to storm the place had been frustrated by the heroism of his little mixed garrison of Egyptian and British troops, ammunition had run pitiably short, and desperate ruses were constantly necessary in order to procure sufficient food.

During that year no word from the outside world had penetrated the beleaguered city, yet every member of the garrison—Gordon most of all—was buoyed up by a sublime faith in Great Britain's power and willingness to fly to the rescue. Each day, from the top of the Govern-

ment House, the Nile was scanned as far as telescope could carry for a glimpse of the long-expected river steamers bearing troops to raise the siege. In each of the many fresh disturbances at the Mahdi's camp the defenders saw the onslaught of an overland relief army.

Though almost a full year had rolled by without sign of these reenforcements, it never for an instant occurred to Gordon or his men that such aid would not sooner or later arrive, and the garrison fell to conjecturing the various possible reasons that might have unavoidably delayed the rescuers.

In their most pessimistic moments they never once dreamed the truth—that the British government, hampered by Gladstone's policy of postponement and compromise, had for months contented itself with sending windy and futile messages on the subject to the helpless Khedive, and had at length countenanced the outfitting of two such expeditions, both of them so utterly inadequate as to be easily annihilated by the Mahdi long before coming within sight of Khartum. Nor did they guess that even now, far to the north, a similar relief army—small and ill equipped for so gigantic a hazard—was slowly working its way up the Nile, fighting for every mile it gained, a force too puny to lift the siege of Khartum, but pushing on, nevertheless, in the hope of aiding Gordon and his men to escape from the death-trap in which they were caught.

Late one afternoon, as Gordon Pasha was making his rounds of inspection, Captain Kelleher, his aide, came hurrying up to him in great excitement.

"Sentry at the north gate, sir," he said as he saluted, "reports approach of six persons across the plain from the direction of the Mahdist camp. Says two of them look, at that distance, like women— *white* women."

"White women!" echoed Gordon. *"Here?"*

Before the aide could continue his report, General Gordon was striding rapidly toward the gate-house. From the parapet above the gate he looked down into the plain below.

The six strangers had advanced closer to the walls by this time, and were distinctly visible.

In the van waddled a gorgeously attired Egyptian, very fat and

very awkward. In one hand he bore a dirty white rag, which he waved above his head from time to time in token of peace.

Gordon recognized him at a glance, and frowned. But his expression turned to wonder as he glanced past Abou at the five who were following wearily in his wake.

Of these five, one wore the tattered costume of a dragoman. The remaining four were clad in nondescript odds and ends of garments that would have been scorned by a rag-picker.

Their faces were all tanned to the color of an Arab's, their hair was long and unkempt, and the two men among them wore flowing beards that had known neither shears nor razor in twelve months.

But it was on the women that Gordon's marveling eyes were riveted. Tanned and weirdly appareled though they were, they were unmistakably white women.

One of them was old and walked feebly, leaning on the arm of the younger of the two men. The second woman was young—a mere girl—and despite her odd attire, showed signs of grace and beauty.

Five minutes later the refugees were safe within the gates of Khartum and found themselves the center of an eager, curious group in the courtyard.

Gordon's eyes, after that first incredulous amazement at seeing Caucasian women in such a place and at such a time, had not strayed from the face of Abou Saoud. Now he stepped forward and confronted his former satellite.

"Why do you come here?" he demanded, with stern displeasure. "I once forbade you to reenter the Sudan. Are you eager for prison, that you—"

"I am come," replied Abou, "to throw myself on the justice and the mercy of the Feringhi. For mine own have cast me out. If that justice and mercy lead to a prison-cell or to the headsman, then be it so. For myself I make no plea.

"Once and twice I sinned against you and betrayed your trust. Death be my portion if it be your wish. But I entreat succor and protection for these four men and women of your own race whom I have brought here for safety. I have brought them to you when I might have cast them adrift, yonder on the plain, and escaped. Let them say if I lie."

"He is speaking the truth," volunteered old Mr. Gault, pressing forward, eager to set their conductor right in Gordon's prejudiced opinion. "He brought us to you after El Mahdi gave us to him as his slaves. The Mahdi drove this man from camp because he dared to speak well of you, sir. Let me explain."

Hurriedly, vehemently, the kind old gentleman gave a sketchy recital of the scene in El Mahdi's tent and the casting forth of Abou.

"And when we were fairly clear of the camp," he ended, "this man turned to us, gave us our freedom, and begged our forgiveness for—"

"Abou Saoud," cried Gordon, flushing, "why did you not tell me of this at the first?"

"To what end, *Saadat-el-Basha* [Excellency]? I had twice sinned again you. How could I think you would credit anything I might say?"

Kelleher and one or two others who had vivid recollections of Abou Saoud in the old slave-trade days glanced at one another in half-incredulous perplexity. But Gordon, whose chief fault as an executive had ever been his readiness to believe the good and his distaste for crediting evil, looked with growing kindliness on his former subordinate.

"I will give you audience later, Abou Saoud," he murmured hastily, as he turned from the slave-trader toward the Americans.

"You are very welcome here, one and all," Gordon added, with the grave, old-fashioned courtesy that was ever the most winning element in his manner. "You look wearied from your long journey. You must rest and eat before I annoy you with questions. I—"

"General Gordon," interposed Madge Brant, stepping forth from among the others and holding out her hand in a frank, childlike manner that struck him as vaguely familiar, "am I so changed that you have forgotten me? I am the American tourist you were so kind to in Cairo last year."

Before she had half finished speaking the general's face was alight with recognition. He grasped her proffered hand warmly in both his own, and smiled down with genuine delight as he recalled the form and features of the American maiden who had attracted so much attention at the Khedivial ball.

It was hard, at first glance, for him to reconcile that memory with the wild garb, unbound hair, and bronzed face of the girl before him.

"Why, my dear Miss Brant," he gasped, "have you dropped from the clouds to brighten our tedious loneliness? A thousand welcomes! And your friends? Are they fellow countrymen of—"

Mrs. Chittenden, Mr. Gault, and Barry Clive were in turn presented to the cordial pasha, who accorded to each a gracious word of welcome and kindness. He then turned to his aide and gave hurried directions that apartments in Government House be set in order for the visitors.

"I am sorry to be forced to offer you siege fare and siege accommodations," he resumed, as he turned again to his guests, "but, such as it is, it gives us all great pleasure to extend to you the hospitality of Khartum."

"General," spoke up Mr. Gault, "if that same hospitality includes a razor, a pair of shears, and some whole clothing, my friend Clive and I can ask nothing better of life."

The old gentleman's eagerness, combined with his rueful glance at his own attire, raised a general laugh, and in that laugh the last vestige of formal restraint between host and guests was swept away.

"The bazaars here—such of them as are still open—should solve the clothes problem with ease," answered Gordon. "Make out your lists, and any sort of costume, from a burnoose and turban to a second-hand tourist suit, shall be brought to you within the hour. And I will send Hassan, my own barber, to you."

"Allah be praised!" sighed Barry, in passable imitation of the fakirs' whine. "For months I have dreamed every night of clothes—clothes without patches, and all made out of the same material instead of a crazy-quilt pattern. I've dreamed of razors, too, and baths. Those three things have seemed brighter in my visions than a peep into the Prophet's Paradise."

The general's glance had caught the strained impatience on the faces of the bystanders during the foregoing colloquy, and had readily translated it.

"One moment!" he said, as the party were about to start for Government House. "I will not weary you with questions until you are rested, but there is one thing that every man here has been burning to ask, and I fear that further delay will make them throw discipline and etiquette to the four winds and shout the query in unison. During

your wanderings, or at the Mahdi's camp, have you heard anything of the relief expedition that is on its way here? And if so, what has detained it, and when may we expect it to appear?"

A feverish stir and whisper ran through the bystanders, and they leaned breathlessly forward to catch the strangers' answer. Madge's eyes grew moist and her heart beat fast. For that subdued expression told her more clearly than could a thousand words the tale of agonized suspense.

How could she or her friends reveal to these heroic fellows the story of the massacre of Hicks Pasha and his men, or of gallant Stewart's fatal, futile dash southward toward the doomed city? There was a moment's pause, none daring to reply, yet all aware of the painful, strained attention with which their hearers awaited the long-deferred tidings.

"You forget, general," said Madge at length, "that we have been prisoners for a year, and have been in the Bishareen Desert, far off the line of march that any English or Egyptian army would take."

At her evasion a stifled sigh broke from a few of the listening men, but Gordon's pleasant smile did not relax. The pasha was a fatalist—as much so as any born Oriental.

Throughout life he had had calm, strongly religious faith in his own destiny and mission. Opposed a thousand times to seemingly annihilating obstacles, this fatalism—or trust in God—had thus far overcome them all. Nor did he doubt the continued ascendency of his star or the timely arrival of the expected relief army.

The man who had ridden, unguarded and alone, into the mighty army of the Wang rebels in China and had bent that murderous host to his wishes could feel no real dread of a Sudanese fanatic's rabble.

"Come," he said, preparing to lead the way to Government House. "Mrs. Chittenden, Miss Brant, here comes Kelleher's *cavasse* [native orderly] with donkeys for you both. Kelleher will escort you. I must stop and have a word with Abou Saoud. Abou—"

He checked himself in bewilderment as his keen gaze wandered over the cluster of faces that surrounded him.

Abou Saoud was nowhere to be seen; neither was Halil, the dragoman. Unobserved, they had long since vanished through the crowd.

CHAPTER XVIII.
A MAN, A MAID, AND MOONLIGHT.

IN the lofty stone veranda of Government House, under the dim glow of hanging lamps, sat Gordon Pasha, one or two members of his suite, and his American guests. Below them, on all sides, lay the sleeping city—for the hour was late—and save for the challenge of an occasional distant sentry, the tropical night lay still as death.

The soft lamplight flickered across Gordon's face, mellowing the hard lines that had not been there a year ago and bringing back to features and figure the semblance of youth. Nor was this youthful aspect due wholly to the light effect.

Ever since the arrival of the refugees, three days earlier, the pasha had been in high spirits. Their advent had lightened his year of loneliness and had freshened him by contact with congenial spirits.

In the four Americans themselves the three days had wrought a physical miracle. Clive and Mr. Gault, clean-shaven and in the garments of civilization, had wholly lost the "wild man" appearance on which Madge had been wont to rally them, and presented the picture of two remarkably healthy, vigorous men in the pink of condition. The tan of a year's suns still rendered their faces the hue of mahogany, and the desert life had given them a freedom of step and ease of carriage not to be acquired by city dwellers.

As for Madge, one must needs have looked a second time to recognize in her the picturesque gipsy girl of the previous week. She and Mrs. Chittenden had procured at the bazaars European garments such as had been in the height of fashion at Cairo seven years before. Still, the costumes were of a distinctly civilized stamp, and as such both women had received them in a flutter of feminine rapture.

Under their influence and that of comparative security, Mrs. Chittenden was rapidly emerging from her recent apathy. She had already recovered enough of her old-time disposition to renew her former complaints and to make one or two delightfully characteristic and unpleasant remarks.

"It is inconsiderate of me to keep you all up so late to-night,"

Gordon was saying. "I beg you will forgive me and place all the blame—as I place all the thanks—on Miss Brant's shoulders: The birthday idea was hers."

"I'll gladly accept the blame for the sake of the thanks," retorted Madge gaily. "I'm glad my silly little plan amused you."

"What was this plan?" asked Kelleher, who had joined the veranda group only a moment or two before.

"Why," explained the girl, "General Gordon happened to mention at dinner that to-morrow is his birthday—your thirtieth or thirty-fifth, general?—I forget which, and—"

"My fifty-second, my dear young lady," replied Gordon, with mock solemnity, "an advanced age that should protect me from such flippant questions."

"But the plan?" persisted Kelleher.

"We got to talking of birthdays in general—as well as in general's—and I said that when I and my brothers were children my father and mother always let us sit up till midnight on the eve of our birthdays as a special treat. Then as the clock struck twelve the rest of the family would all wish us many happy returns of the day and give us our presents before packing us off to bed. A most unhygienic custom for growing children, I suppose, but to us it was always an event with a capital 'E.'

"So, Miss Brant suggested that we import that delightfully inadvisable American practise to Khartum," added Gordon, "and sit up to 'see my birthday in.' It is the first birthday celebration of any kind I've had in thirty years, so I seconded the motion. And in honor of the event I have ordered up the cellar's last two remaining bottles of champagne. At the stroke of twelve the glasses shall be charged and a round-robin of healths drunk."

As he finished speaking two men mounted the broad stone steps leading up from the square before Government House. They wore the uniforms of Egyptian cavalrymen, and were Mohammed Bey Mustafa and Ibrahim Bey Rushdi, captains of the garrison.

Gordon rose from his chair to return their salutes, and excusing himself to his guests, walked with the two cavalrymen to the far end of the veranda.

"Well," he asked as they passed out of ear-shot of the others, "what

news of Abou Saoud?"

"None, excellency," reported Rushdi. "We and our *cavasses* made the house-to-house search you ordered and questioned all who had ever known the man. There was no trace of him."

"Strange!" murmured Gordon. "I cannot understand why he should have deserted the Mahdi and entered Khartum only to leave again at once. Could his courage have given out at the last moment over the fear of possible punishment? But it could scarcely be that; I spoke to him kindly, and I would have taken him back into my service."

"Yet," suggested Mustafa, "I have known Abou Saoud for fifteen years, and I never yet heard of his acting without an object."

"But what object had he in coming here if he meant to desert at once?" argued the pasha. "If he entered the city in order to spy on us, why did he not stay? Or if he is in hiding here for that purpose, how can he ascertain anything regarding our numbers and provisions without going about? If he had stirred abroad some one must surely have recognized him before now. It is a mystery."

"I only trust, excellency, we may find it nothing more serious than a mystery," answered Mustafa.

"We are safe from any harm he can do us," rejoined Gordon carelessly. "Even if he carries away full reports of our condition, he can only tell his master we are faithful, sufficiently provisioned, and too powerfully entrenched for a body of mere dervishes to move us.

"Through all my days," he added, "I shall be proud that, though wealth and honors from El Mahdi would reward a traitor, my garrison, to a man, have remained true to their flag and their general throughout a year of hardship. Many have been the chances to betray us, yet every man has been loyal. It is an honor to command such soldiers."

Meantime, at the other end of the veranda, Barry Clive, taking advantage of a brisk discussion into which Mr. Gault, his aunt, and the rest had been drawn, crossed to where Madge reclined in a long deck-chair midway between the glow from the lamps and the flood of tropical moonlight.

Clive leaned against one of the veranda pillars, looking down at her. In his heart the hopeless love he bore the girl struggled madly for escape in speech.

But remembering her former injunction, he fought back the delirious impulse and stood, in mute adoration, looking his fill on the dainty, graceful, childlike figure in its filmy white draperies. She was another being, outwardly, from the travel-stained maiden of the desert at whose side he had ridden for so many hundred miles. Yet to him then, no less than now, she had been the perfection of womanhood, of all that was gentle, uplifting, lovely.

Madge, returning his gaze, read the love-tale written so clearly in the brown, handsome face, and a great joy possessed her in the reading. She had been so brave in forcing her heart to close its doors against him until he should have had opportunity to test the durability and fervor of his new-awakened regard!

She had been wise in doing so. Oh, very, *very* wise. Again and again she had reminded herself of her wisdom.

Yet as her eyes met his she knew that were he to speak again now her heart would turn traitor and throw wide its gates to him. And despite this knowledge, a fierce yearning possessed her to hear the words of love that she had once checked upon his lips.

But he was silent, and she then saw in his eyes the hopelessness, as well as the all-compelling intensity, of his love; and, seeing it, was miserable; and, woman-like, blamed him for his lack of courage.

"King Cophetua," she said at last, with a nervous little laugh, "you look very statuesque and impressive standing there, but you are not exactly entertaining. Can you find nothing to say in this first *tête-à-tête* we have had for so long?"

Still he was blind to the story her dark eyes told; deaf to the thrill she could not wholly banish from her voice.

"No, Beggar Maid," he replied, with forced lightness, "the discrowned Cophetua can find no words of sufficient wit to entertain his most disloyal vassal. He can only stand and adore."

He made as though to move away and rejoin the others, when she called him back.

"Barry," she whispered.

He paused and returned to her side. But at his obedience her sudden impulse fled, driven away by a swift onrush of shyness. And thus for an instant they faced each other awkwardly. Then—

"You called me," he said.

"Yes," she answered vaguely, seizing on the first pretext that presented itself.

"I want to speak to you about something. About—about your splendid self-sacrifice in inducing Mr. Fitch to leave me the fortune he won from my father. At the time," she hurried on as he was about to interrupt impatiently, "such great issues stood before us, and we were so near to the presence of death, that mere wealth seemed to me a small thing. But—"

"On the very day we reached Khartum you said all this and more," broke in Clive, refusing to be longer silenced, "and I begged you then never to speak of it any more. I—"

"But I *must* speak of it," she insisted. "It was an heroic thing in you to throw away your whole fortune for my sake. It was an act not one man in a million would have had the courage to perform. But now that you are without means, what will you do?"

"*Do?*" he retorted. "I shall do what every sane, normal man of my age ought to do. I shall go to work. I had planned, even before uncle's death, that if ever I got back to America I should be content no longer to lie back on the money of others, but would fill a man's place and do a man's work in the world. Before I left home I was a loafer. And America is no place for loafers. I have a good education; I was admitted to the bar the month before I sailed for the East. With such an equipment and good health, what more can a man desire?"

He spoke earnestly, carried away by the recital of his plans. There was in his incisive, energetic tones no hint of the drawling superiority that had of old so angered Madge.

"You are right!" she exclaimed. "And every one whose opinion is worth having will honor you for your resolve. I *know* you will succeed. I—"

"If anything can make me win it will be your faith in me, Madge. But for you I should always have been—"

"By the way," she broke in irrelevantly, "is Mr. Fitch's will quite safe? You're sure it won't get mislaid?"

"Quite," he answered, a pained surprise underlying his reply. "I carry with me always."

"Would you—I know it's foolish of me, but I am nervous about it, it means so much to me, you know—would you mind very much

giving it to *me* to keep? I should feel safer about it, somehow, and—"

"Certainly," he replied coldly, drawing a wallet from an inner pocket and taking from it a folded slip of paper. "It is yours, of course. Here it is."

"Thank you," she said, receiving it and opening the doubled fly-leaf.

Her eyes ran over the scrawled document by the light of the hanging lamp above her head. She read the brief testament to the end—the will whose provisions rendered her one of the wealthiest single women in the United States.

"I suppose there is no doubt as to its validity?" she questioned as she finished the perusal.

"None," he answered curtly. "It is in correct form, and properly witnessed. I am the only relative who could contest it, and I shall hardly do so. Are you quite satisfied now? "

"I lack only one thing to make me so," she returned, "and that is—*this!*"

As she spoke she had been refolding the precious sheet of paper. Now, at her last word, she tore it across and across. With a low cry of horror, Clive threw out his hand to stop her.

But the girl was too quick for him. Into fifty pieces the will was rent and the handful of scraps tossed over the veranda balustrade.

A gust of warm night-wind snatched up the fragments, and Madge Brant's colossal fortune fluttered broadcast through the Khartum.

"Madge!" gasped Clive. "What have you done? *What have you done?*"

"I have shown how highly I value the fortune whose loss would have impoverished you!" she replied, a little hysterically, her eyes glowing with a light that even blind Barry Clive could scarce mistake.

"*Madge!*"

He was bending above her, his arms outstretched, his whole face kindled by that flame from her dark eyes.

Forgotten were resolution, pride, fear, the presence of others—swept away in the mad tumult of love that surged through him and mastered him.

"*Madge!*" he repeated, his voice vibrant.

The girl had half risen in her chair, whether to meet or to repulse

him he could not know. Her face was white, and her lustrous eyes seemed to fill his whole world.

"Miss Brant!"

Clive was on his feet, erect, dark with rage. Madge sank back into her deck-chair, trembling and weak.

"Miss Brant," repeated Gordon from farther down the veranda, "we are waiting for you and Mr. Clive. The clock is on the stroke of twelve, and all the glasses are filled and ready."

Clive assisted the girl to rise. She felt the touch of his hand, cold as ice, against hers. They came forward together and joined the others. On a wide tabouret stood several glasses which a *sais* had just filled. Gordon, watch in hand, smiled happily on Madge and picked up a glass for her.

"General," interposed Mr. Gault, "with your kind permission, I propose to lead this forlorn hope against the Demon Rum!"

Dropping into a military tone, he ordered:

"Attention, company! Glasses in hand, every one! Wait! There goes the clock!—ten—eleven—*twelve!* Health! To be drunk standing! To our host, General Gordon, God bless him! May he live to respond to the toasts drunk at his hundredth birthday and—"

A distant musket-shot—a scream—a snapping volley of small arms, a chorus of yells, and then, over the ill-paved street leading to the square, the clattering hoof-beats of a horse hard-ridden.

CHAPTER XIX.

THE GRATITUDE OF ABOU SAOUD.

GORDON'S upraised glass slipped from his fingers and shattered on the stone floor of the veranda. His hand instinctively flew to his left side. Mustafa, Rushdi, and Kelleher already had their swords out.

From the house, servants came flocking through the main door, gibbering and shaking.

Mrs. Chittenden shrieked and clung in terror to Madge. At the sound of her outcry Gordon regained his rarely shaken composure.

Turning, he said hastily, but in the same sweet old-world courtesy that never deserted him in his intercourse with women:

"I beg you will not be frightened. It is probably only some outbreak or riot among the native troops. If you will excuse me—"

His suite were already half-way down the veranda steps, and the pasha started to follow them. But on the heels of that first melodramatic, shattering of the night's stillness an indescribable uproar from every quarter of the city had burst forth.

Shrieks, shouts, gunshots, the noise of many thousand voices, split the midnight quiet into a myriad horrible sounds.

Through and above all was audible the maniac battle-yell of the Mahdists.

The horseman whose approach the party on the veranda had heard now burst into the square.

By the vivid moonlight he was easily recognizable to the pasha and his staff, who hurried forward to meet him.

The rider was Raad, Gordon's favorite *cavasse*. He was bleeding from a slash over the head.

"Back, *effendi!*" he roared as he reined back his horse and slipped to the ground. "Back into Government House and make what defense you can! The Mahdi is in the city. Every post is captured, and the garrison surrounded! No, no, for the love of life, *effendina*" (highness), as Gordon would have pushed past him, "turn back! There is no rallying your men. Even now they are under the butcher's hand. Back while there is time!"

Almost simultaneously from each of the three streets debouching into the square a wild, roaring mob surged. Waving torches, brandishing their weapons, calling wildly upon the name of Allah, the Sudanese spearmen (bravest and most dangerous of all El Mahdi's following) dashed across the square toward Government House.

Gordon, calm, fearless, invincible, stepped forward as though to confront them. But Rushdi on one side and the *cavasse* on the other literally forced him backward and up the flight of stone steps leading to the veranda. Mustafa and Kelleher followed closely.

The veranda was reached. Gordon had seen, by this time, the impotence of his fleeting hope of winning a way past that blood-crazed horde and rallying such of his garrison as might remain alive.

As they mounted the steps a loose volley of musket-balls rattled about them. Captain Kelleher halted as though in dazed surprise, then fell dead, his body rolling to the foot of the staircase. There was no opportunity of rescuing the brave Irishman's corpse, for already the Mahdists were half-way across the square.

Issuing concise, comprehensive orders, Gordon arranged for the barricading of the great house, cleared the veranda, and transformed the twenty-five or thirty *cavasses,* servants, and officers who chanced to be in the place at the time from a panic-stricken rout into an organized body of fighting men.

The Americans, who, at the pasha's request, had retired indoors, stood grouped in a corner, viewing with wonder the calm power of the man and the ease and precision with which in a moment he had rendered the building impregnable and had employed each member of his tiny garrison to the utmost advantage.

Long since, the spear-handles of the Sudanese had begun to resound on door and iron window-shutters. The defenders, from window loopholes, poured volley after volley into the mass of assailants. The square without was alive with the Mahdists and aglow with swirling torches. The ceaseless firing resounded from every quarter of the city. "Our men still make a stand in some places," cried Ibrahim Bey Rushdi as the volume of shots increased.

"No," answered Gordon briefly, "our men use the army rifle, not guns that make such reports as those. The fighting is over, and," dropping his voice so as not to be heard by his American guests, *"the massacre has begun!* Oh," his steady voice breaking, "that I should hide her while the men, women, and children who were true to me and who trusted in me to save them are slaughtered like cattle!"

"Raad!" called Mustafa. "It was you who brought us news of this. How did it begin? How did they force their way into the city?"

"There was no 'forcing,' *bey*" (captain), replied the *cavasse.* "They gained an entrance through treachery. The north gate was thrown open to them. They must have crept in unseen—thousands of them—before the signal to attack was given."

"Unseen?" echoed Gordon. "But the sentries—"

"Were slain, *effendina;* slain treacherously."

"I see it!" mused Gordon. "They chose a moonlight night because

on dark nights the guard is doubled. Even by moonlight a whole army could pass unseen along the shade of the grove that lines this side of the river and approach to within a furlong of the north gate. If the sentinels on the gate-house there were disposed of and the gate opened it would not be difficult to bring in quietly ten thousand men, as late at night as this, before the alarm could be given. They doubtless entered in small detachments and stealthily, and disposed themselves about the city to await the signal. And a party would have been told off to silence the other sentries."

The born tactician's brain had at once leaped to the right conclusion, each move in the enemy's game standing clearly revealed before him.

"It was so, Saadat-el-Basha," assented the *cavasse*. "I was riding home from the lower town, where I had been listing provisions in the dock warehouses. The city was asleep. At the stroke of twelve I heard a cry and many shots. Men leaped into the roadway and seized my horse. I broke through them and rode on to give the alarm. Spears were hurled at me, and one of them grazed me. As I passed the barracks they were surrounded and attacked on all sides, and the newly roused sleepers could not hold their own against such odds."

The preparations for prolonged defense were quite complete by now, and armed men still blazed away through each loophole.

Gordon, having seen to the disposing of the little band of defenders, crossed to where the Americans stood.

"It is kinder," he said, "not to deceive you. The city is in the hands of the enemy. We in this house are now probably the sole survivors of its garrison. How long we may be able to hold out here I cannot say. But unless the relief expedition arrives within the next few hours I fear we are beyond mortal aid. For myself, I value my life as nothing, and shall only be giving up weariness for perfect peace. The men with me in this house are soldiers, too, and death is part of a soldier's duty. But with you, my guests, it is different. You are non-combatants all. Nor is this your country's quarrel. So, what faint hope for safety there may be, you shall have it."

"I for one," announced Mr. Gault, "prefer to cast in my lot with yours. I might search a thousand years without finding such company to die in."

Gordon's eyes lighted in the ghost of a smile.

"I thank you, sir," he replied, laying a kindly hand on the excited old gentleman's shoulder, "and I shall always remember your offer. But it seems to me you have a higher duty. These two ladies need defenders. Listen, then, to the idea I have thought out for their welfare and yours.

"Under the south wing of the house is a vault, separate from the main cellars. It is reached by a trap-door in the floor of the presence-chamber anteroom. I have given orders that food and drink be taken down to it. I wish you all to go there and await the issue. If we hold out, well and good. If not, the enemy will loot Government House and depart, for the place will not burn.

"The trap-door is not easy to find, and it may escape their notice. When all is over, and they have left the city, come out and try to make your way north along the Nile. It is possible you may reach some civilized place or fall in with an English or Egyptian detachment. It is a grave risk, I know. But it is your one chance. Let Raad guide you to the vault before the next rush is made."

"Not I!" cried Barry Clive. "I should hate myself forever if I skulked in a cellar while there was man's work to do. I shall be honored, sir, if you will assign me to even the meanest position among the defenders."

"And you would remain here and fight for the mere love of fighting rather than protect the women of your own land from death!" exclaimed Gordon, a righteous anger leaping into his eyes. "You would, for the sake of a little cheap glory, leave them with only one old man to defend them against that host of murderers? My friend, the highest courage rests in enduring, not in mere fighting. Prove that you have that courage."

Clive bowed his head, abashed, speechless, under the sternness of Gordon's eyes and words.

"You are right, sir," he said after a pause. "I was a fool to gainsay you. I ask your pardon."

The wrath was dead in Gordon's eyes. In its place shone the grave gentleness that was the man's real self.

"Good-by!" he said, holding out his hand. "I commit the safety of these ladies to yourself and to Mr. Gault. I know they could find no braver men, no truer gentlemen, to champion them."

He grasped, in turn, the hands of Clive, Gault, and the hysterical old lady. Last of all he turned to Madge Brant.

"Good-by, you brave little girl," he said, an infinite tenderness filling his voice. "Your presence here has made these last days very happy for me. May you in return win all the happiness that life—and love—can afford!"

He stooped and kissed her lightly on the forehead. Through eyes that smarted with hot tears Madge looked up once more into the gallant, grave face of the man who fulfilled all her ideal of the gentleness and purity of chivalry.

With an impulsive gesture she caught up his hand, pressed it to her lips, and hastened away with the others toward the anteroom whence they were to descend to the vault.

Barry Clive, noting the caress, experienced no pang of jealousy. He understood and sympathized with the hero-worship and reverence which Madge had always felt toward Gordon, and he knew it held no trace of mortal love.

Through the uncovered trap-door and down a short, steep ladder the four Americans descended. As the last of them reached the foot the trap was closed above them. They looked about, and saw that they were in a low stone room—or, rather, in two rooms, for a rough wooden partition bisected the apartment—whose only light filtered from a close-screened grating near the ceiling.

In one corner lay a pile of sleeping-mats, bags of meal, strips of dried goat-flesh, and a sack of dates. Near by were a dozen bottles of red wine and a pigskin full of water.

Two revolvers, a brace of Winchester rifles, and a little heap of ammunition were ranged close by.

"Where does that light come from?" asked Mr. Gault curiously. "I thought this was a vault."

He crossed to the screened grating and, rising on his toes, looked through it. The vault was not wholly underground, its ceiling being fully twelve inches above the level of the street. Thus, looking out, unobserved, through the close meshes of the screen, Mr. Gault had an unobstructed view of the greater portion of the square, as well as of the entire veranda, staircase, and front entrance of Government House.

The lurid torch-flare rendered the whole scene bright as day.

The fanatics still surged upward to the attack. The steps and the veranda were filled with screaming, gesticulating Sudanese, who rushed fearlessly forward to meet the hail of death that poured through every loophole of the iron window-shutters.

From above, the refugees could hear he tramp of the defenders' feet, and could even distinguish their various voices as the sound sifted downward through the ill-fitting trap.

Suddenly a roaring report shook the building to its foundations. In place of the orderly routine of the defense, shouts and running steps were heard in the anteroom and the presence-chamber. Then came Raad's cry:

"*Effendina!* They have brought the cannon to bear! The rear door is shattered! It cannot hold in position after the next shot!"

A little hush of despair followed the *cavasse's* words. Then arose Gordon's voice, calm, unemotional, as ever:

"So be it! Unbar the front door!"

"Excellency," cried Mutafa, "what is it you would do? "

"I would not be hunted down and slaughtered like a rat in a drain!" replied Gordon. "Unbar the door!" He moved from the anteroom, and his voice died away.

Mr. Gault, his eyes close against the grating, noted the cessation of firing from the loopholes.

Evidently expecting a trick of some sort on the part of the defenders, the Sudanese gave back from the veranda, leaving it and the staircase deserted as they clustered, yelling, at the foot of the steps and awaited the next move.

One man alone remained on the stairs. With drawn saber he stood there, ready to call back his followers to the attack.

He was a fat man, gaudily arrayed. He turned his head slightly, and Mr. Gault saw his face, powder-stained, bloody, but unmistakable.

"Abou Saoud!" groaned the old gentleman under his breath.

But now the great double doors of Government House swung slowly outward. And at what was there revealed a heaven-piercing shout arose from the whole Mahdist host, followed by as sudden an instant of deathly stillness.

On the threshold, alone, stood Gordon Pasha. Behind him, in the

hallway, could be seen his handful of followers, gripping their rifles, and prepared, at a word from their commander, to fling themselves upon the innumerable multitude that choked the square.

For perhaps five seconds Gordon stood there, solitary, erect, unafraid, his slender, sinewy form sharply outlined against the dark background of the hallway.

In each hand he held a revolver. He looked over that merciless crowd of crazed assassins as unconcernedly as he would have inspected a brigade of his own men on field-day.

Then his gaze fell on Abou Saoud. His expression did not alter, but under his look the slave-merchant's eyes fell and the foul insult on his lips died unspoken. Cowed, he slunk back among his fellow murderers, and Gordon once more bent his grave, gentle eyes on the sea of upturned black faces.

Contemptuous of death, devoid of fear as the Sudanese were, Gordon Pasha's presence and glance held them momentarily in check, as the trainer's eye masters the wild beasts in his care.

"Allah! Allah!" screeched a blind dervish far back in the throng.

The spell was broken.

The seething wave of fanatics, stemmed for an instant, rolled forward again, driven on of its own weight and impetus. Up the stair bounded a hundred men, shovel-blade spears aloft.

Gordon involuntarily lifted his two revolvers. Then as the spearmen surged up the great stone stair the pasha, as though loath to shed unnecessary blood, let his arms drop, inert, to his sides.

The human wave of murder swept about and over him, leaving a tumultuous eddy about the threshold where Gordon had been standing.

CHAPTER XX.

A STRUGGLE IN THE DARK.

MR. GAULT loosed his hold on the grating and sank down on the floor of the vault, burying his face in his hands and weeping like a heart-broken woman.

There was no need for him to speak. His action told all too plainly the story of what he had just witnessed. Were that insufficient, a more terrible proof of Gordon's death was at once forthcoming.

The stone ceiling of the vault clanged and reverberated with the sound of rushing feet. Through the interstices of the trap floated an insensate jargon of delirious rejoicings. The Mahdists, the last obstacle to their triumph forever swept away, plundered the rich furnishings of the Serail, massacring at their cruel leisure such few members of the Pasha's household as fell, still living, into their clutches.

From various parts of the city, shrieks and gunshots could be heard. Resistance at an end, the slaughter became universal.

For six full hours raged the massacre of Khartum. Shuddering in their vaulted hiding-place; fearing at each minute to be discovered by some of the thousands of Mahdists who swarmed through the rooms above their heads; their ears thrilling with the dire medley of sounds from the tortured city—the four Americans waited in silence. They dared speak no word, lest the sound reveal their hiding-place. They could but sit and endure.

Fortunately for them, the trap-door leading down into their vault was in an inconspicuous section of the anteroom and was, furthermore, covered by one of the several rugs that strewed the floor. Moreover, the bulk of the plunderers, as Gordon had foreseen, were desert-bred men to whom a trap-door and its possibilities were utterly unknown.

Day dawned, after an eternity of torchlit night. And with the rising of the sun the distant tumult of slaughter began to die away for lack of victims; four thousand men, women, and children having been meantime sacrificed to the Heaven-Born's glory.

Long before sunrise the ceaseless beat, beat, beat of feet throughout the upper floors of the Government House had died away. Now, save for an occasional chance footstep, the Serail was apparently deserted.

It had not taken long to despoil the house of all that seemed of value in the marauders' eyes and to put the last survivors to the sword. This being accomplished, the Sudanese had deserted the Serail and gone in search of some less thoroughly ravaged district.

Moreover, El Mahdi had given orders that as soon as the task of plunder and murder should be wholly accomplished, the Faithful

were to return to camp, until Khartum could be purified by prayer and other rites from the pollution of infidel residence.

Soon after dawn Clive, without speaking, served out the morning rations, which were eaten in silence. He next carried two of the sleeping-mats into the other part of the partitioned vault, and with a gesture signaled to Madge and his aunt to go and get some rest.

"I don't think," whispered Mr. Gault, as he and Barry were left alone together, "that absolute silence is necessary any longer. There is no one in the room above us; and, even if there were, a whisper or low-spoken words could not reach there clearly enough to be distinguishable above the roar of the rabble outside."

"Perhaps you are right," agreed Barry, "but we have so providentially escaped notice thus far that I did not wish to risk ruining all by any imprudence."

"What are we to do next?"

"If you approve, we'll wait here until nightfall, then trust to darkness and the apparent emptiness of the house to get safely out of doors. The city will have few lights, if any. We can borrow the white burnooses of dead Sudanese; throw them over our European clothes, and make our way to the docks at the foot of the town. There we must trust to luck to steal one of the boats moored along the bank, and start northward."

"Good idea! The only possible idea!" approved the old gentleman. "I —"

"Barry! Mr. Gault!" called Madge under her breath.

They turned to see her emerging from the other side of the partition, half supporting, half carrying Mrs. Chittenden, over whose mouth one of the girl's hands was laid.

The compartment of the vault whither the two ladies had retired for rest was that in which stood the ladder leading up to the trap-door.

Madge's face was alight with excitement.

"The trap-door!" she whispered. "Some one is trying to raise it."

Mrs. Chittenden again opened her mouth, but the pressure of Madge's hand once more prevented her from screaming.

Barry motioned Mr. Gault and the two women to stand where they were, in the farther compartment. Then, noiselessly, he crept through the partition and, from the darkest corner of the vault,

awaited developments.

Unmistakably some one was at work on the trap-door from above. The sound of fumbling and of heavy breathing was audible. At length a line of light appeared in the ceiling. The bar widened as the unseen worker succeeded in lifting the trap to its full scope.

Then, silhouetted against the square of light from behind, a man's head and shoulders came into view. The intruder peered down into the vault, but the contrast between its gloom and the day-lit anteroom was so great that he could see nothing.

His groping hand at length touched the uppermost rungs of the ladder. He drew his body over the edge, and cautiously began the descent.

Arrived at the bottom, he drew forth flint and steel. Once and again he essayed in vain to strike a spark. At length he succeeded, and blew on the glowing tinder.

The same instant he dropped the tinder-box and went reeling backward to the floor, Barry Clive's weight crushing him flat and Barry Clive's fingers driven stranglingly into his throat, shutting off alike breath and voice.

"Mr. Gault!" whispered Clive, panting from his exertion, yet relaxing not one atom of the pressure whereby he pinioned the writhing stranger to the ground, "I have him fast, whoever he is. Run up the ladder and close the door. It's barely possible he was alone and that no one else may have discovered the open trap."

Ere he had finished speaking, Mr. Gault was up the ladder with the agility of a boy, and tugging at the stone slab of the trap-door. He succeeded, after a brief tussle, in drawing it shut; then hurried down to where Clive and his prisoner lay.

"There were no others in sight," reported the old gentleman; "I don't think this fellow had companions. He's more likely some thief prowling around alone after the fighters themselves have gone, in the hope of picking up something they overlooked. Hold him tight and I'll go through his clothes for weapons. So! A pocketful of coins and rings, a box of hasheesh, a Bedouin knife, and a revolver. Queer combination! I'll strike a match and we'll look him over."

The luckless plunderer's struggles had ceased. Breath and consciousness had both fled beneath Clive's muscular throat-grip. The

captive lay motionless.

Clive released his pressure on the throat, but still knelt ready to renew it should his victim prove to be shamming. With a gurgling sound the latter regained his senses and strove to rise. Barry thrust him back.

Mr. Gault found and struck a match. Its flicker revealed the pain-distorted face of Halil, the dragoman.

Barry Clive, who had expected that his late antagonist would turn out to be at the very least a fighting man of the Mahdi's army, growled in disgust. With a powerful wrench he hauled the gasping dragoman to his feet and dragged him into the adjoining and lighter compartment. At sight of him, Madge dropped her hand from Mrs. Chittenden's mouth.

"It's that dreadful dragoman!" squealed the old lady; "he's come back to murder us all!"

The forlorn and cringing condition of the unfortunate Halil accorded so ill with Mrs. Chittenden's notion of his intent that Madge could not repress a half-hysterical laugh. But the two American men were grim enough to counterbalance any comfort the dragoman may have gleaned from her mirth.

Clive drew a revolver and held it to the shivering captive's head.

"Now," he said, "what were you doing here?"

Falteringly Halil started to murmur something about being in search of the beloved Americans, but a pressure of the pistol-muzzle against his temple turned the current of his words. He admitted that, while wandering about in the wake of the army, he had blundered upon the trap-door and, fancying it might lead to some treasure-chamber, had descended into the vault.

"There is more—*much* more—that we wish to learn," pursued Barry. "And you will tell us all of it. And if I so much as suspect you of lying I shall not wait to prove my suspicions. Now speak up! "

It was a rambling confession, incoherent from fright, that a series of cross-questions on Clive's part drew from the dragoman. Briefly it condensed itself into a tale that made the Americans listen open-mouthed.

Going reluctantly back to the beginning, he told of the bargain he had made the year before in Cairo, with Abou Saoud, to deliver

the whole *dahabiyeh* party into the latter's hands. After Darah had stolen the Americans, under cover of the sand-storm, Abou Saoud had taken the forsaken Halil into his service, and, with Abou's retinue, the dragoman had journeyed to the Mahdi's camp.

When the attack on Khartum had failed and the Mahdi was despairing alike of conquering the garrison or corrupting the towns-folk, Abou Saoud had approached the Heaven-Born with the follow-ing plan:

Darah should be lured out of the way and the prisoners permit-ted to enter Khartum. With them should journey Abou and Halil. A scene should first be enacted which would convince the prisoners that Abou was, at heart, Gordon's true adherent and in disgrace with the Mahdi. Thus, by dint of the captives' own representations, the slave-merchant might work upon Gordon's well-known credulity and gain leave to enter the city. Once inside he was to escape Gordon's vigilance and go into hiding in an old haunt of his near the docks, there to remain until an appointed night.

On that night he was to summon the aid of two or three waterside ruffians who would sell their souls for a few medjidie; with their help and Halil's to overpower, without noise, the two unsuspecting senti-nels on the north gate, and to throw open the gate itself to his Mahdist friends. For this honorable service he was to receive the rank of pasha and a monopoly of the Sudanese slave-trade.

"And now," queried Mr. Gault, when the recital was at an end— "now that we have this worthy scoundrel safe, what are we to do with him? If we release him he will bring the whole pack down upon us. We can't very well keep him with us indefinitely. What *can* we do?"

"There is only one thing to do," returned Clive, significantly toying with the revolver. "For the safety of all of us we must—"

"No, no!" begged Madge, seizing the hand that held the weapon. "It would be murder! There *must* be some other way!"

CHAPTER XXI.

THE FLIGHT.

NIGHT had again settled over Khartum, mercifully blotting from view the horrors of the past twenty-four hours. The City of Silence was now a city of the dead as well; its thousands of unburied victims lying where they had fallen; its plunderers for the most part withdrawn to the Mahdist camp.

Khartum had been the last spot in all the Sudan to hold out against the arch-fanatic. Now that it had fallen, there was no pressing need to regarrison the citadel. For the two million square miles of fertile country south of the Sahara, with its eighty million inhabitants, was indisputably El Mahdi's.

And for thirteen long years it was destined to groan under the yoke of fanaticism, until, in 1898, the British government, with Kitchener as its sword, should wreak tardy but terrible vengeance for the murder of Gordon Pasha.

Here and there, as night set in, little groups of men flitted noiselessly through the deserted streets, their bare feet soundless on the dirt road-beds, or stray loiterers lounged along the Serail Square.

At late dusk five white-robed, dark-faced persons moved rapidly across the open space toward the street that leads to the dockyards. All wore Sudanese burnooses—huge garments whose folds rendered utterly shapeless the figures beneath them. One of the party staggered under the load of several heavy sacks.

Two more were of smaller and slighter build. Had it not seemed impossible in such a place, they might almost have been mistaken for women. Close behind the sack-bearer strode two men, one of whom carried in his hand a small object whose nature was concealed beneath his sleeve-folds, but which he at intervals pressed against the head of the lagging carrier of burdens. At such times the reluctant gait would be momentarily changed to a shuffling run.

A few minutes later this odd quintet emerged upon the waterfront. There they paused, and one of the men walked on in advance, making hasty examination of the score or so of deserted boats that lay

moored there.

At length he halted before a stanchly built Nile wherry, whose lines bespoke capacity and a tolerable speed. The burden-bearer was instructed to lay his sacks in the bottom of the boat and to take his place at the forward oars.

"Come!" urged Clive. "There is no time to waste. It was only by a miracle, backed by the audacity of the scheme, that we passed through the city alive. Mr. Gault, will you climb over those provision-bags and rifles in the stern and take the helm? Madge, you and Mrs. Chittenden will sit here in the bow. I'll take the second pair of oars behind Halil. Remember," he adjured the latter, again displaying his revolver, "this pistol will be on the seat beside me, and Mr. Gault carries another in his belt. At the first sign of treachery you will die. And if you shirk your rowing, the same weapons are ready for you. If we *must* keep you with us till we're safe from pursuit, we'll at least see that you work your way."

The boat swung out into the sluggish blackness of the stream. Mr. Gault pointed the bow northward, choosing a course along the shaded western bank. Barry and the dragoman bent to the oars; and the fifteen-hundred-mile journey, through country swarming with direst perils, was begun.

All night they journeyed northward, passing in safety the Mahdi's camp, the scattered vedettes, and minor encampments. Now and again a log-like object would rise to the surface near by, gaze at them with round, lidless eyes, and then with a swirl of churned foam sink out of sight. Once they heard the snorting of a great river-horse wallowing in the reeds near the bank.

Three times they passed, in the uncertain moonlight, at no great distance from boatloads of Mahdists. Once the steersman of a crowded flatboat hailed them.

Mr. Gault's heart stood still, but Barry, pressing the all-persuasive revolver into service again, made Halil stammer forth the watchword and add to it a forcedly cheery salutation.

By dawn they were many miles above the city. Barry, powerful and in perfect condition as he was, felt ready to drop from the prolonged strain, while twice the frailer Halil had swooned at the oars. They put

in at a little cove well banked with trees, whose low-hanging branches offered ample screen for the boat.

Halil was bound and gagged; and throughout the long, hot day Mr. Gault and Madge took turns at standing guard while the others slept the sleep of utter physical exhaustion.

At dusk they moved on again, Clive and Halil forcing their aching muscles and blistered palms to the task of duplicating the former night's record.

Gray dawn was breaking again when they neared a point of land covered by a thick grove of trees that grew close down to the water's edge and ran back for two miles or more to the east. So large a tract of woodland is rare in that almost treeless land, and the prospect of a long day's rest under the cool shade of the interwoven branches was tempting to the weary fugitives. Mooring the boat in the tall shore-rushes, they climbed the bank and stood amid the tangle of under-brush that fringed the rise of ground.

"Lend me a hand at fastening up, Halil," said Barry, "and then let's move inland. From what I can see through these bushes, there's level, unobstructed ground a few yards farther on. It will be good to rest on solid earth once more."

"It's even good to be alive," answered Mr. Gault as they pushed their way through the undergrowth. "To live and to be *free!* To feel we are forever beyond the coils of the 'Serpent of the Nile,' and—"

He checked himself with a gasp.

As he and the others had passed into the open woods, the faint dawnlight filtering dimly through the heavy foliage, the old gentle-man's foot had struck against what looked like a mound. To his horror, the mound had responded to the impact with a grunt, and had with a sudden motion sprung upward, resolving itself as it did so into a Nubian soldier.

The rudely awakened sleeper gave one glance at the invaders, then shouted aloud. At his cry, similar inanimate heaps on all sides came to life and leaped to their feet.

The refugees had blundered upon a sleeping Mahdist outpost!

"Feringhi!" shouted the man they had first awakened, recovering from his amaze and whipping out his saber. Before he could strike a blow, Barry Clive's pistol had spoken and the Nubian toppled over,

sprawling fantastically among the tree-trunks.

"Back!" commanded Barry, "back to the boat! These men are Nubians. They won't dare rush us like the Sudanese. I've killed one, and the rest may hang back long enough to let us reach the boat."

With drawn revolver he menaced the twenty or more black soldiers who pressed threateningly upon the Americans. Most of them were still stupid with sleep, and all had stacked their muskets farther on in the wood before lying down to rest. Moreover, their dead comrade served as a useful object-lesson to restrain any ill-advised rashness.

So, while they pressed close on the little band of retreating Americans, Clive was able to keep them at pistol-point. One of their number had run for the muskets. Until his return they would not risk death at the hands of this wild-eyed, desperate Feringee.

Meantime the party were rapidly making good their retreat toward the boat. Madge, who was nearest the water, was already within three yards of the prow.

"Now, then," commanded Barry, speaking in English, "I'll empty my pistol into the thick of them. As I do so, run for the boat, launch it, and jump in. I'll join you there before they recover from my volley. Ready?"

His finger was on the trigger, his eyes defiantly confronting the semicircle of half-angry, half-cautious faces barely six feet away from his own. Through the wood, some fifty yards behind the Nubians, he could see a soldier running toward them, a sheaf of muskets in his arms.

"It'll be touch-and-go!" thought Clive, hot with the exultation of battle. "Now for it!"

His forefinger contracted on the trigger. But the shot flew high amid the tree-tops. For the pistol had been knocked upward from behind, and two sinewy arms were about him, pinioning his hands to his sides.

In the excitement, unobserved and forgotten, Halil had managed to pick up the dead Nubian's saber and cut through the bonds that fettered his wrists. Retreating toward the river with the Americans (for he dared not provoke a shot by bolting), he had watched his opportunity and had seized it.

Before Barry could shake himself free, or Mr. Gault could shoot down the treacherous dragoman, the Nubians were upon them. In less than a second the entire party were bound and helpless and Halil was rattling off glibly the measure of their crimes against Mahdism and the sum his lord, Abou Saoud, would pay for their recapture.

At the name of Abou Saoud, one of the Nubians raised a cry and set off at top speed through the wood. But on the way he met a man who, evidently attracted by the shots, was hurrying along toward the group on a donkey.

The Nubian rattled off a few sentences of guttural Arabic, and the newcomer, sliding down from his slow-moving donkey, advanced at a waddling run toward the captors and captives.

Even before the bloated face became clearly visible through the lower foliage of the grove, each of the four Americans had recognized him. It was Abou Saoud.

In front of the prisoners he halted, puffing mightily from his run, and stared at them in unctuous delight.

"Allah is indeed propitious!" he said at length, in mock devoutness. "It was but yesterday that I rode northward from the camp of the Heaven-Born, to receive a consignment of slaves that are being brought to me from Nubia. My guards spent the night in this grove while my tent was pitched beyond in the open. I was on my way to summon them to the day's march when—Ah!" he broke off, his eye falling on the dead soldier. "Whose handiwork is that?"

"Mine!" retorted Clive. "I beg you will have the mercy to put us all in like state rather than sell us into slavery!"

"Unfortunately," answered Abou, with perfect suavity, "you are too valuable to kill. But you have slain a servant of mine and for that you must be punished as other unruly slaves are chastised. The *courbash* [whip], Merza!" he ordered, addressing one of the Nubians.

The black, grinning with pleasure, brought forth from a mass of camp-baggage a long, thonged lash.

"As you are Feringee and of gentle blood," resumed Abou, his fingers running lovingly along the thong, "I shall not humiliate you by allowing a rude soldier to strike you. I shall honor you by applying the bastinado myself. Therefore—Stay!" he exclaimed, his eye lighting malevolently on Madge. "You shall suffer by proxy only, *howadji*. The

maiden shall bear the beating for you."

Foaming with impotent rage, Barry flung himself, bound and helpless as he was, upon the slave-merchant. Two Nubians seized him before he could reach his tyrant. With a light laugh, Abou Saoud lashed him across the face.

The cruel whip brought the blood spurting from the bronzed skin. Madge cried out in horror. Mr. Gault, for the first time in his long life, ignored the presence of ladies and cursed the slave-merchant fluently. But Barry did not wince, nor give the faintest sign of the agony he was enduring.

"Tie the girl to that tree," resumed Abou as unconcernedly as though he had merely turned aside to chastise a dog. "Perhaps," he added as the order was obeyed, "a taste of the lash may break her stubborn spirit and render her more salable. Look well, I pray you!" he said to Clive; "I shall do this thing with the skill of an artist. There is a true grace in the bastinado."

Struggling until the cords bit deep into his flesh, Barry writhed like a madman in the strong grip of his two guards. As he saw Abou advance toward the tree to which the girl's dainty body was bound, the strong man lost all control of himself and screamed delirious curses and helpless threats at the torturer.

To these Abou gave not the slightest heed, but, running the thongs again through his fat fingers, shook the lash free and whirled it upward for the first stroke. Madge heard the whiz of the whip through the air and a deadly faintness came over her. Her stanch spirit did not quail, but her tender flesh shrank in anticipation of the approaching horror.

CHAPTER XXII.

THE JUSTICE OF SHEIK DARAH.

THE thonged whip-lash hurtled high in air, poised, and—*fell!* But to the earth, not across the shoulders of the shrinking victim.

Abou stood, agape, staring at something beyond Madge.

Barry, who had shut his eyes to bar out the spectacle he was help-

less to prevent, opened them as he heard the *courbash* fall to the ground.

There, within a spear's length of the torture-tree, sat Sheik Darah, astride his roan charger. Behind him, and from every direction through the grove, were advancing the desert horsemen of the Mekheir.

Even in that moment of stress both Clive and Madge were reminded, with odd irrelevance, of the similar silent, unheralded approach of the tribesmen in the Ibrim ruins more than a year before.

In the tumult of the past few moments none had marked the approach of the Arabs over the soft carpet of the woodland, until the knot of Nubians and their captives were wholly surrounded.

The sheik sat his horse, statue-like, immobile, expressionless, looking down on Abou and the intended victim.

"Sheik Darah!" gasped the girl in an anguish of relief.

At her words the stony immobility of the sheik's face broke up, for the briefest fraction of a second, into a look of infinite tenderness. Then the mask of sternness once more covered it, and he almost seemed not to have heard her glad cry.

The Nubians, hopelessly outnumbered, had drawn together in a frightened group. For the Bishareen Arabs were ill men to cross, and those of the Mekheir were known as the most dangerous of all. Added to which there were scarcely a score of Nubians all told, while the tribesmen numbered a full hundred.

Abou Saoud, throwing off his first amazement, turned as if to give an order to his men. Then, for the first time, Darah spoke. It was the Nubians he addressed.

"Unbind the maiden and the other Feringee!" he said in curt command.

Abou opened his lips to countermand the order, but the uselessness of such a proceeding was already manifest. For, at the word, the scared Nubians had eagerly started to cut the four captives' bonds.

"Tie up that man!" was the next mandate. "There—to the same tree!"

A dozen hands seized the protesting, struggling Abou and hustled him across to the tree to which Madge had been bound.

"Nay," observed Darah, in mild satire, as the slave-merchant began to babble incoherently for mercy, "waste no breath in wailing, before

the lash falls. You will need all your voice for what follows.

"Abou Saoud," he resumed, "I returned to the camp of your master, El Mahdi, last night, from the fool's errand whereon he had sent me and my men. I returned to find Khartum fallen, and your name in all men's mouths. For they spoke highly of the trick by which you betrayed Gordon Pasha, who trusted you. They also laughed aloud at the ruse you and your master devised to draw me out of the way so that these, my captives, might serve as pawns in your game. Abou Saoud, was it wise to make the Sheik of the Mekheir a butt for laughter? Was it wise? Was it *safe*?"

He paused. Abou essayed to speak, but his fear-dried lips refused their office.

"It matters little," went on the sheik. "You will soon find your tongue. I learned whither you had gone, and with a hundred of my men I followed. It seems I am just in time."

His eyes, roving for a moment from Abou, chanced to rest on Halil, the dragoman. A sturdy Nubian, thinking to curry favor, had seized the dragoman by the scuff of the neck as he was unobtrusively creeping away through the undergrowth.

"If I mistake not," said Darah, "that is the Cairene dog who served you in the noble enterprise? Take the vermin away," he commanded two of his horsemen, "and rid the earth of him. Then throw his carcass to the river-wardens [crocodiles]!"

The tribesmen snatched Halil from the Nubian, and dragged him, howling, away, through the trees, toward the river. And a few moments later his howls ceased.

"The Heaven-Born will demand reckoning for whatever injury you do me," Abou found courage to mutter. "I am no longer a mere slave-merchant, but a pasha and—"

"And unlikely to enjoy your pashalik long, I fear. As to El Mahdi, I have left forever the service of a man who could seek to make a dupe of me—of *me*, Darah of the Mekheirs! I am once more my own master. I would that my eyes had been opened sooner, that I might have stood beside that brave man, Gordon Pasha, on his last day!"

"What is my ransom?" sullenly demanded Abou.

"What was the ransom of the ten thousand slaves whom, in your time, you have dragged from free homes and sold to lifelong labor

and shame? What the ransom of those, old or crippled, whom you could not sell, and whom, for your diversion, you flogged to death? As was their fate so shall yours be, Abou Saoud, chief of slave-merchants! Already the spirits of your slain gather to do you honor."

There was a solemn note in the sheik's voice like the boom of a death-knell. Abou Saoud heard, and knew his life was at an end. The apathetic fatalism of the East replaced the grin of mortal terror on his blotched face.

"Your slaves' death shall be your death, O Abou Saoud," continued Darah. "Presently, with this whip which you designed for the Feringee maiden, my men shall beat your spirit on its way to Gehenna. *Tamám!*"

He turned his horse's head and moved away through the trees, signaling his men to follow. The horsemen, leading the four Americans among them, fell in behind their leader.

Clive noted that a dozen of the riders did not accompany the main body, but gathered about the tree to which Abou Saoud was bound. As the intervening trees shut out the group, Barry saw one of the tribesmen cast aside his burnoose, bare his right arm to the shoulder, and pick up the terrible whip. Then the foliage mercifully shut off from the captives the last scene in Abou Saoud's checkered career.

Thus did Darah, Sheik of the Mekheir Bishareen mete out the last justice the Sudan was to know for many a year.

As they passed out of the forest and toward a knoll that commanded a long stretch of the Nile, an Arab scout, who had been riding furiously along the river's bank, from beyond the distant bend far to the north, gained the sheik's side and spoke a few hurried words in an undertone.

The sheik nodded and dismissed him. Summoning the captives, he dismounted and beckoned Madge aside from the rest.

"It is kismet," he began abruptly, "that you once more fall into my hands. In the Mahdi's camp I pleaded with you to let me save you—at a price—and you refused. Now you are mine, whether by your own consent or without it. Yet I would hear you, for your own sake, say that you will be my wife. The lives of these, your companions, hang on your reply. Speak!"

"It was for their sakes as well as for my own," she made answer, "that I once before refused the sacrifice you urged on me. My answer then is my answer to-day. We are in your power, Sheik Darah. It is for you to wield that power justly or to abuse it. I can say no more."

Long and intently he looked at her, the soul in his eyes at utter variance with the curt brutality of the words he had just spoken.

Then, his face hardening as at some sudden resolve, he strode toward the others.

"I have asked Miss Brant to become my wife," he said. "I have offered her wealth and power as the wife of the richest and greatest of the desert princes. The *wife*—as you Feringhi understand the word! Not one of the many wives of a sheik's harem. She refused my plea, although I warned her that on her answer hung the lives of all of you. You have already witnessed my justice once this day. Have you cause to doubt its strength? Then hear my death-sentence on the unbelievers whose presence has been an abomination to me and a pollution to my band for a full year!"

Thus far he had spoken in English, and his hearers had been too amazed by his strange revelation to make reply. Now he addressed his followers in Arabic.

"Take these Feringhi to the summit of that hill and set them with their faces to the north! There shall they await their sentence."

Without another word he mounted his roan and vanished among the trees.

The bewildered prisoners were conducted, none too gently, to the hilltop. There their guards left them.

"What does it mean? Oh, what does it all mean?" whined Mrs. Chittenden in a paroxysm of fear.

"Are we to be stood up here and shot at?" conjectured Mr. Gault. "Or are they going to form a cordon about us, at the foot of the hill, Arab-fashion, and starve us to death? "

"Whatever the form of death, it is better than slavery under Abou Saoud," answered Barry. "If, as he seemed to imply, we shall learn our fate by looking to the north, then let us look there and meet death face to face!"

He turned, as he spoke, and gazed northward, the others mechanically following his lead. As they did so, a simultaneous cry broke from

their lips.

Around the bend of the river steamed an Egyptian gunboat—as strangely out of place in that godless wilderness as a mailed Visigoth in a modern pest-house—and on her decks stood swarms of red-coated English soldiers.

It was the advance-guard of the Gordon relief expedition two days too late!

The gunboat was churning its asthmatic way down the river, toward Cairo and civilization. On the forward deck, beneath an awning, lounged a man and a girl. Across the handsome face of the former ran an angry red welt branded there by a whip-lash.

The girl was still pale, and there were dark circles beneath her eyes from the shock and mortal fear she had undergone. But on the faces of both there was a look of peace and of calm security that had not rested there for many a month.

Two days had elapsed since the gunboat had sighted that pathetic fugitive group on the hillock and had sent a boatload of armed men ashore to their rescue. With incredulity and blank amazement the officers, who clustered about the party as they came aboard, had heard their story.

With an abandon of grief at complete variance with the stolid British character, the rescuers had listened to the tale of Gordon's death and had felt the sick despair of the help that comes too late.

Still, for the sake of visual evidence, the gunboat had made another day's journey up the Nile, until, at a point where the elevation permitted, her commanders had seen through their field-glasses the roofs of the distant City of Silence.

There, above the parapet of the Government House, flapped the green banner of the Prophet. With heavy hearts they had turned the gunboat's prow again northward.

"See!" said Madge, pointing shoreward where a hillock rose black against the red glow of the sunset, "there is the hill where we learned the Justice of Darah! "As they drew nearer both could see, silhouetted against the sky, on the crest of the hill, a mounted Arab.

He was motionless, and was intently gazing at the passing gun-

boat. Though too far away for a single detail of his face to be seen, both Madge and Barry Clive at once knew him.

Long Darah sat there, his eyes devouring the receding vessel. And at last, as the boat rounded the bend, Madge saw him wheel his horse about and ride slowly away into the gathering night.

Madge Brant turned with a half-suppressed sigh from her last glimpse of the strange man with whom her destiny had been so closely linked.

Turning, her eyes met Barry Clive's.

"Madge," he said, striving to keep his tone steady, "look over there to the northwest."

Wonderingly, she obeyed.

"America lies there," he continued, the same note of eager, trembling hope strong in his voice.

"Well?" she queried, still puzzled.

"Do you remember," he went on hastily, lest his courage should not carry him through—"do you remember that when I told you I loved you, you forbade me to speak of it then? And you said: 'When we are free and our faces are set toward America, then speak of this to me again, if you will.' Heart of my heart, we are free! Our faces are set toward home! Madge! Madge!"

"I think," she said dreamily, her big dark eyes raised to his, radiant in a newborn glory of happiness—" I think if I had loved you less, I should not have had the courage to test you so cruelly."

THE END.

Appendix

Publication information
for the stories
in this book

Their Last Hope was serialized in five issues of Argosy, from March 1907 through July 1907.

March 1907
Chapters I through VI.

Front text:
Author of "The Scarlet Scarab," "In the Lion's Mouth," "The Fugitive," etc.

A story of Egypt, in which Americans abroad find the Serpent of the Nile very much at home.

(These two lines appeared at the start of each installment..)

Editorial revisions:
The word unware
was changed to unaware

April 1907
Chapters VII through XI.

SYNOPSIS OF CHAPTERS PREVIOUSLY PUBLISHED.

MADGE BRANT, daughter of the late Henry Brant, once partner of, and ruined by, Jonas Fitch, has gone to Egypt as companion to Mrs. Chittenden, sister of Fitch and a well-known and overbearing New York matron. Accompanying them is young Barry Clive, a spoiled product of riches, Mrs. Chittenden's nephew, and heir both to her fortune and to that of Fitch. They are riding donkeys on the Gizeh Road toward Cairo, and Mrs. Chittenden orders the girl, as though she were a servant, to go to the hotel. Madge complies, though in anger, but loses her way in the Cairo streets and finds herself in a low district known as the "Fishmarket." Clive, who also wants to get back to the hotel, follows her and rescues her from the crowd. She thanks him,

but receives an insult in return, whereupon she calls him a cad and whips up her donkey. Again she loses her way, goes round in a circle, and finds herself once more—this time alone—in the "Fishmarket." A villainous individual, Abou Saoud, lays hands on her, but is driven away by no less a person than "Chinese" Gordon, who takes her back to the hotel.

Meanwhile, Abou Saoud, Halil Sadik-Ali, the party's guide, and a negro named Farragh plot to capture Mrs. Chittenden, Clive, and Madge, by whom Abou is much attracted. Gordon sends Madge an invitation to a levee in his honor at the Khedive's palace, where she makes a big hit, to Mrs. Chittenden's disgust and Clive's embarrassment. He apologizes for his past rudeness and shows some contrition. Gordon, finding they are going south, laughingly asks Miss Brant to visit him in Khartum. The next day they set out up the Nile, Halil guiding them.

Just before the boat starts, Jonas Fitch comes aboard. He attempts to speak to Madge, but is snubbed by her, and retires. Clive becomes even more decent. Otherwise, the trip is practically uneventful until they reach Ibrim, where at about a two hours' donkey ride into the desert are some temples which they decide to visit. They go inland, explore the temples, and are about to return to the river, when they discover a line of villainous-looking mounted natives before them, and another behind. The natives are armed to the teeth, and the little party is entirely hemmed in.

*This story began in the March issue of THE ARGOSY, which will be mailed to any address on receipt of 10 cents.

May 1907
Chapters XII through XV.

Front text:
Author of "The Scarlet Scarab," "In the Lion's Mouth," "The Fugitive," etc.

A story of Egypt, in which Americans abroad find the Serpent of the Nile very much at home.
SYNOPSIS OF CHAPTERS PREVIOUSLY PUBLISHED.

Their Last Hope

MADGE BRANT, daughter of the late Henry Brant, once partner of Jonas Fitch, has gone to Egypt as companion to Mrs. Chittenden, sister of Fitch and a well-known and overbearing New York matron. Accompanying them is young Barry Clive, a spoiled product of riches, Mrs. Chittenden's nephew, and heir both to her fortune and to that of Fitch.

Madge is rescued from a dangerous predicament and a villainous individual named Abou Saoud by "Chinese" Gordon, who later invites her to a levee in his honor at the Khedive's palace, where she makes a hit and gets another invitation from Gordon to visit him in Khartum if she happens to be in that part of the country. Meanwhile, Abou Saoud and Halil Sadik-Ali, the party's guide, plot to capture Mrs. Chittenden, Clive, and Madge, by whom Abou is much attracted. The next day they set out up the Nile, Halil guiding them. Just before the boat starts, Jonas Fitch comes aboard. He attempts to speak to Madge, but is snubbed by her. Clive, during the trip, which is otherwise uneventful, becomes quite decent and gentlemanly. When they reach Ibrim, five of them, including a Mr. Gault, guided by Halil, go inland to visit some ruins. As they are about to return they are captured by an armed party of natives, under Sheik Darah, subordinate to El Mahdi, religious fanatic and most troublesome man in Africa. By the sheik they are taken toward Khartum, where by this time, he says, Gordon is either dead or a prisoner, and where the captives can arrange for ransom, all except Madge, who is intended as a bride for El Mahdi. Clive loses control of himself and threatens the sheik with death in the near future, adding, "And I shall be most actively present at the time to see that the operation goes on without a hitch."

*This story began in the March issue of THE ARGOSY. The two back numbers will be mailed to any address on receipt of 20 cents.

Editorial revisions:
The word thone
was changed to throne

June 1907
Chapters XVI through XIX.

SYNOPSIS OF CHAPTER S PREVIOUSLY PUBLISHED.

MADGE BRANT, daughter of the late Henry Brant, once partner of Jonas Fitch, has gone to Egypt as companion to Mrs. Chittenden, sister of Fitch and a well-known and overbearing New York matron. Accompanying them is young Barry Clive, a spoiled product of riches, Mrs. Chittenden's nephew, and heir both to her fortune and to that of Fitch.

Madge is rescued from a dangerous predicament and a villainous individual named Abou Saoud by "Chinese" Gordon, who later invites her to a levee in his honor at the Khedive's palace, where she makes a hit and gets another invitation from Gordon to visit him in Khartum. Meanwhile, Abou Saoud and Sadik-Ali, the party's guide, plot to capture Mrs. Chittenden, Clive, and Madge, by whom Abou is much attracted. The next day they set out up the Nile, Halil guiding them. Just before the boat starts, Jonas Fitch comes aboard. He attempts to speak to Madge, but is snubbed by her. Clive, during the trip, which is otherwise uneventful, becomes quite decent and gentlemanly. When they reach Ibrim, five of them, including a Mr. Gault, guided by Halil, go inland to visit some ruins. As they are about to return they are captured by an armed party of natives, under Sheik Darah, subordinate to El Mahdi, religious fanatic and most troublesome man in Africa. By the sheik they are taken toward Khartum, where by this time, he says, Gordon is either dead or a prisoner, and where the captives can arrange for ransom, all except Madge, who is intended as a bride for El Mahdi. Clive loses control of himself and threatens the sheik with death in the near future, adding, "And I shall be most actively present at the time to see that the operation goes on without a hitch."

Utterly regenerated by long association with Madge, Barry, who has grown to love her, asks her to be his wife, but is told to wait until they are again at home. Arrived at last at Khartum, the party awaits the pleasure of El Mahdi. Meanwhile, Jonas Fitch, who has been growing weaker, dies, after making Madge, whom he had wronged by cheating her father, his heir. The infidel forces are repulsed by Gordon, and the fanatics clamor for the execution of Darah's captives. Darah proposes that Madge save herself and the others by wedding him, but she indignantly refuses, and they are brought before El Mahdi.

*This story began in the March issue of THE ARGOSY. The three back numbers will be mailed to any address on receipt of 30 cents.

Their Last Hope

Editorial revisions:
"his dack of courage"
was changed to
"his lack of courage"

July 1907
Chapters XX through XXII.

* This story began in the March issue of THE ARGOSY. The four
back numbers will be mailed to any address on receipt of 40 cent.

General Notes
The original story was not illustrated.

Charles George "Chinese" Gordon (1833-1885). Photo taken between
1878 and 1885 by Geruzet Frères. Source: Harvard Art Museum/
Fogg Museum, Historical Photographs and Special Visual Collections
Department, Fine Arts Library.

Human Interest Stuff

A graphic narrative adaptation of the short story from
A Terhune Omnibus,
illustrated by long-time professional comics artist William Messner-Loebs.

Available on eBay.

Will Eisner always said that Bill Loebs was the closest to his own drawing style and story-telling methodology, among Will's many acolytes, in whose number I proudly count myself. "Human Interest Stuff" establishes that Bill can still hit and sustain that exalted high artistic note, adapted from Terhune's deeply affecting short story, with gifted collaborator Rodney Schroeter. It's like having Will back with us again. Bravo!

Dave Sim

I do think you've picked up on the flavor of the Albert Payson Terhune story.

Marilyn R. Horowitz

Rodney Schroeter has delivered a smart script, a page-turner, a winner by every yard-stick. Best of all, he was clever enough to recruit Bill Messner-Loebs as his artist, so you have to stop and stare at every panel. "Human Interest Stuff" is the dope.

Clifford Meth

Rodney Schroeter and William Messner-Loebs have revived that time-honored but half-forgotten pulp subgenre, the sentimental dog story. You will never forget Tatters!

Will Murray

Adapted by Rodney Schroeter
and William Messner-Loebs

Writers
PRESS

I don't suspect I've read a comic book since I was 12 years old—but as they say, sometimes you need to stuff your old ideas and ways of doing things aside and look at something in a new light.

Well, was I ever surprised. The story starts out with action and it just keeps right on truckin' along, keeping the reader, looker, or whatever you call a comic book consumer right on the edge of his chair wondering what's about to happen next.

This is a fine story, no question about it. Makes a good point, in fact several of them. I like the way the story is organized, and I like the way it takes a few twists and turns. Oh, I also like that even the threat of the pen can make some folks squirm a bit—and sometimes do what's right.

Jerry Apps

Once upon a time the comics were fresh, original, emotional, exciting, timely and timeless, interesting, romantic and memo-rable.

"Human Interest Stuff" is the type of story that attracted and attracts me to the comics.

Rodney Schroeter and William Messner-Loebs deserve a 21-gun salute.

Because.

Once upon a time is now.

Robin Snyder

The Woman Tamers

Historical Essays by Terhune

Cheddar Cheese

by Francis Lynde

All books are available from
major bookstores online,
as print books and as e-books.